Also by Liz Tuccillo

He's Just Not That Into You
(cowritten with Greg Behrendt)

How to Be Single

How to Be
Single

A NOVEL

Liz Tuccillo

ATRIA BOOKS

New York London Toronto Sydney

ATRIA BOOKS

A Division of Simon & Schuster, Inc.
1230 Avenue of the Americas
New York, NY 10020

First Atria Books hardcover edition June 2008

ATRIA BOOKS and colophon are trademarks of Simon & Schuster, Inc.

For information about special discounts for bulk purchases,
please contact Simon & Schuster Special Sales at 1-800-456-6798
or business@simonandschuster.com.

Designed by Jaime Putorti

Manufactured in the United States of America

10   9   8   7   6   5   4   3   2   1

Library of Congress Cataloging-in-Publication Data

Tuccillo, Liz.
  How to be single : a novel / by Liz Tuccillo. -- 1st Atria Books hardcover ed.
     p. cm.
1. Single women—Fiction. 2. Dating (Social customs—Fiction.
3. Self-actualization (Psychology)—Fiction. 4. Chick lit. I. Title.

  PS3620.U284H69 2008
  813'.6—dc22   2008010368

ISBN-13: 978-1-4165-3412-9
ISBN-10:   1-4165-3412-1

*This book is dedicated, as is everything I do,
to my mother, Shirley Tuccillo*

How to Be Single

It's the most annoying question and they just can't help asking you. You'll be asked it at family gatherings, particularly weddings. Men will ask you it on first dates. Therapists will ask you over and over again. And you'll ask yourself it far too often. It's the question that has no good answer, and that never makes anyone feel better. It's the question, that when people stop asking it, makes you feel even worse.

And yet, I can't help but ask. Why are you single? *You seem like an awfully nice person. And very attractive.* I just don't understand it.

But times are changing. In almost every country around the world, the trend is for people to remain single longer and to divorce more easily. As more and more women become economically independent, their need for personal freedom increases, and that often results in not marrying so quickly.

A human being's desire to mate, to pair up, to be part of a couple, will never change. But the way we go about it, how badly we need it, what we are willing to sacrifice for it, most definitely is.

So maybe the question isn't anymore, "Why are you single?" Maybe the question you should be asking yourself is "How are you single?" It's a big new world out there and the rules keep changing.

So, tell me ladies, how's it going?

—Julie Jenson

RULE

1

Make Sure You Have Friends

How Georgia Is Single

"I JUST WANT TO HAVE FUN! NOW THAT I'M SINGLE I JUST WANT TO HAVE FUN! YOU SINGLE PEOPLE ARE ALWAYS HAVING FUN!! *WHEN ARE WE GOING TO GO OUT AND HAVE FUN?!!!*"

She is screaming, *screaming* at me on the phone. "I WANT TO KILL MYSELF, JULIE. I DON'T WANT TO LIVE WITH THIS MUCH PAIN. REALLY. I WANT TO DIE. YOU HAVE TO MAKE ME FEEL LIKE EVERYTHING IS GOING TO BE OKAY! YOU HAVE TO TAKE ME OUT AND REMIND ME THAT I'M YOUNG AND ALIVE AND CAN HAVE LOTS AND LOTS OF FUN! OR GOD KNOWS WHAT I MIGHT DO!!!" Dale, Georgia's husband, had left her for another woman two weeks ago and she was obviously a tad upset.

The call came at 8:45 in the morning. I was at the Starbucks on Forty-fourth and Eighth, balancing a cardboard tray of coffees in one hand, my cell phone and this conversation in the other, my hair in my face, grande mochaccinos tilting toward my left breast, all while paying the nice young twentysomething at the cash register. I'm a multitasker.

I had already been up for four hours. As a publicist for a large New York publishing house, part of my job is to cart our writers around from interview to interview as they promote their books. On this morning I was responsible for thirty-one-year-old writer Jennifer Baldwin. Her book, *How to Keep Your Husband Attracted to You During Pregnancy*, became an instant bestseller. Women all around the country couldn't buy the book fast enough. Because, of course, how to keep your husband attracted to you during your pregnancy should be the main concern for a woman during that very special time in her life. So this week we were making the prestigious morning show rounds. *Today, The View, Regis and Kelly.* WPIX, NBC, and CNN, so far that day, ate it up. How could you not love a segment showing eight-months-pregnant women how to strip for their men? Now the author, her personal publicist, her literary agent, and the agent's assistant were all anxiously waiting for me in the Town Car that was parked outside. I held the lifeline to their caffeine fix.

"Do you really feel like you want to kill yourself, Georgia? Because if you do, I'll call 911 right now and get an ambulance over there." I'd read somewhere that you should take all suicide talk seriously, even though I think all she was really doing was making sure I would take her out drinking.

"FORGET THE AMBULANCE, JULIE, YOU'RE THE ORGANIZER, THE ONE WHO MAKES THINGS HAPPEN—CALL THOSE SINGLE FRIENDS OF YOURS, THE ONES YOU ARE ALWAYS HAVING FUN WITH—AND LET'S GO OUT AND HAVE FUN!"

As I continued my balancing act toward the car, I thought about how tired that thought made me. But I knew Georgia was going through a difficult period and it would probably get much worse before it got better.

It's a tale as old as time. Dale and Georgia had kids, stopped having regular sex, and began fighting. They became distant, and then Dale told Georgia he was in love with a twenty-seven-year-old *whore gutter trash* samba teacher, that he met at Equinox. Call me crazy, but I'm thinking hot sex might have had something to do with this. Also, and I don't want to be disloyal, and I would never even *suggest* Georgia was at fault *in any way* because *Dale is an asshole,* and *we hate him now,* but I can't resist saying, Georgia completely took Dale for granted.

Now, to be fair, I am particularly judgmental about the Married

Women Who Take Their Husbands for Granted Syndrome. When I see a very wet man hold an umbrella out to his wife after he has just walked five blocks to pick up the car and drive it back to the restaurant and she doesn't even say thank you, honestly, it makes me very cranky. So I noticed that Georgia took Dale for granted, particularly when she would talk to him in *that tone.* The tone that you can dress up and call what you want, but the truth is it's plain old-fashioned contempt. The tone is disgust. The tone is impatience. The tone is a vocal eye roll. It is the undeniable proof that marriage is a horribly flawed institution let out in a single "I told you, the popcorn popper is on the shelf *over the refrigerator.*" If you were able to fly around the world, collecting the tone as it is let out of all the disgruntled married men's and women's mouths, cart it back to some desert in Nevada, and release it—the earth would literally sink into itself, imploding in sheer global irritation.

Georgia talked to Dale in that tone. And of course that wasn't the only reason for their split. People are irritating and that's what marriage is: good days and bad days. And, really, what do I know? I'm thirty-eight years old and I have been single for six years. (Yes, I said six.) Not celibate, not out of commission, but definitely, fully, officially, here-goes-another-holiday-season-alone single. So in my imaginings, I would always treat my man right. I would never speak harshly to him. I would always let him know that he was desired and respected and my number one priority. And I would always look hot and I'd always be sweet, and if he asked, I would grow a long fishtail and gills and swim with him in the ocean topless.

So now Georgia has gone from semicontented wife and mother to a somewhat suicidal single mother with two children. And she wants to *party.*

Something must happen when you become single again. A self-preservation instinct must kick in that resembles having a complete lobotomy. Because Georgia suddenly has traveled back in time to when she was twenty-eight and now just wants to go out "to some bars, you know, to meet guys," forgetting that we are actually in our late thirties and some of us have been doing that without a break for years now. And frankly, I don't want to go out and meet guys. I don't want to spend an hour using one of the many hot appliances I own to straighten my hair so I can feel attractive enough to go out drinking. I want to go to bed early so I can get up early so I can make my smoothie and go out and run in the morning. I am a marathoner. Not in the literal sense; I run only three miles a day. But as a single person. I know how to pace myself. I am aware of how long a run it can be. Georgia, of course, wants to line up the babysitters and start sprinting.

"IT'S YOUR OBLIGATION TO HAVE FUN WITH ME! I DON'T KNOW ANY OTHER SINGLE PERSON EXCEPT YOU! YOU HAVE TO GO OUT WITH ME. I WANT TO GO OUT WITH YOUR SINGLE FRIENDS! YOU GUYS ARE ALWAYS GOING OUT!! NOW THAT I'M SINGLE, I WANT TO GO OUT TOO!!!"

She is also forgetting that she is the same woman who would always look at me with such pity when I would talk about my single life and exclaim in one breath "OhmyGodthat'ssosadIwanttodie."

But Georgia would do something that all my other happily married or coupled friends would never even think of doing: she would pick up the phone and organize a dinner party and scrounge up some single men for me to meet. Or she'd go to her pediatrician and ask if he knew any eligible bachelors. She was actively involved in my search for the Good Man, no matter how comfortable and self-satisfied she might have felt herself. And that is a rare and beautiful quality. And that is why on that Friday morning, as I was mopping up coffee from my white shirt, I agreed to call up three of my other single friends and see if they would go out and party with my newly single, slightly hysterical friend.

How Alice Is Single

Georgia is right. We're having so much fun, my single friends and I. Really. Oh my God, being single is hilarious. For instance, let me tell you about the sidesplitting uproariousness that is Alice. For a living, she gets incredibly underpaid to defend the rights of the impoverished people of New York City—against callous judges, ruthless prosecutors, and an overburdened system in general. She has dedicated herself to trying to help the underdog by bucking the system, beating the man, and guarding our Constitution. Oh yeah, and every once in a while she has to defend a rapist or murderer that she knows is guilty and whom she often succeeds in putting back onto the streets. Oops. You win some, you . . . win some.

Alice is a Legal Aid attorney. While the Constitution guarantees the right to a lawyer, it unfortunately can't promise that you'll be defended by Alice. First of all, she is gorgeous. Which, of course, is superficial, who cares. Because those jurors sitting in that drab industrial green jury room with the fluorescent lighting, and that eighty-year-old judge presiding over the general misery of it all, well, they'll take whatever aesthetic pleasure they can find. And when redheaded, sexy Alice talks to you with her deep, soothing voice and her thick, I'm-one-of-the-people-but-much-more-adorable Staten Island–Italian accent, you would drive into Sing Sing and break out every last prisoner, if that's what she asked of you.

She was so startling in her legal acumen and plain old-fashioned charisma that she became the youngest law professor at NYU. By day Alice was saving the world, and by night she was inspiring yuppie born-and-bred law students to forget their dreams of nice Manhattan co-ops and Hampton summer shares to go into Legal Aid law and do something important. She was outrageously successful. She made insubordination and compassion cool again. She got them to actually believe that helping people was more important than making money.

She was a Goddess.

Yeah. I say *was,* because I'm kind of lying. The truth hurts too much. Alice is no longer a Legal Aid attorney.

"Okay, this is the *only* time I believe in the death penalty." Alice, being a fantastic friend, was helping me transport books from my office on Fiftieth Street and Eighth Avenue to a book signing on Seventeenth Street. (The book was *The Idiot's Guide to Being an Idiot* and was, of course, a big hit.)

"The only exception to the rule is any man who goes out with a thirty-three-year-old woman until she's thirty-eight and then discovers he has commitment issues; who gives that woman the impression that he has no problem with marriage and being with her for the rest of her life; who keeps telling her it's going to happen, until finally, one day he tells her that he doesn't think 'marriage is really for him.'" Alice put her fingers in her mouth and let out a whistle that could stop traffic. A cab veered over to pick us up.

"Pop the trunk, please," Alice said, forcefully grabbing a box of the *Idiot* books from my arms and throwing them in the trunk.

"That was shitty," I conceded.

"It was more than shitty. It was criminal. It was a crime against my ovaries. It was a felony against my biological time clock. He stole five of my precious childbearing years from me and that should be considered grand larceny of motherhood and be punishable by hanging." She was ripping each box out of my hands and hurling them now. I thought it best to let her finish this on her own. When she was done, we walked to opposite sides of the cab to get in and she continued talking to me over the cab roof without taking a breath.

"I'm not going to take this lying down. I'm a powerful woman, I'm in control. I can make up for lost time, I can."

"What do you mean?" I asked.

"I'm going to quit my job and start dating." Alice got into her side of the cab and slammed the door.

Confused, I sank into the cab. "I'm sorry, what?"

"Union Square Barnes and Noble," Alice barked to the cabdriver. Then to me, "That's right. I'm going to sign up for every online service, I'm going to send out a mass email to all my friends to set me up with any single guys they know. I'm going to go out every night and I'm going to meet someone fast."

"You're quitting your job *to date*?" I tried to say this with the least amount of horror and judgment in my voice.

"Exactly." She kept nodding her head vigorously, as if I knew just what she was talking about. "I'll keep teaching, I have to make some money. But basically, yeah, it's my new job. You heard me."

So now my dear do-gooder Superwoman, Xena the Warrior Princess, Erin Brockovich, friend Alice, is still spending all her time and energy trying to help the underdog. But this time the underdog is herself: a thirty-eight-year-old single woman in New York City. She's still trying to stick it to "the man." But this time the man is Trevor, who took up all that precious time of hers and has now made her feel old, unlovable, and frightened.

And when Alice is asked what she does with all her newly free time that she once used to help keep young, first-time offenders away from Rikers and imminent horrifying physical abuse, she often goes into this little speech: "Besides the Internet, and the fix-ups, I just make sure I go to everything I get invited to, every conference or luncheon or dinner party. No matter how shitty I feel. Remember when I had that really bad flu? I got out of the house and went to a singles night at New York Theatre Workshop. The night after my hand surgery I took some Percocet and went to that huge benefit for the Central Park Conservancy. You never know what night it will be when you meet the man who's going to change your life. But then I also have hobbies. I purposely do what I love to do, because you know, when you least expect it, that could be when you meet someone."

"When you least expect it?" I asked, during one of Alice's diatribes. "Alice, you have decided to quit your job to dedicate your life to meeting someone. How can you ever, *ever* least expect it?"

"By staying busy. By doing interesting things. I kayak in the Hudson, rock climb at Chelsea Piers, take carpentry classes at Home Depot, which you should totally do with me, by the way, I made an amazing cabinet, and I'm also thinking about taking this sailing course at the South Street Seaport. I'm keeping busy doing things I find interesting, so that I can trick myself into forgetting that I'm really just trying to look for guys. Because you can't look desperate. That's the *worst*."

As she is telling people this, she often comes across as a little deranged, particularly because she's usually chain-popping Tums as she says all this. Her indigestion problems stem, I believe, from a little acid reflux condition called "I'm terrified of being alone."

So, of course, who else would I call first when I needed to go out with a bunch of girlfriends and "have fun" than Alice, who is basically a professional at it now. She now knows all the bartenders, doormen, maître d's, bars, clubs, out-of-the-way places, tourist hangouts, dives, and happening scenes in New York City. And naturally, Alice was ready to go.

"I'm on it," she said. "Don't you worry. We'll make sure tomorrow night, Georgia has the best time of her life."

I hung up the phone, relieved. I knew I could count on Alice, because no matter how Alice's life might have changed, she still loved a good cause.

How Serena Is Single

"It's too smoky, no way."

"You don't even know where we're going."

"I know, but it's going to be too smoky. Every place is too smoky."

"Serena, there's a smoking ban in New York; you can't smoke in bars."

"I know, but it still seems too smoky. And it's always too loud at these places."

We are sitting at the Zen Palate—the only place I have ever met Serena at in the past three years. Serena doesn't like to go out. Serena also doesn't like to eat cheese, gluten, nightshade vegetables, nonorganic vegetables, and pineapple. None of it agrees with her blood type. If you haven't guessed, Serena is very, very thin. She is one of those very pretty, waiflike blond girls you see in yoga classes in every major city across America. She is a vegetarian chef for a New York celebrity family, about whom I'm not allowed to speak due to a confidentiality agreement Serena made me sign so that she wouldn't feel guilty about breaking the confidentiality agreement *she* signed with her employer when she gossiped to me about them. Really. But let's just say for the purposes here, that their names are Robert and Joanna, and their son's name is Kip. And to be honest, Serena doesn't say anything bad about them at all; they treat her really well and seem to appreciate her gentle spirit. But by God, when Madonna comes over for lunch and makes a dig about Serena's cooking, Serena has to be able to tell someone. She's only human.

Serena is also a student of Hinduism. She believes in equanimity in all things. She wants to see divine perfection in all of life, even the fact that she literally hasn't had a date or sex in four years. She sees this as perfection, the world showing her that she needs to work on herself more. For how can you really be a true partner to someone until you are a fully realized human being yourself?

So Serena has worked on herself. She has worked on herself to such an extent that she has actually become a human maze. I pity the man who ever attempts to enter the winding corridors and dead-end tunnels that are her dietary restrictions, meditation schedule, new age workshops, yoga classes, vitamin regimes, and distilled water needs. If she works on herself any more, she will become a shut-in.

Serena is that friend you always see alone; the one whom no one else knows. The one who, if you ever mention her in passing, prompts your other friends to say, "Serena? You have a friend named Serena?" But things weren't always like this. I met Serena in college and she used to be just like everyone else. She was always a tad obsessive-compulsive, but back then it was a quirk and not a lifestyle choice. All through her twenties she would meet guys and go out. And she had a long-term boyfriend for three years as well. Clyde. He was really sweet and was crazy about her, but Serena always knew he wasn't the one. She sort of settled into a nice routine with him—and if you haven't guessed, Serena does enjoy her routines. So we encouraged her not to lead him along—never dreaming that he might be the last real relationship for the rest of her wheat-free life. And after Clyde she still managed to date—not aggressively so, but whenever something came up. But around thirty-five, when she never found anyone who truly interested her, she started focusing on other aspects of her life. Which, to be fair, is what many of the self-help books that I help publicize tell women to do. These books also tell you to love yourself. In fact, if you had to boil every self-help book down to two words, it would be "love yourself." I can't tell you why, but this irritates me immensely.

So Serena started focusing on other things, and thus began the classes and crazy diet stuff. Unlike Alice, at least in terms of dating, Serena decided to go quietly into that good night. It's a slippery slope, the decision just to let go of the dream of love in your life. Because if done well, it can make you relax, enjoy your life, and actually allow your inner light to shine brighter and stronger than ever before. (Yes, I am talking about someone's inner light—we are dealing with Serena right now, after all.) But in my opinion, that strategy, if followed incorrectly or for too long, can make your light go out, slowly, day by day. You can become sexless and cut off. Even though I think it might be extreme to quit your job to start dating, I don't think you can ever just sit back and let love just find you. Love isn't that clever. Love isn't actually all that concerned about you. I think love is out there finding people whose lights are burning so brightly that you could actually see them from the space shuttle. And frankly, somewhere between the high-colonics and the African dance classes, Serena's light went out.

But still, she has a calming effect on me. She is capable of listening to me vent about how much I hate my job, with the patience of Gandhi. Besides the books I have already mentioned, I have helped publicize such tomes as *The Clock Is Ticking! How to Meet and Marry the Man of Your Dreams in Ten Days, How to Know if Your Man Really Loves You,* and the runaway hit *How to Be Lovely* (it's supposedly the secret to all feminine happiness).

I grew up in New Jersey, not so terribly far away, just a bridge or a tunnel from the city of my dreams. I moved here to be a writer, then I thought I might be a documentary filmmaker, then I even took a few courses in anthropology, thinking I might move to Africa and study the Masai warriors or some other almost-extinct tribe. I am fascinated by our species, and loved the idea of reporting on them in some way. But I realized I inherited a strong practical streak from my father. I liked indoor plumbing, and knowing I had health insurance. So I got a job in publishing.

But now, the novelty of being able to afford groceries had definitely lost its initial thrill. And throughout all my complaining, Serena listens quietly.

"Why don't you just quit?"

"And do what? Get another job in publicity? I hate publicity. Or be unemployed? I'm too dependent on a steady paycheck to be that free-spirited."

"Sometimes you have to take a risk."

If *Serena* was thinking I was in a rut, I knew things must be really bad. "Like what?" I asked.

"Like—didn't you always say you wanted to write?"

"Yes. But I don't have a big enough ego to be a writer."

In my professional life, I was a bit stuck. My "voice of reason," so relied on by others, only caused me to talk myself out of pretty much everything. But every Friday, Serena would listen to me bitch about my work frustrations as if it were the first time I was bringing it up.

So I thought, why not? My friends have always been curious about her. Why not try to convince her to go out?

"The chances of any of us going out tomorrow night and meeting the man of our dreams is practically zero. So why bother?" Serena asked as she took another bite of her tempeh burger.

In terms of the facts, Serena has a point. I have been going out at night in the hopes of meeting the one guy that's going to adore me for the rest of my life. Let's say I've been doing this for two or three times a week for, oh, fifteen years. I have met men and dated, but clearly, as of today, not the guy that gets written down in my big book of life as "The One." That adds up to a hell of a lot of nights out *not* meeting the man of my dreams.

I know, I know, we weren't just going out to meet men. We were going out to have fun, to celebrate being single and being sort of young (or at least not yet old) and alive and living in the best city in the world. It's just funny how when you finally do meet someone and begin dating, the first thing you both do is start staying home to snuggle on the couch. Because going out with your friends was simply that much fun.

So I couldn't really argue with Serena. The whole concept of "going out" is somewhat flawed. But I continued my plea. "We're not going out to meet guys. We are just going out to go out. To show Georgia that it's fun to just go out. To be out in the world, eating, drinking, talking, laughing. Sometimes something unexpected happens and sometimes, most of the time, you just go home. But you go out, you know, to *go out*. To see what *might* happen. That's the fun of it."

The argument for the benefits of spontaneity and the unknown was usually not the way to Serena's heart, but for some reason, she agreed.

"Fine. But I don't want it to be anywhere too smoky or too noisy. And make sure they have a vegetable plate on the menu."

How Ruby Is Single

And then, there's Ruby.

It was Saturday, at two in the afternoon, and I had come over to Ruby's apartment to try to recruit her into going out that night—and because I knew she might not have gotten out of bed yet.

Ruby opened the door in her pajamas. Her hair was severely matted, almost in a predreadlocked state of knots.

"Did you get out of bed today?" I asked, worried.

"Yes. Of course. Right now," she said, offended. She proceeded to walk back into her bedroom. Her apartment was impeccably neat. None of your cliché telltale depression signs, such as moldy ice cream cartons, half-eaten doughnuts, or weeks of dirty laundry strewn around. She was a very tidy depressive. It gave me hope.

"How are you feeling today?" I asked, following her into her bedroom.

"Better. When I woke up he wasn't the first thing I thought about." She crawled back into her very fluffy, downy, flowery bed and pulled the covers around her. It looked really comfortable. I was starting to think about taking a nap myself.

"Great!" I said, knowing I was about to hear much more than that. Ruby is an adorable, long-haired brunette, a perfectly curvy, feminine creature of soothing tones and tender words. And Ruby likes to talk about her feelings.

She sat up. "My first thought this morning was 'I feel okay.' You know what I mean—that moment before you remember who you are and what the actual facts of your life are? My first thought, in my gut, in my body, was 'I feel okay.' I haven't felt like that in a long time. Usually, you know, I open my eyes and I already feel like shit. Like in my sleep I was feeling like shit, and waking up was just an extension of that, you know? But this morning, my first thought was 'I feel okay.' As if my body wasn't, you know, housing any more sadness."

"That's awesome," I said, cheerfully. Maybe things aren't as bad as I thought.

"Yeah, well, of course, once I remembered everything, then I started crying and couldn't stop for three hours. But I think it was an improvement, you know? It made me see that I was getting better. Because Ralph can't stay in my memory so strongly, he just can't. Soon I'll wake up and it'll take me three whole minutes to start crying about him. And then fifteen minutes. And then an hour, then a whole day, and then I'll finally be through this, you know?" She looked as if she was going to start crying again.

Ralph was Ruby's cat. He died of kidney failure three months ago. She has been keeping me updated on the physical sensations of her profound depression every day since. This is particularly difficult for me because I have absolutely no idea why anyone would pour all their emotional energy into something that can't even give you a back rub. And not only that, but I feel superior about it. I believe anyone with a pet is actually weaker than I. Because when I ask somebody why they love their pet so much, they invariably say something like, "You just can't believe the amount of unconditional love Beemie gives me." Well, guess what. I don't need unconditional love, how about that? I need conditional love. I need someone who can walk on two legs and form sentences and use tools and remind me that that was the second time in a week that I yelled at a customer service person over the phone when I didn't get my way and *I may want to look into that.* I need to be loved by someone who can fully comprehend that when he sees me get locked out of my apartment three times in one month, that that may very well be the Thing About Me That Is Never Going to Change. And he loves me anyway. Not because it's an unconditional love, but because he actually truly knows me and has decided that my fascinating mind and hot bod are worth perhaps missing a flight or two because I forgot my driver's license at home.

But that's not really the point right now. The point here is that Ruby refuses to step out for a cup of coffee, go shopping, or even take a walk with me, because Ruby is a disaster at handling disappointment. Particularly of the romantic variety. Whatever good times she has with some fellow, it will never be worth the amount of pain and torture she puts herself through when it doesn't work out. The math of it simply doesn't add up. If she dates someone for three weeks, and then they break up, she'll spend the next two months driving herself and everyone around her crazy.

Because I'm an expert on the emotional MRI of Ruby, I can tell you exactly what happens during her descent. She will meet someone, a man, say, as opposed to a feline. She will like him. She will go out with him. Her heart will be full of the possibility and excitement that comes with finally finding someone you actually like who is available, kind, decent, and who seems to like you back.

As I said before, Ruby is attractive; very soft, very feminine. She can be inquisitive and attentive, and a great conversationalist. And when she meets men, they like her for all these reasons. Ruby is actually really good at the dating part of dating, and when she is in a relationship, she is clearly in her element.

However, this is New York, this is life, and this is dating. Things often don't work out. And when they don't, when Ruby gets rejected, for whatever reason it may be, and however the bad news is delivered, a process begins. She is usually fine at the Moment of Disappointment. Like when this guy Nile broke up with her because he wanted to get back together with his ex-girlfriend. At the moment of impact, she is philosophical about it. A burst of sanity and self-esteem washes over her, and she tells me that she knows that it just means he wasn't the one, and she can't take it personally and it's his loss. And then a few hours go by and time will push her further away from that moment of clarity and she will start to slip into the Crazy Pit. Her beloved, whom she once saw at normal size, starts growing larger and larger and larger, and in a matter of hours he becomes the Mount Everest of desirability and she is inconsolable. He was the best thing ever to happen to her. There will never be anyone as good as him ever again. Nile did the most powerful thing he could do to Ruby—he rejected her and now he is EVERYTHING and she is nothing.

I've gotten so used to watching Ruby go through this, that I make a point of being around her during those critical few hours after a rejection, to see if I can stop her at the top of the stairs down to Crazy. Because, let me tell you, once she goes down, there's no telling when she's going to come back up. And she doesn't like to sit there alone. Ruby likes to call up her friends and describe in vivid detail, for hours, what it's like in the basement of broken dreams. The wallpaper, the upholstery, the floor tiles. And there is nothing we can do. We just have to wait it out.

So you can imagine that after a few years of these ups and downs, whenever I get the call from Ruby that she has "met this great guy" or the second date went "really, really well," I'm not necessarily jumping for joy. Because, again, the math is simply not promising. If three weeks can add up to two months of tears, imagine how terrified I am when Ruby celebrates her four-month anniversary with someone. If she ends up breaking up with someone after a few years of living together, well, I don't think at this point there are enough years left in her life to get over him.

Which is why she decided to get Ralph. Ruby was tired of being disappointed. And as long as she kept her windows closed and doors not ajar, Ralph would never leave her. And Ruby would never have to be disappointed again. But Ruby didn't know about feline chronic renal failure.

And now, well, now Ralph was the best cat there ever was. Ralph made her happier than any animal or human could have ever possibly made her and she has no idea how she will ever live without him. She still manages to work. She's got her own business as an executive recruiter, and she has clients who rely on her to get their asses jobs. And thank God for them, because she will always get out of bed to help someone in need of a good nonlateral job placement. But a Saturday afternoon is much different. Ruby isn't budging.

Until I told her about Georgia. How her husband left her for a samba instructor and she's devastated and wants to go out and feel good about life. Then, Ruby understood completely. Ruby understood that there are moments when no matter how badly you feel, it's your duty to get out of the house and help deceive a newly single person into believing that everything is going to be okay. Ruby knew, intuitively, that this was just such a night.

How I'm Single

Let's be honest. I'm not doing it any better. I date, I meet men at parties and at work, or through friends, but things never seem to "work out." I'm not crazy, I don't date crazy men. Things just don't "work out." I look at couples walking down the street and I want to shake them, to beg them to answer my question, "How did you guys figure *that* out?" It has become the Sphinx for me, the eternal mystery. How do two people ever find each other in this city and "work out"?

And what do I do about it? I get upset. I cry. I stop. And then I cheer up and go out and be absolutely charming and have a great time as often as I can. I try to be a good person, a good friend, and a good member of my family. I try to make sure there isn't some unconscious reason why I'm still single. I keep going.

"You're single now because you're too snobby." That's Alice's answer every time the subject comes up. Meanwhile, I don't see her married to the handsome gentleman working at the fruit stand on the corner of Twelfth and Seventh who seems to have taken quite a shine to her. She is basing this judgment on the fact that I refuse to date online. In the good old days, online dating was considered a hideous embarrassment, something that no one would be caught dead admitting to. I loved that time. Now the reaction you will get from people when they hear that you're single and *not* doing some form of online dating is that you *must not really want it that bad.* It has become the bottom line, the litmus test for *how much you're willing to do for love.* As if your Mr. Right is definitely, absolutely guaranteed to be online. He's waiting for you and if you're not willing to spend the 1,500 hours, 39 coffees, 47 dinners, and 432 drinks to meet him, then you *just don't want to meet him badly enough and you deserve to grow old and die alone.*

"I don't think you're really open to love yet. You're not ready." That's Ruby's answer. I'm not even going to dignify it with a response—except to say, I didn't know that finding love had become something equivalent to becoming a Jedi Knight. I didn't know there were years of psychic training, metaphysical trials to endure, and rings of fire to jump through before I could get a date for my cousin's wedding in May. And yet, I know women who are so out of their minds they might as well be barking like dogs, who still find men who adore them, men whom they, in their madness, feel they are in love with. But no matter.

My mother thinks I'm single because I like having my independence. But she rarely weighs in on the subject. She comes from the generation of women who didn't think they had any other option but to get married and have children. There were no other choices for her. So she thinks it's just dandy that I'm single and that I don't have to rely on a man. I don't think my mother and father had a particularly happy marriage and after my father died, she was one of those widows who finally got to come into her own—the classes, the vacations, the bridge and book clubs. When I was still just a girl, she thought she was doing me a great service, giving me this wonderful gift of reminding me that I don't need a man to be happy. I can do anything I want, be anyone I want to be, without a man.

And now . . . I don't have the heart to tell her that I'm not really happy being single, and if you want to be someone's girlfriend or wife, and you happen to be straight, you kind of *do* need a man, *sorry, Mom,* because then I know she'd worry. Mothers do not like to see their children sad. So I steer the conversation away from my love life and she doesn't ask, both of us not wanting to reveal or know about any pesky unhappiness.

"Oh please," Serena—who, among my friends has known me the longest—said. "It's no mystery. You dated bad boys till your mid-thirties,
and now that you've finally come to your senses, the good ones are all
taken."

Bingo.

My last boyfriend six years ago was the worst one of all. There are
some guys you date who are so bad that when you tell the story about
them, it reflects just as badly on you as it does on them. His name was
Jeremy and we had been dating for two tumultuous years. He decided to
break up with me by not showing up to my father's funeral. I never heard
from him after that.

Since then, no bad boys. But no great love, either.

Georgia weighed in on this subject of why I'm single on one particularly dark, lonely, regretful night.

"Oh for God's sake, there's no reason. It's just totally fucked. You're
kind, you're beautiful, you have the best hair in New York City." (It's really
long and curly but never ever frizzy, and when I want to straighten it, it
looks just as great. I have to admit, it's my best feature.)

"You're hot, you're smart, you're funny, and you are one of the finest
people I know. You are perfect. Stop asking yourself that awful question
because there is not one goddamn reason why the sexiest, nicest, most
charming man in New York City isn't madly in love with you right now."

And that was why I loved Georgia. And that's how this weekend I
ended up spearheading an outing with my mismatched set of friends to
make her feel like life was worth living. Because at the end of the day, it's
night. And in New York, if it's night there's nightlife, and when there's life,
as most optimists will be happy to tell you, there's always hope. And I
guess that's a big part of how to be single. Hope. Friends. And making
sure you get out of your damn apartment.

RULE

2

Don't Be Crazy, No Matter How You Feel, Because It Just Makes Us All Look Bad

When you're going out for a night on the town with the main goal being to make a friend stop threatening, however unconvincingly, to commit suicide, you must pick your locations carefully. Alice and I discussed this with the deliberation of generals planning a midnight air assault. The truth is, any night you go out, you must do your research thoroughly. Because a bad night out can be demoralizing even for the fittest of us single women. So you must ask a lot of questions. How many men will there be to how many women? How expensive are the drinks? Is the music good? Is this the right night to be there? You have to take all these factors into consideration, and if need be, use graphs, diagrams, and a couple of well-placed phone calls to come up with the right plan of attack. In this case, the strategy was quite simple: places with tons of men. Because the one idea you don't want anywhere near your newly single friend is the one concept that is so all-pervasive, so oppressive, that it will be the first thought any sensible woman will have when she realizes she is now officially single, and that is of course, *There are no good men left*. And then the next thought would be *I'm going to be alone for the rest of my life*.

Now, the big question of whether there really are no good guys left in New York City is something we could probably debate forever, but for now we will leave the reality of that up to the Census Bureau and the matchmaking services. What I'm concerned about, for this particular night, is the *perception* that there are tons and tons of handsome single men out there, literally falling out of the skies, out of trees, bumping into you on the street, wanting to have sex with you. So therefore, in Alice's mind, where to have dinner was an easy choice. It had to be a steakhouse, and the biggest one there is. And that would be Peter Luger in Williamsburg, Brooklyn. Now you may wonder what we are doing taking our newly single friend out to Brooklyn. Well, wake up, sleepy—where have you been? Brooklyn is the new Manhattan and Williamsburg is the new Lower East Side and Peter Luger serves so much red meat that you are guaranteed to find heaps of straight men there (or women beefing up for their next weight-lifting competition). Either way, that makes the odds pretty good for us, and that's all I'm asking for. At a time like this, the perception of abundance is everything, not just with the thirty-eight-ounce steaks, but with the tons of straight men all sitting around large wooden tables in groups of eight and ten, devouring their meat like cavemen.

I don't know if you have ever been responsible for getting people together and deciding where they go for an evening. But if you haven't, let me tell you that it is a surprisingly nerve-racking experience. I say "surprisingly," because if you've never been the one in charge, you'll just be wondering why your normally relaxed friend asked you three times if you liked your tortellini. But if you've ever done it, you understand that even the most confident person turns into a jittery, insecure hostess, obsessed with every joke, eye roll, and aside made by her companions. And if it doesn't go well, it will be seared into people's minds as the night you took them out and they didn't have fun.

Now, the key to having fun is, of course, a great mix of people. So let me remind you of what we're dealing with here: Georgia, a newly single woman toying with the idea of a nervous breakdown; Ruby, who is still mourning the death of her cat; Serena, the girl in the nondairy wheat-free bubble; and Alice, who God bless her, though she may be working on a gastric ulcer from her dating schedule, is my only hope of getting through this in one piece.

You see, none of them know one another very well. They know each other from my various birthday parties throughout the years, but we are definitely not a gang. I met Alice at a spin class five years ago. I worked with Georgia until she left to raise her kids. Serena's my best friend from college and Ruby and I bonded fifteen years ago at a horrific temp job, then we shared an apartment for three years after that. They are basically strangers to one another. In fact, I could safely say that Alice, Georgia, Serena, and Ruby don't really care for each other that much, for no real reason except that none of them is really any of the others' "types." I always wanted a gaggle of girlfriends, always longed for a posse, my little family of friends, but it just didn't work out that way. It would have been nice if at one job I was able to grab a whole bunch of them, like lobsters in a trap. But meeting a group of women who end up living in the same city, remaining friends, and sharing the most intimate moments of their lives is rare and wonderful and definitely something to pine for, or at least watch on television.

"Oh my God, it's so cold, I should have worn a heavier coat. I hate October. October is the most annoying month because you never know how to dress," said "no-body-fat" Serena.

We had decided to meet on Twenty-third and Eighth, and take a cab to Williamsburg together. Everyone seemed to be fairly upbeat, but I could already tell that Serena, who was so out of her element, was going to be the problem. Not that I wasn't worried about Georgia, too, who was wearing a low-cut shirt and a miniskirt. Georgia is a gorgeous woman who can certainly pull this off. She's a slim five seven, with long, light brown hair and bangs that are just a little too long in that way they're supposed to be so they fall perfectly in front of her eyes. She has naturally bee-stung lips that many women would happily inject themselves for, and before the separation, used to always look effortlessly, carelessly hip. Now, however, it was October. And cold. And I could actually see her ass. We all piled into a cab and were on our way.

As Serena wondered aloud if there was going to be anything vegetarian to eat at this place, and Alice was barking orders at the cabdriver, I had an epiphany as to how this entire night might actually turn out okay. I realized there is a divine spirit looking out for us in this world. Because there's this thing called alcohol. And at that moment, alcohol seemed like such a good idea that I knew there must be a God who loved us enough to invent it.

When we entered Peter Luger Steak House it was just as my alcohol-creating God would have intended it: handsome, clearly employed men as far as the eye could see. The knot in my stomach relaxed. I knew that the first leg of the treasure hunt that is called "Running Around New York City Looking for Fun" was going to be a win for our team.

"Oh my God, I'm a genius," Alice said proudly.

"Yay!" said Georgia.

"I love it here," said Ruby.

"I know there's not going to be one thing here that I can eat," said Serena, as we walked past the multitudes of tables heaped with cooked animal flesh.

It's a funny thing about peer pressure: it works at any age. While we were looking at the menus, Serena ordered a vodka tonic. Now that might not seem like much to you, but it was a momentous occasion in my book. And it came to be simply because my three friends, who didn't know Serena at all, told her she should lighten up. And she got embarrassed. After the past three years of my begging her to try a mojito, it was as simple as that. She still ordered a plate of broccoli rabe for dinner, but you couldn't deny that there was magic in the girl posse and it had already begun.

It's always better when you have a purpose, whether in life or simply for a night out, and for this evening the goal was clear: Georgia needed to flirt with someone recklessly. And here we were, in the land of big steaks and bold moves. So as the red meat and alcohol began to flow, it was time to get into wacky-scheme mode.

Alice decided to approach the table adjacent to us, which, coincidentally, had five men at it.

"Hey guys, we're trying to show our newly single friend a good time and thought it'd be fun to crash your table."

Alice is fearless. Once you've had a few murderers lunge at you from across a table and try to choke you to death, walking up to a group of guys is a piece of cake. And because of Alice, there we were, moving our plates and silverware over to the table next to us and squeezing ourselves in very closely with a bunch of cute men. And Georgia, happily, was getting the lion's share of the attention, like a bride-to-be at her bachelorette party. Nothing like putting your romantic stakes right out on the table to get people hopping, and this time she didn't need to wear the plastic condom veil with matching penis earrings. I looked around the table and this is what I saw:

Georgia giggling like a schoolgirl.

Ruby giggling like a schoolgirl.

Serena giggling like a schoolgirl.

Alice giggling like a schoolgirl.

And, when I gave myself a moment to stop worrying if everyone was having a good time, I was giggling like a schoolgirl, too. And I thought, *My God, we are pathetic creatures. We are lawyers and publicists and businesswomen and mothers with blow-dried hair and lipstick, all just waiting for the sun of male attention to shine down upon us and make us feel alive again.*

They taught us drinking games, we made jokes about their ties. Ruby was talking to a man who seemed particularly enraptured with her and every one of the guys told Georgia that she was hot and she doesn't have a thing to worry about. There was gold in that thar steakhouse.

"Oh my God, that was so much fun!" Georgia said, laughing, as we left the restaurant.

"I can't believe I drank vodka!" Serena said, beaming.

"That guy I was talking to wants to come with us wherever we go next!" Ruby said, giggling. "Where are we going next?!"

Now, the thing about being responsible for people's good time is that the stakes just keep getting higher and higher throughout the night, no matter what has happened the moment before. If dinner was a dud, then boy, you have to make up for it with a kick-ass bar or club to go to next. If dinner was really fun, which in this case it was, then you better not blow it by picking a place that brings the mood down. So I conferred again with my own personal Zagat, Alice. We were sticking with the theme "It's raining men" so Alice made her decision quickly. We headed to "Sports," a fancy sports bar with a clearly unimaginative name on the Upper West Side. Ruby and her new guy, Gary, took one cab and we piled into another. Not the cheapest taxi ride but what's money when there's five drunky girls trying to keep their buzz alive?

When we arrived, I knew immediately that this was a misstep. The problem with sports bars hits you immediately when you walk in: men really are there to watch sports. Because if they really had their sights set on going out to meet women—they wouldn't go to a sports bar. Alice was thinking the same thing.

"We should go to the Flatiron instead."

But Serena had already ordered another vodka and Georgia had walked up to the cutest guy in the place and was trying to talk to him. Unfortunately, there was a big Knicks basketball game on—which I don't understand since it was preseason and the Knicks aren't involved in "big" basketball games anymore. Anyway, Georgia was able to grab his attention during a commercial break and she was using those four minutes to get in as much flirting as possible.

Ruby was talking to Gary, who had clearly fallen in love with her and wanted to be with her forever. But unfortunately for Serena, Alice, and me, we were soon sitting at the bar with our drinks, looking at about twenty screens of various sports that we couldn't give a crap about.

But Alice knew something we didn't.

"Oh my God, there's a foosball table over there!" Alice said, way too excitedly.

"I don't play foosball," Serena said, already grumpy.

"Do you think we should go somewhere else?" I said, ignoring the whole foosball idea.

"No, you don't understand. It is an absolute fact that a group of women cannot play foosball for more than ten minutes without guys coming over to play with them."

"You've spent a lot of time proving this fact?" I said, a little reproachfully. Did I happen to tell you that Alice used to be a lawyer who defended the rights of the poor and disenfranchised, making them feel respected and heard, often at the darkest times of their lives?

"Yes. And I'll prove it to you now."

So we took our drinks and moved over to the foosball table. Alice and I played foosball, while Serena watched the clock. It was exactly three and a half minutes before two guys walked up to us. At four and a half minutes, they challenged us to a game.

Alice scares me, sometimes.

She is, of course, brilliant at foosball, so we kept winning and getting challenged, the foosball suitors lining up to get a piece of our foosball magic. We kept drinking and the giggles started again and the next thing I knew, Serena was eating chicken wings off one of our challengers' plates. A game later, she was licking her hot-sauce-covered fingers and ordering a plate of wings for herself. She was a vegan gone wild. I quickly scanned the room and saw Ruby still chatting with Gary, and Georgia still trying to talk to the cute guy between sports highlights. I had never seen Georgia flirt before; she was already married when I met her. But I could tell from just one look that she was trying too hard. She was talking a little too animatedly, listening a little too earnestly, laughing a little too excitedly. She was trying to compete with the Knicks and, even though they suck, she didn't stand a chance. But instead of cutting her losses, she continued to touch his arm, laugh loudly, and order another drink.

As Alice and I continued to beat these two guys (Bruce and Todd) at foosball, I heard Alice, when asked what she does for a living, say in complete earnestness that she's a "facialist." I looked at her with surprise and she shot me a look of "I'll explain later." I had had my foosball and flirting fill and excused myself, getting Serena to stop shoving poultry in her face long enough to take my place, and I walked over to the bar. On one side I heard Georgia squealing, "Oh my God, I love Audioslave!" (like she knows from Audioslave), and on the other, Ruby was saying to Gary, "I loved Ralph, but I mean, he was just a cat, you know?"

Alice eventually walked over to get a drink. I looked at her, scowling with as much judgment and disappointment as I could muster. Alice took the hint.

"Didn't you hear about that study that came out of England? The smarter you are, the less likely you are of getting married. The dumb girls are getting the guys."

"So you say that you give facials for a living, instead of that you're a lawyer who graduated with top honors from Harvard Law School?"

"Yes, and it works."

"What happens if you start dating one of these guys?"

"I'm just getting them interested by appealing to their basest level. Once I have their interest, I slowly sneak the smart in, but by then they're hooked."

Appalled, I turned around just in time to see Georgia grabbing the cute guy's face and kissing him straight on the lips. Kind of like a crazy person. Cute guy's response: not so excited. He did that sort of laughing, sort of muttering "oh ho ho, you're one wild girl" while trying to politely peel her off him. It was a painful moment for all of us.

Serena ran up to us, her face aglow with hot sauce.

"Bruce and Todd think we should go to Hogs and Heifers."

Serena, who before tonight hadn't been anywhere there wasn't Enya or waterfall sounds playing, thought Hogs & Heifers was a keen idea. I realized she was slightly drunk.

"Cool, I know all the bartenders there," Alice replied.

Ruby and her new boyfriend, Gary, thought it was a great idea, too. Again, the entertainment director in me was concerned. Our evening had degraded from Steaks and Vodka to Beer and Wings to Hogs & Heifers. New York is a big, hip, glamorous city, and there was no need to be ending our night in a touristy, outdated biker bar. I told them this, but alas, the horses had broken out of the barn and were now planning to gallop all the way downtown to Hogs & Heifers with or without me. Ruby came up, excited.

"Gary is going to meet us down there; he just had to go pick up one of his friends. Julie—wouldn't it be an amazing story if Ralph died but I ended up meeting the love of my life right after? Wouldn't that be great? Gary's really cute, right?"

"He is totally cute, Ruby. Totally." And he was. He seemed really nice and into her, and by God, people meet and fall in love every day of the week, so what the heck?

Alice, Georgia, and Serena were already outside hailing cabs with Bruce and Todd. Ruby went outside to join them. I decided to go along. My experience with women not used to drinking or staying out late is that by the time they have the cab ride downtown, they'll be sleepy, slightly nauseous, and ready to go home.

Unfortunately, that was not the case. In their cab going downtown, Todd told Georgia about how Hogs & Heifers is famous for women getting on the bar and dancing, and then somehow taking off their bras. Demi's done it, Julia's done it, Drew's done it. It's the thing to do. At least, that's what Alice told me when I got there, explaining how and why

Georgia had managed to already be on top of the bar swinging her bra around. Ruby was screaming and laughing, Serena was hootin' and hollerin' and the place was going wild. Hogs & Heifers is famous for its "biker redneck" aesthetic. The walls are covered with hundreds of women's tossed-off bras for as far as the eye can see. Wherever there might be a tiny bit of wall space left, there's an American flag or cowboy hat. The bartenders are all women wearing tight denim and even tighter t-shirts and the place is packed. Bruce and Todd had disappeared, but I'm sure they were hootin' and hollerin' from wherever they were. It's so odd how all it takes is a few people dancing on a bar to make people feel as if they're having a hilariously wild night out.

Now, you have to understand why seeing Georgia on top of a bar was disturbing to me. Remember, I met Georgia when she was already married. And Georgia and Dale were not the couple you're going to catch groping each other in the kitchen. So I have never actually seen Georgia get her groove on, so to speak, and it wasn't something I ever really missed seeing. I looked at her on the bar, gyrating and grinding, and I remembered back to a day when I went to the beach with Georgia and her two children, Beth and Gareth. She spent the whole day in the water with them, getting them used to the waves. I helped for a while, playing with them for an hour or two, but she stayed in longer than any adult human being should have to, without a complaint. Then she let them cover her entire body with sand, with only her tired, salty face sticking out. That's the Georgia I remember—Georgia, the wife and mother of two.

But now Georgia was allowing herself to unravel. She was single, she was out, and she wanted to have FUN!

The bar was crowded with lots of guys, many from out of town, some bikers, a couple of cowboys (don't ask me), all sharing the common trait of having a deep respect for women and their struggles on this planet. Just kidding. Serena then got on the bar as well, beer in hand, drinking and dancing. Okay, I'll admit it, that was fun to see. Serena, not only in a bar, but *on* a bar and trying to do a two-step. Alice then got up on the bar, too—my own little White Trash Rockettes. Ruby, however, was now standing by the door, checking her cell phone constantly and looking out onto the street, waiting for Gary. She might as well have been sitting on the windowsill, like her pet cat, Ralph, waiting for her master to arrive.

My stomach began to tighten again at the idea that there might be another impending disappointment in store for Ruby.

The longest country song in the world finally came to an end, and Alice and Serena, as drunk but not completely-out-of-their-minds women do, got off the bar. Georgia, however, stayed, not yet ready to leave the spotlight. A large biker man in his fifties, with a bushy gray beard and long gray hair, helped Serena off the bar. I overheard him ask her if he could buy her a drink.

She said, "Yes, and some ribs would be nice as well." I don't quite understand what happened, but somewhere after her first vodka tonic, Serena's sleeping carnivore awoke, and she turned into a pretty, little werewolf. The biker man told Serena his name was Frankie and he was an art dealer who had just finished a long round of the galleries of Chelsea and came in for a break.

"Wow, that just goes to show you. I would never have guessed you were an art dealer. I know nothing about people, Frank." As she spoke she drunkenly slung her arm over Frank's shoulder. "I've been living a sheltered life. And I know nothing. *Nothing.*"

Alice had also gotten the attention of a few men. I guess their spotlight dance was like a thirty-second dating advertisement. So, there I was again, worrying about my friends and not having any fun on my own. I started wondering if it would be okay for me to leave. I was tired of being Judge McJudgey, and frankly, I was beginning a downward spiral of worry and fear. *What would become of all of us? Would we end up with husbands and children? Would we all stay in New York? What would become of me? Would I just stay at my hateful job, doing work that doesn't satisfy me, being single, alone, trying to make the best of it for the rest of my life? Is this as good as it's going to get? A yuppie biker bar on a Saturday night at 2 A.M.?*

But then a guy came up and started talking to me. And that's all it took to cheer me up. Because, I believe you recall, we are pathetic creatures. He was cute and he picked me to talk to and I was flattered as if I was at my first school dance. I forgot all morose or possibly deep thoughts and just started flirting my ass off.

"So what brings you to this place?" he asked. His name was David and he was in town from Houston with his buddy Tom. I pointed to Georgia, who was still dancing up a storm.

"She just split up with her husband and we're trying to show her a good time."

He looked up at Georgia, and he said, "It looks like you did a good job." As if the universal symbol for having a good time is dancing on a bar swinging your bra around.

He then said, "I split up with my girlfriend two months ago. It was really rough, so I understand what she's going through." Was he really trying to talk seriously with me while "Achy Breaky Heart" was playing and women were taking off their bras on the bar? That's kind of sweet. We sat down at a table, and began to have a lovely conversation, the kind you can have anywhere at any time when you're with someone you really like talking to. I told him about our evening and how worried I was about it, and he immediately began to tease me about being a control freak. I love it when they tease. And he talked about being a little bit bossy since he's the oldest of four, and how much he worries about all his siblings. Cute.

I believe we were talking for an hour, though it could have been five hours or ten minutes. I couldn't tell you. I had stopped worrying, thinking, and judging, and was just trying to have a goddamn nice time.

I finally looked up to see a girl gesturing to Georgia to get off the bar. Yes, Georgia was still on the bar, and for everyone there, the novelty had worn off and they wanted someone else to take advantage of that valuable bartop real estate. I saw Georgia shaking her head as if to say "No fucking way." In fact, I think I heard her actually say that. I walked over to Georgia and saw that Alice was now bartending, because randomly, Alice knows how to bartend and decided to help out. I saw Serena nodding out in a corner with the biker art buyer. He was holding her so she wouldn't fall over and while doing so, had a hand firmly over her right breast. I had no idea where Ruby was. Then a guy from the crowd screamed, "Get your tired old ass off the bar, and give that other girl a chance! She's hotter and younger and you can't dance for shit!" And the entire bar laughed. I turned around to see what asshole said it—and it was David. David whom I was just talking to, David. The cute teaser, David.

Georgia heard this, and I could see the words hit her ears, go into her brain, and wash across her face. She was mortified. And at this moment, the Georgia I used to know would have sort of crumpled off the bar and run into the bathroom, in tears. But the new Georgia, how-ever humiliated she might have felt, flipped David her middle finger and refused to give up her spot. The hot girl in question was now pissed and started grabbing at Georgia's calves to pull her off the bar. A very large bouncer, perhaps a giant, got to the bar quickly and tried to keep things calm. And yet Georgia would not get down. She wanted to stay up there and dance to country music until she goddamn felt like coming down. She would stay up there until all her pain was gone and she truly felt attractive and whole and loved again. And if that took her to next Christmas, by God, I think she planned on being up there until then.

Now Georgia started dancing even more suggestively than she had been, like a stripper on speed. It was about as painful a thing to watch as anything you could imagine. Except for perhaps ten seconds later, when I looked over to see Serena vomiting on herself. Oh yes. I was about to run over to her when I saw Georgia try to kick the bouncer, who then pulled her off the bar. The hot girl took this opportunity to call Georgia a cunt, and Georgia, now flung over the bouncer's shoulder, managed to seize the hot girl's hair and tug as hard as she could. The hot girl then slapped Georgia in the face as the bouncer weaved and turned, trying to get these women away from each other. He put Georgia down and one of the hot girl's friends punched her in the arm.

This was when Alice jumped across the bar and started throwing punches at the hot girl, the hot girl's friends, and anyone else who got in her way. You can take the girl out of the fight, but you can't take the fight out of the girl, and until that moment, I had no idea how good Alice was at actual hand-to-hand combat. Frankly, I was impressed. Not much of a fighter myself, I ran to Serena.

"Good, you better deal with her. This bitch is fucked up," the biker art dealer delicately said to me, as he stood up. As if on cue, Serena vomited on herself again. The only saving grace to all this was that she was out cold, so she was spared the humiliation of seeing her entire self covered in half-digested chicken wings and ribs.

"What should I do?" I asked.

"Get her to the emergency room. She might have alcohol poisoning." He looked at her, disgusted.

Georgia and Alice were still pulling and scratching and swinging. I made my way through the crowd trying to avoid physical injury and managed to scream out to Georgia and Alice that Serena might have to go to the hospital and we had to go. They didn't need to agree with me on this, because they were promptly dragged by the scruffs of their necks by two other very large men, and basically thrown out onto the street. Frank had deposited Serena outside as well. "Jesus, I'm fucking covered in her fucking vomit. Fuck." He shook his head and walked back inside. It was a lovely sight to see: Alice and Georgia scratched and bruised and Serena covered in vomit, all underneath a big neon sign that said "Hogs & Heifers." I realized that I didn't know where Ruby was, but I had a hunch. I went back in and walked through the crowd to the ladies' room. I got there to find, exactly as I suspected, Ruby sitting on the bathroom floor, her pretty heart-shaped face crumpled up in pain, her eye makeup dripping down her face. She was sobbing.

"He didn't show up. Why would he say he was going to show up if he didn't mean it?" I sat down on the floor with her, and put my arm around her.

"How do people do this?" she asked. "How do people keep putting themselves out there when they know they're probably just going to get hurt? How can anyone deal with that much disappointment? It's unnatural. We're not supposed to go through life so exposed. That's why people get married. Because no one is supposed to go through life that vulnerable. No one is supposed to be forced to meet so many strangers who end up making you feel bad!"

I had nothing to say to this. I was in complete agreement with her. "I know. It's brutal, isn't it?"

"But what are we supposed to do? I don't want to be the girl who stays home and cries about her cat. I don't want to be the one that's sitting here now! But what can I do? I liked him and I wanted him to come down to the bar like he said he would and he didn't show up and *I'm so disappointed*!"

I scooped Ruby up and walked outside with her. On the way out, I passed David and kind of shoved him. Hard. Made him spill his drink. I was mad at him—he had humiliated my friend Georgia and ended up not being my husband.

When we got outside, I explained to Ruby what had happened with the fighting and the vomiting. Then Georgia told us Alice had already taken Serena to the hospital. We all hopped in a cab and went to Saint Vincent's.

By the time we got there, Serena's stomach was being pumped, which I have heard is not a pleasant experience by any stretch of the imagination. I was thinking that sounded a little severe until the nurse told me Serena had consumed about seventeen drinks during the course of the evening.

Why hadn't I noticed? I was so busy being happy that she was finally letting her hair down, I didn't even see that she was hazing herself. Alice and Georgia came back from getting treated for their wounds and were covered in bandages like a pair of Roller Derby girls.

Something was terribly, terribly wrong. We were beautiful, accomplished, sexy, intelligent single women and we were disasters. If there was a "How To" book to write, it should be called "How Not to Be Us." We were doing it all wrong, this "being single" business, yet I had no clue as to how to do it better.

As my thoughts were giving way to musings of a better life, I looked over to see two women across from us, very animatedly speaking in French. Both were beautiful, slim, impeccably dressed women in their early forties. One was wearing a brown felt duster with large white stitching on the front side and the other was in a short brown suede coat with fringe. Somehow it worked. I never notice shoes, won't even bother, but a nice thin overcoat that makes you ignore anything else being worn, well, that impresses me. These perfect ladies were obviously disgusted about something. Which is so French. As I tuned in with my two years of college French, I got the gist of it: the health care in the States is *deplorable,* this emergency room is filthy, and America basically sucks. I was now curious as to what brought them here. They looked so elegant, so perfect. What could have possibly gone wrong in their lovely French lives to have them wind up in the emergency room? Did one of their friends OD on contempt?

"Excuse me, is there anything I can do to help?" I tried to appear friendly, but I just felt like being nosy.

The two women stopped talking and stared at me. The one with the fringe coat looked at Ruby and Alice with complete superiority and said, "Our friend sprained her ankle." The other one, darting her eyes around us, decided to get curious as well.

"What brings *you* here?" she said in her adorable French accent. I was thinking about lying when Alice just blurted it out.

"We got into a fight with some girls."

"They made me get off the bar I was dancing on," Georgia said. She stared at them as if to say "and I'm ready for another round." The French women scrunched up their noses as if they'd smelled some bad Brie.

They looked at each other and spoke in French. It was something like, "American women, have no [*something*]. Where are their mothers? Did they not teach them [*something*]?"

I understood everything but that one word. Damn that I didn't keep up with my French studies. Oh, fuck it.

"Excuse me, what does *orgueil* mean?" I asked, a little confrontation-ally.

The one in the long coat looked me straight in the eye and said, "Pride. You American women have no pride."

Alice and Georgia sat up straight, ready to rumble. Ruby looked like she was going to cry. But I was interested. "Really? Do all French women have pride? Do you all walk around proud and dignified all the time?"

The French women looked at each other and nodded. "Yes, for the most part, we do." And then they moved to another corner of the emergency room. Ouch. Shamed by the cool French ladies.

But I really couldn't argue with them. We were by no means behaving like the strong, independent single women that we were taught we could be. I wondered how we had sunk so low. It's not as if we didn't have role models. We did. We had our Gloria Steinem, Jane Fonda, Mary and Rhoda, and so many more. We have image after image of beautiful single women who lead fun, fulfilling, sexy lives. Yet many of us—I won't say all, I refuse to say all, but many of us—still walk around knowing that we're barely making the best of the untenable situation of not having romantic love in our lives. We have our jobs and our friends and our passions and our churches and our gyms and yet we still can't escape our essential nature of needing to be loved and feel close to another human being. How do we keep going when that's not what life has given to us?

How do we date, having to act as if it's not the be-all and end-all in our lives, while knowing that one great date could change the course of our lives? How do we keep going in the face of all the disappointment and uncertainty? How do we be single and not go crazy?

All I knew was that I was sick and tired of it all. I was sick of the parties and the clothes and the schedules and the taxis and the phone calls and the drinks and the lunches. I was tired of my job. I was tired of doing something that I hated, but being too scared to do anything about it. I was frankly tired of America, with all our indulgences and our myopia. I was stuck and tired.

And suddenly I realized what I wanted to do. I wanted to talk to more single women. I wanted to talk to them all over the world. I wanted to know if anyone out there was doing this single thing any better than we were. After reading all the self-help books that I have, it was ironic—I was still looking for advice.

The next morning I logged on to my computer and spent the day doing research about single women all over the world. I learned about marriage and divorce statistics from New Delhi to Greenland. I even stumbled across the sex practices in Papua New Guinea. (Read about their yam festival, it's fascinating.) The rest of Sunday I walked around Manhattan and thought about what it would be like to leave it all. As I walked downtown along Eighth Avenue, through all the different neighborhoods and communities, crossed to the East Village and saw all the NYU students rushing around with great urgency, then walked past the South Street Seaport and saw the tourists taking their photographs, and made my way to the Hudson River, I thought about what it would feel like to remove myself from this ball of activity and intensity that is New York. By the time I got back to Union Square, and watched all the people selling or buying things at the farmers' market, I had to admit it: If I left town for a little while, Manhattan would really do just fine without me. It would manage.

So on Monday, I walked into my boss's office and pitched her an idea for a book. It would be titled "How to Be Single" and I would travel around the world and see if there is any place in the world where women are better at being single than here. I mean, we might not necessarily

have all the answers here in America; we could perhaps be taught a thing or two. I knew the first stop would be France. Those women never want to read our self-help books—they don't give a crap about Bridget Jones—and the French version of *The Bachelor* has yet to be made. Why not start there? My boss, Candace, an extremely unpleasant woman, around sixty, very well respected and quite feared, replied that it was the worst idea she had ever heard.

"'How to Be Single'? Like they need to be good at it because they're going to be single for that long? That's depressing. Nobody wants to be single. That's why you always have to give women the hope that they soon *won't* be single, that the man of their dreams is right around the corner and the horror will soon come to an end. If you want to write a book, write one called 'How *Not* to Be Single.'" She said this without looking up from her computer.

"And, by the way, who cares what they're doing in France or India or Timbuktu for that matter? This is America, and frankly we do know best and I couldn't give a fuck what they're doing in Tanzania."

"Oh," I said. "Then I guess that new statistic that there are officially more single women living in America than married ones means nothing to you?"

She peered at me from over her glasses.

"Continue."

"And that maybe women need a book that's not about how to get a man or keep a man, but how to cope with a state of being that's inherently filled with confliction, emotion, and mystery?"

"I'm still bored," Candace said as she took her glasses off. I continued.

"And that maybe women might want to read a book that helps them deal with something that might be long-term, and not sugarcoat it for them? It's a fact that all over the world women are getting married later in life and getting divorced more easily. Maybe women might be interested in a global perspective on something that's so private. Maybe they would find it comforting."

Candace folded her arms over her chest and thought for a moment.

"Comforting is nice. Comforting sells," she said, finally looking up at me.

"And I'll pay for all my travel expenses," I added. After all these years, I knew what to say to really sell something.

"Well, the idea is certainly getting less unbearable," she said, begrudgingly, as she grabbed a notepad. She wrote down something on the notepad and passed it to me on the desk.

"That would be your advance, if you're interested. Take it or leave it."

I looked at the figure on the piece of paper. It was incredibly low. Not low enough for me to walk out in a huff, but not high enough for me to appear grateful. I accepted the offer.

That evening, I went back to my small one-bedroom apartment, sat on my couch, and looked around. I still lived like I was twenty-five. I had my books, my CDs, my iPod. My computer, my television, my photos. I have no talent for decorating. No personal flair. It was an extremely depressing place. And it was time to go. I got on the phone and cashed in all my stocks, leaving me with a very meager sum of money. I then went on Craigslist and by the time the week was through I had someone subletting my apartment, had a "round-the-world" plane ticket (basically the airline version of a Eurail Pass for the entire world), and I had explained to my mother what I was doing.

"Well, I think that's fantastic. I always thought you needed a break from the nine-to-five. It's time you do something outside the box," is all my incredibly supportive mother had to say. But then she added, "Just don't go anywhere too dangerous. I have no need to hear about you getting blown up in some marketplace."

Then, right before I left, I called up my four dear friends and asked them to please look out for one another. I asked Serena, Ruby, and Georgia to make sure Alice didn't overdose on Tums or dating. I asked Alice, Georgia, and Serena to make sure Ruby got out of the house, and I asked Alice and Ruby to make sure Serena and Georgia didn't leave the house at all. I found out that at least one of those concerns was already taken care of.

"I've decided to become a swami," Serena said, over the phone.

"I'm sorry, what?" was my witty reply.

"I've quit my job and I'm going to renounce all my worldly desires and take a vow of celibacy at my yoga center. The ceremony is next week—can't you postpone your trip to make it? I've invited Georgia, Alice, and Ruby, too."

I lied (yes, I lied to a soon-to-be member of the clergy) and told her I couldn't, I had a big meeting in France with someone about my new, exciting book and I just simply couldn't change my plans. And then I hung up the phone and got ready to get my ass out of New York. Was I going crazy? I wasn't sure. It may have seemed like an insane thing to do at the time, but somehow . . . staying in New York would have been even crazier.

RULE

3

*Decide What You Believe In
and Then Behave Accordingly*

"Well, I've lined up four women for tonight. They're excited to talk to you."

"They are? You really did that for me?"

"You told me that you wanted to talk to single French women, so I got you single French women."

Steve is my oldest friend in the world. I met him on the first day of my freshman year of high school. He sat behind me in home room. I turned around and told him he looked exactly like Jon Bon Jovi and we have been lifelong friends ever since. We stayed close even when we went to different colleges, and even when Steve moved away to study harpsichord and orchestra conducting in Paris. There were never any romantic notions between us, which never seemed odd to us, and then somewhere during his junior year abroad, Steve realized he was gay. He now lives in Paris, travels the world conducting operas and accompanying singers, and nothing pleases him more than being a wonderful host to his visiting friends and getting junk food—Twinkies, Sno Balls, jelly beans—brought to him from the States.

He took a sip of his coffee and smiled at me. He shaved his head ten years ago when he realized he was going bald, and now he sports a very trendy, I wouldn't say beard, but more like a hair pattern on his face. He has a thin line of hair that follows along his jawline, like an outline of a beard. Somehow the whole effect is quite distinguished— which is crucial when you're a thirty-eight-year-old man who works in opera. I took a bite of the most delicious croissant known to mankind and wondered how I ever thought I wouldn't eat bread while I was in Europe.

"They suggested you meet them at Régine's, which is a great idea."

"What's Régine's?"

"It's this place where hundreds and hundreds of the most beautiful young women in Paris go on Saturday nights starting at eight. To be together and talk."

I was confused. "Hundreds of French women all go to a nightclub to get together and talk? That makes no sense."

"I don't get it, either. But apparently the women have three hours just to be alone, unbothered. They even get a free buffet. After eleven P.M. the men are allowed in. They supposedly line up to get in because they know hundreds of beautiful women are inside. It's a genius marketing idea, really."

"But," I say, my mind already in research mode, "they go just to be together? That's weird."

"We don't have that in the States?" he asked.

"No, women don't need a special night where they get to be alone together. We can do that any day of the week."

After consideration, Steve said, "Well, I don't think French women travel in packs like you girls do in the States. Maybe this is their chance to make new friends."

This was exciting. I'd only been there for a few hours and already I was onto a big cultural difference: *French women like to go out in droves just to be somewhere without men.* I started to think about the ramifications of this. Are French men so aggressive that the women need a place to be away from them? Are French women so antisocial in their daily lives that they need a place to make friends? I couldn't wait to figure it all out.

"It's sweet of these women to agree to talk to me. But I don't know what I'm going to ask them. This is all new. Maybe I can just get them all drunk and see what happens."

"French women don't get drunk," Steve said.

"They don't?" I asked, disappointed.

"They might have a glass of wine or two, but I've never seen a French woman drunk."

"Well, then, difference number two. No drunky French ladies." I took a big sip of café au lait.

"Don't worry. Women are women. Get them all together and eventually they all start talking."

"I sure as hell hope so." I downed the rest of my drink. "Can I take a nap now? Please? Is that breaking the laws of jet lag?"

"You may take a nap now. But only for a few hours."

"Thank you, *mon chéri,* thank you."

And with that, Steve took me to his two-bedroom French flat and put me to bed.

It was a mob scene outside Régine's. What seemed like hundreds of gorgeous young women were all converging on this one nightclub. They were prompt, dressed up, and wanting desperately to get in.

"These women are herding themselves in here just to make new friends? This is insane!" I said to Steve as we got shoved by some six-foot-tall beauty (who I'm sure was *definitely* going to get in).

Just then, we heard a high-pitched voice yell "Steef! Steef!" Charging through the crowd was a short, stocky woman, wearing simple black trousers and a t-shirt. She did not look dressed for a night on the town.

"That's Clara," Steve explained. "She handles all of the business affairs for the Paris opera house. When you told me what you needed, I called her first—she knows everybody."

"*Bonsoir,*" said Clara as she walked up to Steve and kissed him on both his cheeks. Steve introduced us, then leaned his face out to me to kiss, and said, "*Au revoir.*"

"Really? I'm on my own?" I said. I was suddenly overcome with shyness.

"You know the rules, no men allowed . . ." Steve said. And with that we kissed and he was off. Clara then immediately grabbed me and barreled her way to the doorman. She spoke to him forcefully, and got us both into the club.

As we walked down a long set of stairs, and my eyes adjusted to the darkness, I asked, "But what about the other women? How will we find them?"

"I'll get them later. Let's just sit you down at the table."

The club itself seemed to be all red velvet banquettes and pink lighting. And there were women as far as the eye could see, as if I had thrown a bomb into a lake of pretty ladies and these were the ones who had floated to the surface. I was so impressed. I had no idea that French women would fight and haggle and risk possible humiliation with a doorman just to have a precious few hours to be alone with one another. This was a triumph of female kinship. Of course, later they got to meet men. But here it was, eight o'clock, and there was a long line for the buffet table and the banquettes were getting filled up. They had a little roped-off area where some French makeup company was giving free makeovers. This was fantastic. My first day in Paris and I'd already hit on a stereotype-debunking cultural trend: French women needing to be French women together. Maybe this wasn't such a crazy idea after all.

A buff, shirtless waiter in tiny little harem pants walked by with champagne, *free* champagne. Nice touch, love it, fabulous—I helped myself to one as Clara came back with three women: Patrice, Audrey, and Joanne. I stood up to say hello, but Clara shooed me back down and they all came and sat in the banquette. Greetings were exchanged. Patrice was a pretty book editor in her thirties with hair pulled up in an elegant do; Audrey was a very sexy brunette opera singer, with long wild hair and a wraparound dress that showed off her big, lovely—lungs; and Joanne, a jewelry designer, seemed to be about forty-five years old with brown hair in long, cute braids dangling messily down each side of her face. Clara, though not as elegant as the others, was pretty in a farm-girl kind of way. I took out a little hardcover journal I had bought in New York that I thought I would make my notes in. I was trying to appear professional. They looked at me expectantly. It was time I explained myself.

"I'm thirty-eight and single and live in New York. I met these French women in a hospital emergency room, not that that's important, and they seemed to, well, know something that we Americans don't know. About how to be single?" It felt so silly coming out of my mouth, but luckily Joanne piped right in.

"Oh please, we don't have any answers. I mean, c'mon." She dismissed the idea immediately with that superior French accent of hers. The others seemed to agree.

"Really? You don't have anything you can teach me?" I asked. They all shook their heads no again. I decided I should try to dig a little deeper. After all, they were a captive audience.

"For instance, they talked about French women having pride. Does that make sense to you?"

"What do you mean?" Patrice asked.

"Well. Let's say you go out with a guy on a date—"

Patrice stopped me. "We don't go on dates here."

"You don't?"

All the women shook their heads again. No dates.

"Well, what do you go on, then?" I asked, confused.

"We go out, we have a drink, but we don't call this a date. We are just having a drink."

"Yes, but if you like the person, if it's a man you're interested in, isn't it a date?"

The women just shook their heads at me, no.

"But let's say a man you work with asks you to go have a drink, and it's a man you really like. Wouldn't you be a little excited and maybe, let's say, get a little dressed up?" I could see from their expressions that I was already losing them. "And then wouldn't that, in fact, be a date?"

They kept shaking their heads. Clearly *date* was not one of the American words the French co-opted. I was getting nowhere so I changed my tack.

"Okay, what if you've slept with a guy. Someone you liked. And then he doesn't call you. You would feel bad, yes?" The women all shrugged some version of yes.

"So would you ever, in a weak moment, call him and say you wanted to see him again?"

They all started shaking their heads no violently.

"No, never," Audrey said.

"Absolutely not," Patrice said.

"Not really, no," said Joanne.

Clara shook her head also. "No."

"Really?" I said, surprised. "You wouldn't be tempted?"

"No, of course not," said Audrey. "We have our pride."

And they all nodded in agreement.

So there it was again. Pride.

"Well, who taught you about this? This idea of pride?"

"My mother," Clara said.

"Yes, my mother," said Patrice.

"Our world, our culture. It's in the air," said Audrey.

"So a man, a boyfriend, starts pulling away from you, starts calling you less and less, tells you that maybe he's not ready to be in a relationship, what would you do?"

"I wouldn't call him again."

"I would think it's his loss."

"I would not bother with him."

"Even if you really like him?"

"Yes."

"Yes."

"Yes."

"Yes."

I was sitting there staring at four women who were good at accepting rejection—these ladies didn't seem like they were from France, they seemed like they were from Mars.

Elegant Patrice tried to explain it to me. "Julie, you have to understand, it's not that we don't feel things; we do. We fall in love, we get our hearts broken, we're disappointed and sad, but we've been taught that you must always have your pride. Above all."

Again, much nodding in agreement.

"So does that mean you all love yourselves or something?" I blurted out. They all smiled, but this time they differed.

"No," Patrice said.

"Not necessarily," said Audrey. "We've just learned how to hide our insecurities."

"Yes," said Joanne, the beautiful forty-five-year-old with the braids. "I do love myself. Very much."

"Don't you worry about getting older and there not being enough men to go around and all that?"

"No," said Joanne. "There are many men. You just go out, you meet them. All the time."

The other women agreed. And just when I was about to ask where all these men were, a figure passed our banquette dressed like Lawrence of Arabia. As he walked down toward the dance floor, all the women started turning in his direction. The lights on the dance floor started to swirl and Middle Eastern music began to play. Women started to scurry toward the dance floor. Audrey rolled her eyes.

"Ah. The strippers are here." The dance floor was now lined with women standing and watching.

"Strippers?" I asked, surprised. "There's strippers?"

"Didn't Steve tell you? That's why all the women come here at eight. To eat free food and see the strippers."

I was aghast.

"So you mean all this is, is a French Chippendales? Steve made it sound like the women came here to make new friends."

The women all grimaced. "Please," elegant Patrice sniffed. "Who needs to do that?"

So maybe we're not so different after all. We went to the dance floor and checked out the action. I might as well have been at the Hunk-o-Rama in Brooklyn. The two men dancing were taking off their flowing robes until they were in nothing but itty-bitty g-strings. Then they pulled two women out of the audience and sat them on chairs on the dance floor and began dancing and rubbing their *Jean-Pierres* in these women's faces. All the women in the club were screaming and cheering. These women were making friends all right. I couldn't wait to tell Steve. Where had all the cool, detached Parisian attitude gone? It was a good lesson. Sometimes even French women need to strip off their pride and go whoop it up for a night.

About an hour later, we walked upstairs to leave as hordes of men were charging in like bulls out of the pen. Outside was now a mob of men desperately trying to get in.

"This is ingenious. You let in only the most beautiful women, give them free food and drinks, get them loose and crazy with strippers, then send in the men and charge them tons of money. It's diabolical," I said as we walked out of the club, the cool air hitting my face.

"You have to meet the owner, Thomas. He's a bit of a celebrity here. He owns three restaurants and two nightclubs, plus many other venues all over the world. He's very interesting," Clara said, elbowing her way through the crowd. "And he's my brother," she added.

"Your brother?" I asked, surprised.

"How do you think we got in tonight?" Clara asked. I tried not to take that personally. "I know he's here. I just texted him to come out and say hello. He would be good for you to talk to. He has some very interesting theories on the subject." Clara scanned the crowd. "Thomas! *Viens ici!* Over here!"

Now how I remember it is that the crowd began to part in slow motion as a tall, slim man emerged out of the sea of people. He had short, black wavy hair with pale skin and shimmering blue eyes. He looked like royalty. I took one look at him and thought, *Dashing. This is what they mean when they talk about dashing.*

"Thomas, this is the woman I told you about, who is doing research on women and being single," Clara said, politely speaking in English.

"Ah, yes," Thomas said, looking right at me. "So, what did you think of my night here?"

"I think you're an evil genius," I said, smiling. He laughed.

"This is very accurate. An evil genius, yes." He looked at me. "And why are you doing this? Tell me."

"For a book that I'm writing. About single women? About how to be . . . single?" I sounded like an idiot.

"Ah! So much about single women in the States! Relationships, that's much more interesting."

"Um . . . yes, but single women are interesting, too."

"Yes, but sometimes a bit obsessive, don't you think?"

I felt this perfect stranger was insulting me and I didn't really know how to defend myself.

"So what is the problem? Too many single women and no men? Is that it?" He couldn't have made it sound more trite if he had tried.

"Well, yes, I guess that's the main problem, yes. I'm not sure."

He continued on: "But you American women, you idealize marriage so much. Every movie, there's a wedding in it. Or some man is running off a pier or getting in a helicopter to propose to the woman he loves. It's infantile, really."

My eyebrows raised. "As opposed to the French films where everyone is cheating on everyone?"

"That's reality. That's complications. That's life."

"Well, if you don't like it, I guess you can always stop watching bad American films . . ." I responded, quickly.

"But it helps me feel superior," he said, smiling.

"It doesn't seem like you have a problem with that," I said, glaring at him a bit.

Thomas burst out laughing. "Ah, good for you, Miss Single Woman. Good for you!" He then put his hand on my shoulder, apologetically.

"I didn't mean to offend you. I just meant to say, everything is changing. All over the world. It's very difficult to understand what any of it means anymore, single, marriage, any of it. No?"

I didn't know exactly what he was talking about. "I live in America. We don't really know what's going on all over the world."

"Well, then it is perfect that you are taking this trip, isn't it?" he said, his blue eyes sparkling at me. "Have dinner with me. I will explain to you more. I love discussing these things."

Startled, I turned to Clara to see if I had heard him wrong. Clara laughed. "I told you, he has a lot to say on the subject." I didn't know how to respond. Thomas took that as a yes, and I guess it was.

"Come. I'll take you to another club of mine."

We got out of Thomas's car and walked a half a block to a nondescript town house. He pressed the buzzer and a gentleman in a suit and tie answered the door. He greeted Thomas deferentially and ushered us into a dark, elegant room with a long wooden bar and crystal chandelier. Opposite the bar, well-dressed people were seated eating dinner and drinking champagne on black leather banquettes with a golden brass railing separating them from the rest of the room.

"This is your place as well?" I asked, impressed.

"It is."

"Well, this is quite different from men in g-strings and lukewarm tortellini," I joked. We sat down at a little banquette in the corner.

"Yes," Thomas said, smiling as if he had a secret. I wasn't quite sure what was happening; why Thomas had invited me out or what we were doing there. But who really cared? This was a fantastic way to spend my first night in Paris. As the champagne arrived, I dove right in.

"So, was there anything else mildly insulting you wanted to say about American single women? Or were you done?" I was trying to be sassy but cute.

Thomas shook his head and laughed. "I'm sorry if you found me insulting. I will try and behave myself from now on." He looked around the club. "I invited you here to give you a different perspective. To show you that everyone is trying to figure it out. There are no easy answers to any of it."

"Wow. In the few minutes you've known me, I've shown myself to be that ignorant? Thank you for being so concerned with my world perspective."

"We French have to do what we can." Thomas looked me straight in the eyes and smiled. I blushed. I couldn't help it, but I did. He was fantastic.

"For instance, I have an open marriage."

"Excuse me?" I said, trying to sound nonchalant.

"Yes. An open marriage, is how I think you Americans describe it."

"Oh. That's interesting."

"It's one way to go, to deal with this problem."

"What problem?" I asked. The waiter brought us tiny cups of some kind of thick, warm amuse-bouche soup.

"Of boredom, of stagnation, of resentment."

"And you solve that by sleeping with other people?"

"No. We solve that by making no rules for ourselves. By being open to life. When you get married, you tell each other that from that day forward, you will never be allowed to have sex with someone else, to feel passion, to explore a spark, an attraction. You are beginning the murder of a part of your essential nature. The part that keeps you alive."

"But . . . doesn't that make things complicated?"

"Yes, sometimes very much so. But as I said, that is reality. That is life."

"I don't understand. Do you just say, 'Hey, honey, I'm going out to have sex with someone else, see you later . . .'"

"No. We are polite. You must be polite. But for instance, right now I know my wife has a boyfriend. He is not so important to her; she sees him once a week or less. If it truly bothered me, she would be done with him."

"But it doesn't bother you?"

"It is just sex. Just passion. It is life."

I downed my champagne. "It sounds like a little too much life for me. You're giving me a headache." The waiter came and took our orders.

Thomas smiled mischievously. "For example: this club. We have a very nice restaurant. But upstairs, it is a place where people can have sex."

"Um. What?" Thomas poured more champagne into my glass.

"You heard me. It's what you call a sex club—for couples. Everyone must come in with a partner."

"You mean, these people, all around us, are going to go upstairs later and . . . with each other?"

"Most likely, yes." Thomas looked at me. He became quite polite. "I don't want to offend you; I just thought you'd be interested to know."

"No. I'm very interested. I am. I've never had dinner at a sex club before . . ."

Thomas then looked down at his hands, folded at the table. He looked up at me. "If you want to take a tour, I'd be happy to show you around."

I looked straight at Thomas. He shrugged his shoulders. I believed it was a bit of a dare. And I hate backing down from a dare. And besides, it's all in the name of research, right?

I took another gulp of my champagne and set down my glass with purpose. "Sure. Let's go."

We got up. Thomas and I walked toward the bar area. It was only then that I noticed the television at the bar was showing women in lingerie, dancing. Thomas took my hand and walked me toward a dark corner of the room. There I could see a spiral staircase, with a delicate iron railing. He looked at me for a moment and smiled. We began to walk up it, slowly. I have to admit, I was curious. And slightly nervous. When we landed on the second floor, I looked around. I could see it was a long, dark room, but couldn't make out much else. Thomas walked me over to the men's room right by the stairs. Okay, it's a men's room. Then, the women's room. Nice bouquet of flowers by the sink, whatever. And then he opened a door.

"This is the shower room." I peeked in and saw a large tiled room with a single showerhead in the middle of it.

"It fits six." I stood there staring, until he took my shoulders and pointed me toward the other end of the floor. We passed a room with no door, and which had a giant platform bed in it. No one was in there. We began to walk down the center of the long room. It was then that I started hearing, um, noises. The lighting was low, but what I think I saw, and I couldn't testify to this under oath, but what I *think* I saw, was three people on one side of a large platform having sex. The only woman, I believe, was on her back, spread-eagled. On the other side of the room there was a couple having sex against a wall. I put my head down, and tried not to let out a shocked American gasp. At the end of the room, there was another staircase, thankfully, leading down. As I descended, I could hear Thomas laughing behind me.

"You're lucky. Things haven't really started up yet."

"I'm not going to act shocked, no matter how much I am," I said, laughing.

"And that is why I find you so appealing, Miss Tough New Yorker."

As we sat back down, our dinner arrived. I was now very curious. "Now tell me what's so great about that idea," I asked, my elbows firmly on the table, my whole body leaning in.

Thomas shrugged. "It's one way people are trying to keep their marriages exciting."

"By sleeping with other people in front of each other?" I asked a little sarcastically.

Thomas suddenly turned serious, speaking to me as if I were a rude, slightly dim child.

"Julie, have you ever slept with someone for over three years? Over ten years? Over twenty years? Someone you share a bed with every night, have children with, the diapers, the illnesses, the homework, the tantrums, hearing about their bullshit work problems, every day, in and out?"

I was shamed and silenced. I hate the "what's the longest *you've* been in a relationship" card. But he had a point. I felt like a pilgrim. A very immature pilgrim.

"Then, how can you judge?" he said, softening. I drank some more champagne and looked around at all the proper people. I couldn't help but imagine them upstairs without their pearls and silk shirts and wool jackets doing God knows what to one another.

"Isn't this just asking for trouble? Don't you have a lot of divorces that come out of this place?"

"On the contrary. Most of these couples have been coming here for years."

"No pun intended," I said. Thomas gave me a sympathetic smile.

"I thought Paris was supposed to be such a romantic place, and tonight all I'm hearing about is sex."

"No, Julie. You are hearing about people who are trying to keep their love alive. As opposed to you Americans who get fat and stop sleeping with each other, or lie to each other and have affairs with their neighbors."

"You make us sound like one big *Jerry Springer* episode."

"I exaggerate to make a point," he said, smiling. "What I am saying is that marriage is not the only way to go. And a monogamous marriage is not the only way to be married. Everything is moving toward freedom, in whatever form that takes. Being single is going to be just one of many life choices."

"But come on, wouldn't most people agree it's better to be in love and in a relationship than not?"

"Yes, definitely. But how many people do you know that are in a relationship and in love?"

Of course, I've thought about this before. "Not that many."

Thomas folded his hands in front of him, very professorially. "There are only two interesting lives you can lead, in my opinion. You can be in love. That, to me, is very interesting. And you can be single. Also, a *very* interesting life. The rest is bullshit."

I understood exactly what he meant.

"Are you in love with your wife?" I asked, deciding to be nosy.

"Yes, absolutely."

A surprising pang of disappointment hit my chest.

"And we try not to become bored of each other. Because we are in love. And because of that, it's a very interesting life. For instance, the minute you called me an evil genius, I wanted to spend more time with you. Because you seemed funny and interesting and you are beautiful."

I started to sweat a little.

"That doesn't mean I'm not in love with my wife, or that I don't want to be married to her. It just means that I'm a man and I am alive."

I tried to make a joke. "Listen, if you think that kind of talk is going to get me into that jungle gym upstairs you better think again."

Thomas laughed. "No, no, Julie. Tonight, I am just enjoying your company. Entirely." He looked at me, shyly. I could almost swear I saw him blush.

"You know, I think the jet lag is kicking in a little," I blurted out, awkwardly. Thomas nodded.

"Of course, this is your first night in Paris. You must be quite tired."

"Yes. Yes I am."

Thomas pulled up in front of Steve's apartment and turned off the engine. I suddenly got very nervous, not knowing what to expect next from this French fellow. "So, thank you for the ride and the champagne and the sex, I mean you know, the eye-opening . . . you know . . ." I was stammering a little.

Thomas smiled at me, amused at my awkwardness.

"I believe you will be going to the opera on Tuesday and then to the gala? Yes?"

"What? Oh yes, Steve mentioned it. He's conducting."

"Fantastic. I will be there with my wife. I will see you then."

And with that he got out of the car and opened my door for me. Besides the whole showing-me-people-having-a-three-way, he was the perfect gentleman. He kissed me on both cheeks and sent me on my way.

Back in the States

They all got dressed up for the funeral. It was a happy occasion after all. Serena's old self of ego and desire and attachment to this material world was about to die, and Georgia, Alice, and Ruby agreed to all go to the funeral to celebrate. It was ninety minutes out of the city, at an ashram near New Paltz, New York, and Georgia had offered to drive. Ruby was late to meet them at the garage, because she is always late, which immediately irritated both Alice and Georgia, because they are never late and they didn't want to be driving up to New Paltz to watch Serena become a swami in the first place. But they had promised me, and though they weren't about to take a vow of celibacy at the altar of Siva, they did worship at the altar of friendship and keeping promises.

At first, there was an uncomfortable silence in the car. It was nine in the morning, they were all tired and cranky, and none had any idea what they were about to get themselves into. However, if you know anything about women, you know that something about the confinement and intimacy of a car will eventually get even cranky ladies gabbing.

Alice soon began laying out for Georgia her belief system for being single. She verbally drew for Georgia all the maps and diagrams that spelled out the basic tenets of her dating dogma: You have to get out there, you have to get out there, you have to get out there. As they drove up 87, Alice taught Georgia about Nerve.com and Match.com, about not spending too much time emailing these guys, but instead making a date for drinks or coffee, never dinner. She taught Georgia about immediately deleting the guys who use sexual innuendo in the first couple of emails and not feeling bad if she doesn't want to respond to guys she feels are too old, short, or unattractive for her.

As Georgia exited the Thruway, and started driving along tree-lined roads and past farms and cows and goats, Alice told her about rock climbing at Chelsea Piers, about kayaking and trapezing on the West Side Highway. She explained to her about the hottest clubs and bars and what nights you should go where.

Georgia, already on a steady IV of panic and mania, really didn't need any more pumping up. Though it was only an hour and a half in an Acura driving upstate, it could well have been forty-eight hours trapped in a

Motel 6 with a bunch of Scientologists depriving you of sleep, food, and phone calls. By the time they pulled up in front of the Jayananda Meditation Center, Georgia was fully brainwashed on the Gospel according to Alice and she was hooked.

In the backseat, Ruby slept the whole way. She woke up just as Alice pulled into the gravel driveway.

"Does anyone know what we're actually going to be seeing here?" Ruby asked as they drove past the sign for the center.

"I have no idea," Georgia said.

"I just hope we don't have to do any crazy chanting," Alice added.

They got out of the car and smoothed out their rumpled outfits. Georgia and Ruby were both wearing dresses with stockings and boots, and Alice had opted for a more professional-looking blazer and pants set. As they followed the smattering of people walking down a grassy hill on a little stone path, they saw that they were clearly overdressed. The other guests were wearing flowing shirts and skirts, the men had various displays of facial hair, and the women were mostly sporting unshaven legs. There were a few Indian men in orange robes and sandals. As Georgia, Alice, and Ruby got to the bottom of the hill, they saw where the ceremony was to take place. A few yards away there was an open-air stone temple. It was circular, with marble floors and stone pillars and pictures of various Hindu figures on the walls. People were taking off their shoes and sandals outside the temple. Incense wafted in the air.

"This is really weird," Georgia whispered.

They wrestled their footwear off and walked in. They immediately took on an air of solemnity befitting the occasion. In the middle of the temple was a stone pit, with a small fire quietly burning in it. The "congregation" all began sitting on the floor, cross-legged. These three ladies were not dressed for the lotus position, but they gamely arranged their skirts and pants in some fashion that let them put their pretty asses on the cold rock floor.

An elderly Indian man in orange robes who seemed to be the head swami started reading from a book in Sanskrit. There were two other male swamis flanking him, an older Italian-looking swami and a really hot fortysomething swami. Next to him was an extremely overweight female swami. They stood silently as the head Indian swami

kept reading. Eventually, the initiates were brought out. There were five of them: three men and two women. And one of those women was Serena.

Alice, Ruby, and Georgia let out a collective gasp when they saw her. She had shaved off all her hair. All, that is, except for a little belt of hair trailing down her back. Her beautiful blond hair. Gone. Only a skinny little bird of a thing remained. Serena. In an orange sari. When Serena had called Alice the day before to give her directions, she explained to Alice what she was doing. She believed her calling was to spend the rest of her life meditating and being of service, all in the hopes of achieving some kind of spiritual enlightenment. Serena believed she was done with this material world, and was ready to give it all up. Alice hadn't really understood what Serena was talking about, but now, seeing her in the orange robe and no hair, Alice realized Serena was not kidding around. The initiates stood quietly as the swami finished reading a section of the book. Then the hot swami began to speak. He seemed to be the translator, the temple PR person designated to explain to everyone what was going on.

"I want to welcome everyone here today to this funeral. This is the day these students become sannyasins. They will take vows of poverty, of celibacy, of detachment from family, from friends, from all the pleasures in this physical world. This fire represents the funeral pyre . . ."

"He is really hot," Georgia whispered. "What kind of accent do you think that is?"

"I'm not sure," Alice whispered back. "Australian?" Ruby glared at them. They closed their mouths.

". . . where their old selves will be burned away, to make way for their new self as a sannyasin."

And with that, the old Indian swami picked up some scissors that were lying on the ground and as each initiate kneeled before him, he cut off the last remaining strands of their hair and threw it in the fire. After that was done, the five almost-swamis sat down cross-legged on the floor. One by one, the overweight lady swami placed three cones of incense on each of their heads; Serena was the last. Georgia, Alice, and Ruby watched this, perplexed. A girl they had only met on a few occasions, who last time they saw her she was getting her stomach pumped, was

now bald and balancing incense on her head. All six of their eyes widened with dismay as they watched the Indian swami light the cones, one by one. The hot swami explained:

"As the cones of incense burn down to their scalps, these five new sannyasins will meditate on their new path of abstinence; the burning cones may form a scar on their heads, creating a permanent symbol of their new commitment to self-denial."

Alice gasped. Ruby raised her eyebrows, and Georgia just rolled her eyes. Serena looked out into the crowd and smiled. She seemed to be almost glowing. Something about the look in her eyes took their collective breath away. Peace. Calm.

Imagine that.

"I invite you to all meditate with our sannyasins for a few moments."

All eyes in the temple closed. But Georgia looked around as everyone began breathing in and out slowly. She started contemplating the idea of the burning off of the self. If Serena could cast off her old self, so could she. She didn't have to be mad at Dale. She didn't have to be humiliated that she recently broke the promise she made to 230 of her closest friends and relatives and broke up with the man she was supposed to love till death do they part. She could let go of the feeling that she was a failure in her marriage, and therefore at life. She could let go of the agony of knowing that someone with whom she had shared intimacies and embarrassments and joy and sex and the birth of two children had found someone else he'd rather be with.

As she sat there, with a tiny rip tearing up the side of her skirt, her inner voice said, *I can let it all go. I don't have to be a bitter, divorced lady. I can do it any way I want. And I want to date young, hot guys.*

Alice meanwhile felt the pangs of her crossed legs cramping up, but she couldn't help but notice how nice it was just to sit still for a moment. Peace. Calm. To breathe. To stop. She closed her eyes.

Yes, her inner voice said. *I've passed my knowledge on to Georgia. She'll make a valiant and loyal student. It's time for me to stop. I'm fucking exhausted.* Alice kept breathing in and out, in and out, slowly, until her inner voice finally said, *It's time for me to marry the next man I meet.*

In Ruby's mind's eye, much to her surprise, she was holding a baby in her arms, surrounded by all her friends and family in a halo of love and

acceptance. Her eyes popped open in shock at the sudden image of her motherhood.

"While the sannyasins meditate, feel free to join us in the main house for some curry and chapatis."

After they drove back to the West Village, where Georgia parked her car, Ruby, Georgia, and Alice said their polite good-byes.

In a contemplative mood, Ruby decided to walk to a park and get some fresh air. But she didn't walk to just any park. Bleecker Street Playground is a mere thousand square feet, but it is chock full o' children—running, climbing, digging, screaming, giggling, fighting, feuding children. There were big brightly colored pails and trucks and wheelie things they can sit on and motor with their little children feet. There were mothers and nannies, all shining with the glow of West Village chic. There were a few fathers, all handsome with their salt-and-pepper hair and well-gymed biceps. Ruby stood looking in at it all, her hands on the bars of the fence that protected those inside from molesters and kidnappers. She walked to the entrance, a big metal gate with a big sign that said "Adults not admitted without a child." She ignored this and, trying to feign the look of a beautiful-mother-now-looking-for-her-adorable-child-and-beloved-nanny, walked right in.

She scanned the park. She wasn't quite sure what she was looking for, but she knew this was the place where she was going to find it. She sat down next to two mothers; white, slim, really good highlights in their hair. She was gathering information, soaking it all in: the kids, the moms, the nannies, everything. Suddenly, there was an eruption in the center of the park, near the monkey bars. A four-year-old devil-girl, with long, ringleted brown hair, screamed and beat on a poor defenseless little boy, throwing him down on the concrete and then wailing at the top of her lungs. Her face was red and her eyes were almost rolling in the back of her head, as if she were the injured party. A young woman ran over to the little girl and hugged her. Another woman raced over and picked up the little boy, who was now also wailing. The monster's mother scolded her demon child, but it clearly was not penetrating. This bad seed was already in the Land of Tantrum, screaming and crying and hitting her mother. When the two mothers sitting next to Ruby saw the look of horror on Ruby's face, they just shook their heads, and almost in unison, said two words that would explain everything: "Single mother."

Ruby nodded sympathetically. "That's so sad," she said, egging them on.

"It was a one-night stand. She got pregnant and decided to do it on her own. It was very brave," said the slim woman with the blond highlights.

"But now, even with help from her sister and babysitters, it's a nightmare," said the other slim woman, with the red highlights.

"A nightmare," said the blonde, to emphasize the point. Ruby couldn't stop herself.

"Well, I know I could never do it. Could you?" Ruby said innocently. From the expressions on their faces, she knew the answer, but she decided to keep going. "I mean, could you even imagine doing it on your own?" She tried to appear as casual as possible, but she waited for their answers as if the Lost Ark was about to be opened.

"Never. Not a chance. It's too hard. Too lonely."

"Absolutely. I would kill myself."

Just as Ruby suspected—being a single mother is even more depressing than being single. But what about the joys of motherhood? The intimate relationship between a mother and child? The gratification of raising a human being from birth and putting them out into the world?

"But don't you think it would still be nice to be a mother? Even without a husband?"

"Not worth it. I'd rather die."

The blond-highlight mom spelled it out. "Just imagine doing everything by yourself. Even if you had all the help in the world, at the end of the day it's still just you worrying if they're sick, deciding what school to go to, teaching them how to tie their shoelaces, ride a bike. You're the one who would have to take them sledding, who would have to organize all their playdates, who would have to feed them and put them to bed every night. You would be the one who would have to make sure they got to school on time, make their lunch, deal with their teachers, help them do their homework. You would get the call if your kid was sick in school, or in trouble, or," she said a little more pointedly, "had a reading disability."

"Right, and imagine if you had a really sick kid, like with cancer or something," said the red highlights.

"Oh my God, just the thought of being in the hospital, having to call a friend or a family member to sit with you, alone, being that kind of burden on everyone. If I was single, that image alone would make me wear five condoms every time I had sex."

"Then imagine being a single mother with a teenager."

"Right, you have to discipline them, set boundaries, deal with drugs and dating and sex, *and,* add to that that now they hate you."

"And if you had a girl, imagine going through menopause and seeing your daughter blossom and become sexually desirable just at the moment you're shriveling and drying up and becoming sexually useless."

These ladies were getting really dark now, even for Ruby. She tried to appear unfazed and attempted to interject some optimism into the conversation: "Well, you might not still be a single mother by the time they're teenagers. After all, you could meet someone."

In unison, the two mothers stared at Ruby. "Like you'd ever have the time," the blonde said. And the redhead said, "Who would want you? These men in New York could have anyone they want. Like they're going to pick a woman with a child?"

Ruby's optimism now came out in a whisper. "Well, if a man fell in love with you, he wouldn't care . . . ?"

The two mothers again looked at Ruby, as if she was a simpleton. The blond woman then asked Ruby, "Well, what do you think? Could you do it alone?"

Ruby looked out into the playground at children she considered for the most part to be adorable, well dressed, and well raised. She thought about the playdates and the homework and getting them to bed and the childhood cancer. She thought about how depressed she got just when a guy didn't call her after two dates.

"No. I couldn't. I could never be a single mother."

The mothers nodded in agreement. Here in the children's park in the West Village, three women were in complete agreement about what they believed in: *Being a single mother would really, really suck.*

Ruby walked all the way up Broadway. She was around Seventy-sixth Street when she made peace with the fact that she would never be a single mother. Guess she could check that off her list now. They were right, and they should know—it was too hard. So then the only thing left for her to do was keep dating. But how? It was so depressing. As she walked, she thought about Serena. Serena believed in God and spiritual enlightenment so much that she renounced everything and burned incense on her scalp. That was pretty hard-core. It made Ruby wonder what she believed in. *Should she pack it in, too? Should she just stop dating and start caring about other things?* It was not such an unattractive thought. But as Ruby walked and thought, she realized she wasn't ready for that just yet. She still had a little more fight left in her. And by Ninety-sixth Street, it finally came to her. She needed to get back on the horse, to love again. She needed to not be afraid to get emotionally involved again. She had to dive back in.

It was time to get another cat.

Now she was walking with a purpose; she was going to go back to the animal shelter where she had adopted Ralph. Her time for mourning was over.

The shelter was a two-floor concrete bunker on 122nd Street and Amsterdam, in a neighborhood that was a little dangerous. It didn't make Ruby scared as much as nostalgic for a bygone era. We don't have that many streets left anymore. By the time she got there, Ruby was proud that she was doing something as life-affirming as choosing to love again.

As she opened the door to the shelter, the smell of animals hit her immediately. It was a suffocating smell, one that made you want to walk right back out the door. But Ruby walked to the counter to a young Irish-looking girl with frizzy hair in a barrette on top of her head. The walls were covered with cheerful posters of animals reminding you "To love me is to spay me," or "Give me an $8 ID tag today, save the $300 reward fee later!" The cement walls were covered with paintings of dogs and cats, but really it was of very little use. The place felt like a bomb shelter no matter how many puppies you painted on the walls.

Ruby told the girl that she wanted to adopt a cat and was buzzed through a door that led to a flight of stairs. The stench of animals got stronger as she walked up the steps. As she opened the door to the second floor, the sound of one dog howling filled her ears. It was a sound that cut right through her; a keening that seemed to be coming from the pit of the dog's soul. Its familiarity made Ruby dizzy. *That's the sound I want to make every morning when I wake up,* Ruby thought.

It was macabre walking through that industrial hallway, with that howling—very *One Flew Over the Cuckoo's Nest,* but with dogs. Ruby quickly walked into the narrow room that had the cages of cats. She closed the door and the dog's cries were muffled a bit. She looked at the cats, one by one. They were all cute and soft and slightly lethargic. But she could still hear that damn dog losing it. Ruby stopped at one cat that was exceptionally adorable, almost a kitten with white and gray fur, named "Vanilla." When Ruby stuck her finger in the cage, Vanilla playfully grabbed at it with her paws. That was that—she would adopt Vanilla. She walked out of the room to tell the man at the front desk about her decision. As she walked down the hall, the crazy dog kept baying. Ruby decided she had to take a look at that thing. She opened the door into the cuckoo's nest. She passed what seemed like cage after cage of pit bulls. She finally got to Loud-Mouth. Ruby looked at the description that was taped on her cage: "Kimya Johnson is a four-year-old white pit mix who was adopted out as a puppy. We recently found her as a stray, and we haven't been able to locate her owner. She's a very nice, friendly and snuggly dog, and appears to be housetrained. Well, her former owner's loss will be a new owner's gain. Perhaps that new owner will be you?"

Ruby's heart sank. Getting adopted from the pound only to be brought back again. Talk about abandonment issues. Kimya was standing up, her front paws on the cage, howling her little heart out. She might as well have been clanging the cage door with a tin cup. Just then a young girl of about sixteen walked into the room. She was wearing the brown uniform of a staff member, with a pin that said "Felicia" in blue Magic Marker, and underneath it, "Volunteer."

"She's so loud, right?" she said in a thick Hispanic accent. "That's why nobody wants her. She's so loud."

Ruby looked at Felicia. This was no way for a volunteer to talk. Kimya kept crying.

"She's so cute, though," Ruby said, trying to be kind.

Felicia looked at Kimya and smirked. "Yeah, but she's too loud. That's why I think they're going to put her down tomorrow. She's so loud. Dang."

Ruby quickly looked at Kimya. "Really? Tomorrow?" Her voice squeaked.

Felicia sucked her teeth. "That's what I heard." She shrugged her shoulders.

Ruby was aghast. "Well . . . aren't you supposed to be trying to convince me to take her?"

Felicia looked at Ruby blankly, taking a nice long pause for dramatic effect. "Well, do you want her? 'Cause you can have her if you want her."

When Ruby shot back, "My building doesn't allow dogs," Felicia rolled her eyes, smirked, waved her hands in exasperation, and walked out the door.

Ruby stared at Kimya. For one moment, Kimya got quiet. She looked at Ruby, her black pink eyes pleading for help.

Ruby walked quickly out of the room and down the flight of stairs. She walked up to the girl at the counter.

"I'm sorry I can't adopt Kimya. I'm really sorry. But I really would get kicked out of my building. You have no idea how strict my co-op board is."

The girl at the counter looked at her blankly.

"But I can adopt Vanilla," Ruby said proudly. "And I'd like to volunteer here once a week."

The woman looked surprised. She handed Ruby another form. "Great. Orientation is this Wednesday at seven."

Ruby smiled brightly. "Terrific. Thanks." As she waited for them to get Vanilla, she breathed a sigh of relief. She knew she would be great at convincing people to take unwanted strays. She would save the lives of dozens of dogs and cats. They needed her here.

•　•　•

Georgia went home that night, put on a pair of two-hundred-dollar jeans, a tight-fitting cashmere t-shirt top, and a pair of trendy little motorcycle boots, and off she went to Whole Foods Market to do some grocery shopping.

In the car that day, her new dating guru, Alice, told her that the Whole Foods in Union Square is a great place to meet really cute guys on a Saturday evening. You can sit and watch a cooking demonstration or stop at an organic-wine tasting or just go searching for homemade hummus and the love of your life.

As Georgia wheeled her cart around this high-end supermarket, she noticed that she felt great. It might have had something to do with watching Serena's funeral, because she felt centered. Optimistic. Dale had the kids all weekend, so she was free to just be a single person in the world; a single person who was attractive, fun, smart, and truly excited to be alive. How hot must that be? As she rolled by the organic greens, she realized that she didn't have to believe a single thing that she had ever heard about finding love in New York. There was no reason she had to buy into the belief system that there are no good men left, that the men in New York are all dogs, that every second that ticks by she gets older and less desirable. She didn't have to believe any of that. Because that was not her experience. She met Dale in New York, at Columbia. She was in grad school for journalism and he was a business major. They had been together ever since. So until she had personally experienced that there were no good men anywhere in the world, she would assume the opposite. As she pushed her cart past the overflowing mountain of cheeses, the French ones, the Italian ones, the ones that come in wheels, the ones from goats, she realized she can simply choose to drive around the entire landfill of presumptions and fears associated with dating in New York. Until it happened to her, none of those stories mattered. She was a blank slate, filled with optimism, unfettered with bitterness; and because of that she felt that she had an edge over most of the single women out there. Men were going to pick up on her joie de dating vivre, and it was going to be irresistible.

She made one lap around the whole store, taking her time enjoying the tour of healthy food. She was now standing over a row of organic beets, pondering how desirable she was going to seem to all of mankind, when a tall, slim man came up to her. He asked her if she had ever cooked beet greens. She looked up and smiled. He had curly brown hair, parted in the middle with just enough scruff on his face to look sexy, but not as if he was in a band.

See? she thought to herself. It doesn't have to be so hard. She then sweetly explained to this cute gentleman that she had, in fact, cooked beet greens, and that they are delicious fried with just some oil, garlic, and salt.

"Wow, thanks. I'm trying to cook more, you know? Eat more greens."

"Well, that's great. They're supposed to be very nutritious."

Then this cute man smiled at Georgia, a sort of devilish and sheepish smile combined, and added, "How was that for an opening line? I've been following you ever since the organic chocolate section but I couldn't think of anything smart to say. But then you landed in the beets and I thought, Ah! Beet greens! Now that's a conversation starter!"

Georgia laughed, blushing, and quickly said, "It was perfect. Didn't seem forced at all, very natural, yet charming."

The cute man extended his hand and said, "Hi, my name is Max."

Georgia shook his hand and said, "Georgia, nice to meet you." And after they talked for about twenty minutes, next to the beets, they made a plan to go out to dinner soon. Georgia left Whole Foods, with three yellow peppers for eight dollars and her newfound optimism validated. She thought to herself, *This dating thing is going to be a breeze.*

* * *

That night, Alice, our Special Forces of dating, was on her next "op." His name was Jim and he was a fix-up, from a friend of a friend who had been forwarded the famous Alice Email. The Alice Email was a mass email, similar to what you'd send out to the public at large when looking for a good cat sitter. The Alice Email, however, was about looking for a good man. She sent it to all her friends, and asked them to send it to all of their friends, a sort of viral marketing manhunt. Because of it, she ended up meeting a lot of men she might never have met. Unfortunately, she wouldn't have wanted to meet most of them, but that hadn't bothered Alice one bit. She had been out there and that was the name of the game. Jim was an electrical engineer from New Jersey. He was thirty-seven, and from his emails, seemed to be intelligent and friendly. They were going to meet at a small bar in Noho where Alice took all her first dates. It's a tiny, dark, Turkish wine bar with beaded velvet lamps and overstuffed couches. If you can't manage to muster some kind of romantic connection in this place, with its dim lighting, and huge goblets of red wine, then it isn't going to happen anywhere.

As Alice walked to the bar, she thought about the countless dates she had been on this year. She thought about all the men she had met, and wondered why none of them had been the guy for her. There had been a few tiny relationships, a couple of affairs, but for the most part none of these men were guys that she wanted to spend time with. She wondered briefly if this numbers game was really working for her. She was certainly meeting a lot of men, but maybe by increasing her odds, all she was doing was increasing the odds of just meeting guys that she wasn't attracted to. Maybe love is so special, so magical, that it has nothing to do with numbers. Maybe it's just destiny and luck. And destiny and luck have no need for odds. Up until that moment, Alice always thought she believed in the odds, in math. But looking back on the past year, it gave her pause. All those men . . . A wave of exhaustion shimmered over her. She shook it off, and put on her prettiest smile, ran her fingers through her hair, and walked into the bar.

Alice looked around and saw a man sitting on one of the sofas and seeming to be waiting for someone. He was approaching cuteness, but was not actually someone you would say was cute; a little too pasty, a little too soft in the face.

She walked up to him and asked, "Are you Jim?" He immediately stood up and put out his hand and smiled a warm, open smile.

"Alice, so nice to meet you."

She could tell immediately that he was a good man.

They began to talk about the things people talk about on first dates: jobs, family, apartments, where they went to school. But as they talked, as is the case with all first dates, only 70 percent of their brains was talking, listening, and responding to what the other was saying. The other 30 percent was wondering, *Do I want to kiss this person? Do I want to have sex with this person? What would my friends think of this person?* Jim asked Alice a lot of questions about herself, in the way that sweet men do when they really like you. As Alice told her stories and laughed at his almost funny jokes, she could tell from the way he looked at her that he found her adorable.

"What do you mean, you have a trick that makes you able to hear yourself snoring?" he asked, already laughing at her very personal admission.

"Seriously, if you can remember, right before the moment you actually wake up, to make sure you don't alter your breathing—like you almost pretend you're still sleeping, but you're actually awake—you can catch yourself snoring."

Jim just looked at Alice, shook his head, and laughed. He was completely smitten with her. Now this wasn't a new event for sexy, redheaded Alice. Men found her adorable all the time. But because of her usual take-no-prisoners approach to dating, if Alice didn't return the sentiment, only 25 percent of her brain was listening to the man, and 75 percent of her brain had paid the check, caught a cab home, and was now watching *Seinfeld* reruns. If she was interested in the guy as well, then Alice would work as hard as she could to be even more adorable while looking as if she was not trying to be anything but herself. But tonight, she was just allowing herself the enjoyment of being admired by someone. And it felt warm. Relaxing. She started getting tingly and buzzed from her second glass of wine, but she was also tipsy off of this new discovery: sometimes it's okay not to try so hard.

Back in France

The scene was fantastic. As I stepped out of my cab, I saw glamorous, well-dressed men and women getting out of taxis or rushing down the street toward the Palais Garnier. I walked up the stairs of the opera house and turned around to look out at the scene. Paris. How clichéd to be impressed. But I was. It's an unbelievable gift to be able to travel. It just is. That there are these gigantic steel machines that manage to lift us into the sky—that seems an impossible achievement in itself. But then to have the time and the finances to take advantage of it. How thrilling. How thrilling to be somewhere different—where every sight and smell seems strange and exotic. Paris, where I'd been so many times before, was still a foreign city to me. The cafés, the bread, the cheese, the men with their ruddy faces and gray mustaches—and the smell. It smells old and earthy. European. I love it.

We were seeing the opera *Lohengrin*, the story of a princess who dreams about a knight in shining armor coming to her rescue, and when he appears, all she has to do is never ask him who he is or where he's come from. Of course, eventually she can't take it, and she asks him, thus losing him forever. Just like a woman.

As I gazed over the whole mise-en-scène I heard a woman's voice call out to me loudly. "Allorah, Julie. Hallo! Hallo!" Audrey and Joanne, all dressed up, were walking up the stairs toward me. Steve had gotten us all tickets together.

Audrey smiled and asked, "How did you enjoy our talk the other night? Was it helpful?"

"Yes, very helpful," I said, as we entered the opera house. "I was surprised how well French women handle rejection."

"Yes, I was thinking about this," Joanne said, as we walked through the lobby.

"I do believe it has something to do with our upbringing. I think in the States, perhaps, it is considered very bad to fail, to be bad at something. Parents never want to tell their child that they aren't fantastic, they never want to see their child lose. But here," Joanne pursed her lips and shrugged her shoulders, "if we are bad at something, our parents tell us we're bad at something; if we fail, we fail. There is no shame about it."

We gave our tickets to the ushers and walked in. Could it be true that if our mothers and our teachers hadn't coddled us so much in our childhood we would be better able to handle rejection?

I was too busy chatting with Audrey and Joanne to really pay attention to where I was. But then the place hit me full on. We were now in the audience of the Palais Garnier, one of the two theaters that house the Opéra National de Paris. It was opulence to the highest degree. Balcony upon balcony, red velvet seating and gold leaf everywhere you looked. The stage was concealed by a red velvet curtain, and over it all there was a chandelier that, according to the program's notes, weighed ten tons. We sat in our seats and I looked around.

As if I hadn't already seen enough beauty, grandeur, and Parisian charm for one evening, Thomas entered the row behind us with the tiniest, most elegant woman I had ever seen. She had long, blond, straight-as-a-sunbeam hair that fell just below her shoulders. She was wearing a powder blue dress one might describe as a "confection"; it poufed out at her waist and made her look as if she should be on top of a jewelry box. I could swear I smelled a waft of her tasteful perfume from where I sat. Thomas smiled and waved. He pointed me out to his wife; I saw him leaning over to her and whispering in her ear. She smiled and waved graciously to me. I suddenly felt like Andre the Giant and wished I had dressed better.

The orchestra began to play and Steve stood up out of the orchestra pit. He bowed to the audience and they applauded madly for him. My dear high school friend began waving his arms around and it seemed the orchestra was doing exactly what he told them to do. It was very impressive. The opera began and we settled in for the story of a princess who could have had it all if she had been able to keep her damn mouth shut.

When the opera was over twenty-seven hours later, or maybe just four, we were ushered to a room behind the backstage area. It was another gold leaf and rococo extravaganza and it was very old-world Parisian and very grand. I watched proudly as Steve was greeted and congratulated by his adoring, well-educated public. Thomas came into my view as I made my way toward a waiter who was passing out champagne. Thomas saw me and walked over. We took our champagne together.

"Where did your wife go?" I asked, casually.

"She decided to go home. Opera gives her a headache." He looked around at the crowded room, and then his eyes landed squarely on me.

"Would you like to take a walk?" Thomas asked, not breaking his gaze.

"Now?" I asked.

"Please. This is so boring. We must get out of here."

"I can't . . . my friend Steve, I'm his date . . . I couldn't."

I pointed to Steve, who at that moment was talking very closely to a fresh-faced young man in his mid-twenties.

"I believe Steve might have another date this evening. But I'll ask his permission." And at that, Thomas grabbed my hand and pulled me over to Steve.

"No, please," I said, feeling his surprisingly rough hand in mine.

As we walked up, Steve looked away from his gentleman friend and saw Thomas standing there holding my hand.

"You must be Thomas," Steve said, slyly.

Thomas registered this comment with a smile.

"Yes, I am, and I was wondering if I could borrow your friend for the evening. It seems she is the only one I want to speak with tonight, and it is such a warm evening for October, I would love to take advantage."

"Of her?" said my asshole friend Steve, smiling.

"No, no, of course not," Thomas said, laughing. "Of the weather. Of the evening."

"Oh. Of course. Of course."

Thomas shook Steve's hand. "You did an extraordinary job tonight. Bravo, Steve, really." He then put his hand on my back and gently guided me toward the door.

As we walked along the Avenue de l'Opéra, I couldn't help but get right to the heart of the matter.

"Your wife is very beautiful."

"Yes, she is."

I didn't really have anything to say after that. I just felt it was important for her to be brought up.

"What does she do? For a living?"

"She owns a lingerie shop in the Eleventh Quarter. Very successful. All the models and actresses go there."

I thought to myself, *Of course she owns a business that celebrates femininity and sexuality. I'm sure she looks perfect in very little clothes.*

Let me get this out of the way as quickly as I can. I'm a woman living in a large city in America who watches television and goes to movies, so, yes, I hate my body. I know how politically incorrect, clichéd, unfeminist, and tired that is. But I can't help it. I know I'm not fat, I am a respectable size six, but if I dig just a tiny bit, I have to admit to myself that I'm absolutely sure the reason I don't have a boyfriend is because of my cellulite and my huge thighs. Women are crazy, let's move on.

"Would you like to sit down and have a coffee?" Thomas asked. We were in front of a café with seats available outside.

"Yes, that would be nice."

A waitress handed us plastic menus, the kind with the little photos of croque-monsieurs and steak frites.

"So, tell me, Julie. As a single woman, what is your biggest fear?" I looked up at Thomas, startled.

"Wow, you're not one for small talk, are you?" I laughed, nervously.

"Life is too short and you are too interesting." He slanted his head, giving me his full attention.

"Well, I guess it's obvious. That I won't ever find someone, you know. To love." I looked down at my menu, staring at the photograph of an omelette.

The waitress came over again and Thomas ordered us a bottle of chardonnay.

"But why should you be so worried about finding love? It will happen. It always does, doesn't it?"

"Ummm, yeah. Actually no. It doesn't feel that way to me and my friends. Back home, the statistics are telling us that it's very hard to find a good man, and that it's only going to get harder. It seems a little bit like a crisis." The waiter came with our bottle of wine. Thomas approved it and the waiter poured two glasses.

"Yes, but with anything in life, you must ask yourself, Am I a statistical person? Or a mystical person? To me, it seems one must choose to be mystical, no? How could you bear it any other way?"

Mystical versus statistical—I had never thought about it that way. I looked at Thomas and decided I loved him then and there. Not in the real sense of love. More in the "I'm-in-Paris-and-you're-handsome-and-saying-smart-things-about-life-and-love" love. He was married and I would never sleep with him, but he was definitely my kind of heartthrob. "That's an interesting theory" is all I said.

We drank our wine and talked for another three hours. It was four in the morning when we had visited our last café and walked all the way back to Steve's apartment. I felt rejuvenated and flattered and attractive and smart and funny. As we stopped by Steve's door to say good night, Thomas kissed me on both my cheeks.

Then he smiled mischievously at me. "We should have an affair, Julie. It would be so nice."

I then began to have a prolonged coughing fit that happens when I suddenly feel exceptionally nervous. It also gave me time to think of what to say.

When I was finally done hacking, I said, "Yeah, well, you know, I don't know if I believe that I'll find the love of my life any time soon, and I'm not sure if I believe I'm a mystical person or a statistical person, but I do believe I shouldn't sleep with married men."

Thomas nodded. "I see."

"No matter if their wives approve of it or not. Call me provincial."

"Okay, Miss Julie Provincial," he said, smiling at me. "Tell me, how long will you be here in France?"

It was then that I realized I hadn't made any actual plans about how long I was staying or where I should go next.

As I stood there I wondered, *had Paris taught me enough about how to be single?* I did learn about pride. And something about the different types of marriages that exist. Maybe I had learned all I needed to know for now. Maybe it was time for me to go.

"I don't know. I might go to Rome next."

Thomas's eyes lit up.

"You must! Paris is very nice, yes, but even we French understand— Rome is . . ." He rolled his eyes in reverence. "I am part owner of a café there. You must go. I know many single women there."

"I'm sure you do," I said, sarcastically. I heard how it sounded before I was even finished with the sentence. It sounded so hard, so cynical, so New York.

Thomas looked at me, earnestly and slightly annoyed.

"You know, Julie, if you dislike yourself so much that you think I must be like this with every woman I meet, that's for you and your therapist. But please, don't paint me as some pig. It's not fair."

Properly scolded, I didn't have a sassy retort.

"Please let me know if you need my help with Rome. It will be perfect for you," he said politely. "In fact—I think it's just what you need."

As I watched him walk away, I realized what I believed in for this moment at least: sometimes the princess really should just shut the hell up.

Back in the States

A week after Georgia had given Max her number at Whole Foods, she didn't know whom to turn to. Because I wasn't around, and because they were the only single women she knew, she called up Ruby and Alice, who agreed to meet her at a West Village Mexican restaurant that served five-dollar margaritas.

"I mean, why would a man ask for your number and then never call you?" Georgia asked Ruby and Alice, incredulous. "Please explain this to me."

Ruby and Alice hadn't even had a chance to get their coats off. They stared at Georgia, frozen, not knowing how to answer.

"Really. I didn't come up to talk to *him,* I didn't ask him for *his* number. I was minding my own business. But then he asked for my number, and I got excited. I looked forward to seeing him. Going on a date with him. Does this happen a lot?" Ruby and Alice looked at each other. Ruby couldn't help but ask, "I'm sorry, but have you never dated before?"

A waiter came over and took their drink orders. It was going to be frozen peach margaritas all around.

"I had a steady boyfriend all through college, and then I met Dale at grad school, so, actually no. I never have really dated before. I listened to Julie and all her stories, but I guess I wasn't really paying that much attention, since I was, you know, married." Georgia suddenly looked very guilty. And confused. She looked up at Alice and Ruby, her eyes searching for answers.

"Tell me, are men really that shitty to women in New York?"

Ruby and Alice looked at each other again. They were facing the same dilemma you face when a friend's about to get her wisdom teeth pulled and she asks you how it was when you had it done. Do you tell her the truth and say you spent two weeks in excruciating pain, swollen like a chipmunk, or do you lie, let her find out for herself, and secretly hope it goes better for her?

Ruby sipped her margarita, which was the size of a small car, and thought about it for a moment. She thought about how many days and nights she spent disappointed and crying over some guy. Alice crunched on a greasy, delicious corn chip, and thought about how many men she had dated, of how much time she put into this whole dating venture. In that brief moment, they both thought about what they actually believed about dating and looking for love in New York. Ruby began.

"No . . . no, it's not like all guys are shitty. You can't think that, you mustn't think that. There are really, really great guys out there. It's just that, well, it can be rough out there, and you have to sort of, well, protect yourself, you know? But not protect yourself so much that you seem, brittle. But you have to be careful, you have to take it all very seriously . . . in a sense, but then not at all, you know?"

Georgia looked at Ruby, confused. Ruby realized she was not helping in any way. Alice, because she was a former trial lawyer, was much more comfortable breaking the bad news to Georgia, straight, fast, and with no salt around the rim:

"Listen, Georgia, the truth is some guys in New York really do suck. They're not really out there to meet the woman of their dreams, to settle down and get married. They're out there trying to have sex with as many women as they can, while they keep looking for the next woman who's going to be prettier, hotter, better in bed. Now as for this guy, Max. He could just be going around collecting women's numbers just because it makes him feel like a big man, to know he can get women to give him their number. He could be doing it just for sport."

Georgia listened to Alice in rapt attention.

"And the only protection we have against this is our resilience. Our ability to go back out there and try to meet someone else; to be able to recognize, weed out, fend off, and recover from all the bad guys out there, just to get to the one good guy. That's our only defense."

Georgia took a big gulp of her frozen margarita. "Well, okay. But I don't think these men should be allowed to get away with . . . ow! Brain freeze. Brain freeze!" Georgia's face suddenly scrunched up as she threw her hands to her head. She sat there for a moment until her face relaxed as the sensation passed away. For a moment she looked truly deranged.

"Okay, anyway, I don't think they should be able to get away with it that easily. I think they need to be retrained. If none of us ever tell them how it makes us feel, they'll think that they can keep going around asking for women's numbers and never calling them. But we have to let them know that it's not okay. We have to take back the night!"

At that, Georgia picked up her pocketbook, got out her wallet, took out twenty dollars, and threw it on the table.

"Thank you for all your help. Drinks are on me."

Ruby asked, fearfully, "Where are you going?"

Georgia put on her jacket and got up from the table. "Whole Foods. I'm going to wait for him there until he shows up. And then I'm going to try and be a catalyst for change in New York!"

Georgia stormed out of the restaurant, leaving Ruby and Alice there, alone, not knowing exactly what to say to each other.

Georgia prowled the Whole Foods aisles like a cougar searching for an unsuspecting hiker. There was no reason why Max should be at Whole Foods on this night, at this time, but Georgia was on a mission. She was hoping that the sheer force of her will might conjure him to appear in the organic greens section right this very minute. She walked up and down the aisles thinking about how she would talk to him, calmly, teaching him how his actions affect others, and so making the world a safer dating place for all of womankind. She walked up and down the aisles for two hours. It was now ten o'clock at night. She had memorized every section in the store, and was now starting to become familiar with all the items in each section, when she saw him by the frozen edamame.

He was talking to a young pretty blond girl who was holding an NYU backpack. Another one of his victims. Georgia didn't waste a minute to pounce. She bounded over to Max and stood right in front of him and the cute NYUer.

"Oh, hey—hi. Great to see you here," Max said, perhaps with a touch of discomfort in his voice.

"Hi, Max. I just wanted you to know, that when you take a woman's number, to call her, and then you don't, it can be hurtful. Most women don't just give their number to just anyone. Most women rarely feel that much of a spark to someone they're talking to, to want to take it further. So when they do give you their number, there's sort of an unspoken agreement, or expectation, that you'll actually call— because, just to be clear, you're the one that asked for the number in the first place."

Max now started looking around the store, his eyes darting nervously. The NYU girl looked at Georgia blankly.

"I'm sure you think you can do that because you have been getting away with it. But I'm here to tell you that you actually can't anymore. It's ungentlemanly."

Max just looked at his sneakers and muttered, "Jesus, don't get all psycho on me."

Of course he went straight for the psycho defense. Men always like to go straight to the psycho defense. For that reason alone we should never go psycho on a guy: just so we'll never be proving them right. ANYWAY, Georgia now got a little pissed.

"Oh, of course you're going to call me psycho. Of course. Because most women don't confront men and their bad behavior, because they've already been so beaten down, they're sure it won't make any difference. But this time, I just wanted to enlighten you. That's all."

By this point, people were glancing over at them. The NYU girl wasn't budging; she was enjoying the show. Max was losing his cool.

"Okay fine, psycho, are you done?"

Georgia now got pissed. "LISTEN, DON'T CALL ME A PSYCHO. YOU WILL NOT INVALIDATE MY FEELINGS LIKE THAT."

The NYU girl, who up to this moment had been silent, began to speak.

"Yeah, I don't think you should call her a psycho. She's just telling you how she feels."

"Oh great, another psycho," Max said.

"Don't call me a psycho," the NYU girl then said, a little more loudly.

"Don't call her a psycho," Georgia said, even more loudly than the NYU girl. Luckily for everyone involved—except maybe the highly entertained onlookers—a short Hispanic man in a crisp white shirt came over to break it up.

"I'm sorry, but you're going to have to leave the store right now. You're disturbing the other customers." Georgia looked around. She looked back at Max, haughtily.

"Fine, I'll leave. I think he's gotten the message." Georgia began to walk proudly out of the store, her head held high. She didn't even notice the smirks and the people giggling at her as she stormed out the exit door. But as she walked down the street and looked back into the window of Whole Foods, she couldn't help but notice that the NYU girl was still standing there talking to Max. And that Max was laughing and making that circular motion with his finger at his head that signifies "crazy."

Georgia turned away from the window. She walked down the street, trying to remain prideful, trying to maintain her dignity. She got two more blocks and began to cry. She thought yelling at him was going to make her feel so much better. And it did for that five minutes when she was screaming. But she was still a freshman at being single, and so no matter what she thought she believed, she still had a lot to learn.

4

Get Carried Away

(Even Though It's Impossible to Know When You Should
and When It's Just Going to End in Disaster)

A lice had always prided herself on how well she knew New York; she could be a tour guide for this grand city from the Bronx to Staten Island because she knew the ins and outs of the place like no other.

But that was before she had a boyfriend. It was only then that she was reminded that there was a whole other New York out there that existed only for couples. In this past year of professional dating, Alice had gained access to the hottest bars, nightclubs, restaurants, and sporting events that the city has to offer. But because she had not had a boyfriend, there had been a whole other side of New York to which she had not been given admittance.

For example, there was the Brooklyn Botanic Garden, where she was with Jim. Okay, so he wasn't really her boyfriend; it had only been two weeks. But after that first date together, she had decided to let him adore her for as long as they both were enjoying it. They had taken the No. 2 train out to Brooklyn together and were now walking through the tropical pavilion and the bonsai museum, holding hands. It was divine.

They stopped at a little lecture being given about the golden ginkgo trees.

A white-haired little woman was talking to a group of people about how you can distinguish a ginkgo from other gymnosperms by its fan-shaped, bi-lobed leaves. Alice started to think back on these past fourteen days with Jim. They had discovered other couple hot spots, such as the Hayden Planetarium on the first Friday of the month (when it stays open late), the Bronx Zoo (who would ever go without a child or a boyfriend?), and the skating rink at Chelsea Piers (Alice had always wanted to go but could never drag anyone with her). And now she was at the Botanic Garden learning about bi-lobeds.

This is just so cute, Alice thought. *Being in a couple is cute.*

The lecture over, they walked down a pathway strewn with leaves. Jim took Alice's hand and a rush of pure joy warmed her. She was aware that it probably wouldn't have mattered if the hand were attached to the arm of Ted Bundy—holding hands felt fucking great. Holding someone's hand meant that you belonged to them. Not in some profound irrevocable way, but for that moment in time, you were attached to someone. As they walked along the path, Jim said, "We should go apple picking next weekend."

"Cute," Alice said, happily.

They walked toward the Japanese garden pond. The air was cool, but not cold, with the bright sun warming everything up. It was a perfect fall day. They sat under a little pagoda looking out onto the pond. For someone who thought she knew everything there was to know about dating, Alice was shocked to discover what an amazing time she could have with someone she wasn't crazy about. She decided to check in with herself again as to why she wasn't falling in love with Jim yet. He was attractive. His manners were impeccable, which, Alice realized as she got older, was an important thing to her. He was fun, and sometimes even a little silly, which she always loved. And she really liked his laugh. And he thought she was hilarious. He moved in a little closer to Alice. She put her head on his chest. Last week, when they had sex for the first time, she was relieved to discover that she kind of enjoyed it.

If she hadn't, that would have been the deal breaker in this crazy scheme. But the sex was nice. Fine. If there was a worry that it wasn't hot

enough, there was also that whole other area in human experience cor-
doned off for couples only: regular sex. The experience of consistently
having an intimate, physical connection with someone. Of not having to
worry when the proper alignment of mutual attraction, safety, and appropriate circumstances (him not being a jerk, him not being the ex of a
friend who's still in love with him, him not being a friend of a friend so if
it doesn't go well it's a disaster so you might as well not even try it, etc.)
would allow you to have sexual intercourse. There is nothing worse than
looking through your datebook and realizing you haven't had sex in over
six months and it went by in what seemed like a day. And then the worry
that another six months could go by in a blink without your naked flesh
getting anywhere near someone else's. Because of Jim, that worry was
now out of the equation, and if it wasn't bodice-ripping, chest-heaving
sex, that was fine, Alice reasoned—because it was regular. And that more
than made up for any heat that might be missing.

Alice noticed two little turtles swimming in the pond. They weren't
the kind you raise in a box with a plastic palm tree and feed hamburger
meat. These were bigger, hearty things, and they were swimming in the
small pond that must have seemed endless to them.

She kept thinking about Jim, about how nice this all was, and how she
hoped to God that she would be able to fall in love with him. But she also
knew enough to give herself a break. She wouldn't beat herself up just because she wasn't able to fall in love with every nice guy she met. If Jim
wasn't going to be the great love of her life, it didn't mean Alice was afraid
of commitment, or that she only liked guys who were emotionally un-
available, or any of the nonsense people like to blame you for. If Jim
wasn't the one, that was no one's fault, it was just life. But as she sat there
and thought about how nice and cute things had been these past two
weeks, she desperately hoped that he might do just fine for a very, very
long time.

Alice turned to Jim, who was staring out into space. He had been
acting a little odd the whole morning; his usual laid-back manner had a
tiny little pulse running underneath it. He kept bouncing his right leg up
and down, now making the whole bench vibrate. Alice put her hand on
his crazy leg, and asked what the matter was.

"I'm just a little nervous, that's all."

"Why?" Alice asked.

"Because I need to talk to you."

Alice's heart started beating faster. Men don't usually say things like that unless it's bad news or . . .

"I just wanted you to know that I'm having a better time with you than I've had with any other human being in my entire life."

Alice's heart started beating even faster and her breath quickened the way it does for everyone on the planet when another human being is about to go through the embarrassment of revealing a large emotion to them.

"And I just want you to know that you're the one for me. And however fast or slow you want to take this, it's fine with me. If you want to get married next week, I would happily do that, and if you want to take it really, really slow I'd do that as well. Not as happily, but I would."

Alice looked directly at Jim. It was hard to imagine him looking more vulnerable than he did at that moment. She glanced back at the pond and saw her two turtles sunning themselves on a rock. She decided to let herself get carried away. "I've been having an amazing time, too. I know we don't know each other very well, but I want to give this a go, too."

Jim let out the breath he'd been holding in for the past three and a half minutes, and smiled.

"Great. That's great."

"I don't really know what to say besides that right now. Is that okay?"

"Yeah, sure, no, that's fine. Great. I'm just glad you didn't punch me in the face and throw me in the pond."

"Now, why would I do that?" Alice said, sweetly. They kissed. She was happy, safe, content. Because sometimes after swimming around and around in a long black lake, it's nice to get to sit on a rock and sun yourself for a while.

On to Rome

It was ten minutes before the flight and I was hyperventilating a bit. Well, actually a lot.

It's odd when you realize suddenly that you have a new crazy thing about yourself. They say you get more fearful and phobic as you get older, but it's still shocking when you realize you have to add on one more thing to your list of Crazy. I had not a care in the world when I boarded the plane. But now, as I sat in my seat and the minutes ticked by, I became increasingly nervous. How *do* airplanes stay up? What does keep them from just crashing into the earth? Wouldn't that be completely terrifying to be conscious all those minutes that the plane is plummeting to earth? What would I be thinking about . . . ? And as the physics of air travel became even more implausible to me and I was convinced I would never make it to Rome alive, I began having what I imagine was a panic attack. I started sweating and breathing heavy. Why now? I have no idea. I'd traveled from New York to Paris without a care in the world. Perhaps a therapist might say I was nervous about venturing out on my own, to a strange city, with no one that I knew meeting me there; that I was planning on doing all this "research" in Rome, but I didn't really know how I was going to start. Maybe it finally hit me that I had quit my job and left my home without really that much of a plan in place. Whatever the reason, I realized: who better to talk to in this moment than my very own guru? Luckily, I got her on the phone.

"Okay, so Julie, close your eyes and breathe from your diaphragm," Serena said in a soothing swami voice. "Imagine a white light emanating right out of your belly button and radiating out into the plane."

I was imagining. "It's a white light of peace and safety and protection and it's filling up the plane and then the sky and then the whole world. And you are completely safe." My breathing started to calm. My heartbeat slowed down. It was working. I opened my eyes. And Thomas was standing right in front of me.

"Well, hello, Miss Provincial. I believe I have the seat next to you."

A jolt of surprise zapped through my body, Serena's hard work ruined in an instant. "Um . . . Serena, I have to call you back."

"Okay, but I've been meaning to tell you. You should go to India. I mean, their spirituality, their culture—everyone says going to India is a really powerful experience."

"Okay, I'll think about that. Thanks."

"No, really. They say life-changing."

"Okay. I'll talk to you later. Bye, and thanks!" I hung up. I looked up at Thomas, who was emanating his own special brand of white light.

"What are you doing here?"

"I decided to go with you. I thought I could do some business there." He made a gesture with his hand, asking me to get up so he could sit next to me. I stood up into the aisle.

"Of course I don't usually fly economy class," Thomas said as he moved into his seat and we sat. "But I decided to make an exception." As he buckled himself in and looked around, he added, "My God, coach. It's such a tragedy."

He saw I was having trouble piecing it all together.

"I got your itinerary from Steve. Plus, I know someone at Alitalia." He smiled at me and squeezed my wrist. I blushed and got out a piece of mint gum and popped it in my mouth. The announcements about the plane taking off began and I tried to hide the sweat and the panting. How mortifying would it be to have my first panic attack in front of Thomas? There's New York Quirky, and then there's New York Crazy. Just because it was starting to dawn on me which one I was, that didn't mean he had to know right off the bat. While he was busy trying to find a comfortable place to put his knees, and the flight attendants were coming around checking our seat belts, I let out a tiny cry. Thomas looked alarmed.

"Sorry. I'm just. Something's happening. I feel a little like I'm dying. Or drowning. Something. Sorry," I whispered.

Thomas leaned closer to me. "Has this ever happened before?" I shook my head no.

"You are having some kind of panic episode, yes?"

I nodded. "Yes. I think so." I clutched the armrests tightly on both sides of me, but accidentally grabbed on to Thomas's arm. I leaned forward and started gasping for air.

"Excuse me, is everything all right?" the flight attendant asked Thomas.

"Yes, of course. She just has a stomachache. She'll be fine." As the flight attendant walked away, Thomas reached into his bag.

"Julie, you must take one of these, right away. Please. It will calm you down."

I threw myself back onto my chair and gasped, "I can't believe you're seeing me like this. This is mortifying."

"We'll worry about that later, but for now, just take this pill and swallow please, quickly."

"What is it?"

"Lexomil. France's Valium. We eat it here like candy."

I swallowed the tiny white pill dry. "Thank you so much," and I took another gasp of air. I started feeling calmer already.

"You'll probably be falling asleep soon." He put his hand on top of mine. "It's a shame, we won't get a chance to talk," he said, his blue eyes twinkling.

You really are close to someone when you sit next to them in coach. It's like you have to actually make an effort not to bump your lips into them.

Soon enough, I fell asleep.

I woke up to Thomas tapping the back of my hand, quite hard, and saying in his sweet French accent, "Julie, Julie, it's time to wake up. Please."

Like deadlifting four-hundred-pound barbells, it took every ounce of my strength to open my eyes. In a haze I saw beautiful Thomas in the aisle, looking unruffled and slightly amused as a flight attendant hovered over him.

"*Signore,* we have to leave the plane. You must get her off." It was then that I saw that the plane was on the ground and the cabin was absolutely empty. I groaned loudly and put my hands to my eyes to somehow shield myself from the humiliation. Why wouldn't they just let me go back to sleep?

Thomas gently guided me out of my seat. I steadied myself, grabbed my purse, and tried to pull myself together as quickly as possible. As we walked past the many, many rows of seats to the door, I asked Thomas, "Just tell me this—was there a drooling situation going on?"

Thomas laughed and said, "Julie, you don't want to know." He steadied me out the door of the plane.

Later that afternoon I awoke in a room at some kind of pensione. I was a little disoriented, so I got up and looked out my window onto a piazza with a huge circular building off to one side—the Pantheon. I had no memory of getting there. Thomas told me later that I had gone through customs and been mistaken for a drug addict, had all my bags searched, and then passed out in the cab with my head in his lap. That Lexomil doesn't kid around.

On the desk I found a note: "I am next door at a café with my friend Lorenzo, please come by when you wake up. Kisses, Thomas." I shakily got into the shower, fixed myself up, and went out to find Thomas.

Next to the hotel was a tiny café, right on the piazza. Thomas was with a man in his early thirties who was speaking animatedly, gesturing wildly. Thomas saw me and stood up, his friend getting up as well.

"How are you feeling, my Sleeping Beauty?" Thomas asked.

"Fine. A little groggy."

"I'll get you a cappuccino immediately." Thomas waved over a waitress and we all sat down.

"This is my friend, Lorenzo. He's heartbroken and telling me all about it."

Lorenzo was a handsome Italian man, with big, tired eyes and long brown hair that he grabbed and pushed back whenever he was exclaiming something, which was often.

"It's awful, Julie, awful. My heart is broken, you don't understand. Crushed. I'm crushed." He pushed back his hair. "I don't want to live, really. I want to throw myself off a building. She just left me. She told me she doesn't love me anymore. Just like that. Tell me, Julie, you're a woman. Tell me. How is this possible? How can a woman love you one minute and destroy you the next? How can she have no feelings for me overnight?"

Luckily my cappuccino came just then, so I could get a little caffeine into my system.

"Um . . . I don't know. Was it really that sudden?"

"It was! Three nights ago, we made love, she told me she loved me. That she wanted to spend the rest of her life with me. That we should have babies together. Then, yesterday she calls me up and tells me she doesn't want to be with me."

"How long were you together?" I asked.

"One year. One beautiful year. We both agreed that we have never been in such a good relationship. How is this possible, Julie, tell me. Just three nights ago she told me she loved me. Just three nights ago. I can't sleep. I can't eat. It's terrible."

I looked at Thomas, wondering what I just stepped into. As if reading my mind, Thomas laughed and said, "Lorenzo's an actor. He's very dramatic."

"*Ma no,* Thomas, c'mon," Lorenzo said, offended. "This is no exaggeration. This is a real tragedy."

"Was your girlfriend an actress as well?"

"No. She's a dancer. You should see her body. The most beautiful body you have ever seen. Perfect breasts. Perfect. And these long legs, like art. Tell me, Julie, tell me. How can this happen?"

Thomas saw the dazed expression on my face and decided to egg him on. "Please, Julie, you must help him."

I was still a little slow from my drug overdose, but I tried to think as quickly as I could.

"Do you think she met someone else?"

"Impossible! We saw each other all the time."

"Are you sure? Because that could be—"

"No. It's not possible. I know all her friends. Her dancing partners, too. No."

"Well, is she psychotic?"

"No. She was perfectly fine. Sane."

"Maybe," I said slowly, "she wasn't really in love with you?" Lorenzo banged his hands on the table.

"*Ma no*—how could that be? How?" He was truly looking for me to explain.

"Well, if she's not seeing anyone else, she isn't psychotic, and she just changed her mind about you, then maybe she wasn't really in love with you. Or maybe she just doesn't know what love means."

This type of American analysis simply didn't compute for Lorenzo. He just shrugged his shoulders and said, "Or maybe she just fell out of love with me."

"Do you think that love is so fleeting that it can just go away? Just like that?"

"Of course I do, Julie. It finds you, like magic, like a miracle, and then it can go just as fast."

"You really think of love as a mysterious emotion that comes and goes like magic?"

"Yes, of course. Of course!"

Thomas said gently, "I believe you would call my friend a romantic."

Lorenzo threw his arms in the air. "What other way is there to live? Julie, don't you believe this, too?"

"Well, no. I guess I don't," I said.

"Tell me, then. What *do* you believe?"

Thomas leaned in. "Now this is getting interesting."

Again, that question. I stalled, sipping my coffee. I have spent a good deal of time in therapy analyzing why I've been attracted to the people I've been attracted to. What "buttons they push" in me that makes me want them in my life. I've spent a good deal of time analyzing why my friends are attracted to the types of men they are attracted to. I've watched them swear that they've met their soulmate, that they've never felt this way before and that it's destiny—and then break up with that soulmate in less time than it takes to get a sofa delivered. I've watched friends—smart, levelheaded friends—get married, and then I've watched in shock as their marriages fell apart. And I've watched absolutely ridiculous couples stay together for ten years and counting.

And I've been so busy looking for love and being frustrated that I can't find it, that I have never really defined it for myself. So I sat at this little café as the sun went down, and pondered.

"I guess I don't really believe in romantic love," I finally said. Thomas raised his eyebrows and Lorenzo looked as if he had just seen a ghost.

"What do you believe in, then?" Thomas asked.

"Well, I believe in attraction. And I believe in passion and the *feeling* of falling in love. But I guess I don't think that that's necessarily real."

Thomas and Lorenzo seemed shocked.

"Why? Because sometimes it doesn't last?" Thomas asked.

"Because *most* times it doesn't last. Because most of the time it's about what you're projecting onto a person, what you want them to be, what you want yourself to be, so many things that have nothing to do with the other person."

"I had no idea," Thomas said. "It seems we have a very big cynic here."

"This is a disaster, truly," Lorenzo said, throwing his hands in the air. "I thought I had it bad."

I laughed. "I know! I didn't know what a cynic I was until this moment, either!"

"But Julie," Thomas asked, concerned, "how can love ever find you if you don't believe in it?"

I looked at them both staring at me with great concern, and then—I burst out crying. Funny how that happens. One moment you're a strong, independent woman talking about love and relationships. And the next moment someone says an arrangement of words that somehow destroys you.

"No! Julie. It was not meant to be—no!" Thomas was horrified. "Please, it was nothing!"

I put my hand over my face. "No, I know, don't feel bad. I don't know why . . . I'm just too . . . please. Don't worry about it. Really." But as I spoke, the tears rolled down my face. There it was again, the question that always seems to pop out of the subtext when I least expect it. *Why are you single? Why don't you have love?* And now, in Rome, one answer: *because you don't believe in it.*

"I'm just going to go to my room," I said, starting to get up.

Thomas grabbed my hand as Lorenzo said loudly, "*Ma no,* Julie, come on! You can't run back into your little room to cry. That's unacceptable." Thomas added, gently, "How are we ever going to be friends if you run and hide every time you have an emotion?" I sat back down.

"I'm sorry. It must be the Lexomil or something."

Thomas smiled. "Yes, I'm sure. You're relaxed. Your defenses are down."

I turned to Lorenzo, embarrassed. "I'm so sorry. I'm not usually like this." He looked at me with admiration.

"Women! They are fantastic. Look at you. You feel, you cry. So fluid. *Che bella! Che bella!*" He waved his arms around and laughed. I burst out laughing as well, and Thomas looked as happy as any man could look.

•   •   •

After we went to another restaurant for dinner, and I had the best pasta carbonara I've ever tasted, with large strips of bacon in it—not chunks, not bits, but actual *strips* (you wouldn't think it would work but it did)—it was time to go to sleep. Lorenzo went home, and Thomas and I walked back to the hotel, passing piazza after beautiful piazza, the Trevi Fountain, the Spanish Steps. Rome is so old, so beautiful, it's hard to take it all in. When we got to the hotel, Thomas walked to a motorcycle with two helmets locked to it. He got out a key, unlocked them, and handed a helmet to me.

"And now," he said grandly, "you must see Rome by motorcycle."

"When did you get this?"

"It's Lorenzo's. He has a few. He lent it to me while you were asleep."

I don't like motorcycles. Never have. Because here's what—they're really dangerous. And it would be cold. I don't like to be cold. But the thought of explaining that to him and seeming once again like an unspontaneous, unromantic, panicky American, well, it just exhausted me to the core. So I took the helmet and got on the bike. What can I say. When in Rome. . . .

We drove fast, by random Roman ruins and by the Forum. We wound through tiny streets and raced along the main thoroughfare and up a street that led straight to Saint Peter's Square.

There I was, on the back of a dangerous vehicle that was going very fast with a driver who, let's face it, did have a few glasses of wine at dinner. I was cold. I was frightened. And very vulnerable. I imagined the motorcycle crashing, Thomas losing control as we took a turn, our bodies sliding into oncoming traffic. I imagined some official calling my mom and telling her what happened, and her or my brother having to deal with the horror and hassle of getting my body shipped home.

And then, as we rocketed back toward the hotel, we circled around the Colosseum. It struck me: none of these structures are surrounded by walls or gates or plate glass. They stand unprotected, waiting to dazzle us, accepting their vulnerability to any graffiti artist or vandal or terrorist that might want to come around. And I thought to myself, *Well, if this is how I'm going to go, it's a damn good way to go.* And then I wrapped my arms around Thomas a little tighter and tried to drink in every ounce of magnificent Roman splendor.

• • •

When we got back to the hotel, Thomas took off his helmet and helped me take off mine. There's nothing less sexy than wearing a motorcycle helmet, truly. We walked through the lobby and into the elevator. I was suddenly jarred back into the world of dynamics and morality and innuendo and not knowing where Thomas was sleeping that night. And as if he had read my mind, Thomas said, "My room is on the third floor. I believe yours is on the second, yes?"

I nodded. I had managed to remember my room key and my room number. Thomas pressed the second- and third-floor buttons and the doors closed. When they opened again, Thomas gave me a polite kiss on both my cheeks and said, "Good night, my dear Julie. Sleep well." I walked out of the elevator and down the hall to my room.

Back in the States

Georgia knew exactly what she was supposed to do. Dale was coming over in a few minutes, and she knew the cardinal rule that everyone, no matter how romantically inept, knows: you always try to look extremely hot when you are meeting with an ex. But on this particular morning, Georgia had said "fuck it." She wasn't going to bathe and blow-dry for Dale. Fuck him. She wasn't trying to woo him back. Fuck. Him. He can go live with his underage samba dancer.

Georgia and Dale were meeting to talk about how they would officially share custody of their children. No lawyers, no fighting. Two adults with no agenda except for the well-being of their kids.

When she opened the door, Dale walked in looking, well, hot, unfortunately, but fuck him. The first thing he did when he came in was look up and see that the little door of the smoke alarm was open, and the battery gone.

"Jesus, Georgia, you didn't get a battery for the smoke alarm yet?"

"Shit, no, I've been meaning to."

"Well, don't you think that's kind of important?"

"Yes, I do, but I've been kind of busy around here, you know."

He shook his head. "Don't you think that should be high on the list of priorities? A battery for the smoke and carbon monoxide detector in the house our children live in?"

Georgia knew that this could blow up right away into a fight, and that hip, well-educated New Yorkers don't have to have fights with their exes over stupid things. But she didn't care.

"If you'd like, you can turn around right now and go to the hardware store and get a battery for the smoke and carbon monoxide detector that's in the house our children live in. You are welcome to do that if you like."

"I'll do it after we're done talking, okay?"

"Okay. Thanks so much."

They both took a breath. They walked over to the kitchen table and sat down. There was a long silence.

"Can I get you anything? Coffee? Soda?"

"I'll have a glass of water," Dale said, as he got up from his chair. But Georgia was at the refrigerator. This was her house now and Dale knew better than to get up and help himself to a glass of water. As Dale sat back down, she poured a glass of water from the Brita, then walked over and handed it to him. He took a sip. Georgia sat down across from him, her hands folded on the table in front of her. She felt that if she just kept her hands folded in front of her, things couldn't get that out of control.

As it stood, Georgia had full custody of the kids, with Dale seeing them whenever they both agreed to it, and whenever Georgia needed a break. But they knew it was time to set up some rules.

"I was thinking that maybe you could have the kids during the week, and I got them on the weekend."

The sarcasm leaped out before Georgia even had a chance to stop it.

"That sounds great. I get to get them to school and help with their homework and make sure they have dinner and go to bed and *you* get to go out and have fun with them?"

Georgia didn't even know what she was fighting for; it actually sounded like a good arrangement. Let Dale take the kids on the weekend so she could go out and have fun. Dale didn't need the weekends to go out and have fun because he was home with his samba dancer having hot samba sex every night of the week. But she didn't feel like agreeing with him yet. She felt like being pissy, and she felt like getting one thing perfectly clear.

"She can never be with my children. You know that, don't you?"

"Georgia."

"Seriously, if I hear that she was around the kids, I'll go apeshit on you."

"We'll talk about this later," Dale said, his head down, trying to sound neutral.

Georgia's hands were no longer folded. They were now flapping around, helping her make her points.

"What do you mean we'll talk about this later? Like I'm going to change my mind? Like two weeks from now I'm all of a sudden going to be like, 'Hey, can you please bring that Brazilian whore around my children to show them who broke up their mommy and daddy's marriage?'"

"She didn't break up our marriage, Georgia."

Georgia got up, the civility of sitting down to discuss something at the kitchen table now broken.

"Oh, like you would have left on your own with no safety net? Right. You left the minute you knew you had someone else to be with."

Dale didn't wait to respond. "Maybe that's true, but that doesn't mean that our marriage wasn't over long before that."

Georgia was now pacing and her voice had gone up a couple of decibels in volume. "Really? Okay. How long before? How long was our marriage over before you met the samba dancer? A couple months? A year? Two years?" Georgia stopped right in front of Dale, who was still sitting. "How long!?"

There's an expression that if you have to go through hell, the best way is to drive right through it. Dale decided to do just that.

"Five years. It started going bad for me five years ago."

Georgia looked as if she had just been electrocuted.

"You mean right after Beth was born? Then?"

"Yes, if you must know, then. Yes."

Georgia began pacing again. She was a wounded animal now—wild-eyed and unpredictable.

"So you're telling me that for the past five years that we've been living together, you didn't love me anymore?"

"Yes."

Before Georgia was able to stifle it, she let out a little yelp. She tried to swallow it, hoping Dale might have only heard it as a gasp. She walked over to the kitchen counter, shaking. But being a strong, wild animal, Georgia gathered her wits and went right back on the attack.

"Well, bullshit. You're just saying that to make yourself feel better, so you don't have to actually deal with the truth. And the truth is that you got lucky enough to find someone really hot who wanted to fuck you and so you ditched your marriage and your children for it. You're going to tell me that you haven't been in love with me in five years? I say bullshit. You weren't in love with me when Gareth rode his bike for the first time without his training wheels and you picked me up and twirled me around in your arms and kissed me? You weren't in love with me when you got your promotion and I got the kids to write cards that said 'Congratulations, Daddy' and we papered them around the house and had a big dinner for you when you came home?"

"I loved you, but no, I wasn't in love with you anymore. We never had sex, Georgia. Ever. Our marriage was passionless. It was dead."

Georgia was holding on to her hair at the roots, trying somehow to compose herself. Since the breakup of their marriage, there were tears, there was shouting, but they had never had the "face-to-face" talk. This, apparently, was it.

"So that's what this is all about? Hot, sweaty sex? That's not what a marriage is, Dale. That's what an affair is. A marriage is two people building a life together and raising children and sometimes being bored."

"And sometimes having sex, Georgia. WE NEVER HAD SEX."

"THEN WHY DIDN'T YOU TALK ABOUT IT WITH ME?" Georgia shrieked. "WHY DIDN'T YOU TELL ME THAT YOU WANTED MORE SEX? WHY DIDN'T WE GO TO COUNSELING OR GO AWAY FOR A FUCKING WEEKEND? I THOUGHT EVERYTHING WAS FINE."

Dale got up from the table.

"HOW COULD YOU THINK EVERYTHING WAS FINE? WE DIDN'T HAVE SEX. I'M TOO YOUNG NOT TO HAVE SEX, GEORGIA. I STILL WANT PASSION AND FIRE AND EXCITEMENT IN MY LIFE."

"FINE. LET'S HAVE SEX. IF THAT'S ALL IT IS LET'S HAVE SEX RIGHT NOW." Georgia stood with her greasy hair and her sweatpants, her arms outstretched. Dale started backing up, shaking his head.

"Georgia, come on."

"What? You don't think it'll be all hot and sweaty right now? You don't think you can find fire and passion with me?" Georgia was sobbing between bursts of fury.

"You don't just want *sex*, Dale, you want *new* sex. If you wanted sex with me, you would have tried to have sex with me. But all you want is new, hot sweaty sex." Georgia was poking him as she spoke, jabbing at his shoulders and his chest.

Dale put his jacket on. "This isn't going anywhere. We were supposed to be talking about the children."

"Yes." Georgia followed him, standing very close. "The children you left because you need to have HOT, SWEATY SEX."

Dale spun around and grabbed Georgia by the shoulders. "I HATE TO TELL YOU THIS, BUT I LOVE MELEA, GEORGIA, AND YOU'RE GOING TO HAVE TO GET USED TO THE IDEA THAT SHE'S GOING TO BE IN MY LIFE FOR A LONG, LONG TIME."

Dale then basically picked Georgia up by her shoulders and moved her out of his way, practically sprinting to the door. Georgia was officially unhinged.

"SHE'S NOT GOING TO GET NEAR MY KIDS, DO YOU HEAR ME??"

She followed him into the hallway, as Dale flew to the staircase, clearly not wanting to wait for the elevator. Georgia shrieked down at him as he raced down the stairs.

"WHAT? AREN'T YOU GOING TO COME BACK WITH BATTERIES FOR THE FUCKING SMOKE DETECTOR THAT YOU'RE SO CONCERNED ABOUT?"

Dale stopped at the bottom landing and looked up at Georgia glaring down at him from three floors above.

"Get it yourself, Georgia." And he slammed the door.

Back in Rome

While Thomas had business meetings, he had thoughtfully arranged little appointments for me to meet with some of his female friends to talk about love and men and relationships. I was here, after all, for research.

Right away, I learned some very important things about these Italian women. First of all, none of them had slept with Thomas. That might not have been the most monumental cultural or anthropological discovery, but it was pretty interesting to me. I never asked outright; all you have to do is ask a woman how she knows someone and you can usually tell from the expression on her face what's up.

The second thing I learned is that they seemed a little shy, which was surprising. In the land of Sophia Loren and . . . actually, there aren't a lot of new Italian actresses who come to mind, which come to think of it, might support my argument . . . I was surprised at how reticent they were in talking about their feelings. Of course it could have just been the women I met, but it was striking. But soon enough, I started noticing another trend.

In their conversations about their relationships, Italian women often mentioned slapping. For example, "Oh, I got so mad that I had to slap him." Or, "I slapped him and then I walked out the door, I was so angry." It seems these timid women weren't so retiring when it came to a little bit of physical abuse. Of course, I only spoke to a few Italian women, and I normally don't like to generalize, but what would stories about a trip around the world be without generalizing? Even so, I don't want to perpetuate a stereotype. But it was of note.

On my third day, I met Cecily. She was just five feet tall, weighed about eighty pounds, and barely spoke above a whisper. And yet in that whisper, she casually let slip that her last boyfriend got her so mad at a party that she slapped him and went home.

"Um, you slapped him right there? At the party?"

"Yes, I was furious. He was talking to this one woman all night long. It looked like he was going to kiss her, they were so close. It was humiliating."

"You're about the fourth woman I've talked to who's mentioned slapping her boyfriend."

Her friend Lena chimed in, "That's because they make us so mad. They don't listen."

We were sitting at a busy café right near the Trevi Fountain. I was eating a chocolate-filled croissant that was covered in powdered sugar.

Cecily tried to explain. "Julie, I'm not proud of this, I don't think I should slap. But I get so upset. I don't know what else to do!"

"I understand, I do," I said, completely lying. Because the truth was, it's something I would never dream of doing. Yes, because I was taught hitting is bad, and that one must learn how to control one's more violent impulses. But also, I could just never imagine the audacity. *Not that I would want to, really.* But still, I've been beaten down to the point where I wouldn't ask a man to put lotion on my back for fear of seeming too needy. So the thought of feeling comfortable landing the palm of my hand across some guy's face was beyond my imagination.

Lena added, "We can't help it. We get so angry, we need to slap."

Cecily understood the expression on my face.

"Do women slap in the United States?"

I didn't want to sound superior, but I didn't want to lie, either.

"Um . . . I'm sure some women do, but it doesn't seem as common as it is here."

Lena then asked, "Have you ever slapped?"

I shook my head, picked at my sugary croissant, and said no. They both took this in, quietly.

After a moment, Cecily asked, "Julie, but certainly a man has made you so angry that you *wanted* to slap him, yes?"

I looked down at my cappuccino. "No."

They both looked at me with pity. I looked back up at them with envy.

"Then you have never been in love," Lena said.

"You might be right."

They both looked at me as if I had revealed the most tragic secret in the world.

"This is a tragedy. You must go out in Rome and fall in love immediately," Cecily said, quite seriously.

"Yes, tonight," Lena said. "You've wasted too much time already."

"Is it that easy? To just walk out your door and decide to fall in love?"

Lena and Cecily just looked at each other and shrugged.

"In Rome, it just might be," Cecily said, smiling.

Lena added, "At least you should try and be open to it. Be open to losing yourself in love."

"Losing myself? I thought that was a bad thing."

Lena shook her head. "No. That's where you American women have it wrong. Trying to be so independent. You have to be willing to lose yourself, to risk everything. Otherwise, it's not really love."

Finally, these shy women had something they wanted to teach me.

Later, when I went to meet Thomas for dinner, I was still rattled. Those women—those timid, passionate, jealous, temperamental women—made me feel so dry inside, so emotionally limited. How does one start believing in love? How do you turn off your brain and everything you've seen and heard in the past twenty years? How do I all of a sudden believe that these crazy large emotions are not just a bunch of hormones and illusions? How do I suddenly believe romantic love is a real, concrete thing and that I'm entitled to it? I was worried that I was starting to think like a self-help book as I walked into a small restaurant on the Piazza di Pietro. Thomas was already there at the bar, a glass of wine in his hand.

The last few days spent with Thomas had been so simple, yet so extraordinary. Innocent, unbroken happiness. There had been dinners and drinks with his friends, and we'd seen a lot of Lorenzo, whose girlfriend had not returned any of his calls, and who was insisting he was ready to be hospitalized. There had been walks and talks and heated debates and lots and lots of laughter. There were more motorcycle rides, and late-night glasses of Prosecco. It's funny how fast you can feel like you're in a couple. It only takes a matter of days before you're thinking "we" instead of "I."

And through all this, he had not made a pass at me once. Not once. For the past four nights, he politely kissed me good night on my cheeks and then went to bed. Not that I wanted him to make a pass. I mean. Not that I would have done anything. I mean. Not that . . . whatever.

As I sat down, I asked him right out, "Have you dated an Italian woman, and did she ever slap you?"

He laughed. "This is what I love about you, Julie—you're not very good with the small talk, either. We share this trait."

All I heard was that he said he loved something about me.

"I have been with a few Italian women, but they never slapped me. I think they know that a French man might slap them back."

"It seems like the Italian men take it in stride."

"I don't know about that. I don't think they like it. But I do hear of it happening quite often."

I shook my head. "Fascinating." I was already getting a little tipsy off my one glass of red wine.

Thomas's cell phone rang. As he listened he began to look concerned.

"Now please, calm down. You will do no such thing. Now stop it. I am coming right over. Yes." I thought it might be his wife, wondering when he was getting his ass back to Paris. Thomas put down the phone.

"It's Lorenzo. He is threatening to throw himself off the balcony of his apartment."

I grabbed my jacket and purse and we were off.

When we got to his apartment, Lorenzo was distraught. He was crying, and it looked like he hadn't slept all night. There were a few broken dishes on the floor.

"She called me today, Thomas. She wasn't angry, she didn't meet anyone else, she just doesn't want to be with me anymore. She told me to stop calling her! It's over! It's really over!"

He grabbed his long floppy brown hair, sat in a chair, and sobbed. Thomas sat on the chair's armrest and tenderly put his hand on Lorenzo's back. Then Lorenzo jumped up and ripped his shirt off, buttons flying, and threw it in a ball on the floor, leaving him in a white t-shirt.

"I'm going to kill myself. Just to show her."

Why he needed to do it in just his t-shirt, I'm not sure, but it got our attention. He ran to the balcony and opened the doors. Thomas ran over to him and grabbed him by the arm, pulling him backward. Lorenzo broke free and went for the window again; Thomas caught him. They both fell to the floor and Lorenzo crawled toward the window while Thomas held on to his leg. Lorenzo tried to kick Thomas with his other leg, around his head and shoulders.

"*Basta*, Lorenzo!"

"Leave me alone, leave me alone!"

"What should I do? Should I call for help?!" I chimed in.

Thomas managed to get on top of Lorenzo. It was a ridiculous sight. Lorenzo was now lying on his back, thrashing around as Thomas sat on his stomach, scolding him loudly. "Please, Lorenzo, this is too much. I won't get up until you calm down. And I mean really calm down. Please."

After a few minutes, Lorenzo's breathing slowed.

"Um, can I get either of you a glass of water?" I asked, with clearly nothing else better to say. They both surprisingly nodded yes. I ran to the kitchen and got two glasses of tap water. Thomas drank his while still on top of Lorenzo, and Lorenzo managed to drink his while still lying on the floor.

Lorenzo tried, or pretended to try, to throw himself out a window over a woman. Was that crazy? Wars have been started, empires jeopardized, over love. Songs are sung, poems are written, all because of love. Historically speaking, it seems to be very real, this feeling. And in this moment, seeing Thomas sitting on Lorenzo, coming to his rescue, it was hard not to think Thomas was perfect. It was hard not to project all my hopes and desires and assumptions right onto him. He was dashing, he was interesting, he was able to comfort a male friend who was crying his heart out without batting an eye. But he was also able to tackle him to the ground like a linebacker. He was a great friend and a fully realized man.

It's so funny, but when it happens, it really does feel like you're physically falling. And I wanted to feel every moment of it, to get lost in it. Why not? Before I knew what I was doing, before I could talk myself out of it, I ran toward Thomas, knelt on the ground next to him, wrapped my arms around him, and gave him a big kiss on the lips. Lorenzo, looking up at us from the ground, started clapping.

"*Brava Americana.* You are beginning to understand a few things."

I stood up quickly. Thomas looked up at me; he was beaming, almost proud.

"I was just trying to, you know, break the tension," I said, backing away from them.

"No! Don't ruin it with excuses. No," Lorenzo said, still on the floor. "It was *bellissima. Si.*"

It might have been bellissima, but I was now embarrassed. Did Lorenzo know Thomas's wife? How many women had he seen throw themselves at Thomas? Did he even want me to kiss him? There was no way to lose myself in love when I had this kind of mind as my compass. I walked to the kitchen and got a glass of water for myself.

I glanced over and saw Thomas look at Lorenzo and speak sternly in Italian. Lorenzo seemed to say something that reassured him. Thomas slowly stood up. Lorenzo slowly got up and sat calmly on his sofa.

Not to take any chances, Thomas gave Lorenzo a dose of the magic Lexomil and after about twenty minutes, Lorenzo was asleep.

We walked back to the hotel, unusually quiet. Finally, Thomas broke the silence.

"So. My dear Julie. I'm very sorry to say this, but I believe I should be getting back. I think Lorenzo will be fine, and I'm finished with my work here."

So that was the response to my dramatic display. He needed to leave town. It served me right. Shame on me for humiliating myself like that. I had made a fool of myself. I knew it—getting carried away did not suit me at all.

"Oh, of course. Yes. That makes sense. Well, thanks! Thanks for everything."

I hoped to sound cheerful, trying to be like a French woman and keep my dignity. Of course this had to end, of course it was going to be over soon. There was no need to get all weepy about it. We were walking by the Colosseum again. It's just crazy, Rome. You'll be walking and chatting and feeling this and that about whatever the hell, and then you'll just turn your head and be like, *Oh hi, two thousand years ago.*

"How long will you stay here?" Thomas asked.

"I'm not sure. I have to decide where to go next." I really had to get better about planning this trip.

We stopped and took a long look at the Colosseum, ancient and glowing.

Thomas turned to look at me. "So tell me, Miss New York. What is going through that busy mind of yours right now?"

"Nothing."

"Oh really? Somehow I have a hard time believing that."

"I just, you know, feel a little stupid, that's all. I mean I kissed you because I thought I should try to get carried away, like everyone is telling me. But it felt dumb. You're married, first of all, and so handsome and charming, you must have . . . I just don't want to look like a silly . . ."

"But tell me, Julie, how did this week feel to you? Tell me that."

I thought for a moment. I didn't really want to tell the truth. I had had a perfect time and I felt like I was falling in love with him. I don't even know what that means, but it's how I felt.

"Stop thinking, Julie, just tell me."

You really shouldn't stand in front of one of the great wonders of the world and lie. Even I could sense that. So I told the truth. What did I have to lose? "It felt fantastic. Like . . . like a miracle. Like hours flew by in seconds and I never ever wanted to leave your side. Everything you said seemed so interesting, so funny. And I just loved looking at you, your face. I loved just being near you. Sitting near you, standing near you. And then when I saw you wrestling Lorenzo, it just made me completely adore you."

Thomas walked up closer to me. "And can you believe that during this week, I felt the exact same way?"

"Well, I never wrestled Lorenzo, so . . ."

Thomas raised his eyebrows. "You know what I mean."

I looked at him, and wanted to say, "No, actually, I can't. Because things like this don't ever happen to me. And I don't think that I'm so great that I can really understand what you would find so captivating about me, so, no, I don't believe it one goddamn bit." But instead, I thought about the hours we'd spent together, the meals and the talks and thoughts shared. It felt very real. And mutual. I thought about the Italian women and their telling me to lose myself in love. I guess people do meet and fall in love or in infatuation without much reason why. It just happens. And all you can rely on is how you feel, because it might not make any sense. You just have to trust the feeling and the moment.

"It's hard for me to believe that, but I guess I can try" is what I ended up saying. And then Thomas put his arms around me and kissed me. In front of the Colosseum with its history and decay and majesty, we kissed. Like two teenagers. Like two people who believed in the wonder of love.

I woke up in Thomas's bed the next morning. I looked over and saw him sleeping soundly. I thought about the night before. How we came back to the hotel and went into his room. How I let myself get carried away. I scanned my mind. How did I feel? Guilty? Yes. Yes, I felt guilty. Even if it was okay with the both of them, he *was* someone else's husband. So, I felt guilty. But did I regret it? No, I did not. Then I felt guilty for not regretting it. How else did I feel? Happy? Yes. Definitely. I felt happy. I had allowed myself to enjoy a moment. I looked over at Thomas and knew that I had felt something, something like falling in love, and it felt real and I hadn't hurt anyone. And that was enough for now. I was ready to leave Rome. I had learned all I needed to learn here.

5

Figure Out the Whole Sex Thing—
When You Want It, How to Get It, Who to Do It With

(Just Make Sure You Have It Every Once in a While; Just My Opinion)

I t seemed like a good idea at the time. Georgia and I were in Rio de Janeiro trying on expensive bikinis at a boutique in Ipanema.

Georgia came out of the dressing room to show me hers: a little orange number with white piping and little silver hoops on the hips and right in the middle of her cleavage, holding all the fabric together. Very sixties, very Bond girl. I forgot what an amazing body Georgia has—so had Georgia, it seems, because she was very excited about it.

"Look at me. Look how hot I am. Like she's the only one who's hot? Please. Look how hot I am!" She twirled around and looked at her tight little butt in the mirror and said to the salesgirl, "I'll take it." Then she turned to me, still dressed and clutching a modest two-piece, trembling slightly.

"Now it's your turn."

I believe I told you. I hate my body. And just when I've convinced myself that it's all in my mind, I turn around at the mirror and realize—no, it's all in my butt. Acres and acres of cellulite. In that bikini store, clutching my little two-piece, I felt so debilitated by my cellulite that I should have been given a wheelchair.

Georgia was on a mission. She had called me in Rome to tell me all about her fight with Dale. She was upset and said she needed to get away from it all. That wasn't so surprising, but when she suggested going to the home country of the Other Woman, I was confused. That didn't seem so much like getting away from it all as diving right into it. But I agreed. Her parents had been dying to take care of the kids, so they flew in and she took off.

I used my round-the-world pass to go back to Miami, where I met Georgia, and we flew to Brazil together panic-free. I had heard so much about Rio, about its sexiness, its fun, its danger, I was excited to see it all for myself.

But Georgia had something to prove. It was clear the minute I met her in Miami and we shared a plate of deep-fried stuffed mushrooms at one of those classy airport restaurants.

"What's so great about her? Oooh, she's Brazilian. Oooh, that's so exotic. Well, guess what? I'm a sexy American. That's hot, too." She shoved a forkful of the cheesy mushroom situation in her mouth. "Damn, that's good."

So now Georgia was prancing around in the store like a happy little Creamsicle trying to prove whatever she needed to prove in as little clothing as possible.

So, first off, let me tell you my thing about two-piece bathing suits: they're underwear. Why don't we just admit that? For some reason, when you put sand and water and sun together, you're allowed, even pressured, to go out in public in your underwear. You're expected to expose yourself to friends and family members, sometimes even colleagues, in a way you would never do in any other given moment in time. If Georgia were walking around *this very same store* in her underwear, I would say, "Hey Georgia, put on some clothes. You're walking around in your underwear, that's weird." But because the underwear is orange nylon, it's okay.

I don't want to wear my underwear in public.

My solution has been to wear a cute little bathing suit top with men's surfing trunks. All problem areas covered, even when swimming. The only problem is that I can get away with this for maybe another two years before I overhear some kid at the beach saying, "Who's that weird old lady dressed like a boy?"

As Georgia changed, I explained my philosophy on the bathing suit situation until she cut me off.

"We're in Rio. You're going to wear a bikini on the beach. Go try it on. Seriously. Enough."

Her tone was so perfectly "I'm the mother, do as you're told," I had no choice but to do so. As I was changing behind a curtain, I heard Georgia speaking to the saleswoman, trying her best to cheer me on.

"Women in Rio love their bodies, right? They are proud of their bodies and like showing them off, right?"

"Oh yes," I heard the young saleswoman say. "In Rio we worship our bodies."

I looked at myself in the mirror. I didn't think I would be hanging this sight up on an altar and praying to it any time soon. And then I got really sad. I'm simply too young to hate my body. I'm going to be old in like two minutes, and my body really will be difficult to love. But now, well, it's fine. Why shouldn't I admire it? It's mine and it keeps me healthy and I should accept it, just the way it is. There are people who are sick or disabled and would kill to have a strong, healthy body, and the last thing they're worrying about is their fucking cellulite. It's a show of ungratefulness to my health and mobility and youth to hate my body so much.

And then I turned around. There was so much cellulite on my ass and thighs it made me want to throw up on myself.

"Goddamn it!" I said. "The lighting in here is just as bad as it is in the States. Why do they do that with the overhead lighting? To make us want to kill ourselves instead of buy clothing? I don't get it!"

"Julie, just come out, you're exaggerating."

"No. No way. I'm putting my clothes back on."

"Julie, for Pete's sake, come out. Now," Georgia said in that tone, and by God, it worked again. I walked out and they looked me over.

"You're crazy. You look fantastic. Look at your abs. They're insane."

"Ooh, very nice, miss, very nice," said the saleswoman.

"Oh yeah?" I said, angrily—my need to prove my point overshadowing any vanity I had left. I turned around and showed them the rear view. "Now what do you think?"

Here's the bummer about women: it's so easy to tell when we're lying. Not about the big things; when we're prepared to lie we can be masters. But about small things, like this? God, we're transparent. Georgia's voice immediately went up two octaves.

"Oh please, what are you talking about?"

"Oh, I think you know what I'm talking about."

"You're insane."

"Really, I'm insane? You mean I don't have cellulite from the back of my knees up to the top of my thighs? You mean that's just some crazy 'cellulite hallucination' I've been having for the past five years?"

"It's not as bad as you think. Really."

"See!? I just went from 'fantastic' to 'not as bad as you think.'"

I noticed the salesgirl suddenly went mute. "So, what do you think? I look terrible, right?"

She was silent for a moment. Torn, I realize now, between her job as a bikini saleswoman and her civic duty. She took a deep breath and said, "Maybe you don't need to go on the beach. There are other things to do in Rio."

Georgia gasped loudly. I stood there with my mouth and eyes wide open, speechless. Finally, I got out, "Wha . . . ?"

Georgia jumped right in. "How could you say that?! I thought you said the women in Rio all loved their bodies, worshipped their bodies."

The saleswoman remained calm. "Yes, but these women all work out, they diet, they do liposuction."

"So you can only love your body if you've had liposuction?!" Georgia screamed.

I was seeing stars. I managed to mumble, "So I shouldn't go to the beach because of my cellulite?"

"Or wear a wrap if you do."

"So, you're telling me that my cellulite shouldn't be let out in public."

The young, thin, surely undimpled salesgirl shrugged. "This is just my opinion."

"Oh my God, I think I'm going to faint," I said, seriously.

Georgia was fit to be tied. "That's a horrible thing to say to someone. You should be ashamed of yourself for talking to her that way. You're a

BIKINI SALESWOMAN, for God's sake. Where's your boss? I want to talk to her."

"I am my boss," she said quietly. "I own this store."

Georgia clenched her fists while I watched the room spin in my own cellulite shame spiral.

"Well, fine. We're out of here. We're not going to buy anything in your store. We're not going to give you a dime." Georgia pushed me back in the dressing room.

"Come on, Julie, let's get dressed and go." I got my clothes on quickly and we walked to the door, Georgia still furious. Just as we got to the street, she turned around and went back inside.

"On second thought. No. You can't tell us who's allowed to wear a bikini on the beach and who's not. No one hired you to be Rio's Cellulite Police. Fuck that. I'm going to buy that bikini she was wearing. And she's going to wear it at the beach and she's going to be hot." I tried to protest, because Rio would have to freeze over before I put a bikini on my body. In fact, I wasn't sure if I would ever let anyone see me naked ever again.

Again, the saleswoman just shrugged. "That is fine with me." Georgia looked at me with a that'll-show-her look. "Don't worry, it's my treat." She then looked over at the salesgirl, who was wrapping up my bikini, and said a little more sheepishly, "And I'll take the orange one, too, while you're at it."

Four hundred and eighty-five dollars later—two hundred and forty-two dollars and fifty cents of which will never see the light of day, nor sand nor water—we walked out of the store.

Yep, we really showed her.

So there we were on the beach, right across the road from our hotel in Ipanema. Georgia was in her James Bond swimsuit, and I was in my men's surfing trunks, bikini top, ski pants, and parka. Just kidding. I was still recovering from this morning's shooting, I mean *shopping* spree. As we lay in silence, I could hear the sounds of three women laughing and talking in Portuguese. With my eyes closed, I could pick out the different voices. One was deep-throated and immediately drew me to it. Another was smooth, light, and feminine, and the third was more girlish. The deep-throated one was telling a story and the other women were laughing and chiming in. I opened my eyes, rolled to my side, and looked at them. The woman telling the story was tall and tan, young and lovely . . . Actually, she was tall and black, really black, her skin the color of onyx— she was gorgeous. Her two friends were equally beautiful. One had red curly hair that flowed way past her shoulders, and the other had short jet-black hair in a cute little bob. They looked to be in their late twenties and were all wearing tiny string bikinis. Georgia sat up and saw me watching them.

"I wonder if they like stealing husbands, too."

"Georgia . . ."

"I'm just curious. Why don't you ask them? For your research. Ask them if they like stealing women's husbands."

"Stop it."

The women saw us looking at them. The tall, deep-throated one looked at us a little suspiciously. I decided to be outgoing and introduce myself.

"Hi. We're from New York, and were just listening to you speak Portuguese. It's a beautiful language."

"Oh, New York, I love New York," said the woman with the short black hair.

"It's a wonderful city," I said.

"Yes, I go all the time for work, it's fantastic," said the deep-voiced one.

"Are you here on vacation?" asked the redhead.

"Sort of," I said.

But Georgia, being the good, pushy friend that she is, said, "Actually, my friend Julie is here trying to talk to single women. You all seem so sexy and free-spirited. We wanted to know your secret." She was smiling. I didn't think the ladies noticed any sarcasm in her voice, but I knew it was dripping all over.

They all smiled. The redhead said, "It's not us, it's Rio. It's a very sexy city."

They all agreed.

"Yeah, blame it on Rio," Georgia said. Then she added under her breath, "Or maybe you're just all whores."

"Georgia!" I whispered, glaring at her.

The deep-voiced one said, "We were just talking about that. Last night

I was out and this boy came up to me and said, 'Oh, you are so beautiful, I need to kiss you right now!' And then he did!"

"Now this is not the unusual part. This happens all the time in Rio," said the redhead.

"It does?" I asked.

"Yes. All the time," said the black-haired woman.

"Really?" Georgia said. Now she was interested.

"The funny thing is," continued the deep-voiced one, "that I decided to try it out on this boy Marco, who was so cute. I went up to him and told him that he was so sexy and I had to kiss him right now. He then grabbed me and kissed me for ten minutes!" The other girls started laughing.

"And then she had a *fica*," said the black-haired girl, giggling.

Then the deep-voiced girl said something in Portuguese, seeming to admonish her friend.

"Please, they're from New York."

"What's a fica?" I asked.

The deep-voiced woman sort of pursed her lips to the side and shrugged. "A one-night stand."

"Oh! Great," I said, not knowing what my response should be. But I was trying to bond. "Was it fun?"

"Yes, it was fun. He's from Buenos Aires. So hot."

"Buenos Aires, that's where all the good men are. We never date men from Rio," said Red.

"No, never," said Deep-voiced.

"Why not?" I asked.

"Because they can't commit."

"They are cheaters."

"Wait a minute!" The black-haired lady started laughing.

"Anna is engaged to a boy from Rio. So she doesn't like to hear these things!"

"Not all Rio men are cheaters!" said the black-haired woman, whose name was apparently Anna.

"Well, congratulations," I said. "I'm Julie, by the way, and this is my friend Georgia."

"Ah, like the state!"

"Yes," Georgia said, crisply. "Like the state."

"I'm Flavia," said the deep-throated one, "and this is Caroline," gesturing to the redhead, "and Anna."

Georgia went right in there. "Tell me, Anna. Are you afraid other women are going to try and steal your husband?"

"Georgia!" I shook my head. "Please excuse my friend; she has no manners."

"I'm from New York," she said. "We like to get to the point."

Flavia joked, "No. Women don't steal husbands. Husbands like to stay married forever, and cheat."

"Besides, it's not just the other women we have to worry about so much. It's the prostitutes," said Caroline.

"Prostitutes?"

"Yes, these men love the prostitutes. They all go together. For fun," Caroline said.

"It is a problem really," Anna said. "I worry."

"You worry that your husband is going to go to prostitutes?" Georgia asked.

"Yes. It's very common. Maybe not now, because we're in love. But later. I worry."

Flavia spoke up. "Who cares if he fucks a prostitute? I mean, really. If he sticks his dick in some other woman, who cares? Especially one that he's paid. He's a man, she's a hole. He fucks her. That's what men are like. You're not going to change them."

This is what I love about women. We have no problem just getting into it.

"I don't care. I don't like it," Anna said.

Caroline now joined in. "Anna, please. He's marrying you. He's going to have children with you. He's going to take care of you when you're sick, you're going to take care of him. So what if he goes to a prostitute?"

"If he cheats, I won't leave him, of course. I just don't like it."

Georgia and I looked at each other, surprised.

"If you found out he goes to a prostitute or sleeps with other women, you wouldn't leave him?" Georgia asked.

Anna shook her head. "I don't think so. He's my husband." She began to frown. "But I wouldn't like it."

Georgia and I gaped at each other.

Flavia smiled. "It's very American, this idea of fidelity. I think it's very naïve."

I've heard this before. And I thought about my participation in Thomas's infidelity. A wave of guilt shimmered through my body, and then I just felt sad. I missed him and even though I wished I didn't want him to call, I wished he would call.

Caroline agreed. "Men weren't meant to be faithful. But that's okay; it means we can go out and cheat, too."

Anna looked up at us, sadly. "I try to be realistic about things. I want to be married forever."

Georgia looked at the three of them. I couldn't tell if she was about to start a beach brawl or invite them out for a piña colada. She decided on a new line of questioning.

"So tell me. Are there male prostitutes for women?"

The three women all nodded their heads.

"Yes, definitely," Flavia said. "It's not as common but yes, they have them."

"There are agencies for them," said Caroline.

Georgia's eyes lit up. "Well, at least there's something for the women, too. At least there's an equality in that."

Flavia said, "You two should come out with us tonight. To Lapa. We're going out dancing."

"You'll get to meet Frederico, my fiancé," Anna said. "It will be fun."

"Samba dancing?" I asked, excited.

"Yes, of course, samba," Flavia said.

"Will there be kissing at this place?" Georgia asked.

"Oh, definitely," said Caroline.

"Then we're there!" said Georgia.

You know you're in Rio's Lapa district when you see the large concrete aqueduct towering above you. It was built in 1723 by slaves—a massive structure of archways that once brought water from the Rio Carioca. Now it's the giant doorway to the best party in town. Flavia and her two friends picked us up at our hotel in a minibus. Not very chic, but it seems the minibus is the preferred mode of transportation for rich American tourists when they come to Rio (usually accompanied by an armed body-guard or two). But Flavia borrowed the car from her company, a well-known photography studio. The driver, who we later found out was Anna's brother, Alan, was a tanned, good-natured guy with an easy smile, and not a word to say to anyone. And tonight, this minibus was ready to party. Caroline, Anna, and Flavia were already drinking when we got into the car. They opened the cooler and showed us a big pile of Red Bulls and a bottle of rum. They mixed us drinks and we were on our way.

Twenty minutes later we passed through the aqueduct archway that leads directly onto the main street of Lapa, where all the clubs, bars, and restaurants are. Samba music filled the air, and there were people every-where. It was a giant block party. We parked and walked up the cobble-stone streets. I bought a chocolate bar from a young child selling candy from a box he was carrying, with a strap around his neck. There were a few transvestite prostitutes standing on the corner. Many of the clubs had large windows that allowed you to look inside, often to the sight of bodies bouncing to the rhythmic music. It all felt surreal and a little dangerous. We went into Carioca de Gema, a smallish club packed with people of all ages.

There was a Brazilian woman singing, with two drummers behind her, but no one was dancing yet. We headed to the back room, where we found a table, and Flavia ordered us some food. I began to get the im-pression that she knew everyone in the place. And why shouldn't she? As she walked into the club and kissed everyone hello, Flavia was the star of the show—she was wearing tight denim jeans that perfectly conformed around her round Brazilian butt, and a tan halter top that had tiny beads running all down the sides. Flavia was beautiful, tough, fun-loving, and always ready with the good, hearty laugh. The more I saw her in action, the more I liked her.

When the food came, it was a large plate of dried meat, onions, and what appeared to be sand. Don't ask me how dried meat, onions, and sand could taste so good, but it did. Flavia ordered us caipirinhas, but with vodka in them, not cachaça, the official drink of Brazil. We were under strict orders from Anna's brother, Alan, to stay away from the stuff.

I saw Flavia at a distance, talking to some women who looked at me curiously. I had no idea what she was saying, but I didn't mind. I was too busy shoveling the delicious sand in my mouth and listening to the music and reminding myself that I was, in fact, in Rio, at a nightclub. How cool was that?

Georgia was swaying to the rhythmic beats of the drums. She leaned over and said, "I better get kissed tonight!" A couple in their sixties was standing in front of us, listening to the music. They started doing that crazy thing with their feet, the fast, beautiful, and mysterious step that is samba dancing. It was fantastic. We couldn't take our eyes off them. Flavia came over to us.

"Julie, I have some single women for you who'd like to talk to you about what it's like to be single in Rio."

"Really? Now?" I asked, surprised.

"Yes, I'll bring them over."

For the next hour, my new cultural attaché, Flavia, brought single woman after single woman over to me. I drank and ate sand and meat and listened to the music and heard their stories. I scribbled in my book as fast as I could.

Now, I know that I was just one woman talking to a tiny fraction of the population of women in Rio, but they all seemed to be in agreement about one thing: The men in Rio suck. They don't want to commit and they don't need to. There are beautiful women in bikinis (without any cellulite) everywhere they turn. Who needs to settle down? They are eternal bachelors. Or if they do settle down, they cheat. I'm not saying all men from Rio are like that; I'm just telling you what they told me.

So what is a single woman in Rio to do? They work out a lot. And they travel to São Paulo, where, everyone seemed to agree, the men are more sophisticated, more mature, less childish than the men of Rio.

But they all also agreed that the men of Rio are fantastic kissers and passionate, sexy, skillful lovers. They were all in such vocal agreement about this, that while I was too shy to ask them what made them so good at it, I couldn't help but get very curious. Particularly because all evening there was a tall, dark, and gorgeous man with large, muscular arms standing quietly in the corner staring at me. I was beginning to understand why fica was the first Portuguese word I had learned.

The women also spoke about "husbands," and men they were "married to," and it took me a while to realize that they might not actually be

legally married, but were using it as a term to mean a long, serious relationship. I asked Flavia about this later.

"Oh yes, we use it to mean any long relationship, when you live with
someone."

It's all pretty confusing. Living with someone can be referred to as
"married," but "married to someone" can also mean "I sleep with prostitutes."

Anna's Frederico arrived. Introductions were made and he sweetly
apologized to Anna for being late. He was tied up at his popular hang-
gliding business near Sugarloaf, a big rock in the middle of the city, well
traveled by the tourists.

"Excuse us, we must dance now," Frederico said as he took Anna's hand
and led her onto the dance floor. Anna, who had before this been somewhat quiet and soft-spoken, suddenly began to beam. She started moving
her feet and shaking her ass and she became instantly the most adorable
creature I have ever laid eyes on. And Frederico kept up—working his
crazy feet and twirling her around. How could any two people not have
great sex if they could dance like that together? This city was awesome.

"I'm going to walk around," Georgia said, and got up from our table. I
think all the sweat and sexy dancing was getting to her.

I looked up and saw that Flavia was talking to someone; he was
touching her on the arm and leaning in to talk to her. I turned to Caroline, who was sitting next to me.

"Hey, who's the cute guy that Flavia's talking to?"

"That's Marco, the fica from last night. He called today and she told
him to meet her here."

"Interesting. The fica calls . . . how often does that happen?"

"Not very often, I think. But sometimes."

"In the States, some people think that if you want them to call again,
you shouldn't have a fica first."

Caroline rolled her eyes. "This is your puritan ethics. In Rio, a fica,
not a fica, he might call you, he might not—it doesn't matter how you
meet."

Flavia and Marco came over to us, and she introduced us all. He had
long black hair and lots of stubble. He had a big dopey smile, and a lot of
energy.

"Ah, New York! I love New York! I love it!"

That's all he could say to me in English, and he said it to me all night long. To which I would reply "Rio! I love Rio!" It wasn't much, but it was still fun.

I spotted Georgia milling around the crowd. For a moment I didn't understand whom or what she was looking for. She was sort of shuffling around, fluffing her hair, looking a bit lost. I watched her for a little while longer, while she made a loop around the whole bar area, stopping by any cute guy or two. It was then that I realized what she was in search of—she was on a kiss hunt. I wasn't sure if kisses were something that you were supposed to look for, but I did admire her tenacity.

Anna came back to the table without Frederico and stood by the table, dancing in place.

"What the hell are your feet actually doing?" I asked, a little tipsy on my second caipirinha.

"Come, I'll show you." I stood up and she started slowly, moving her feet around, back and forth, heel to toe, toe to heel. I was copying her, getting the hang of it, until she started going a little faster and adding her wiggling ass to the mix. Then she lost me. But I just faked it, bouncing my feet and shaking my butt. I think I more resembled a fish flapping on a sidewalk than a samba dancer, but it got a smile out of the tall, dark drink of cachaça in the corner, so it was worth it. We all continued dancing by our table, the music throbbing, the singers singing in shouts over the drums, whipping the crowd into a sweating, bouncy-feet mass.

Georgia, meanwhile, bumped into Frederico, who was on his way to the men's room. He asked her what she was doing all the way over there, away from her friends.

"I heard people like to kiss a lot in Rio. I'm waiting for someone to try and kiss me."

Frederico smiled. He was extremely handsome: young, tan, with a little beard on his chin and wavy brown hair. With his brown eyes and nice white teeth, he looked like a Latin pop star.

"Well, I'm sure it won't be long. This is Rio after all." And with that he smiled and walked away.

Georgia had learned her lesson; she wasn't going to be the aggressor this time. She had learned from the sports bar that night that the fun wasn't grabbing someone and kissing them. The real rush was someone choosing to kiss *you*. So she kept walking around, wetting her lips and trying to look kissable.

I was still dancing, aware that my man in the corner kept looking over at me. While I continued my stomping, I saw Flavia and Marco walk over to talk to him. She put her arm on his shoulder—of course, Flavia, mayor of Rio, knew him. When Flavia and Marco came back over to us, I asked, "You know that guy?"

Flavia smiled. "Yes, he's an old friend of mine."

"What's he doing in the corner?" I asked.

"He works here, doing security."

I nodded and thought to myself, Hot.

"What—do you like him?" Flavia asked, smiling. We both turned and looked at him, which he immediately noticed. I quickly looked back at Flavia.

"Well . . . he's just . . . sexy, that's all," I said.

"Paulo. He's really sweet, too. He's like a brother to me," Flavia said.

I gave him another look. He saw me and smiled. I smiled back. As I turned around, I felt a sudden pang of something. Guilt. It was the strangest thing. I felt guilty for being attracted to Paulo because I had only recently slept with open-married Thomas. Just thinking about Paulo and smiling at him made me feel slutty. I had recently had sex with a man whom I was kind of crazy about. A man who, let's just be honest, also hadn't called me since, and whom I probably would never see again. But still, I had recently had sex with someone, and it was odd thinking about being attracted to someone else so soon after. I wouldn't have known this was a problem for me, since I don't have this kind of conundrum in New York.

Another reason to travel, is all I have to say about *that.*

Georgia walked back up to us, frustrated, just in time to see Frederico start making out with Anna. Georgia rolled her eyes, jealous and re-pulsed at the same time. She sat down next to Alan the Silent One.

"Tell me, Alan. Do you go to prostitutes?"

I laughed, surprised, and looked at Alan to see what his response would be. Alan simply smiled, leaned over to Georgia, and gave her a wink.

"Really. Well, I guess it's the quiet ones you always have to look out for," Georgia said, sipping her drink, unfazed. But she wasn't done. "But what if you ever caught Frederico cheating on your sister. Would you kill him?"

Alan looked at Georgia like she was from another planet. Or the United States. He laughed and shook his head. I was now completely engaged in this conversation.

"Really? Why not?" I asked.

Alan took a drink from his beer and said, "We men, we have to stick together."

Georgia raised her eyebrows. "Are you kidding me? Even if it's your sister?" Alan just shrugged and drank from his beer. Georgia looked at him and then at Caroline. "I don't understand. If brothers aren't even looking out for their sisters—then who is?"

Caroline also shrugged. "I guess no one."

Georgia and I stared at each other, depressed. I checked my cell phone and saw that it was 3 A.M. We all agreed it was time to go.

We were at the exit buying CDs of the music we had just heard when I saw Paulo make his way through the crowd. He seemed to be looking for someone. I walked out the door and onto the street. I looked back to see if I could get a last glimpse at him. Just then, he walked out of the club and landed his sights right on me. He walked up to me and put his hand out.

"Hello, my name is Paulo. You are very beautiful." My eyes widened and I started to laugh, looking around to see if Flavia had set this up.

"Well, thank you . . . my name is . . ." and before I had a chance to say another word, Paulo put his velvety lips on mine. Softly, gently, as if he had all the time in the world and had waited his whole life for this moment. When he let me go I blushed and kept my eyes to the ground, not wanting to look up and see who might have seen.

"Give me your cell phone, please," he demanded sweetly. As if in a trance, I took it out of my bag and handed it to him. I kept my eyes directly on his shoes, while he programmed his name and his number into my phone, gave it back to me, and walked away. When I got the nerve to look up, Flavia, Alan, Caroline, Frederico, Anna, and Georgia were all looking at me, laughing and clapping. Even Marco began to laugh.

I walked up, blushing.

"Well, at least one of us got kissed this evening," Georgia said, smiling. And at that, we went back under the aqueduct and to our hotel. The party, at least for tonight, was over.

When I woke up around noon, Georgia was sitting at the little table in our suite, flipping through something, drinking a cup of coffee.

"What are you doing?" I asked groggily, sitting up in bed.

"I'm looking through a portfolio of male prostitutes," Georgia said, calmly.

I rubbed my eyes with my fingertips. I thought I'd try again. "What did you say?" I asked.

"I'm looking through a portfolio of male prostitutes I got from an agency. I had to pay a hundred bucks just to look at it."

"What? What are you talking about?"

Georgia kept flipping pages. "I asked Flavia about it last night, and she gave me the name of an agency. I called them this morning and they sent it over."

"Georgia, you're not really going to have sex with a prostitute."

She looked up. "Why not? Wouldn't it be great to have sex with someone and have absolutely no expectations. You couldn't feel bad about them not calling, because they're a *prostitute*."

"But don't you think it's kind of . . ."

"What, gross?"

"Yeah. Kind of."

"Well, maybe that's something we have to get over. I think it's a great idea, paying for sex. I know a lot of women who really need to have sex. I think it would be good if we could get past the whole gross thing."

"And the whole AIDS thing, and the whole 'aren't they all gay' thing?"

Georgia put her coffee down. "Listen. I don't want to be one of those single women who hasn't had sex in three years. I want the charge of someone on top of me. Kissing me. Holding me. But I don't want to have sex with assholes who pretend they like me when they really don't. I think hiring a prostitute is the way to go."

"But you're paying them. Doesn't that take the fun out of it?"

Georgia shrugged her shoulders. "Maybe." She was still formulating her theory. "That's what I want to find out. Because I think that's how to be single. To try and stay sexually active, at any cost."

"*Literally* at any cost," I couldn't resist adding, still appalled. "It's different for women. The men are going to be penetrating us. It's weird."

"Julie, come look at these guys. They're not gross. They're hot."

I sighed and swung my feet out of the bed, traipsing over to the kitchen table in my flannel boxer shorts and t-shirt. Georgia passed the book to me.

"Well, I thought I'd have bagels for breakfast, but I guess it's going to be stud muffins instead," I quipped.

Georgia wasn't amused. I looked at the photos. There were shots of men in suits, and then the same men with their shirts off. As I flipped through the pages, I had to admit that while they were cheesy, in a hunky, coiffed, and slightly gay kind of way, they weren't terribly gross.

And I could imagine the innocent side to all this. Maybe they were just men who happened to possess an innate talent for pleasuring women, a talent that they'd decided to use for financial gain. Maybe they thought of themselves as sex social workers or *extremely* personal trainers. Perhaps because it was men, we didn't have to see this paid exchange as a kind of victimization. These men on page after page in suits and ties and bathing suits looked like the pleasant male strippers we saw in Paris. Overly built, a little corny, and willing to please. Of course, looking at them in another way, they also looked like they could be your average neighborhood serial killer.

"I guess they don't look so bad," I said.

"I told you. I'm going to do it. If no one kisses me tonight, I'm making the call first thing in the morning. I want to have some kind of physical contact with a man before I leave tomorrow night."

I kept my mouth shut, thinking about how I would have to get someone to kiss her tonight or else. Georgia added, "Flavia invited us to a big party tonight, at some samba school. I told her we'd love to go. She's picking us up at eight."

"Does that mean someone's going to teach us how to samba?" I asked hopefully.

"Well, if they don't, you can always ask my husband's girlfriend,

Melea, when you get home. I bet she has quite a following," Georgia said as she sipped her coffee. "I wonder if it's going to be a whole room full of husband-stealing samba teachers. Wouldn't that be fun?"

She raised her right hand and pushed her hair behind her ear. I had never woken up with Georgia before, and without makeup and with the sun hitting her face, she looked young and so beautiful. At that moment, her future seemed to hold so much possibility for happiness and light. I wished she could have felt it. But I knew, as she thought about Dale and Melea, that I was the only one in the room who could see what was possible for my divorcing, grieving, funny, slightly crazy friend.

Back in the States

Wearing Jim's pajama bottoms and a tank top, Alice stood in Jim's kitchen and poured herself a glass of water, pondering this whole phenomenon of regular sex. As she drank the water, she admitted to herself that there was now a fly in the ointment.

Having sex with someone all the time only works if you are truly excited about them. Then it's just the world's best thing. But if you happen not to be in love with that someone, it might become a problem. The last couple of times Alice and Jim had sex, she realized she was bored. He didn't do anything wrong, he was perfectly good at it all. But she was simply not passionate about him. As she stood at the counter, she thought about how dreary it would be to have passionless sex for the rest of her life.

Alice wanted desperately for it to work out. And Alice is a problem solver; there's not a difficult situation in the world she can't make right. If she knew more about geophysics, she'd beat this whole global warming thing in a heartbeat. As Alice put the glass in the sink, she was convinced that the problem of having passionate sex with Jim just simply couldn't be that hard to solve.

Alice walked down the hallway and into Jim's bedroom. Jim was in bed, reading. He looked up and smiled.

"Hey, baby," he said.

"Hey," Alice said. Even in Jim's pajama bottoms and a tank top, she looked hot and Jim couldn't help but notice. Alice looked at him for a long moment, wondering what passion actually was; what are its ingredients, what are its component parts? When describing someone, people always say, "They're a very passionate person." But what does that mean? Alice walked over to her side of the bed and sat on it, her back to Jim as she thought. *It means they are excitable*, she thought. *They are enthusiastic. They get worked up over things they believe in strongly.* Jim put his hand on her back and stroked it. Alice was excited about being in a relationship, excited about not dating, about feeling secure. She was excited about what a nice man Jim was and how much he seemed to love her. Alice closed her eyes and tried to direct all that excitement to her groin area. After all, emotion is just energy. So she could take that energy and make it sexual. She felt Jim's hand on her back and let her thoughts flow. It's nice to be touched. It's nice to have sex. She turned around to Jim and put her hands on each side of his face and kissed him deeply. She climbed on top of him and pressed her body forcefully against his. He put his hands under her shirt to touch her breasts. She sighed with pleasure.

Alice smiled to herself. She didn't need to be passionate about Jim to have passionate sex. *Because she's a passionate person.* She believes passionately in rights for the underprivileged. She is passionate about being against the death penalty. She is passionate about world peace. She kept kissing Jim deeply as she hugged him tightly. She tilted her body just enough to roll Jim on top of her. She pulled off his t-shirt. She tugged off his boxer shorts. Jim took off her pajama bottoms and put his hand in between her legs. Alice gasped with excitement. She thought about how she was going to have someone do that for the rest of her life. She gasped again, louder. Jim could not have been more excited—he had never seen Alice like this. He was hard, breathing heavily as he entered her. Alice wrapped her legs around his back and tugged at his hair as they kissed—passionately, tongues and teeth and lips, and shallow breaths. Alice was moaning loudly. She loved penises, she loved penises inside her and she was going to love Jim, who grabbed her and lifted her up to him. She was straddling him now, as they sat up and were rocking back and forth. He was kissing her neck and as Alice was moving up and down, a thought flashed across her mind: *how will I ever keep this up?* They kept moving and Alice was groaning, concentrating on coming when another thought flashed across her mind: *this is taking a lot of energy.* Jim kept thrusting and kissing while Alice had the best idea she'd ever had in her entire life. An idea that made her understand how it was all possible, how she could keep this up forever and ever and how it wouldn't have to take so much energy: she could just think about Brad Pitt. It was an obvious choice but she didn't care. She went through his entire oeuvre. She thought about Brad Pitt's slim torso in *Thelma and Louise,* his muscular torso in *Fight Club,* and his really muscular torso in *Troy.* She thought about how he threw Angelina Jolie against a wall in *Mr. and Mrs. Smith.* As she got close to coming, Alice realized she could think about Brad Pitt for the rest of her life. It was a free goddamn country and no one would ever need to know. She could think about Brad Pitt and Johnny Depp and even Tom Cruise—who she knew was weird, but she loved buff torsos, no matter what the torso happened to believe in. When her inner passion wasn't enough, they would always be waiting in the wings. And as she imagined Brad Pitt in gold metal armor jumping through the air in slow motion, she came.

"Oh my God!" Alice screamed. Jim only had two more thrusts in him until he came as well—he had been having a hard time containing himself up to that point, what with all the excitement going on.

"Oh my God," Alice said, catching her breath as a new thought flashed across her mind: *I can do this! I am really going to be able to do this.*

· · ·

Now, as any dieter knows, the minute you tell yourself that you're not allowed something, that is precisely when you can't stop thinking about it. Serena hadn't had sex in four years and her sex drive, due to lack of attention, had driven far, far away. So the minute she was told she would never be allowed to have sex again, well, that was just the thing to kick-start her lifeless libido.

Serena was now stationed at a yoga center in the East Village. This particular yoga organization had branches all over the world and Serena managed to get stationed in a beautiful brownstone less than two miles from where she used to live. Walking around the East Village with her shaved head and her orange outfits, she was aflame with the most dirty thoughts imaginable. Each morning, as she sat cross-legged on the floor of the meditation room, the scent of incense wafting through the air, her mind raced with thoughts of naked flesh and men on top of her. She had a recurring dream in which she was walking down a New York City street and just kept grabbing men and making out with them as they walked by. She would wake up sweaty and shocked. Serena had just assumed that for her, taking a vow of celibacy was merely a formality. This deluge of pornographic thoughts took her completely off guard.

That is why it was so easy for everything to happen the way it did. One of the jobs given to Serena, now known as Swami Durgananda, was to wake up a little earlier than everyone else and prepare the altar plate. This meant getting up at 5:45, cutting up some fruit or arranging some dates and figs on a platter, and then putting it on the altar as an offering to the Hindu gods before group meditation began at 6:00. And every morning, Swami Swaroopananda, otherwise known as the "hot swami," would be at the kitchen table, reading a book and looking hot. At 5:45 in the morning. Serena wasn't yet sure what the rules of engagement were for swamis at the center, but as she opened the refrigerator to decide what to offer up to the gods, she decided to say something.

"Is this when you normally like to read? Early in the morning?" Serena whispered softly.

He looked up at Serena and smiled. "Yes, it seems like the only time I have to read is at this hour."

"Wow. You actually wake up early to read. That's impressive." She took out a pineapple and put in on the counter. She got out a long knife and started skinning it. He went back to his book. As she chopped up the pineapple she would steal glances at him. For a man of Vishnu he was really built. Was that really just from doing yoga? Were swamis allowed to go to the gym? She didn't think so. His face was hard to describe, but it was the face of a real man. His head wasn't completely shaved—it was more of a very close buzz cut, and it was a look he was made for. He looked like he could maybe have been an army sergeant—tall, with a muscular chest and long, ripped arms. And his orange swami robes, instead of making it all seem silly, made him seem, well, super orange hot.

They would talk only briefly, but Serena didn't need much to fan her flames of desire. Each morning she got up a little earlier just to talk to him. And every morning, he'd be sitting on a stool at the counter, quietly reading, little circular glasses on the tip of his nose.

Tuesday at 5:30 A.M.:

"Good morning, Swami Swaroopananda."

"Good morning, Swami Durgananda."

"How's your book? Are you enjoying it?"

"Yes, it's one of the better ones I've read about Pranayama." He put his book down this time. "By the way, how are you adjusting to your new life?"

Serena made her way to the refrigerator. "It's been surprising, some of the things that come up, you know, when you're trying to calm the mind."

Swami Swaroopananda crossed his arms over his chest and looked at Serena. "Really? Like what?"

Serena felt her face get red and she wondered if, without hair, her entire head would blush as well.

"Oh, just the flotsam and jetsam of a cluttered mind, you know. So, how long have you been a part of this organization?"

And then they began to really talk. He told her that he was from New Zealand (*that's the accent*) and he'd been a swami for eight years. He told her about how his meditation practices had gotten so intense, the experiences he was having were so blissful, that he felt compelled to take the next step and become a renunciate. Serena wanted to know more. While they talked, Serena assembled quite an abundant offering plate.

Wednesday at 5:15 A.M.:

"Good morning, Swami Swaroopananda."

"Good morning, Swami Durgananda. How are you this morning?"

"Very well, swami." Serena started getting out flour and honey and walnuts. She was going to make her famous banana nut bread for the offering this morning. After all, she had to do something with all her time while pretending she wasn't flirting with a man of the cloth, forgetting entirely that she was now a woman of the cloth herself. Besides, she reasoned to herself, what better way to start the day than with the nice aroma of banana bread floating around them while they meditated? And besides, they could have the rest of it for breakfast. She began mashing the bananas in a bowl.

"How is your meditation practice going? You mentioned a lot of thoughts coming up, yesterday. Do you have any questions about the practice itself?"

The only question Serena had now was how she could have sex and still be celibate, but she knew that wasn't something she should say. So she made something up.

"Well, yes, I do, swami. When I meditate, I feel my thoughts slow down; I feel calmer, more at peace, more in touch with a higher power, so that's good. But I don't have any visions. No white lights, no colors swirling in my mind. I'm just meditating, you know?" Serena was now pouring flour and sugar in another bowl. She cracked an egg and started mixing it up by hand.

Swami Swaroopananda closed his book. "That's perfectly normal. There shouldn't be a goal to your meditation; that's the antithesis of the practice. The point is merely to be still. Everyone's experience is going to be different. The last thing you should be hoping for is fireworks when you're meditating."

Serena smiled. She poured the mashed bananas into the batter and stirred them together.

"Now, speaking of fireworks, Swami Durgananda, tell me. Have you been thinking a lot about sex lately?"

Serena looked up from her stirring. She wasn't sure if she had heard right. By his expression, which was serious and unembarrassed, it seemed like this was a normal spiritual question. She turned to the cabinets. While her back was to him, she admitted, "Well, actually, yes. I have been thinking a lot about it. Like not being able to think of anything else, really." She pulled out three loaf pans from a top shelf and brought them to the counter. She tried not to look at Swami Swaroopananda, but couldn't resist. She peeked up and he was smiling at her.

"You shouldn't be ashamed, that's part of the process. Your mind is just reacting to your body's desires. It will quiet down soon enough."

"I hope so. It's just like when I'm fasting. I can't stop reading cookbooks the whole time." She poured the batter into the loaf pans and pushed them one by one into the oven. Serena looked at the clock. It was only 5:30. She had no idea she could make banana bread that fast. There were still thirty minutes before meditation.

"I guess I'll go in and start, you know. Meditating."

Swami Swaroopananda closed his book. "Don't rush off. Why don't you sit for a moment. Let's talk some more. Where are you from?"

Serena smiled and shyly sat on the stool next to Swami Swaroopananda, also known as Swami Swaroop. He looked at Serena closely, and for the next thirty minutes he asked her questions about her family, the jobs she'd had, and what her favorite music used to be. In the basement of this yoga center, the smell of banana bread in the oven, as she sat next to a man wearing a bright orange dress, both of them basically bald, Serena realized she hadn't been on this great a date in years.

By the following Monday, Serena was baking fresh, yeasted, wake-up-early-so-you-can-make-the-dough-let-it-rise-and-punch-it-down-and-then-do-it-all-over-again bread. And he would always be there, sometimes reading, sometimes watching, but always talking to her. By the end of the week, they were mixing and kneading together.

For that past week and a half, Serena couldn't think about anything else but him. The beatific, blissed-out expression on her face, which might have been construed as spiritual awakening, was really just dumb puppy love. All day long, all night long, she thought about seeing him the next morning. And then in the morning, when she was with him, it wasn't so much that she was talking and listening to him as she was *absorbing* him. During meditation and yoga and chanting and working, she was supposed to be trying to become one with God. But instead, each morning as she made the most elaborate altar offering plates in the history of the Jayananda Yoga Center, Serena was becoming at one with Swami Swaroop. The way he said things, the opinions he had, seemed so in tune with how she thought and felt that when the words came out of his mouth and hit her ears it was like they mutated into a warm ooze that spread throughout her brain.

It was joy. For every minute that she was with him, she felt the undeniable sensation of joy. The thought of adding sex to this intense emotion had almost become too much for her to fathom. *Almost* too much for her to fathom. And in the meantime, the entire yoga center was gaining weight, gorging at breakfast on hot bread, walnut loafs, and muffins.

On Thursday, at 4:30 in the morning, as she walked into the kitchen, Serena looked for him, her heart beating fast, worried that for some reason he wouldn't be there. But he was standing by the counter. He smiled shyly at her. Long gone were the formal greetings of "Good morning, Swami Swaroop" and "Good morning, Swami Durga." They had now been replaced by two people who met each other in the morning by beaming wordlessly at each other.

All the kneading and rising and mixing had to lead to something. And on this morning, Swami Swaroop walked up to Serena, took her by the shoulders, looked to make sure no one else was around, and kissed her on the lips. Serena wrapped her arms around his neck and kissed him back, deeply. Now, her eyes closed and her body finally touching his, Serena finally saw the white light, the one everyone talks about, of unity, peace, and divine happiness. Finally.

So Serena still got up at 4:30 in the morning, but the altar plate went back to being a few dried-up grapes and a couple of figs. They had finally figured out what else they could be doing during that time, and they were doing it everywhere they could get away with it: the pantry closet, the furnace room, the basement. If Serena was the kind of girl who could get out of control over a couple of buffalo wings, you can imagine what she was like now that she was having sex with someone she was madly in love with. Eventually, they couldn't wait until the morning, and were recklessly finding places to meet during the day as well. When Swami Swaroop took the center's van to Hunts Point to do grocery shopping, of course he needed help and why not ask Swami Durgananda? So there, too, in the back of the van on the side of a road in some industrial wasteland in the South Bronx they unleashed their forbidden swami love. It may have taken a vow of celibacy to do it, but Serena finally had a sex life. Her dry spell was officially over.

Back in Rio

When they talked about this samba school party, I had an image of a dance school with mirrored walls and ballet barres, and maybe some streamers draped around and some punch in a punch bowl, with instructors available to teach the newcomers samba. But no. Flavia, Alan, Caroline, Anna and Frederico, Georgia, and I drove in the minivan to one of the poorest neighborhoods, called Estácio, far from the fancy tourist areas of Ipanema and Leblon. We parked by a massive concrete structure that looked like it used to be an airport hangar, except that it was painted blue and white and covered in beautiful graffiti artwork of stars and beams of light. In big white graffiti letters was the name of the samba school, G.R.E.S. Estácio de Sá. People were pouring into the place, and we joined the flood into what can only be described as a huge high school dance and block party combined. The place was the size of a football field. Everyone was walking around with plastic cups of beer, and the floor was already littered with empty cups and cans. The excitement of knowing I was about to witness something that most tourists would never get to see already had my heart racing.

But that was nothing compared to what the drums would do to me. From the moment we entered, the loudest, most vibrant drums I'd ever heard shook the building, cutting right through my heart. From a raised set of bleachers about forty drummers were whipping the crowd into a frenzy.

We made our way up some stairs to a little VIP balcony that looked out over the entire scene. At the far end of the hangar were two singers on a raised stage, shouting out joyfully. This was not the crowd of young people at Lapa, dressed up for a night on the town. These were men in jeans and t-shirts, shorts and sneakers. There were women wearing some of the tightest jeans I have ever seen stretched over a human form, and some skirts that were so short I wanted to throw a jacket over them and send them to their rooms without supper. It's true what they say, the Brazilian women do have the most beautiful butts, and tonight they were all on display. Most people were sambaing, talking, drinking beer. And there were others dressed in red and white outfits just milling about. I wasn't quite sure what this place was, and what we were doing there, but I knew I would never have gotten to see it if it weren't for our new best friend, Flavia.

"I don't understand: why do you call it a samba school?" I asked loudly, over the drums.

"Each neighborhood has a school where they drum and do samba. Each school picks a song that they're going to do at Carnival, and then they compete with all the others."

"So they're kind of like neighborhood teams?"

"Yes, exactly. This one is my samba school. And in a few minutes they are going to present for the first time the song they'll be competing with at Carnival." Flavia looked down to where the masses of people were and suddenly smiled. "There's Marco!"

Marco looked up and saw Flavia and waved. Flavia turned to me, a tough smirk on her face. "I don't mind that he's here," she said, trying not to seem at all happy. She motioned for him to come up the stairs. "I better go and make sure the bouncers let him up."

I looked over at the drummers and tried to find Anna. This was her samba school, too, and she was going to be drumming with them to-night.

The song they were playing stopped, and the drums began again, slow at first, it seemed, to get everyone's attention. People started to move toward the center of the room, the whole space newly energized. Frederico turned to us and said, "Come, let's go on the dance floor." Georgia, Frederico, Alan, and I made our way down the stairs. The drums were now at full speed and the whole space was pulsating, jumping, in united celebration.

We all began dancing. Well, Frederico and Alan began dancing. Georgia and I sort of wiggled around a bit, trying to shake our asses as best as possible, but the samba is really not a dance you can fake. Then the dancers paraded out. There were dozens of them, and the crowd parted, making a wide lane for them to dance through. They were all wearing their "team" costume: red and white sequins. The women came out first, in tiny red skirts and high, high heels, dancing so fast, their lower bodies moving so rapidly, it seemed that they were vibrating in some kind of sexual ecstasy. Their arms were flying around, their legs were whirling, and their asses were shaking so fast they could have whipped butter.

Following the young gorgeous women, in their tiny skirts and their bikini tops, were the little old ladies. They were also dressed in red and white, but their outfits were knee-length skirts, short-sleeved tops, and hats. They came out in a single line and formed a frame around the young women, or more accurately, a defensive perimeter against any wolves who might come in and devour these beauties whole.

They danced like women who had seen it all. They no longer needed to shake their asses and wave their arms around, though I'm sure they had done their share of that. Now, they more paraded about. I don't know what the rest of their lives were like, and I'd hate to imagine how difficult they were, but I knew that at this moment, they were in the midst of celebration. They were red and white peacocks strutting and prancing for everyone to see, proud of themselves and their neighborhood and their song.

Georgia, Frederico, and Alan had meanwhile gone to get beers. As they were waiting in line, far away from the dance floor, Frederico leaned over to Georgia and said, "You don't need to look for someone to kiss you, beautiful Georgia. I would be happy to make love to you any time you ask."

And at that, engaged Frederico kissed single, horny Georgia, as Anna's dear brother Alan laughed and drank his beer. Frederico was sexy, young, Brazilian, and gorgeous. Georgia's revenge fantasy had been to come to Brazil and steal someone away from his wife. Now Georgia had her chance; Frederico was the male Melea and he wanted her. Georgia, new to dating, still instinctively understood one of the cardinal rules of being single: *We ladies have to have each other's backs.*

So Georgia gently pushed Frederico away and said they should get back to the party. It was then that Georgia answered the question of who was looking out for the women in Rio—and sadly, the answer was her. Then she turned back to Alan and put her finger right in his face. "And you. Shame on you. You're her brother."

We all met up when we rejoined Flavia and Marco on the balcony. The queen and king of the samba school were now dancing down the center of the madness, the man in a crisp white suit and a white hat, the woman in a red gown and a crown. People were swirling flags around them as they danced separately, and then together, hand in hand.

Just then something flew into the air from down below. I didn't see what it was, but Flavia grasped her face and stumbled a few steps backward. Caroline was right there, holding Flavia's arm and asking what happened. On the floor near Flavia was a full can of beer. Someone had thrown it up toward us either in wild abandon or with a more malevolent intent. Either way, Flavia was the one who ended up getting hit in the face. Caroline sat her on a chair, and I watched as tough, deep-throated Flavia scrunched her lips up in a smirk and tried not to cry.

Everyone was trying to figure out what the hell happened, as Flavia's eye started to swell up. Caroline had gone to get her some ice, and Georgia was rubbing her back. Anna was now there, and when she saw what had happened she got down on her knees and started to stroke Flavia's hair. But Flavia just leaned over and picked up the offending can of beer and put it to her eye, to stop the swelling. Marco stood there a little helplessly. This woman, whom he barely knew, was hurt but he wasn't quite sure what to do or what his role should be. So he just sort of paced around, running his fingers through his hair. After the shock wore off, Flavia told everyone that she was fine. Anna suggested it was time to leave, and we piled into the minibus—Georgia, Flavia, Marco, Alan, Anna, Frederico, and myself.

So, considering it was Rio and it was three in the morning, the only reasonable thing to do was go to Pizzaria Guanabara, a local restaurant. As we walked in, I saw grown-up men and women, completely sober and well dressed, all gathered civilly eating pizza as if it were eight at night, some with their children.

We all sat down and talked and tried to make Flavia laugh, while she iced her puffy eye. She was a good sport in the truest sense of the word, not a trace of self-pity. Looking at her, I felt I had learned something else about how to be single: *There are some nights you might have to take a can of beer to the face. That's just the way it is, and it's best not to be a wimp about it.*

Flavia started to fold herself gradually into Marco, leaning into him as he put his arm around her. He had found his place, encouraging her body to nuzzle against his and draping his arm around her, letting her feel protected. She may be the toughest, coolest girl in Rio, but she had been wounded, ambushed. No matter how many girlfriends were around to help at that moment, nothing would beat the feeling of a strong chest against her cheek and muscular arms enveloping her.

Later, when we dropped them off at Flavia's house, Marco helped her out of the van, and put his arm around her sweetly. One more thing about being single: *On the unfortunate night when you're the one who gets the can to the face, you never know who might be there, ready and willing to comfort you.*

When Alan finally dropped us off at the hotel, the only ones left were

Georgia and me. Georgia looked at Alan and said, one last time, "Shame on you."

● ● ●

"You're having sex with a fellow swami?" Ruby asked, confused. She and Alice had been summoned by Serena to a diner on Twenty-fourth and Eighth, and frankly, they all felt a little embarrassed. Not because of Serena's admission of swami sex, but because Serena looked like one of those Hare Krishna people that you never even see anymore at the airports—and everyone was staring at them.

Ruby added, "Didn't you just take a vow of celibacy?"

"And didn't you have sex before taking your vow, like—never?" Alice asked, not very tactfully.

"I hadn't had sex for four years."

Ruby looked at Serena with great sympathy. Alice kept interrogating the witness.

"So, you have no sex, take a vow of celibacy, and now you're having sex?"

"It's not like that," Serena said, defensively. "I fell in love. I could have fallen in love with someone I met at a coffee shop, or at a class at school—I just happened to fall in love with someone I met being a swami. This is big, it's a once-in-a-lifetime thing."

The ladies didn't know what to say to this. They were still trying to ignore the fact that everyone was staring at Serena.

"Well," Ruby said, "I guess priests and nuns fall in love all the time."

Alice took a sip of her Diet Coke. "And it's not like any of this is real, right? It's kind of a make-believe religion, isn't it? No one is going to tell you that you've sinned and you're going to hell or anything?"

"Hindus don't believe in hell. Just karma."

Alice picked at Ruby's french fries. "So if you break your vows, do you believe that in the next life you would come back as an ant or something?"

"More like a hooker, probably," Serena said, guiltily.

Alice laughed. "It's true, you'd probably come back as a dirty street whore."

Serena wasn't amused. "I called you guys because Julie is gone and I

have no one else I can talk to. I made this really big commitment and I think I made the wrong choice."

The ladies sobered up.

Alice asked, "Have you asked him how he feels?"

Serena put her head in her hands. "He feels guilty. He feels terrible."

Ruby jumped in. "Does he want to leave the church? I mean, temple, or whatever you call it?"

"He's not sure. He said this has never happened to him before."

Alice grabbed two french fries and stuffed them in her mouth. "If it really is love, you two should forget everything and go for it. It's love, for God's sake. That's a miracle. Nothing else matters."

"But it doesn't really mean anything. There are lots of people who fall in love and can't make it work. In the Hindu religion they talk a lot about how this whole world, this existence is an illusion. I'd probably fall in love with *anyone* who was the first person I slept with in four years. He's been a swami for eight years. How can I talk to him about this when there's no guarantee it will work out? Falling in love doesn't mean anything."

Alice hoped Serena had a point. She hoped being in love didn't mean anything. She hoped respect and kindness and a little Brad Pitt would win the day for her and Jim. Maybe being in love is just infatuation and passion and no one should make a big life decision based on that.

Ruby thought about all the men she thought she was in love with, with whom she had fantastic sex, and with whom it didn't work out. They all meant nothing to her now. Serena was right. It is an illusion. Before the words got out of Ruby's mouth, Alice had said them.

"Maybe you shouldn't do anything drastic right now. It's still so new, you have no idea what's really going on with you two. You don't want to get ahead of yourself."

Serena nodded her head, relieved. "You're right. You're right. That's a good plan. I should just wait."

They sat in silence, somewhat satisfied that at least this problem could be solved. Ruby took a sip of her coffee and glanced out the window. She saw two thirteen-year-old boys dressed in hip-hop clothes, pointing at Serena and laughing. Ruby looked away quickly, pretending she didn't see a thing.

Back in Rio

The next morning, I woke up to see Georgia lying on her bed, staring at me.

"I'm going to hire a prostitute today."

"And good morning to you."

"Why not? I don't have to be at the airport until eight. I have lots of time."

And with that, she opened the Prostitute Book to a page she had earmarked and picked up the phone. She dialed without hesitation. In a very businesslike voice, she asked if she could see Mauro at one o'clock that day. She gave the address of the hotel and our room number, agreed to the price of five hundred dollars, and hung up the phone. We sat in silence for a moment.

Then she burst out laughing. "I can't really go through with this, can I? I'm a mother, for Pete's sake."

I breathed a sigh of relief. "No, you can't. I'm glad you've finally come to your senses. Call them back."

And then Georgia gave it a second thought. "No, actually, I think I will do it. I want to know if I could enjoy having sex I've paid for. And besides, we *are* in Rio after all . . ."

I couldn't believe it. Georgia was actually planning on having sex with someone she hired. I was mortified, nervous, irritated, and—I'll admit it—slightly impressed.

At noon, Georgia and I started getting ready for her "date" with Mauro. We had agreed that I would be there when he arrived so we could both check him out before she was left alone with him. I was partially hoping that she would chicken out at some point before he showed up. This did seem a bit insane. But until then, we carefully decided what she should wear. After looking through her suitcase full of sundresses, shorts, high heels, and evening wear, a decision was made: jeans and a t-shirt. For some reason, we didn't want her to seem too eager. I wanted her to wear something that, if for some reason the mission was aborted, she wouldn't feel silly in. I mean, what's worse than sitting alone in your hotel room in some skimpy negligee after you've just sent a male prostitute home without sex? Jeans and a t-shirt felt right to us both. Because after all, isn't that what the five hundred dollars is for? So she could have sex and not have to worry about how she looked?

At one o'clock on the dot, the concierge announced that a Mr. Torres was there to see Georgia. "Thank you. Could you please tell him to come up in five minutes?" Georgia said in a monotone and then hung up the phone. And then we both screamed and started running around the room.

"What do we do? What do we say when he comes in?" I shrieked as I jumped onto the sofa.

"First we have to let him know that you're not staying, that we're not trying to get a two-for-the-price-of-one-type situation."

"How do you say that without it sounding . . . I don't know!"

"This is crazy! Am I crazy? I'm crazy!!" Georgia said, now pacing, trying to compose herself.

"Wine! You need to be drinking! How did we not think of that before?" I was now getting into it—the train was chugging down the track and I was curious to see where it was going to take us.

Georgia raced to the minibar. She uncorked a mini bottle of wine and chugged. She passed it to me. Somehow I needed to get loaded, too.

"What are we going to talk about?" Georgia asked, nervously. "Normally on a first date you ask questions like 'So what do you do for a living?' 'Do you like your job?' 'Where do you live?' But what am I going to say to him?"

I took another swig of the chardonnay. "I don't know. Just talk about Rio, ask him questions about Brazil. Ask him what that stuff is called that we like so much. The stuff that looks like sand."

"Rio and food. Okay."

I finished off the little bottle of wine and then opened another one.

"I'll pour two glasses, one for you and one for him."

"Okay, okay, right, that's a good icebreaker." Georgia got out two glasses. Then she stopped.

"Wait, what if he doesn't drink?"

"A sober prostitute? Do you think?" I said as I poured the wine, my hands shaking.

"You're right, you're right." Georgia put the full glasses on the counter.

"Now we have to have a plan. We need a code word for if one of us gets a bad vibe from him."

"Got it, right," I said, now just pacing. "How about, um, samba dancing. I'll say that we went samba dancing and it was fun."

"No, that's too positive. I'll get confused and think you like him."

"Okay, how about, 'We went samba dancing and it was too hard for us to do.'"

"That's good, samba dancing, bad, means he's bad, got it. Now what if I get a good vibe from him and I want you to leave?" Georgia was now looking at the mirror, fluffing her hair. She turned around and ran into the bathroom. She took out a bottle of Listerine and started to gargle.

"Just be honest. Say, 'Well, Julie, I guess you should be going to that appointment of yours.'"

"Okay, good." Georgia, now back in the room, took a big gulp from her glass of wine. She made a face. "Eew, Listerine and chardonnay, ecch!" She ran and spit it out in the bathroom and rinsed her mouth again.

Then I asked, "But what if you tell me to leave, but I have a bad feeling about him?"

"Then, after I tell you to leave, say, 'Okay, but hey, can I talk to you for a minute about something?' and then we'll go into the hallway and talk." Georgia came back into the room and took another gulp of wine. She made no face this time, and kept gulping.

"Okay, that sounds good." I stopped pacing. "All right. I think we're ready." And as if on cue, there was a knock on the door. Georgia and I froze. Then we ran to each other and excitedly grabbed each other's hands.

"I'll open it," I said, in a burst of courage. I walked over and put my hand on the doorknob. Before I turned it, I looked back at Georgia. We both screamed silently at each other. I turned and opened the door.

Right out of a board game from the seventies, there he was, our Mystery Date. Mauro. I don't know what it is about these Brazilians, but he had a dazzling smile that immediately put you at ease. He could have been a soap star with his small pointed nose and short-cropped hair with a little product in it. He was young, around twenty-seven. Coincidentally, he was wearing jeans and a t-shirt. My first thought was, *Not gay and not a serial killer.* My second thought was to ask, *What's a nice guy like you* . . . But instead I said, "You must be Mauro. Please come in."

He smiled and entered the room. Georgia had a smile plastered on her face so wide I thought her skin might crack. In order to avoid any confusion, I said, "I'm leaving soon. I just wanted to say hi and make sure everything's . . . okay."

Mauro nodded. "Yes, that's fine. Of course."

Georgia walked over holding out a glass of wine. I could see her hands were trembling.

"Would you like a glass of wine?" Her voice seemed much calmer than her hands.

"Yes, that would be nice." He took the glass and said, "Please, sit down, let's relax." We both immediately sat down like obedient puppies. Georgia and I were on the couch, and Mauro sat in an armchair to the right of Georgia. I realized that in the midst of all our nervousness, we had forgotten one important thing: it may have been our first time doing anything like this, but it definitely wasn't his.

"So, how are you enjoying Rio?" he asked, cheerfully. As Georgia talked about the beach and Lapa and whatever else she was saying, I tried to just soak Mauro in. He didn't seem like he hated his job. He didn't seem like he was on drugs or had some big guy wearing furs and a fedora waiting for him downstairs to beat him up and take his money. He seemed perfectly content to be here with us. Maybe he was relieved; Georgia is beautiful, even in a t-shirt and jeans. Maybe he simply liked having sex with women. Why not make money from it? But how does he get it up anyway for all these women? That's not something you can actually fake. What about the really unattractive ones he must meet? Does he have an IV drip of Viagra somewhere? I had so many questions, I couldn't resist.

"So, tell me, Mauro. Do you enjoy this line of work?"

Georgia stared at me, her wide eyes trying to telepathically shut my mouth.

Mauro just smiled. Again, this probably wasn't the first time he'd encountered a nosy lady.

"Yes, very much. It's not easy to make a living in Rio, and I love women," he said, pleasantly. I looked him over again and he still felt safe to me. But there was something about him that seemed vaguely empty. Vacuous.

I pressed on, "Is it difficult for you to have sex with women who are—you know, not . . . attractive?"

Mauro just raised his eyebrows and shook his head. "No woman is unattractive when she is being pleasured."

Granted, it was a line right off the first page of the Male Hookers Manual, but it worked. The next thing I heard was "Julie, don't you have to get to your appointment?" I looked at Georgia, who was now trying to transport me telepathically out the door. Women are really just as easy as men when it comes to sexual arousal. But instead of porn, we just need a man who can lie to us and tell us we're beautiful no matter what.

"Yes, of course, I really do have to go." I got up from my chair, and so did Mauro. He was trained well. "It was so nice meeting you." I got my purse and put on a little jacket and walked to the door. I turned back to look at Georgia. She wiggled her fingers at me in a wave and grinned. I knew she was going to be all right. Perhaps better than all right.

I decided to take a walk on the beach to kill some time. From the sand, I looked out at the two shapely green mountains jutting out of the ocean, the mountains that many have compared to the shape of a Brazilian woman's buttocks.

I couldn't escape it. Even the mountains had a better ass than me.

As I walked along the beach, I thought about Thomas, about our time together. Maybe I had imagined it all, the connection, the romance. As I walked past the women in their string bikinis with their asses hanging out, I tried to see if there was any cellulite to be found. Not so far.

As I walked looking at all the perfect, smooth bodies, I wondered if the reason Thomas hadn't called me was because of my cellulite. He must have slept with me because he felt some connection, but then later on, when he thought back on the horrors that he had seen and touched, he came to his senses. I sat down in the sand and wondered when it ends. When do I get to feel like I'm great just the way I am? It's just too much to ask me to love myself on my own. Heterosexual women need men to tell them they're beautiful and sexy and fantastic; we just do. Because every day the world is telling us that we're not beautiful enough, not skinny enough, not rich enough. It's too much to expect us to be able to feel good about it all with just a few affirmations and a couple of candles. But as I started to get sucked into a vacuum of self-pity and despair, I remembered something: that guy Paulo had given me his phone number.

I had almost forgotten this delightful piece of information, but like someone clutching at a life preserver, I grabbed my phone and looked up his number. I dialed. I couldn't help myself. It was, after all, Rio. And Thomas had never called me.

Then I remembered that Paulo didn't speak English. I decided to text him, so if he happened to be around someone who knew English, they could help him out. I typed into my phone, "Hi, Paulo. Would you like to see me today?" Then I shut my phone and wondered how things were going with Georgia.

Were we disgusting? Sleeping with prostitutes, sleeping with married men, having one-night stands. Was this any way to be single? Before I could really ponder this any further, my phone beeped, telling me I had a text. It was Paulo. He said he could meet me at my hotel in ten minutes. As Thomas would say, "You must say yes to life." And one of the best things about being single is that you get to say yes to life *as often as you feel like it.*

I raced back to the hotel and used my credit card to get an extra room. Thank God, they had one room available. I texted Paulo my new room number and he came right over. When I opened the door, his eyes were sparkling.

"Hi, Paulo!" I said, not knowing how much he could understand. But before I could say anything else, he had wrapped his arms behind my back and kissed me. His tongue was soft as a feather and touched mine slowly and gently. We stood there, suspended together in time by our lips and our tongues. It was as if all his concentration was going into these kisses, making sure his tongue never made a wrong move. We stood in the middle of the room for about fifteen minutes, kissing. He was the best kisser I had ever had the privilege of laying lips on.

Then he wrapped his arms around my waist and picked me up. He was lifting and kissing me, and it made me feel tiny. Delicate. He put me back down, and he started kissing my neck, softly. He touched my head, my hair, massaging my shoulder as he kissed. Then he gently turned me around, lifting up my hair and kissing the back of my neck, keeping our bodies close. His hands ran slowly over my breasts, down to my waist and under my t-shirt. I turned my head back to him and he leaned in and kissed me, all the while caressing my breasts with his hand. His left hand was now slowly moving down my leg, over my thigh. He slipped his hand under my long, loose skirt, and gently guided it up. Our breathing was getting faster and I let out a gasp as his hand found its way between my legs. My right hand was on the desk, balancing myself as he pressed his body against mine. He raised my left leg onto the chair by the desk. My left arm was behind me, running over his ass, his thighs. I could feel his hardness pressed right on the small of my back. He was running his fingers between my legs, searching, exploring. I was breathing very heavily now. He took both hands and slowly pulled my skirt and underwear down my legs. I stepped out of them as he pulled my t-shirt over my head. Then he took his own shirt off. I could feel his warm, smooth skin against mine. I wanted to turn around and rub my hands all over his chest, throw my arms around his waist, and look into his face, but I didn't dare move.

And then, as if this man weren't genius enough, he took his hand and reached into the back pocket of his shorts, and pulled out a condom. My mind was already dreading the moment when we would have to pull away from each other, someone mumbling something to the effect of "Do you have a . . . ?" "Shouldn't we get a . . . ?" But I was spared. Paulo was a gentleman and an amateur porn star and he pulled out the condom, unwrapped it, and put it on.

I imagine there are women who are really good at the whole condom transfer situation; the unwrapping and uncoiling and putting it on their waiting man. But not me. Since about age thirty-five, condoms represented to me the grave possibility of a lost erection. I don't know if it was the men I was with or something about me, but there were so many lost opportunities once the condoms came out that they began to terrify me. After a certain number of these mishaps, I just refused to go near them. I would use them, of course, but my hands would not get anywhere near one. It was going to be the man's problem. He would have only himself to blame for his lost erection. ANYWAY, Paulo had his erection, his condom, and his groove on and he gracefully slipped himself inside me. His head was next to mine, his arms, his shoulders, his biceps were all around me, enveloping me. He whispered into my ear, "You are so beautiful." He kissed my ear. Then, his tongue slowly licked my earlobe and moved its way around, his hot breath tickling me. He was a one-man band, this fellow, as his right hand was again between my legs, hitting just the right spot, his tongue was giving me goosebumps down my neck, and he was also inside me, moving and thrusting gently, perfectly. All while standing up, thank you very much. I felt like I was in a three-way with every sensitive, sexual area being touched or kissed, but this lovely man was doing it all by himself. I was making loudish noises that I've never heard come out of me before. He didn't miss a beat as my body twisted and arched and I orgasmed. I turned around to face him and kissed him deeply on the mouth. He picked me up and carried me to the armchair, where he sat down with me on top of him, still inside me. I wanted to give him an award. He put his hands on my hips and set the rhythm. Now it was my turn to do some work, and I moved with his guidance, willing my thighs to stay strong—a charley horse would be so impolite right now. I watched his eyes close, his concentration now all going to his pleasure. But then he looked up and pulled me toward him, kissing me, his hands in my hair. We moved together, with my arms around his neck, kissing and panting, until suddenly he grabbed the arms of the chair, pulled my legs around him tight, and stood up. He walked me over to the bed and put me down. For a moment I got paranoid. Was I not doing it right? Had I gotten the rhythm wrong? Sometimes, on top, it's hard to get in the right . . . I pushed that thought away as his body pressed down on me, my legs wrapped around his torso. His eyes opened once in a while to look into mine and he would smile and kiss me. He was on his own now, knowing exactly how to move to make himself come. Which he did, in Portuguese, saying, "Meu Deus, meu Deus!"

He rolled on his side, and I rolled over to face him. We kissed softly, our arms and legs curled around each other. After twenty minutes of this, he whispered in my ear, "I must go now." And about three minutes after that he was dressed and kissing me good-bye. He said to me softly, "I like you," and then he was history. I lay back on the bed to think about how I felt about all this, but I didn't have much time to ponder because Georgia called on my cell phone. It was safe to return to our room. *Well, weren't we the swingers*, I thought to myself.

When I got back, the bed was thankfully made and there were no visible signs of sex anywhere. Georgia was packed and ready to go to the airport.

"Hey, Julie," she said, not giving anything away.

"Hey," I said as I sat on the couch. I decided not to be coy. "Well, how was it?!"

Georgia sat in the armchair and thought about it for a good two minutes. "I have to say, it's really not bad to pay for sex."

Georgia didn't look any different. I realize that's a strange thing to notice, as if paying for sex would somehow be immediately traceable on one's appearance. If that were the case, there'd be a lot more wives filing for divorce all across America. *Anyway*, I waited for her answer.

"It was a good thing. A very good thing."

"Well, tell me about it!!"

"Okay, okay." Georgia was being very serious, as if she were an astronaut describing what it was like to walk on the moon. "He was amazing in bed. Like, truly a professional. He was able to stay hard a really long time, he was really strong and threw me all around the room—in a good way—and it was really satisfying."

"So, it was good," I said. "It was a good thing. Are you happy you did it?"

Georgia thought again. "Yes. I am. I mean, it was physically perfectly satisfying." She got up from her armchair and walked over to a mirror by the desk. She grabbed a lipstick from the desk and started applying it.

"And . . . ?"

"And . . . that's it. It was completely physically satisfying. If I have a complaint, I'd say it was a little cold. Not cold like harsh, or unfeeling. Cold, like . . ."

"Like you were having sex with a prostitute."

Georgia started to laugh. "Exactly. Like I was having sex with a prostitute."

Just then the phone rang. Georgia's taxi was here. "But you know what?" Georgia said. "'Completely physically satisfied' is not a bad way to leave a room."

I smiled. It was not a bad way at all.

It was time for Georgia to go. I walked her to the taxi and gave her a big hug. I thought about how nice it would be just to get in the car with her and go home. But I resisted. She handed me a piece of paper.

"This is the number of my cousin Rachel in Australia. She's really fun and knows everyone there."

"What? Australia?"

"It's just a thought."

"You have family in Sydney, Australia? That's kind of far away."

"I know, but don't you have that pass thingy?"

"Yeah, but that seems too far. I don't want to have an anxiety attack and run out of Lexomil, and then be flipping out over the South Pacific."

"Here." Georgia handed me a little plastic bag with some pills in it. "Take some of my Xanax. Just to supplement the Lexomil. They're amazing."

"But I'll be flying alone. That's a really long trip."

"But once you get there, you'll know my cousin Rachel. She'll help you with everything you need."

I looked down at the little Baggie. I definitely had enough medication for the trip. "Well, I read there was a man drought there. It *would* be a good place to go for my research."

Georgia looked at me with that look, and spoke to me with that tone. "Julie. Go."

I immediately obeyed.

RULE

6

*Make Peace with the Statistics Because There
Really Isn't Anything We Can Do About Them
(Or Is There?)*

I always assumed that we live in a world where, if one wanted to go from Rio de Janeiro, Brazil, to Sydney, Australia, one would just hop on a plane, perhaps have a little stopover in, say, New Zealand, and then be on one's merry way. But when I got my itinerary printed out at the front desk of the hotel, it read like an issue of *National Geographic*. Flying from Rio, I'd have a layover four and a half hours later in Santiago, Chile. That sounded cute. I would then take a five-hour flight from Chile to Hanga Roa. Where is Hanga Roa, you ask? It's the "capital" of Easter Island. Where is Easter Island? It's off the coast of Chile, in the South Pacific. The natives call it Rapa Nui, population three thousand, and it's famous for the mysterious giant sculptures of scary stone men that line the coast. It's supposed to be a lovely place to visit, with snorkeling, horseback riding, mystical ruins, and spectacular hiking and views. But I would only be spending an hour at the airport, waiting for my connection to Papeete, Tahiti. Getting to Tahiti would take another five hours, with me arriving at 11:30 at night. And then after waiting in Papeete till three in the morning, I would take the eight-hour flight to Sydney.

I handled most of my 22.5 hours of air travel masterfully, mixing my drugs like a skilled pharmacist. I took Tylenol PM to Chile, then again to Easter Island. I popped a Lexomil to Tahiti and a Xanax to Sydney. It was genius.

This time it wasn't *during* my flight that I started breathing heavily, sweating, and becoming dizzy. The drugs worked quite well for that. No, this time it was in the various airports where I almost lost my mind.

I had decided to start reading about this supposed "man drought" plaguing Australia and New Zealand during my layovers at the various airports. So I printed out all the articles I could find online and read them. In airport bars and waiting areas throughout the South Pacific, I got the bad news: that a thirty-two-year-old New Zealand woman had as much chance in 2004 of finding a male partner her own age as an eighty-two-year-old woman did; that there are five women to every man in Sydney, Australia. Then there was the British report that stated that for every sixteen-point rise in a woman's IQ, there is a 40 percent drop in her likelihood of marriage, not to mention the oft-quoted advice given to Australian women in their twenties to "tag and bag" their men before they hit thirty, because after that it's anyone's guess if you'll ever be able to meet a guy, let alone get him to commit.

By the time I was headed to Papeete, I no longer was panicking about plunging through the clouds, spiraling down to my death, those last few minutes turning into an eternity and so giving me time to realize that these would be my last minutes on earth, that I would never again see my friends, my family, that I would never fall in love and have children, that my life was about to be over. No, that no longer worried me. It was now scary enough just reading about being a single woman over thirty-five. As I got on my flight to Sydney and popped the Xanax, I was confounded. Whatever happened to the idea that there was a goddamn lid for every pot? People have to stop saying that shit. Because here's what—the statistics are telling us that there definitely is *not* a lid for every pot. It sounds like a lot of the lids have left the kitchen to go find better pots elsewhere, or maybe to meet younger, prettier pots. Whatever the reason—it seems like there are a lot of big empty pots hanging out in the kitchen these days.

The Xanax was trying to take hold as my mind was racing, obsessing, worrying. What's going to happen to all these women? If there isn't a guarantee that there's a pea for every pod, then what are these women supposed to believe? That they might not ever fall in love, get married, have a conventional family? Or do some of them realize that they'll have to settle: not everyone gets to have love in their life, so they should just make the best of it? And what are they supposed to think about the idea of never ever having someone in their life whom they really love, who loves them back, deeply and passionately? And when I say "they," I mean "we." And when I say "we," I really mean "me."

So my question is, How sad are we supposed to think this is? On the one hand, we are told by movies and love songs, and our own personal experiences at times, that a life without love is a tragedy; it's one of the worst fates imaginable. On the other hand, we're also told that we're not supposed to need a man in our lives. That we're vital, fantastic people who are fabulous the way we are. So which is it? Is it a tragedy if we never have the love we're all still searching for, or is that an old-fashioned, antifeminist notion? Or has love been completely overrated? Maybe not overrated, but *oversimplified*. Maybe we should stop watching films and listening to music that makes it seem like people are falling in love and living happily ever after as often as they buy chewing gum. They should tell us that it's more like winning the lottery. Lots of people play, but very few actually win. Depending on which study you look at, 43 to 51 percent of all American marriages end in divorce. In fact, the average American will spend more years *unmarried* during their adult years if they live past the age of seventy. And a new census study shows that married couples who head households have officially become a slight minority.

The lights inside the plane were now being shut off. I love that about night flights. The flight attendants turn into camp counselors and decide when it's "lights out," subtly forcing an entire cabin of grown-ups to go to sleep. But I couldn't. Even with the Xanax, I was obsessing over the idea of statistics in general. What were we supposed to do with these hateful things? I mean, any woman living in New York City can tell you about the little statistic from 1986, when *Newsweek* told us that if you were over forty and living in New York you were more likely to get hit by a terrorist attack than get married. But then, lo and behold, twenty years later, after many forty-plus women moved to Vermont, or married guys they didn't love, or spent thousands of dollars on Marianne Williamson courses or plastic surgery, or just woke up every morning in sheer terror because of that damn statistic, *Newsweek* published an article saying, basically, "Ooops! We were wrong! Sorry. You guys actually have a fine chance of getting married. Everyone, go about your business now, carry on."

But here are my statistics. One: every man I know, see, or hear about, poor, boring, bald, fat, arrogant, or whatever, unless he's actually a shut-in, can get a girlfriend whenever he wants. And two: I know dozens of smart, funny, gorgeous, sane, financially stable, professionally fulfilled, fascinating, fit women in New York in their mid-thirties to mid-forties who are single. And not just single like "in between boyfriends" but single for years. When I hear of a couple breaking up, I know that the man will be in his next relationship much sooner than the woman.

I took out my trusty vinyl sleep mask and put it on. Because I knew it looked really good on me. Just kidding. I was trying to shut my brain off. Because here's the other thing. This little monologue I've been doing? It's been performed for many years. Not just by me, but by many women before me, women my mother's age, and perhaps even before that. And the complaint remains the same: *There are not enough good men out there.* So what does one do? How do you be single when the statistics (and reality) are telling you that you are doomed?

I arrived at the hotel tired and cranky; after more than twenty-four hours of traveling I just needed to get to bed. As the bellhop got my suitcases out of the cab, I turned and looked into the distance.

Even in my haze of drugs and sleep deprivation, I couldn't help but be a little dumbstruck at the sight of the Sydney Opera House, jutting out into the harbor like a little miracle. I really don't have much of a passion for architecture in general, but seeing it up close, I was surprised at how breathtaking I found it. I had never before seen a building that seemed to be such

an organic extension of a city's natural landscape. Apparently the architect, Jorn Utzon, designed the roof to look like a "ship at full sail." And that's what I saw—the Sydney Opera House setting sail right before my eyes.

My hotel was right on the wharf, and even though all I wanted to do was go to bed, I had to stand there, as my suitcases were taken into the hotel, just to soak it all in. As I did, I became sure that, statistics be damned, I was going to have a great time in Sydney. The ride from the airport had been pleasant, the weather warm and the sun shining. Sydney seemed modern, yet quaint, English yet Pan-Asian. The gloom and doom I felt on the plane had lifted. I had overindulged in statistics and they had made me sick. The reality of Sydney was a different situation altogether.

As I entered my room, the good news was that it was really great-looking, with a view of the water and lots of space. The bad news was that there was someone already sleeping in one of my double beds. I let out a little gasp and froze in my tracks. Assuming I had barged into someone else's room, I slowly backed up, trying to get out before I woke the person up. Then I heard a sound I would be able to recognize anywhere: Alice's sleep-breathing. It wasn't really a snore, it was much more delicate than that. It was like a loud purr. I knew it from trips we took to the Bahamas and New Orleans. I walked closer to the bed and saw I was right: it was Alice, sound asleep. I didn't know how she got there, but there she was. I lay down on the other bed and passed out.

When we woke up, Alice explained that Georgia had called her from the airport in Rio to tell her what a good time she had. Alice, who's a little competitive and never likes to miss a party, asked Georgia where I was going next and decided to join me. Now, I wasn't sure what was going on with Jim at this moment, but I didn't think it was a good sign that Alice, in the middle of a new relationship, decided she just *had* to go halfway around the world. So, being a friend, I had to ask.

"So, tell me about this Jim guy, how's it going?"

Alice bobbed her head and sort of half smiled. "He's great. Really nice. I mean, oh my God, so nice." Alice quickly got out of bed. "Should we go get something to eat? I'm starving."

That night, we met Georgia's cousin Rachel for a drink at the hotel bar. We were sitting at a table outside, overlooking the harbor. The water was sparkling and the wind was balmy and that darn opera house was showing off again. It was heavenly.

Rachel was a thirty-year-old Australian girl-about-town. She was bubbly and upbeat, with long curly blond hair. She worked as a publicist for a very successful family-run company that owned many restaurants and hotels all throughout Sydney. She talked really fast and sort of through her nose, as people with Australian accents sometimes do. We were drinking a lovely Australian rosé, and she was telling us all about the night to come.

"It's going to be an absolutely brilliant party, it is. This man, whose birthday it is, he's really rich. His family made their money in cattle. It's a big deal that we're getting to go. My friend Leo got us the invites. Isn't it absolutely brilliant?"

"Yes, we're so excited," I said, politely.

"And the guys in Sydney are just gorgeous, they *are*."

"But what about this man drought?" I asked. "Is it true?"

Rachel nodded her head vigorously. "It does seem like the men have the pick of the litter. That's why I'm never going to leave my boyfriend. No matter how much of a tosser he is."

"Is he not nice to you?" I asked, guessing at the meaning of *tosser*.

"Not at all. But he's absolutely *yummy*."

When we got to the party, it was already in full swing. The most beautiful men and women in Sydney were there, all in their Saturday-night coolest. The women were in cute little tops and jeans or flowing dresses, with their hair all fluffy and flipped, their lips glossy and pink. The men looked slick in their jackets and jeans and groomed hair. The folks in Sydney knew how to dress for the occasion—it could be called "casual-fabulous." The private club seemed to be going for a Paris opera house aesthetic, all in red velvet, gold leaf, and murals.

As we made our way to the bar, a tall man with black hair that had a lot of product in it came over to us. Rachel told us that this was our host, Clark. He kissed Rachel on the cheek.

"So these must be the ladies from New York?"

"Yes, this is Julie and Alice."

He looked at me. "Are you the one interviewing single women all over the world?"

"Yes, I guess I am," I said, a little embarrassed.

"Brilliant," he said. "Can I get you three some Sammy's? That's what everyone's drinking tonight."

"Perfect," Rachel said, and he leaned over to order.

"What's a Sammy?" Alice asked Rachel.

"A Semillon. It's a local white wine. It's not big in the States, but it's everywhere in Australia."

Clark brought the wine over.

"Would you like me to introduce you to some single ladies that you might like to talk to?"

"Sure," I said, taking my little journal out of my bag.

Alice took my wrist. "No, not right now," she said. "It's time for Julie to talk to some single men." She then led me toward a crowd of men. Then she added, "Man drought my ass. Statistics don't mean anything. I'll prove it."

Soon enough, Alice had made friends with a group of four young men, all in business suits. She had the whole group in rapt attention as she started telling how she once got a judge to let a drug dealer go because of a lack of evidence, and the drug dealer promptly offered to thank her by giving her an ounce of blow. They were enthralled and impressed.

"That's awesome, really," one of the exceptionally handsome men said.

"It's impressive, to be so young and so accomplished," another said.

Jim back home must have been doing something good for Alice, because at that moment she didn't feel the need to lie or minimize herself in any way. She felt good enough about herself to just blurt out the truth. "Well, I'm not that young. I'm thirty-eight."

All the blokes looked incredulous. The exceptionally handsome one said, "I thought you were around thirty-two!"

"I reckoned you were about thirty," the shorter, stockier one said. Their two mates murmured in agreement.

"No. Thirty-eight." And then Alice had to drag me into it. "Julie here is thirty-eight, too."

Now, let's be honest, the only correct response from any man at that moment would be a gigantic display of disbelief, which they all thankfully made.

I always feel so guilty at how pleased I am when someone thinks I look much younger than I am. As if it's such a disgrace to just look your age. Every time I say "thank you" when someone says I look much younger than I am, I always think, *We both just acknowledged that it's terrible for a woman to be old.*

"Wow, you both look great for your age," the short, stocky one said. Somehow, just by the detached way he said that, I suddenly felt ancient. The music started to get louder and people were begining to dance. Suddenly, two of the men seemed to have somewhere else in the room they urgently needed to be. The exceptionally handsome blond man wasn't going to get away that easily. Alice asked him to dance. He said okay, and then, the shorter, stockier man and I stood there and stared at each other until I asked him if he wanted to dance. He politely said yes.

Alice and I got on the dance floor with these two men. Now, I don't want to brag, but Alice and I know how to dance. We don't go crazy on the dance floor, nothing embarrassing, mind you, we're just two girls who have a little bit of rhythm. "Groove Is in the Heart" was playing, and who doesn't love to dance to that? Alice and I were boogying away, shaking our hips and moving our feet, clapping our hands a bit, but the men were just shuffling their feet a little. Okay, they're not dancers, that's fine. But it immediately put a damper on the boogying vibe. I started to shake my hips a little less, move my feet a little slower. Alice, on the other hand, kept at it, dancing closer to the handsome guy, putting her hand on his hip for a moment, then taking it away and swirling around. She wasn't making a fool of herself by any means. She was just out there having fun. But Handsome Guy didn't seem to want to play along. I was still having fun because I love the song, but it was hard not to notice that Short-Stocky Guy was looking above my head as he danced with me, not making eye contact with me at all. Now, here's what I love about dancing: it's a time when you can feel free and sexy and flirty with someone you might not necessarily even be interested in. Like kissing in Rio, it's a great way to rev up your sexy engine without having to actually sleep with someone you don't want to.

So I was looking at Short-Stocky Guy, smiling, trying to be friendly and flirty. He had very closely cropped hair and a big round, ruddy face.

He smiled back at me, briefly, and he went back to sort of staring four feet over my head. It was pretty disconcerting. So when the song ended I was planning on just getting off the dance floor and away from Stocky Guy. But then "Hey Ya" by Outkast came on, and I really, *really* love to dance to that. So I kept dancing, not giving Stocky Guy a chance to slip away.

As I was bouncing up and down, I made a moment of eye contact with Stocky Guy and smiled. He just sort of ignored me and again turned his attention to four feet above my head. In that split second I knew exactly what was going on: *He did not find me even remotely sexually attractive.* Of course I've felt that before, on dates, in conversations, but never on the dance floor doing my sexy moves. A wave of humiliation came over me.

"You're reading too much into it," Alice said later as we waited for our Sammy's at the bar. "He didn't like to dance. I had the same experience with my guy. That's why he just swayed back and forth to the music. You don't see me taking it personally."

"Alice, he stared above my head the whole time. ABOVE MY HEAD." I was practically shrieking.

We drank our wine, which was delicious. The music was still really great for dancing.

"Let's go dance by ourselves," Alice suggested. "Fuck these guys."

I looked around at all the beautiful people. This was my first night in Sydney and I was damned if I was going to have a bad time because of some Above-the-Head-Starer. We set our wine down and headed out to the dance floor.

I was still on a roll. Yelling over the music, I said, "I'm telling you, if I was on fire, that guy wouldn't have gone near me to put it out."

Alice yelled back, "I'm telling you, Julie. Some guys just don't like to dance! It has *nothing* to do with you."

Just then, my eyes glanced past Alice. There was the short-stocky-above-my-head guy doing the cabbage patch with a twenty-two-year-old blond pixie. He was perspiring, he was dancing so hard. From the expression on my face, Alice turned around and saw him. She turned back to me, speechless. Then, at the same time, we looked to our left and saw Exceptionally Handsome Guy grinding a woman on the dance floor. He had his hands on her hips and his pelvis was thrust close into hers. He must have met her about three and a half minutes ago. His hands moved toward the side of her face and he kissed her. They stopped dancing and they just began making out on the dance floor. Alice saw this. And this is another reason why I love Alice. She knows when to admit defeat. She leaned in to me and said, "Let's get the fuck out of here."

Back in the States

The cutest thing about Georgia's date was that he was nervous. Shy. This was Sam's first date since his divorce four months ago and he seemed like a boy at his high school prom. They had been set up by Alice, who knew Sam from her days in Legal Aid. Now that she and Jim were "exclusive," Alice had a lot of extra time and energy to dedicate to finding other people boyfriends.

They were at an out-of-the-way little restaurant on a block Georgia had never heard of, Tudor Place, which was slightly elevated above the rest of the neighborhood. This allowed for a 360-degree view of New York at night, with one side featuring the United Nations building looming above like a giant. Georgia was entranced. The restaurant was all candles and drapery, which made the room feel as if you were in some sheik's love tent. Sam took charge and ordered a bottle of wine for them, which impressed Georgia immediately. Dale knew a lot about wine and she had to admit, it was something she always liked about him. Actually, it was something she always liked about *them*. Before the kids, they would take wine-tasting classes at the local wine store and once even went to Sonoma for a wine-tasting vacation.

Tonight Sam ordered a lovely Shiraz, and then he began his adorable, completely winning confession.

"This is my first date since my divorce, and I'm really, really nervous. I tried on three different shirts before I left the house." He was smiling, his eyes looking at his hands, which were drumming nervously on the table.

Georgia liked him already. An honest, vulnerable man who knew about wine.

"Well, you look perfect."

And he did. He was a tall beanpole of a man, with beautiful sleek brown hair, that came down just past his ears. He looked a little like James Taylor, if James Taylor still had hair.

"Thank you." Sam looked up at Georgia, and then back down at his hands.

"Alice told me that you were really beautiful and smart, so I knew the pressure was on." Sam now looked straight at Georgia. "I just didn't know how beautiful you actually were going to be." He nervously pushed his hair back away from his face. "Thanks for agreeing to have dinner with me. I really appreciate it."

Georgia laughed. "I'm not doing it as a favor. You sounded nice on the phone and Alice said you were great."

Sam laughed, embarrassed. "Right. I guess I shouldn't sound so pathetic, right? It's just, going through a divorce, and the unhappy years of a marriage, well, it kind of undermines your confidence, you know?"

Georgia nodded slowly and said, "Oh yes. I know."

But what she was really thinking, while she looked at him, was, Guileless. He was completely without guile or pretense. He was a grown-up, openhearted man who told her she was beautiful and practically blushed. She wanted to dart him, cage him, and bring him back to her place, where she could keep him to herself, unspoiled by the outside world. As they ate their dinner, she learned that he was from the Midwest, which perhaps explained a lot. His manners were impeccable. He was kind to the waitress but he also had a dry sense of humor that amused Georgia to no end. Best of all, when he spoke of his ex-wife, it was clear that it pained him to say anything bad about her; it was well into the conversation before Georgia got out of him that his wife had cheated on him. Many times. They talked and talked, sharing their personal stories about their marriages and how they ended, and besides being completely smitten, Georgia was totally impressed. Somehow this man managed to make being a beleaguered, cuckolded, mistreated husband—hot. He was noble and kind and funny with just enough self-awareness of the absurdity of it all to be utterly charming about his disastrous wreck of a marriage and fifteen lost years. They finished dinner and ordered another bottle of wine. They drank that and were both officially a little drunk. He waited while Georgia got in her cab and kissed her good night. And then, with complete sincerity, Sam told her he had had a great time and would love to see her again. They made a date for exactly a week later, which seemed like a long time away to Georgia, but she knew he was new to this whole dating thing, so she didn't want to push. Georgia went upstairs to her apartment, paid the babysitter, and went to bed, happy. There was hope now and hope's name was Sam.

Back in Australia

I got up early the next morning to search for more statistics. I couldn't get enough of them. While I was surfing the Web for "man drought," there was one writer whose articles kept coming up. Her name was Fiona Crenshaw from Tasmania (a small island off the coast of southern Australia) and she wrote articles for the single ladies of Australia. She did it with cheeky Australian humor, but was adamant that no matter how bad the drought, the ladies must remember that they're *Goddesses,* that they mustn't settle, and must stay positive. She gave one woman the earth-shattering advice that—get this—*she has to love herself.* Isn't that novel? Apparently, as long as you love yourself the men are going to start lining up in droves.

This irritated me immensely. I sat on my bed, listening to Alice purr, and felt furious. Here's a woman who was reciting the statistics in her columns, but telling the ladies to love themselves and "stay positive" anyway. If there were a starving village, with no food in sight, no one in their right mind would tell the village that all they had to do was love themselves and think positively and food would show up. But love has a mystical quality about it that makes us feel we can ignore the cold hard facts—one of them being that there aren't enough men out there.

Luckily, I didn't have to think about this for long, because our hostess, Rachel, called to brighten my day.

"My friend, Will, wants to take you out on his boat today. Can you two make it? It seems like it's going to be a super day for that."

"Really? He wants to take us out on his boat?"

"Yes, he's a businessman, so he loves doing all this networking rubbish."

"But he knows that Alice and I aren't necessarily . . ."

"Oh please, you're writing a book about dating. Who doesn't love that? He's going to bring some of his mates on board so you can get the male perspective on it."

"Well, that's awfully nice . . ." I wasn't used to all this generosity. I'm a New Yorker and we're all too busy to be that accommodating to anyone.

"See you at two at the hotel. The boat will pick you up right there." And she hung up.

His boat was a Donzi—a speedboat that looked very expensive and went very fast. We were rocketing around the harbor, our skin getting pushed back on our faces as the wind hit us, our hair getting knotted and gnarled. Will showed us where Russell Crowe lived (good going, Russell) and he pointed out the building that Rupert Murdoch owned. He also had brought along two of his mates, John and Freddie. They were in their early thirties, handsome, and, from what I could gather, extremely rich. John was the first swarthy man I had seen in Sydney, looking almost Italian. Freddie was a member of the family that Rachel worked for. In his own right, Freddie owned or partly owned five or six restaurants or hotels in downtown Sydney alone. He reminded me a bit of Lance Armstrong: tall, slim, confident, and kind of an asshole. He had narrow eyes and the ability never to crack a smile or look at you directly. I took one look at these handsome, rich gentlemen who live in the middle of a man drought and saw them as one thing and one thing only: *kids in a candy store.*

So that was the attitude I took when Will finally slowed the boat down and I was able to sit down for a chat with these blokes. Will poured us all champagne, and Rachel had brought some tiny "nibbles"—itsy-bitsy pieces of black bread with salmon and crème fraîche on top. They were delicious. I asked the men if any of them had girlfriends. They said they didn't. I asked them if it was because there were too many options, and they all just laughed and shrugged. Well, Freddie didn't laugh because he was too cool to laugh.

"So that means yes," I said.

They all just shrugged again, sheepishly. But John tried to explain.

"It's not like that. I want to settle down, I do. To fall in love. But I just haven't met the right girl yet."

"But don't you think that you might be having a hard time meeting the right girl because you're never quite sure if there's another right girl coming right after her?"

Will spoke up this time. "No, when you fall in love, it just hits you, doesn't it? You just know. There could be five hundred supermodels and you wouldn't give a toss."

The others agreed. I really had only one question that I had wanted answered. It was about the damn statistics.

"What does it feel like? To not have to worry about finding someone to love?"

John looked at me, surprised. "What do you mean? I worry. I'm not sure."

Will agreed. "I work all the time. When do I have time to meet anyone?"

John added, "Just because there's lots of women around doesn't mean I'm guaranteed to meet someone I can fall in love with."

Will poured himself a little more champagne. "In fact, it can be more depressing really, meeting all these women, and none of them being 'the one.'"

There was no way Will was going to get me to feel bad for him because there were too many women. I pressed on. "So you're saying it's just as hard for you to find love here in Sydney as it is for the women?"

The two men nodded. Freddie was just staring out into the ocean, stone-faced. I didn't let it drop.

"But wouldn't you have to agree that the odds of you falling in love are better, simply because you're meeting more people who might be 'the one' than the women are? Don't you think that has to help your odds?"

John said, "I don't think it works that way."

Will said, "All it takes is one."

These men had an entirely different way of viewing the statistics than I did. Apparently, to these men it doesn't matter if there are a lot of fish in the sea. Finding the one fish to love for the rest of your life is difficult no matter where you swim.

Alice continued the interrogation.

"So have any of you ever been in love?"

They all nodded their heads. Will began. "When I was a teenager I was in love. I got my heart crushed. I had a girlfriend when I was nineteen who just trampled me."

John agreed. "I treated my girlfriends well when I was young. I brought them flowers, wrote them love poems."

Will laughed and John went on, embarrassed. "I couldn't help it, I was a romantic! I had a girlfriend when I was twenty-one whom I would have married. I was head over heels for her. But she broke up with me because she said I was getting too serious."

I wondered where this woman was now. I hoped she wasn't single and living in Sydney.

Alice looked at Lance Armstrong. "So, Freddie. You've been awfully quiet."

Freddie just looked at Alice and shrugged. "It was the same for me. I got crushed when I was younger. But I figured it out. Until a woman is around thirty, thirty-two, she has all the power. We hit on them, we fight over them, we chase after them. Then, around thirty-two, thirty-three, it all shifts. We get the power and they're the ones fighting and chasing after us. I think it's just payback. For all the shit they put us through when we were younger."

The other men looked at Freddie, not really disagreeing, but not wanting to start trouble. Alice narrowed her eyes, shifted in her seat, and calmly took a sip of her champagne. I dove in.

"Would any of you consider going out with an older woman? Someone in her late thirties or even forty?"

"I prefer the strategy of 'divide your age and add four,' if you know what I mean," Freddie said, not really joking. The other guys laughed.

I did the math. That meant that they all wanted to date nineteen- or twenty-year-olds. I was considering jumping off the boat right then and there.

Freddie added knowledgeably, "We don't meet single older women when we're out, because there aren't any."

Alice quickly said, "Excuse me?"

In a cool, slow tone, as if talking to two imbeciles, Freddie explained, "There aren't women that age out at my clubs and restaurants because they're all married."

I had to step in now. "Are you telling me that you think all the women over, like, thirty-eight are married? That's why they're not at your clubs?"

"Yeah. Of course." The other guys agreed.

Alice, confused, said, "You're saying there are literally no single women in Sydney who are over, say, thirty-eight?"

Freddie nodded his head confidently. "Yes."

I stared at him for a minute and then cleared my throat. "Do you realize that the statistics, with which I'm quite familiar, don't support that at all?"

Freddie shrugged. "I own half the bars and restaurants in this town. Who are you going to believe, the statistics or me?"

I was unable to stop talking. "Do you think, Freddie, that the reason you think there aren't any women over the age of thirty-eight who are single is perhaps that you're just not noticing them? That they might be invisible to you?"

Freddie just shrugged. "Maybe." Alice and I looked at each other. This was the biggest confession we had gotten out of any of these blokes all day.

"Well, you two don't have anything to worry about for years, so what's the fuss?" Will asked. "How old are you ladies? Thirty-one, thirty-two?"

Even here, on this boat with these men, it made me feel good to hear that. Damn me to hell. This time, Alice didn't feel the need to correct him.

That night, Alice may have blow-dried her hair and put on her heels and mascara, but she might as well have been wearing khakis, hiking boots, a safari hat, and carrying a rifle. She was out to track down where all the women over thirty-five were.

We went to one of Freddie's places, wittily called "Freddie's World." It was a cavernous space with a huge circular bar in the middle and throngs of people mingling about. And there seemed to be no man drought here.

"You fan out to our right, I'll go left. We'll meet up by the archway up ahead."

I went right, my eyes peeled for any woman with light lines on her forehead and creases stretching from the bottom of her nose to the corners of her mouth. All I saw were baby-faced cuties, with under-thirty radiant skin. I got to the archway as Alice came up.

"I went up to two women who I thought might be over thirty-five. They told me they were twenty-seven. One of them almost punched me and the other one left to go cry in the bathroom." Alice looked around again. "Otherwise, I came up with nothing."

"Let's go to one of his restaurants," I said. "I mean, women over thirty-five still have to eat, don't they?"

We walked a few blocks and found Freddie's Fish, a very trendy sushi restaurant that wrapped around the whole corner, with high windows to show all the beautiful people eating rice and raw fish inside. Luckily, we were seated at a table in the middle of things. The table next to us was empty, but by the time our sake had arrived, four women, all of whom had forehead creases and expensive handbags, sat down next to us. Jackpot.

After they ordered, we tried to look at them and smile every once in a while, to appear friendly. Alice hid our low-sodium soy sauce in her bag so she could ask, in her thickest Staten Island accent, to borrow theirs. They took the bait.

"Are you from New York?"

"Yes. Yes, we are," Alice said. "My friend Julie is writing a book about being single all over the world. Sort of a self-help book with a world view."

The women were interested. One of them asked, "So, you've come to Sydney to do research?"

"Yes, I have."

"What have you found?" asked another.

"Well, I haven't learned anything yet, but I have some questions," I said, shyly.

The four women leaned toward Alice and me. They were all very pretty. One of them smiled and said, "Okay. Shoot."

Alice jumped in. "Where do you women go out to meet men? Bars?"

"No, no," said one. "I never go to bars."

"Never," said another one.

The third one said, "I go out sometimes with a few of my other friends and it's usually pretty depressing."

"The men our age, they act like we're invisible."

Alice banged her fist on the table. "I knew it! Do you go to any of Freddie Wells's clubs?"

"It's hard to avoid them," the fourth one said. "But I've pretty much stopped. I'm thirty-seven and I started feeling completely over-the-hill."

Everyone else agreed. "Now we just go out to dinner."

"Or if it's a function for work."

"Otherwise, I just stay home."

Maybe Freddie was right after all. Maybe this was the Town of Lost Women, where ladies over a certain age are forced to stay home and watch television. I looked at these beautiful, vital, stylish women talking as if they were ready to play shuffleboard and get cataract surgery.

I had to ask: "Do you ever think about moving? Somewhere where there are more men?"

"Or where they have bars for people over twenty-five?" Alice added.

One of them said, "I was thinking of moving to Rome."

"Yes, Europe. There I think the men will fuck you when you're fifty," another one said, hopefully.

The other women seemed heartened by this concept. I thought this might be correct. Maybe that could be another bestselling self-help book: *Places Where Men Will Fuck You When You're Fifty.*

"But really. How could we? Just pack up and leave our home because our love lives are so bad? That seems ridiculous," one of the women said.

As we sat eating our edamame and drinking our sake, I thought about me and my friends. Our love lives could be considered disasters. But I would never dream of suggesting any of us leave New York to find a man. Or would I? Shouldn't we all be taking these statistics a little more seriously? We finished our sushi, and being appropriate women in our late thirties in Sydney, we went home and went to bed.

Back in the States

Georgia's week was filled with two quick, witty emails from Sam, a brief phone conversation, and even a text saying "gr8t talking to u!" The text struck Georgia as a bit out of character for the sweetly unhip Sam she met a week ago, but she didn't give it more than a passing thought. She was just relieved that she had a romantic prospect—no matter how far-flung. This thin strand of hope can get you through a lot of days of making your children's lunches alone, and going to bed alone and imagining your husband having sex with a young, nubile dancer with sinewy thighs. Georgia had a prospect, and even when Sam emailed her, asking if they could push back their date a couple of days because something "came up," she didn't even notice. All she cared about was that he didn't cancel on her, that he was still a prospect.

They met at a bar in Brooklyn. Sam suggested it since it was close to his apartment. Georgia didn't mind. Why shouldn't she be the one to travel? Living in Brooklyn, he must be on the subway all the time. He had to wake up in the morning for work, and had had to travel farther the last time they met. It only seemed fair. But when Georgia walked in, she was surprised at how young the crowd seemed; it felt like your standard college pub.

And the minute she saw Sam, Georgia could tell something was different. He looked literally flush with . . . something. Confidence. That's what it was. He seemed much more confident than just a week and a half ago. She let that observation pass and kept focused on the task at hand: being delightful.

"You don't mind if we just sit at the bar, do you?" Sam asked, casually, *confidently.*

"No, no, of course not, that's fine."

Sam pointed toward one lone stool at the corner of the bar. "Here, why don't you sit there?"

Georgia was a little confused. "Oh. Okay, well . . . don't you want to . . . ?"

"No. I've been sitting all day; it'll be good for me to stand for a bit." Georgia sat down dutifully on the stool and looked at Sam as he leaned against the bar.

"What can I get you? They have great Guinness here."

Georgia couldn't help but notice the demotion: from restaurant to bar, banquette to stool, wine to beer.

"That would be great," Georgia said. Sam gave the bartender their order and turned back to Georgia, smiling. The smile that last week was sheepish and tentative was now radiant. He was wearing the same kind of clothes, but they looked different on him now. Trendy. They chatted pleasantly, he standing, while Georgia sat. Georgia had not been dating enough to know why this felt incredibly awkward. Why shouldn't he stand if he wanted to? It's a free country.

"So, how have you been since we last saw each other?" Georgia asked, casually, sipping at her Guinness.

"Great. Really great."

"That's wonderful. So what's been going on that's so 'really great'?"

"You know. I'm just getting out there, you know. Meeting people, finding out who I am without Claire. Spreading my wings. It's exhilarating."

"Exhilarating. Wow. That's great. Exhilarating. Well, you can't beat exhilarating, can you?"

"No. You can't beat exhilarating!" Georgia thought about her life since getting a divorce from Dale. Well, she did sleep with a Brazilian prostitute. She guessed that could be considered exhilarating.

Sam took a big gulp of beer and wiped his lips with his sleeve. Georgia looked at him, not knowing if she wanted to know more, but unable to stop herself.

"So. What makes things so exhilarating?"

"Well, it's really fascinating, actually. I've been meeting all these women, you know?"

Georgia raised her eyebrows. Sam explained himself.

"Well, both of us, we're going out, we're meeting people, you know? We're getting back in the game, seeing where we fit in the whole scheme of things, right?"

Georgia nodded politely. "Yes. Exactly."

"So I'll admit. I've been doing some online dating this week. Like every night of the week. I just decided to just jump in headfirst. Whoosh!" Sam made a big diving motion and then a big splash with his hands.

"Whoosh!" Georgia mimicked, agreeably.

"And it's amazing what I learned. I mean, my wife didn't sleep with me for years. So I guess I assumed it was because I was actually physically repellent. But now I've been dating, and women want to see me again. They don't mind that I have two kids or only make sixty thousand bucks a year. They want to see me again!"

Georgia gave him the response he wanted. "That's great, Sam! Good for you!"

Sam leaned in and grabbed Georgia's arm. "The truth is, all my life, I never got the girls. I was the nice guy who all the girls said they just 'liked as a friend.' And then they would go out with the assholes. Well, guess what? Those girls are now unmarried women in their thirties and forties and me, the nice guy with a decent job? I might as well be Jesus Christ himself."

Georgia felt her stomach turn. A complete flip-flop as the words "Jesus Christ himself" came out of Sam's mouth. She leaned against the bar, trying to remain calm. She knew that this was probably the truth, but so far no one had spelled it out so unrepentantly. In New York, in terms of dating, nice guys over forty do in fact finish first. They are as miraculous as loaves and fishes falling out of the sky. Georgia felt herself flushing, with tears forming at the rims of her eyes. "You know, I'm not feeling very well."

Sam immediately became concerned. "What? Really? I'm so sorry. Can I get you anything? Water?"

The thing was, Sam really was a nice guy—which is exactly why he was such a deadly dating agent in New York.

"No, that's okay. I think I'm just going to get a cab and go home, if you don't mind. I'm so sorry." But in fact, Georgia wasn't that sorry. Sam had so many dates lined up he probably would be relieved to have a night off. She now understood the whole standing-up-at-the-bar thing. He had been dating so much his ass hurt. Or maybe he knew he was going to have to dash to his next date that evening and didn't want a stool to slow him down. Georgia got up. Sam helped her put on her jacket, walked her outside, and waved down a cab.

"Will you be okay?"

Georgia looked at him, a dull pain filling up her entire body. "Don't you worry. I'm fine. I think I ate something bad at lunch. It's been bothering me all day."

Sam opened the cab door and Georgia climbed in. "Okay, I'll call you in twenty minutes to make sure you got home safe. Is that all right?"

"Yes, of course. Thanks," Georgia mumbled. She turned her head so he wouldn't see that she was now crying, her sadness washing over her. Georgia had just learned another important lesson about being single. You might be out there dating to meet the love of your life, but the other person might be just wanting to eat a nice steak on a Saturday night—or just trying to "dive in." She felt humiliated. How could she have thought it was going to be so simple? A nice guy meeting her, liking her, and wanting to be with her. This was New York, and she felt the statistics were now spitting in her face.

Being true to his word, Sam did call exactly twenty minutes later to see how she was. He really was nice. What an asshole.

· · ·

Two hours into her first shift as an animal shelter volunteer, Ruby watched as they took three dogs to their deaths. They didn't necessarily say that was what was happening, but she could tell. A man in a white coat would take the dog out of the cage and leave the room with it. The dog would never come back. Ruby was horrified. She knew that was what they did here, that was their policy, but she had no idea that it happened so often. It felt so random, so cruel. As the third dog was being taken out of its cage, Ruby stopped the young man.

"Excuse me, sir?"

The young man looked up at Ruby, with the door opened.

"Could you please tell me—how do you choose?"

The young man closed the cage door, almost as if he didn't want the dog to hear.

"You mean, who we . . . take?"

Ruby nodded.

This was obviously an uncomfortable subject. He cleared his voice. "We decide by their adoptability, so we take into account their age, their health—and their temperament."

Ruby shook her head. "Temperament?"

The young man nodded.

"So, the crankier the dog, the more chance that he'll get put down?"

The man nodded. He clearly wasn't happy about it, either. He smiled at Ruby politely, and then opened the cage door again. He took out Tucker, a German shepherd mix. He didn't make a peep, but he did look skinny; sickly. Ruby was now fighting back tears.

"May I hold Tucker, please? Just for a moment?"

The young man looked at Ruby. He studied her face and ascertained that he didn't have a nutcase on his hands. He led Tucker out of the cage and walked him over to Ruby. Ruby kneeled down and gave Tucker a big hug. She petted him and whispered in his ear how much she loved him. She didn't cry, she didn't make a scene. She just eventually stood up and let him go.

As she did, the strangest thought came across her mind, a thought she wasn't necessarily proud to have: She was glad that she decided to volunteer at this shelter. And not because she felt she could do good here; not because she felt the animals needed her. No. *If I can do this and not lose my shit,* she thought to herself, *I'll be able to do anything—and that includes dating again.*

Eventually, this became the routine. Ruby became the Sister Mary Prejean of the animal shelter. She would make sure that the last face they saw before they met their maker was a face of love. So whenever Ruby worked, which was once a week, on Thursday evenings, if there was a dog that was about to be put down, that young man, Bennett, would walk the dog over to Ruby. She would then administer his or her last rites, which was a big, big hug and lots of long, whispered affection. Then they were walked into the room, where they were given their injections and put to sleep.

* * *

Meanwhile, Serena was meeting her man everywhere: in broom closets, pantry rooms, and even in the ladies' room of Integral Foods on Thirteenth Street.

The one thing they never risked doing was meeting in one of their rooms. That's the first place one looks for you if they need you, and there was no good way she could explain sneaking out of Swami Swaroop's closed bedroom. But every other enclosed space was fair game. If the purpose of becoming a swami was to help her feel a powerful, all-encompassing love that made her tap into God's transcendent spirit, then those crazy sannyasin vows completely did the trick.

While she sat meditating on this particular morning, after already having a brief tête-à-tête with Swami Swaroop in the basement bathroom, her thoughts replayed the whole scenario: her ass on the sink, he in front of her, then both of them on the closed toilet seat, then them against the wall. These were definitely "extraneous thoughts" that the meditation leader would be wanting her to clear from her mind. But as hard as she tried, Serena couldn't. Because she was in love. And because this was her first time, she was struck by how perfectly apt those words were: *in love.* Serena loved this man so much that she felt as if she were floating in a bubble. A bubble of love. That she was existing, every moment of every hour, *in* love. And it was, ironically, the most spiritual experience she'd ever had. No yoga class, no meditation course, no ten-day juice fast had ever gotten her as close to the exultation she felt as this brand-spanking-new sensation of being in love.

During this meditation, she let herself say all the things she wanted to say to herself. "*This is what everyone has been talking about. All the love songs and the poems and the films. This is what life is all about. Being in love. Loving someone. Having someone love you.*" And as she let her breath go in and out, slowly, she went even a step further. "*I had no understanding of what it meant to be alive. Without love in your life, it is meaningless.*" There. She said it. And she meant it. How could she ever, *ever,* go back to living in the world without this feeling? This is everything, this is life, this is truth, this is God. Luckily, she didn't have to live without it. Because Swami Swaroop wasn't going anywhere. Oddly, she still called him Swami Swaroop. At their most intimate moments, she might say, "Oh, Swamiji," but that's as civilian as it ever got. And Mr. Oh Swamiji seemed to be existing in the same bubble of love, always wanting to be with her, touch her, talk to her. Sneaking a glance, a smile, a touch. He even gave her a gift, a secret sign that she was his: a tiny black string. He tied it around her ankle and told her that every time he saw it, he would know that they were bound together. To Serena, this proved that he was in love as well, and she was content to let things float on as they were.

The only thing that slightly diminished the joy of this cosmic commingling of souls was the fact that she had not yet expressed the enormity of her emotions to anyone. With my traveling, we kept trading phone calls, and she hadn't spoken to Ruby, Georgia, or Alice in a while. She certainly hadn't said any of this to Swami Swaroop. And it was starting to get to her. This joy was lodged inside her, warming her, uplifting her, but it also needed to be let out. It needed to be put into the world, as a truth, as a reality, so she could soar even higher than she already was. So that the love had a place to go, out of her heart, and into the world.

It was her turn to teach the first yoga class of the day. It was early, at seven thirty, and made up of just six very dedicated women and one man. She was guiding them through their Pranayama, their breathing exercises, telling them to inhale through the right nostril, pinch the other one closed with their left thumb, and reverse the process. As they moved through this chakra-stimulating process, Serena made a decision. She was going to tell Swami Swaroopananda how she felt. Serena felt it was disrespectful to the universe, to God, not to acknowledge the blessing that had been bestowed upon her.

This particular yoga center was very old-school. This was not cardio yoga or yoga done in a room the temperature of Hell. This was good old-fashioned yoga, and now they were doing their leg lifts. "Left leg up, and down. Right leg up, and down." As she spoke, her mind wandered. She planned how she was going to talk to him. She decided she would break the cardinal rule and go into Swami Swaroop's bedroom after class. She would gently and sweetly just tell him what they both already knew and felt. She would describe the depth of her emotions, not to ask for any decisions or commitments, but just wanting a release from the secret. It should be a celebration, this feeling, and she needed to be able to celebrate it, even if only between the two of them. Just then, as she looked out onto her class and all the legs that were being raised in the air, she saw something that made her gasp. It sounded something like this: "Now both legs, up, and down . . . up, and . . . kahhh!"

Of the twelve raised female legs in the yoga class, four of them were sporting little black strings around the ankle.

Serena immediately tried to control her breathing—she was a swami and yoga teacher after all. She recovered enough to say, "Excuse me. Now both legs up, and down, up and down."

She searched her mind for an explanation. Maybe it was some kind of new trend that Britney Spears or some other celebrity created to honor some disease. Wait! Don't the people who are into Kabbalah wear little strings? These women were all Kabbalists. That's the answer. She got through the class, peacefully and with equanimity. She comforted herself with the knowledge that these women all changed in the same dressing room before and after class—surely they would have noticed the strings. Swami Swaroop knew she taught these women yoga, he knew she was bound to see their ankles during a leg raise or shoulder stand. What kind of man would give all the women he slept with a black string? No. There was some other explanation and she was in love and she was still going to tell him how she felt.

Right after class, Serena looked in the different yoga rooms and offices to see if he was around, but didn't see him anywhere. She went to his room and heard the familiar sound of Swami Swaroop's heavy breathing, doing his morning Pranayama. She walked in without knocking.

The first thing she saw was the black string. On the ankle of Prema, the nineteen-year-old intern who worked in their tiny bookstore/boutique. That string was raised high above Prema's head. Swami Swaroop was on top of her on the bed, thrusting and Pranayamaing away. He looked up and saw Serena staring at him. With incredible equanimity, her breath slow and steady, even as her heart was racing and her hands were shaking, Serena quietly shut the door, making sure she didn't disturb anyone at the center.

She then walked lightly down the stairs to the basement and slipped into the dressing room. There were three women left there—three whom she saw with strings on their ankles. They all looked like they were just about to leave.

"Hi, Swamiji," said the thin twenty-two-year-old girl with the light brown hair and the long brown hairy armpits. She was putting her coat on. "That was a great class."

"Yeah, really great," said the thirty-five-year-old blond-haired woman. She was now wearing a business suit and putting on her lipstick in the mirror.

"Thanks, I was just . . . was there a sweatshirt in here? Someone called and said they left it."

The ladies, including a fifty-something woman with an outrageously hot buff body, all started helpfully looking. Serena didn't know exactly what she wanted to do or say, but she knew she had to do or say something.

"Wow. That's so funny. I noticed in class you all have black strings around your ankles. Are you all into Kabbalah?"

The women looked at one another and smiled mischievously.

"I think that's a red string," the hairy-armpits girl said.

They all started giggling. The fifty-something politely said, "Actually, we belong to a different kind of cult."

"Really?"

The women looked at one another, not saying another word. They all started collecting their bags and getting ready to scurry out of there as quickly as possible. The blond business-suit lady opened the door to the dressing room, about to make her exit.

Before she realized it, Serena had kicked the door shut and was keeping it closed, her right foot flat against it. The black string on Serena's right ankle was now completely in view. The women's eyes got wide at the sight of it. The hairy-armpitted girl was incredulous. She pointed at Serena.

"But . . . you're a *swami*," she said, outraged.

"So is Swami Swaroopananda!" Serena shouted back. "I don't get it! You all knew about each other and didn't care? Did he hit on you all at once and you guys decided to go for it as a group?"

The buff woman spoke, calmly. "Swami Swaroop came on to me about six months ago, actually, in this very dressing room."

Been there, done that, thought Serena, as the twenty-two-year-old at the same time giggled, "Been there, done that!"

"Anyway," the buff hottie continued, "when he gave me the string, I thought it was sweet. Soon enough I saw Gina had one," she said as she gestured to the blonde, "and so did Ricki," as she gestured to the armpit.

"I didn't care because I'm married; it's just for fun. We talked about it one day in the dressing room and we had a big laugh."

"He's so hot," Ricki said, "we were happy to share."

"Share? Hot? He's a swami?!"

The blonde smiled naughtily. "His spirituality, the forbidden nature of it. It's very hot. But you must know that. You're a swami, too, so that's doubly taboo."

"Doubly taboo. Yeah. That's super hot," said Ricki, who was now less incredulous and more jealous.

The women all looked at Serena enviously and it seemed for a moment that they wished that they had shaved their heads and been sworn to celibacy and orange clothes just to get the added naughtiness of it all.

"So, you're all basically his harem, is that what you're saying?" Serena asked, outraged.

The women all kind of smiled. The blonde shrugged. "Guess you're a part of it now, too."

Serena shook her head furiously. She reached down and grabbed the string around her ankle and pulled. And pulled some more. It wouldn't budge. It's amazing how durable a piece of string can be sometimes. She pulled a few more times until it seemed that she might start cutting through skin. Then she scanned the room, desperately looking for a sharp object. Nothing.

"Does anyone have a fucking key?" Serena the Swami shrieked.

The blonde quickly handed over her house keys. Serena took them, using a single key to start sawing away at her ankle string. The women watched, a little alarmed, as Serena tried to emancipate herself.

"Here's what I'm not a part of. Anyone's fucking harem. This is fucking *bullshit*." And as she said *bullshit*, the string broke. Serena turned and immediately stormed out, leaving the women standing there.

She ran back up the stairs to Swami Swaroopananda's bedroom, but it was empty. Serena remembered that he taught a meditation class at that time.

Oh, fuck it, she thought. And she raced back down the stairs to the Kali Room and opened the door. Three women and two men were breathing in and out; Swami Swaroopananda was now in class leading them in an "om." Serena walked in and threw the piece of string at him. It fell right in front of her, invisible, with the result that she looked more like she had just angrily pawed at the air. Swami Swaroopananda opened his eyes and Serena saw that at that moment, underneath the powerful spirituality that he might be always emanating, there was also a slight twinge of fear. She picked up the string and threw it at him again. It again fell right in front of her. Swami Swaroopananda blinked.

"I loved you. Did you know that? *I loved you.*"

Swami Swaroop got up to somehow stop the impending train wreck. But Serena turned and stormed out of that room as well. She ran all the way back up the stairs to Swami Swaroopananda's room again. She walked in and opened up his closet, taking out every single orange thing in it. She then raced down a flight of stairs to her own room, now taking all her own orange clothes and adding them to the pile. The heap of orange clothing was towering about three feet over her head, and she wasn't able to see very well, but Serena managed to carry it all down and out the front door, down the brick steps, and then dump it all on the sidewalk. Swami Premananda, the heavyset swami, had followed her out of the building.

"Swami Durgananda, please, you're creating bad karma for yourself. You are attaching too closely to your ego."

"Kiss my orange ass," Serena said.

By this point, Swami Swaroop and his students were outside on the stoop looking at Serena.

Serena looked up at Swami Swaroop and said, "Yeah, right, you burned up your desires for God." She then looked at the center's van parked right next to her. There was a "clergy" sign on the dashboard. It had taken the Jayananda Center a long time to get the city to agree to give them clergy status, and it helped them immensely with parking in New York. As her last act of defiance, Serena reached in the half-open window, scraping her arm and almost dislocating her elbow as she grabbed the sign, pulled it out, and ripped it to pieces in front of her little audience on the stoop.

"If you're a member of the clergy so is Howard Fucking Stern," Serena said as she ripped and ripped and ripped. She then started to stomp on the orange pile of clothes as if trying to put out a fire.

So, this was how Serena's career as a swami came to a spectacular end. The students and Swami Swaroop went inside, and Swami Premananda asked Serena to immediately pack her things and go before she had to call the police. Serena was only too happy to oblige.

Back in Australia

That night, the jet lag was at it again. At four in the morning, I got up and reread one of Fiona's columns in the *Hobart News*. In this piece, she was telling a woman to mentally spoon herself—she needed to wrap her self-love around herself every night before she went to bed. I wanted to kill this woman.

She had an email address where one could contact her, and since it was four in the morning and I was an angry and bitter woman, I decided to write. It went something like this:

"Don't you think it's a little irresponsible of you to tell women that all they have to do is love themselves and be optimistic and love will find them? What if they live somewhere where there are literally no men? What if they are older or overweight or unattractive? All they have to do is love themselves and be confident and filled with joy and someone will appear to love them? Really? Can you guarantee that? Can we call you when we're eighty years old and tell you how it worked out for us? And if you were wrong, can we come and punch you in the face?"

I didn't send that one. I sent this one.

"Don't you think it's a little irresponsible of you to tell women that all they have to do is love themselves and be optimistic and love will find them? What if they live somewhere where there are literally no men? Do you really think the statistics, the reality of it all, means nothing? That we can all, if we shine brightly enough, not be one of the statistics?" I then went on to explain that I was writing a book about single women, and I was single myself, and this was of great interest to me.

I finally got to bed around six. When I woke up at ten, Alice had left a note that she was at the free breakfast downstairs. I got up and checked my email to see if Ms. Fiona had anything to say for herself. She had.

"Julie, I'd like to talk to you in person, if you fancy. It's a much better way to explain myself. Could you take a little day trip to Tasmania so we can chat?"

Well, that was awfully civilized. I wondered if she did that for every disgruntled reader. Maybe she was one of those people pleasers, always trying to make sure no one was mad at her. Or maybe it's because I mentioned that I was from New York and I was writing a book. That seemed to be opening up a lot of doors for me.

I went down to breakfast. Alice was there, with a large pot of coffee next to her, making an awful face.

"I just tried Vegemite. I've been looking at it now for days, and I thought it might be time to try it. Jesus, that stuff tastes like ass." She took a big gulp of water and then added, "Yeasty ass."

I poured myself a cup of coffee. "Alice, how would you like to go to Tasmania with me today?"

"That's a real place?" she asked seriously. Again, Americans, not so great with the geography.

"Yes, it's a real place. I want to go talk to a woman there who writes about dating in Australia. She's really, like . . . cheerful."

Alice looked at me. "Cheerful? About dating in Australia?" She put down her piece of toast dramatically. "This I've got to see."

Back in the States

Georgia decided not to take things lying down. She was still new to dating, so she felt that somehow she would be able, with the sheer force of her will and clever strategy, to win. So she came up with a plan. The first step was to call up Sam and see if he could fit a dinner at her place into his busy dating schedule. She knew that he was a good guy, so if necessary she would appeal to his good manners. She picked up the phone, ready to leave a message. But he picked up.

"Hey, Georgia, how are you? Are you feeling better?"

"Oh. Hi, Sam. I am. I'm so sorry about the other night. I was wondering if I could make it up to you."

"Oh, there's no need . . ."

"Well, I want to. I was wondering if you'd like to come over for dinner some night when the kids are with their father."

"Sure, that would be great. I actually had plans this Saturday night that fell through. Would you be free then?"

"That would be great. How about eight o'clock?"

"Great."

Georgia smiled, satisfied, and gave him her address.

Saturday night came and everything was going according to plan. Georgia was making her famous Chicken Riesling for dinner, and the smell of the chicken, cream, and herbs was permeating the apartment. She also had hundreds of dollars' worth of flowers bought by Dale's credit card, placed in conspicuous places all around the apartment. Note cards from the person who had supposedly sent the flowers were placed perfectly casually near each bouquet, along with remnants of some ribbons and paper in which they had arrived. She had the Shiraz breathing and she looked gorgeous. Everything was perfect. The doorbell rang and Sam was there, holding a tiny bouquet of flowers.

"Hi!" From his expression Georgia knew what he was thinking: she was prettier than he remembered.

"Wow. You look great!"

"Thanks." Georgia ushered him in the door. He gave her his tiny bundle of six roses, just as he noticed the huge bouquets of flowers that seemed to be everywhere.

"Wow, I guess you must like flowers," Sam said, sort of awkwardly, looking around. For a moment Georgia saw a little bit of the insecurity she had seen on their first date. Her plan was already working; she had caught her enemy off guard. Georgia acted out an "embarrassed fluster" with the ease of Julia Roberts.

"Oh, those . . . it's a long . . . guys . . . you know, sometimes they get, you know . . . overenthusiastic. They're nice though, aren't they?"

"They're beautiful."

"But yours are beautiful, too, oh my God. Beautiful. Let me put them in water."

Georgia took Sam's minuscule bouquet and put the six sad roses in a vase. She couldn't have predicted he would have brought her flowers; that was just a little gift from the heavens.

"So how have you been? Good? Busy, I'm sure," Georgia asked as she put the roses out on the counter.

"Yes. Definitely busy. But it's nice to be here."

"I'm so glad you're here. It's hard making plans with so much going on for the both of us. It's amazing this was even able to happen. Please, have a seat."

Georgia motioned to the stool by the counter of her beautiful open kitchen. He sat down as commanded and she gave him a glass of Shiraz. This time he would be the one sitting while she was standing. While she put the finishing touches on the meal, they laughed as she told stories of disastrous meals she had made in her day. So far, a great date.

Then Sam told a story about one of his kids. It was rather involved, about a parent of one of the kids on his son's Little League team. It was an amusing story, and he was telling it confidently. Georgia was laughing when the phone rang. Like clockwork.

"I'll let it go to voice mail. Keep going, please."

"So the man went crazy, screaming and yelling, and he had this ice cream in his hand . . ." Just then, a desperate male voice came out of Georgia's answering machine.

"Hey, Georgia, this is Hal. Just wanted to let you know I had a great time last night. I hope I'll get to see you again soon. How about Wednesday? Are you free Wednesday? I can't stop thinking about—"

Georgia "raced" over to the machine. "I'm so sorry, it's . . . I thought I'd turned down the machine . . ." She adjusted the phone, then turned to Sam, an actual blush on her cheeks. "I'm sorry. Continue, please."

Sam just looked at her, a little surprised.

"Wow. He's got it bad."

"No, it's just, we went to this play that was really funny and it just was a great . . . never mind . . . it's not—please, what happened with the ice cream?"

Sam stood up from his stool and leaned on the counter, him on one side of it, her on the other. Suddenly, the counter seemed like a big desk and he was on a job interview. Or an audition.

Sam laughed nervously. "Right. So anyway, the coach told him that if he didn't calm down, he was going to kick his kid off the team for good.

The guy took the ice-cream cone and just flung it right at the coach, like a two-year-old. Then his kid just ran over to him and said . . ."

Just then the answering machine picked up and another man's voice was heard, deep and commanding—the voice of a CIA operative or president of the United States.

"Hey. Georgia, this is Jordan. I really enjoyed our having drinks the other night and I was hoping I could see—" Georgia feigned surprise and irritation at herself.

"I'm so sorry, I must have turned the ringer off instead of the machine, this is so rude . . ." She went to the phone and fiddled with some more buttons.

"It's off now. It's completely off," Georgia said sheepishly. "I'm *so* sorry."

"It's fine. No problem," Sam said. Georgia noticed that Sam was truly flustered at this point. He didn't even comment on this particular man's message, and Georgia chose not to explain it. She thought it was best to let the other man's desire hang in the air.

"So what did his kid say?" she asked sweetly.

Sam looked at Georgia and then back down at the counter. "Nothing. It was nothing."

"Well, dinner's ready anyway."

They began eating, but everything was different. For one thing, Sam was now really looking at her. Women spend so much time wondering how the men they're with feel about them; they'll analyze emails, replay phone messages. But the simple fact is that all you have to do is watch how he looks at you. If he looks at you as if he doesn't want to take his eyes off you for fear that you might disappear, then you are with a man who really likes you. And now, that was how Sam was looking at Georgia. At the pub he barely made eye contact. Now he was staring at her, hard.

Georgia had pulled off a feat that Wall Street brokers and economists would be in awe of. In just one hour, she had raised her stock by manufacturing "demand" out of thin air, and it looked like there might be a bidding war. She made herself seem to be the one thing that everything in our culture wants her to believe she is not: valuable. And all it took was a couple of hundred dollars' worth of flowers and phone calls from the gay couple down the hall. She watched Sam try to impress her with his jokes, nervously running his fingers through his hair. She smiled to herself when he touched her arm to make a point or she felt his eyes follow her as she went to get more wine. At the end of the date he only stopped kissing her when Georgia told him it was time to go.

Now, you may ask, did Georgia feel badly that it was all a lie? That she had to create an entire reality in order to feel good about herself? Did she feel badly that none of this was true? That she actually sent herself flowers to get some midwestern cornhead's attention? No. All she felt in this moment was proud. She saw reality and she refused to kid herself about it. With clearheadedness and foresight, she'd understood the power shift that had occurred with Sam and his new view of the world and then did something about it. She made herself into a "catch" and she felt that someone should give her a medal for it. Women are fucked, the numbers are against them, time is against them, and if their only recourse is to completely fabricate a personal life in order to jump up a notch in the brutal dating pecking order, then that's just fine.

Sam called her the next day. His voice sounded nervous, probably wondering if hot, sought-after Georgia would even take his call.

"Hey, Georgia. It's Sam."

"Hi, Sam!" Georgia said, warmly. "How are you?"

"Great, great," Sam said, trying to sound cheerful, but not too eager. "Listen, I just wanted to let you know that I had a really great time last night and I was hoping I could see you again soon."

Georgia had already decided what she was going to do when this call came (which she knew it would). "Listen, Sam, I had a great time, too. But I just got off the phone with Hal, and we've decided to see each other exclusively."

Sam cleared his throat. "Oh. Okay. Wow. Well, I'm really disappointed, I'm not going to lie, but I appreciate you telling me."

She knew her decision was a risky one. She had cut off the only dating prospect she had. And, as I've made clear, we love the dating prospects. But at the end of the day, Georgia wanted to be with someone who didn't have anything to prove to himself, who didn't need to play the field, and didn't need competition to notice how valuable Georgia was. Besides, flowers are really expensive.

• • •

Unfortunately, Serena had let go of her apartment, something no one in New York should ever do, whether for a relocation, a marriage, or a baby. Only if you're dead, then maybe you can give it up. Even then, try not to.

But Serena did. So now she was hairless and homeless. As I had sublet my apartment, and Serena didn't have money for a hotel, she didn't really know what to do. So she called up the one person who would understand the depression into which she was about to plunge. She called Ruby and asked if she could crash at her house. Ruby, being Ruby, immediately agreed.

When I heard what happened, via a text message, I thought it might be best to do a conference call. I even asked Georgia to come by to make sure the two of them were going to be okay together. I worry sometimes.

Alice and I were still in Sydney, packing to take our trip to Tasmania. Ruby was sitting at her dining room table with Serena and Georgia. They were all on speakerphone and I shouted my disbelief.

"A guy who's not supposed to be having sex with anyone was having sex with at least five different women!?"

"Who were all more than happy to share him. THEY WERE ALL MORE THAN HAPPY TO SHARE HIM," Serena shouted back.

Georgia just shook her head. "Wow. Now celibate guys are having harems. It's the end of the world."

"Maybe they should just start euthanizing us all," Ruby said, almost to herself.

Everyone gasped, even me, on the phone.

"What?!" I said, hoping that my connection had made me misunderstand.

"I mean it," Ruby said matter-of-factly. "Just like with the dogs. Maybe the mayor's office should just start killing off all women who are ill-tempered, not in perfect health, have bad teeth, or whatever. To give the good candidates a better chance at finding a suitable home."

We were all stunned into silence. Clearly things at the animal shelter had started to get to Ruby.

Serena finally asked, "You're the one I've decided to live with to cheer me up?"

Georgia said, "Ruby, I don't know you very well, so please forgive me if this comes out wrong, but if you don't pick up the phone and quit that volunteer job right this minute I will have to punch you in the face."

"Seriously, Ruby, that was the worst thing I have ever heard anyone say in my entire life," I added.

Georgia started to laugh. "I can't believe you actually said that."

Serena started to giggle. "You actually suggested that the city start *gassing* us."

Ruby threw her head down on the table and started laughing, starting to see how far she'd fallen. "Oh my God, and I still kind of believe it. I'm losing my mind!"

Alice and I were in our hotel in Australia, listening to them all scream with laughter.

Georgia took out her cell phone. "Gimme the number. Of the shelter. Now."

Ruby did as she was told. Georgia dialed her cell phone and handed the phone to Ruby. Ruby began to speak.

"Hello? This is Ruby Carson. I'm a volunteer there. I wanted to let you know that I won't be coming in again. It's very bad for my mental health, thank you." She quickly hung up as Ruby and Georgia burst into applause.

"I couldn't hear—did Ruby just quit her volunteer job?" I asked from the other side of the world.

"Yes. Yes, she did," Georgia said. "Now we just have to get Serena a job and our mission for tonight will be accomplished."

"Can you go back to your old job? With the movie star?" Alice asked.

Serena shrugged. "I'm sure they hired someone else."

I piped in on my end. "But Serena, from everything you told me about them, they sounded really nice. You seemed to really like them."

"It's true," Serena said into the phone. "I've actually missed them a little. Joanna really was sweet to me. And Robert was really fun to be around."

Georgia got out her phone. "Call them and find out. What's their number?"

Serena hesitated.

"Please, I'm not going to sell it to *People* magazine. I'm just trying to get you a job."

Serena gave Georgia the number. Georgia dialed and handed the phone to Serena.

"Hello, Joanna? This is Serena." Everyone watched as Serena listened to the voice on the other end. Serena's eyes began to light up.

"Well, actually, it's funny you ask. It didn't really work out for me at the yoga center. So I was wondering if you were . . . really? Oh. Wow. Great. Yeah, I'll come by tomorrow and we can talk about it. Okay. See you then."

Serena closed Georgia's phone, looking puzzled. "They don't have anyone."

Georgia clapped and said, "That's amazing!"

"Yeah," Serena said. "But I don't know . . . she sort of sounded sad."

"What?" I said, the sound having dipped out for a minute.

Serena leaned into the phone and said again, louder, "*She sounded sad.*"

Back to Australia

The flight to Tasmania was only an hour and a half long. I imagined it would be an island wilderness with kangaroos hopping around, and aboriginal tribespeople greeting us with their didgeridoos. But Hobart, the capital of Tasmania, is quite civilized. It's a quaint, colonial-feeling town on a picturesque harbor. Short sandstone buildings line the streets, renovated into pubs and shops. Sadly, I even saw a Subway sandwich shop there.

I had emailed Fiona before we left Sydney, telling her that we'd be coming. She kindly offered to meet us at the local pub to talk. I was still suspecting she had an agenda—being a New Yorker, I had to assume she couldn't be doing this just to be nice.

I have to admit, my mood was not very good. It's one thing to read the lousy statistics, it's another to watch them played out with above-the-head-staring men, women who feel over the hill at thirty-five, and young men who are dividing by two and adding four. In New

York, there's not much difference between the way a twenty-five-year-old behaves and a thirty-five-year-old. In New York, if you're pushing forty, you can be so busy having a good time it doesn't even faze you when you get an invitation to your twentieth high school reunion. But in Sydney, my bubble of self-delusion officially burst. For the first time in my life, I felt old.

We met at a harborside Irish pub with a long wooden bar and a giant sign that said "Fishmonger."

As soon as we walked in, we heard, "Now these must be my New York girls!" A woman walked toward us with her arms outstretched and a big smile on her face. She was exactly as I imagined, with a round, open face and pale Britishy skin. She had thin, light brown hair that was pulled back in a ponytail. She was absolutely pleasant to look at—appealing, innocuous, and a bit bland. She looked us over. "Why you're absolutely gorgeous!" I immediately felt guilty for thinking she looked bland. She ushered us to the bar. "Come on now, if you're here in Hobart, you're going to have to have a pint. Have you tried the James Boag's?"

"No," I said. "I don't really drink beer."

"Me neither," Alice said.

"But you must try just a bit. You're at the docks. We can't have you sipping wine down here, now can we?" Both Alice and I were thinking, *Why yes, yes you can,* when Fiona went to the bar and ordered beers for us. She waited until they came, paid for them, and gave them to us.

"Now tell me, do you think I'm an absolute idiot for the things I write? Are you here to tell me off? Come on, let's have it then." She was so warm and open, I didn't have the heart to get all combative with her.

"I didn't come here to yell at you, it's just . . ."

"I seem too much all sunshine and lollies, is that it?"

"It's just that you telling women to love themselves and they'll find love seems, I don't know . . ."

"Like a lie," Alice jumped in to say. "It's statistically impossible. Even if we all started marrying gay men, the numbers still wouldn't work out."

Fiona took the criticism in stride. "The statistics are very compelling. Did you hear that someone suggested we give our blokes tax incentives just to stay in Australia? What kind of rubbish is that? They already think they're God's gifts, the men here." Fiona waved at some women walking into the bar. "Katie! Jane! We're over here!" She looked back at Alice and me. "Just try and get a man to take you out on a proper date; it's like trying to make a koala run." Katie and Jane came over and Fiona kissed them both on the cheeks and introduced us all.

"I'm just telling them dating in Tasmania doesn't exist."

Jane and Katie nodded knowingly.

"Well, what do you do instead?" Alice asked, curious.

Fiona took a gulp of beer and laughed. "Well, we go down to the pub, get drunk, fall on top of each other, and hope for the best. It's a frightful situation, really."

We all laughed. Fiona kept waving and kissing people hello. She greeted each person with something flattering, and with each person she really seemed to mean it.

I realized that we were in the presence of one of those people God has blessed with an abundance of serotonin and a joyful disposition. You know. A happy person.

"And it's true. I do tell my readers that if you just love your life and are filled with that, then you're going to be irresistible—and the men are just going to come out of the woodwork."

I couldn't help but become insistent. "But that's simply not true. I know dozens of single women who are fantastic and ready and charming and shining and they can't find boyfriends."

"And they're not too picky. They don't have unrealistic expectations," Alice chimed in. She knew a loophole when she saw one.

It was starting to get crowded and the music was up loud, so Fiona practically shouted at us. "Yet!"

"What?" I asked.

"They haven't found boyfriends *yet*. It's not over for them, is it?"

"No. But, that's their reality now."

"And tomorrow everything could change. That's what I think about. Tomorrow everything could change!" As if on cue, a guy in a t-shirt and long cargo shorts walked over to Fiona and said hello to her. She greeted him warmly and kissed him on the cheek. "This is Errol. We fell on each other last summer and were together for three whole weeks, isn't that right?" Errol smiled sheepishly. She playfully pinched his ear. "He was a real wanker to me. Weren't you, Errol?"

"I was an asshole. It's true." Then he walked away.

"So tell me, Julie. What do you think I should tell people? What do you think we should believe?" Fiona asked, good-naturedly.

There it is, that question again. What do I believe in? I looked around the bar. It was a sea of men and women, predominantly women. And the women looked as if they were trying a lot harder than the men.

"That maybe life isn't fair," I said. "That just as not everyone is guaranteed to win the lottery or have perfect health or get along with their family, not everyone is guaranteed to have someone love them." I was on a roll now. "Maybe then we can start a new way to think about life. One that doesn't make it so tragic if love happens to be the thing you end up not getting."

Fiona thought about it for a moment. "I'm sorry, ladies. If I told my readers that, I'd be responsible for the first mass suicide in the history of Australia. There would be hundreds of girls floating facedown in the Tasman Sea."

Alice and I looked at each other. It did sound pretty dark, even to us. "Besides, I think it goes against human nature," Fiona said. "We all want to love and be loved. That's just the way it is."

"Is that human nature, or is that Hollywood?" Alice asked.

A band started to play on a tiny stage set up in the back of the room. They were a lively Irish band, and soon the dance floor was full of drunken white people jumping up and down.

I thought out loud. "Maybe our true human nature is to be in a community. That's the only thing that seems to endure. Much more than marriage, that's for sure."

Fiona got very serious. She stood up and placed a hand on each of our shoulders, looking squarely at us. "I have to say this, and I really mean it from the bottom of my heart. You both are gorgeous women. You are smart and funny and hot. To think that you would end up with no love in your lives is absolutely bullcrap. It's just not possible. You two are goddesses. I know you don't want to believe me, but it's true. Beautiful, sexy goddesses. And you shouldn't consider, even for a moment, that you won't have as much happiness in your life as you can possibly stand." With that, Fiona turned to get another beer.

My eyes started to water up. Alice turned to me, her eyes a little teary as well. She was good, this one.

The music and the dancing became even more raucous and Alice grabbed my hand and dragged me onto the dance floor to jump up and down. Fiona came with us, along with about ten of her closest girlfriends. I watched her, laughing and twirling and singing along to some lyrics I couldn't understand. No matter what I say, no matter how smart I am, I could clearly see that Fiona was happier than me. She had inoculated herself against the poison of the statistics that had weighed me down all week. As I watched the sweat start forming on her cheeks, and her face lit up with laughter, I had to admit it. She was one of those people that everyone wants to be around, and at the end of the day, people who are positive and optimistic are simply more attractive than people who are negative and pessimistic. Alice put her arm around me and pretended to sing a song that we couldn't understand the words to. "Fly into my flah flah baby baba ba . . . yeah." Fiona was dancing with Errol and Jane and Katie, making them laugh by trying to do a hip-hop step. Alice said loudly into my ear, "I like her. She's cool."

A handsome, rugged-looking guy then walked onto the dance floor, making his way through the crowd and right toward Fiona. When she saw him, she threw her arms around him and he gave her a big kiss on the lips. They spoke for a few moments together, their arms wrapped around each other. He went up to the bar, and Fiona saw the curious expressions on our faces and came up to us to explain.

"We just met a few weeks ago. His name is George. I'm absolutely mad about him. He's lived in Hobart his entire life, but we'd never laid eyes on each other till last month. Isn't that the strangest thing?"

Alice and I just looked at her, confused. "Were you not going to tell us about him?" I asked, amused.

Fiona just shrugged, laughing. "Don't you hate those women who think they know everything just because they managed to meet a nice guy? I'd rather die than have you think I was her!"

I looked at Fiona, impressed. She had the ultimate weapon in her arsenal, and she didn't use it. She purposely chose not to play the "well, look how well it worked for me" card. She wanted to make sure I didn't feel that my point of view was any less valid than hers just because she had a boyfriend and I didn't. This truly made her a goddess, and taught me another important rule: *When you finally do fall in love, don't you dare be smug about it.*

In our taxi back to the Hobart airport, I couldn't stop thinking about Fiona. It would be dishonest if I didn't admit that she had been right, in a sense. She shone her light so brightly that a man did actually appear out of the woodwork of Hobart for her. Did that mean I believed that that would happen to everyone who behaved like her? No. Did I suddenly think everyone is guaranteed love in this life? No. Did it make me think that you should ignore the statistics and just make sure you're absolutely adorable? No.

But here's what I did learn from Fiona and Australia about statistics and being single: *One hundred percent of all human beings need hope to get by. And if any statistic takes that away from you, then it's not worth knowing.*

And take trips as often as possible to places where you know there will be lots of men.

Hey, there's nothing wrong with trying to help your odds.

It was time for Alice to get back to New York. In our hotel room in Sydney, as I watched Alice pack, I became filled with homesickness. I missed my bed, my friends, my city. Also, Sydney had rattled me. The farther I got from Fiona and her glow, the less hopeful and optimistic I became. I made a decision.

"I'm going home. I'm going to go home and back to my job and work off my advance and be done with this. I can't do this anymore."

Alice sat on the bed, deciding what she should say.

"I'm sorry you're feeling this way. But I think this has been good for you. You've always been so responsible, you've always had a desk job. It's good for you to not know what's going to happen next."

To me, it was excruciating. I felt unbearably lonely.

"I feel just so . . . frightened."

Alice nodded. "Me, too. But I don't think it's time for you to go home. I just don't."

As I walked Alice to her cab, she asked, "Why don't you go to India? Everyone seems to have some kind of spiritual awakening there."

"Serena said the same thing. I'll think about it."

As the cab pulled away, Alice called out, "Keep going, Julie! You're not done yet!"

I watched her drive away, and was again filled with an unbearable loneliness. *Why was I putting myself through this? And why hadn't Thomas ever called me?* Now this wasn't a new thought; I had thought it every day since Italy, because as I might have mentioned before, I am a pathetic creature and when we women have a connection with someone, geez, it's hard to let it go. The good news is, I never called him. Thank God. Thank God. Because here's a rule I've learned about how to be single, a rule I learned the hard way and didn't have to travel around the world to find: *Don't call him, don't call him, don't call him.* And then, just when you think you have the perfect excuse to call him, *don't call him.* Right now, I was seriously considering calling him.

Just then, the phone rang. I answered it and a man with a French accent was speaking to me.

"Is this Julie?" he asked.

"Yes, it is," I said, not believing what I thought I was hearing.

"It is Thomas." My heart immediately began racing.

"Oh. Wow. Thomas. Wow. How are you?"

"I am well. Where are you? Singapore? Timbuktu?"

"I'm in Sydney."

"Australia? That's perfect. Bali is very close."

"Bali?" I repeated, shifting my weight from one foot to the other nervously.

"Yes. I have some business I need to do there. Why don't you meet me?"

My heart skipped a beat. "I don't know about that . . ."

Then Thomas's voice became much more serious. "Julie. I made a promise to myself. If I could go three days without thinking about you, without wanting to pick up the phone to ask when I could see you again, then I would never call you. I wasn't able to go one day."

It was a shocking thing to hear someone say. Especially in Sydney, where my self-esteem had taken a beating, where my light was on its last watt.

"Julie. Please don't make me beg. Meet me in Bali."

I looked around Sydney Harbor and thought about statistics. What were the odds that a handsome French man would want to see me in Bali? What were the odds that it would ever happen again? And what about the wife?

So I asked, "But what about your wife?"

"She knows I'm going to Bali, but the rest, she doesn't ask."

I said yes. Because on the rare occasion that the odds happen to be in your favor, how can you say no?

Admit That Sometimes You Feel Desperate
(I Won't Tell a Soul)

When Alice arrived back in New York, she was a changed woman. Sydney had done something to her. She was scared. Although she was impressed with Fiona, it didn't stay with her long. As she thought back on the past six months of dating and Australia and the man who didn't want to dance with her, she had to admit to herself: it's hell out there. She had made the best of it, she had given it her Alice-who-can-do-anything all, but the thought of ever having to date again was too much for her to bear. She was so relieved to be with Jim that it almost bordered on delirium. Was she in love with him? No. Was this the man of her dreams? Absolutely not. But she appreciated him to the point that it was almost like being in love, almost like he was the man of her dreams.

And so Alice, redheaded, Staten Island superhero Alice, was ready to settle. Never in court, not a chance, but now, in her life. She saw a flash of a vision of her future without Jim and it truly scared her.

She was walking down Prince Street, thinking all these things, as she headed to meet Jim for the first time since she had gotten home from Sydney. She turned the corner and there he was, in the window of a nice little dive bar, the only one still left in Soho. He was on time, of course. He saw Alice through the window and smiled and waved. She smiled and waved back, picking up her pace so that by the time she was inside she was at a gallop. She threw her arms around him and kissed him hard on the lips. He laughed, surprised, and wrapped his arms around her.

When they finally broke apart, Alice looked at him with utmost seriousness. "Let's get married," she whispered. Jim pulled away, putting his hands on her hips and looking directly in her eyes.

"Are you serious?" His voice was slightly breathy from shock and excitement.

"Absolutely," Alice said, smiling and laughing. She hugged Jim as if she would never let go. Jim picked her up, right there in the bar, and twirled her around as she laughed and buried her head in his neck.

So what if it wasn't exactly how she imagined it would be? Sure, there was no knee and ring and proposal, and she was the one who had asked. But he did scoop her up in his arms and let her know that he felt like the luckiest guy on earth.

As she laughed and twirled she thought to herself, *I really do love Jim. I do.*

On the Way to Bali

I was on the plane from Tokyo to Denpasar, Bali, when it happened. I had been in a nice, sound Lexomil sleep when I suddenly woke up. I was seated on the aisle. The shade on the window on my row had not been closed, so I was able to look out at the utter blackness. Something about all that blackness, that abyss right when I woke up, started my heart beating. Fast. I started breathing heavy, my chest suddenly heaving up and down. I was gasping for air as though I was being strangled. My neighbor, a pudgy Asian man in his twenties, was asleep, his little blue blanket tucked around his chin, his head resting against the black window. The poor thing had no idea there was a crazy lady next to him. I looked around. Everyone was pretty much asleep. I assumed it would really freak them out to wake up to the sound of an American woman screaming at the top of her lungs. I leaned over, propping my elbows on my thighs, and held my head in my hands and tried to breathe. But it felt like there was blackness all around, about to swallow me up whole. Tears formed in my eyes and I desperately tried to hold them back.

Of course, I didn't want to cry because I didn't want to disturb my fellow passengers, alarm the flight attendants, embarrass myself, or otherwise cause a scene. But there was a much more pressing and vainer reason why I didn't want to start tearing up. When I cry, even if it's one drop, my eyes puff up like two Jiffy Pop containers and the circles under my eyes become instantaneously jet-black and loop down practically to my chin. My main concern was that I was meeting Thomas at the airport in Denpasar, and I wanted to look pretty. There, I said it.

I wondered if there was a way to cry without making a sound or producing tears. I tried it for a few seconds, contorting my face in this crazy silent sob while blinking rapidly so as not to let any water well up. I can't even imagine what I looked like. Of course since I was in the middle of a panic attack and had no control over myself, this didn't work. I started to cry. I was crying because I was having a panic attack, and I was also crying because I knew I was going to look hideous now. We only had thirty minutes left on the flight and were going to have to belt ourselves in soon for the descent. I decided to go to the bathroom, where at least I could go crazy in private. I managed to gain control of myself enough to walk down the aisle, past all the men, women, teenagers, children, and babies, sleeping. I walked as fast as I could to the bathroom and went in. I sat on the toilet and released an immediate sob and then kept going. I tried to do this as quietly as I could; I had enough self-protection remaining that I didn't want an international incident. I started rocking back and forth on the toilet seat, my arms wrapped around myself like a disturbed little child. I grabbed at my hair. I crumpled farther in to myself. At some point I looked in the mirror and saw my hundred-year-old turtle face. I cried even harder. I felt lost, suspended in the air, in darkness. I didn't know where I was going or what I was doing—with Thomas, with love, with my life. I felt catastrophe was imminent.

I splashed some cold water on my face. It never helps. Ever. Why do people tell you to do that? They announced that we had to get into our seats for landing, so I stood at the sink and willed myself to calm down. I closed my eyes and focused on slowly getting my breathing back to normal. I started to relax. In a minute I was completely fine, as if nothing had happened. I walked to my seat and sat down quietly in my chair. I looked over at the cozily sleeping neighbor and felt victorious. Yes, I had an attack, but this time, no one noticed. I was able to contain it to the bathroom. I knew I looked like hell, and no amount of makeup was going to change that. But for now, this was good enough.

In situations like this, when you're seeing someone you haven't seen in a while, and the stakes are maybe a little high, and there's a nervousness and a feeling of not knowing what to expect, I think the first second you lay eyes on them is everything. That's the moment when you realize exactly how you feel about that person, and how your time together is going to go. I was now at baggage claim. I glanced at the clock on the wall. It was midnight. There were a lot of tired tourists waiting for their bags, and a lot of drivers milling about, hoping to catch a fare.

Then I saw him.

He was standing a little bit away from everyone else. He was wearing a brown t-shirt and jeans, and he was waving at me, his blue eyes sparkling. He was smiling, but not too broadly, just enough for me to know that he was delighted to see me. In a flash I was running up to him and hugging him. He wrapped his arms around me and held me, kissing my head. There we were, holding each other, kissing and smiling. We must have looked like the greatest of lovers.

He took my face in his hands and looked at me. "Now, tell me. How was your flight?"

I looked him straight in the eyes and I lied. "It was great. I didn't have any problems."

He examined my face and said, "Really? You look like you've been crying." I broke away from him and just sort of looked down at my feet. I lied again, saying, "No. It was fine, really. I'm just tired."

Thomas looked at me closely and smiled. "Okay, I'll pretend I believe you. Now let's get out of here!"

We got to our hotel at around two in the morning. A porter took us down a little stone pathway. When he opened the door to our accommodations, I couldn't help but gasp.

Thomas had reserved a huge villa for us, twice the size of my apartment. The walls were all glowing in light brown wood and the bamboo ceiling above seemed to go on forever, coming to a point high above our heads. There were marble floors and a king-size bed, which faced a private balcony. One side of the villa was all windows, looking out over endless rice paddies. Even at night, the view was stupendous.

"This is . . . this is so beautiful. I can't believe it!" I stammered. No one had ever taken me somewhere so beautiful. No one could ever afford to take me somewhere so beautiful. I turned to Thomas and just stared at him in wonder. He took me in his arms and kissed me.

Now how do I describe what happened next? Okay, let's just say that sometimes in life, after years of just coasting along, trying to make the best of a bad situation, keeping your chin up, sometimes the heavens give you a reward, a tiny little prize for all your hard work. Life gives you a brief taste of how simply glorious it all can be. You don't know how long it's going to last and you don't really care, because you know at that moment you have stumbled upon a little pond of bliss and you're not going to take a minute worrying about when you have to get out of the water.

What I mean to say is that for the next eight days, we didn't leave the hotel. We barely left the room, but if we did, it was only to have a meal. I can't even remember the last time that happened to me. The truth is, I don't have boyfriends that often. I have dates, I have flings, I have "situations." But I don't have men, one after the other, whom I cart around as my boyfriend, and then break up with for some reason or another and say later to my friends "What was I thinking?" Unfortunately, I always know what I'm thinking, and they do, too. So no one is really able to kid themselves for too long, and things pretty much end quickly and relatively painlessly. *Anyway*, all this is my way of saying that it had been a long time since I had spent a lot of time, day in and day out, with one man. It had been a long time since there was anyone with whom I wanted to spend a lot of time and who wanted to spend a lot of time with me. Someone I wanted to wake up with, have sex with, talk with, eat with, have more sex with, etc. It was sad that it felt so unusual. It made me realize how, when you're single, you really do get used to a lack of that kind of intimacy in your life. *Anyway,* what I am trying to say is that the week was unbroken happiness for me.

During that time, Thomas made nine phone calls, six about business, and three to his wife. He would always leave the room when he was talking to her, so I didn't know if she asked him when he was coming home or how he might have answered her. While he spoke with her, I would sit on the bed feeling a bit ashamed and deeply uncomfortable. I couldn't help wondering what kind of marriage they had. He was in every way a supremely intelligent man, one who did not suffer bullshit and valued honesty. But when it came to his marriage, was it real? If your spouse can go off with someone else on a whim, how can you think you really have a marriage? Or was I just minimizing his marriage in order not to feel like a dirty slut?

Eventually, I couldn't help myself—I asked him if his wife was wondering when he was coming home. He told me that they had an agreement—they could disappear for two weeks in a row, but no longer, no questions asked. Then, it was time to come home.

It was an interesting little arrangement, and now at least I knew when our time was up. I no longer had to wonder when our little honeymoon was going to be over. Two weeks, then "Selamat tinggal," as they say in Balinese.

On one of these days, while Thomas was making his calls, I was on the phone with my mother, just letting her know that I was safe and healthy. As I was getting off the phone with her, I heard my cell phone beep with another call coming in. I took it. The voice on the other end was distinct, superior, cold. It was Candace, my publisher, calling me from New York. A tiny jolt shot through me. I sat up a little straighter.

"Hello, Julie, this is Candace. I was just checking in to see how the work was going."

"Oh. Hi. Hello, Candace. Um. The work is going great. Really. I'm learning so much, it's amazing."

"Well, that's nice to hear. I was worried that you hadn't just taken off with some Italian and was spending all our money vacationing in *Capistrano*," she said with a perfect Italian accent.

"No, no, of course not. I'm working very hard. Very hard." At that moment I looked around and Thomas was in just a towel, heading to the little wading pool just outside our bedroom. I began to perspire a bit.

"Well, good. I realize the decision was made somewhat impetuously by me, but we did give you a check, and you did sign a contract, so I just want to make clear that we expect you to honor that."

"Of course," I said. Thomas then plunged into the pool, making a huge splashing sound. I put the phone close to my chest to try to muffle the sound. "I am happy to honor that. I'm gathering so much information, it's going to be an amazing book."

I made a few more assurances to her about how hard I was working, how many women I was talking to, and then I got off the phone with her as quickly as I could. I then tried to put the conversation out of my mind just as fast. I mean, I was on *vacation*, for God's sake.

So eventually, on our eighth day in Bali, we decided to venture outside our hotel and take walks. We strolled down Monkey Road and looked at some of the local art galleries. At one little café we sat and shared a plate of *ayam jeruk:* fresh chicken sautéed with garlic and coconut milk, the local specialty. As we sat staring into each other's eyes and smiling (I was glad to be far from home, so no one saw this moronic kind of behavior), a couple pulled up on a motorcycle. He was a young man, around twenty-five, and she was an older woman in her fifties. They put their helmets on the bike and sat down near us, talking and holding hands. Then she leaned over and kissed him. I stopped staring at Thomas and started staring at them.

Thomas watched me watch them, and smiled.

"Ah, the anthropologist has a new subject." I looked away from them. I had no idea how obvious I was.

"Well, it is interesting, no?"

Thomas looked at them. "Tell me, what do you see?"

I glanced at them quickly. The woman was attractive, but not young-looking. She was in the full bloom of her middle age, with a thick midsection, untoned arms, and gray hair swept up on her head with bobby pins. The boy was beautiful. His black hair was parted in the middle and came down a little past his ears, in a bob. He had a delicate face, but thick eyebrows and big brown eyes that gave him a sense of intensity. He had a skinny body, but even so, it seemed muscular, taut.

"A man taking advantage of a woman," I said.

"Ah. So you see a desperate woman being tricked by a young man."

"Maybe."

"That's very interesting. I see a woman taking advantage of a man."

"Really?" I asked.

"Maybe. It might be that she is here to have a very good time, but she might be making the boy think that she loves him; that she's going to take care of him forever. Then she will go back home to London or Sydney or Detroit, satisfied, but he will be left here. Alone."

"Like the men usually do."

"Yes, like the men usually do."

I pondered this for a moment.

"Isn't it sad we assume it has to be one or the other?"

"What do you mean?"

"We both immediately assumed, because of the age difference, that one of them must be taking advantage of the other."

"Well, yes, of course, Julie. I mean, we're not idiots, are we?"

I laughed at that declaration, and Thomas put his hand over mine. He looked me right in the eyes, gleefully. "Your laugh! Your smile. It's all quite addictive, really."

I looked down at the table. I tried hard not to feel anything.

We walked to the center of Ubud, to the famous temple of Puri Saren Agung, to see a performance of a traditional dance called Legong. As we strolled past cafés and trinket shops, Thomas brought up the couple again.

"You know, Bali is quite famous for this type of situation. Women go here, in droves, for this."

"They do?"

Thomas nodded. "Not usually in Ubud, but in Kutu. That's where they all meet."

"Where's Kutu?"

"It's on the beach, near the airport. It's a very touristy town, with everyone trying to sell you things. That's where all the Balinese gigolos go to meet the women."

"That makes me sad."

"Why?"

"Because I wish the women didn't feel like they had to come here to get someone to have sex with them. It's so . . . desperate."

"Ah yes, and there is nothing more sad than a desperate woman, correct?"

"Well, it's sad when anyone is feeling desperate . . . but yes, it does feel a little tragic."

Then we walked in silence. All I knew about Bali was that it was an island flourishing with the arts, and there was no word in the Balinese culture for "artist," because art was something done by all so there was no need for any delineation. And the people made this art—danced, painted, played music—all in honor of the Hindu gods and their temples. That's what I knew about Bali. Not that it was a place to bang Bali boys.

"Speaking of Kutu, I think we might need to leave here and go to Kutu tomorrow, if you don't mind. It's time I did a little business." He stopped on the road. "Even though this has been absolutely wonderful." As he put his hand on my cheek and kissed me, I got a little queasy; I wasn't used to all this pleasure. I told him I'd be happy to do whatever he needed. Then, suddenly insecure, I wondered if he was hoping to get away without me.

"I mean, unless you were thinking that you wanted to go alone. I mean, I don't want to assume . . ."

He put his arms around me and whispered in my ear, "Shut up, Julie, you are annoying me," and kissed me again.

We walked through a large courtyard and saw that the performance was already taking place. The audience was sitting in a horseshoe on the ground, and the performers were entering from one of the courtyard's gates. It was all women in colorful blue and gold saris with large gold headdresses, their eyes accented with thin eyeliner. The choreography was so precise that everything down to the hand gestures and the fan movements was performed in perfect unison. I noticed that the couple from the restaurant was there as well. I tried to see if she looked like she was in love with him. They weren't making any physical contact at the moment so I tried to glean clues about who might have the upper hand by watching how they looked at each other as they watched the performance. It was hard to tell. I looked back up at the dancers. As I listened to the live gamelan music that accompanied them, I noticed that even these dancers' eye movements were choreographed. Every look, to the left, to the right, up or down, was planned. I looked at Thomas. His eyes were sparkling with interest and wonder at all that was going on. I could tell it was all being absorbed into that brilliant brain of his, then getting swirled around with all the knowledge from his French education and mixing in with his overall perceptiveness and wisdom, so that eventually he would say something about this experience that would be utterly fascinating to me. Thinking about leaving Ubud, and then Bali soon, I realized that soon this whole affair would be over. He would go home to more love, more sex, more intimacy, and more companionship. I would go to my next adventure alone. It was clear who had the upper hand in this relationship.

After the dance ceremony, as we walked out of the gate that led us out to the road, I saw the couple again, kissing on the street a few feet away.

When they finally broke apart, the woman smiled at me and said in a thick Australian accent, "Didn't we see you two at the café today?"

Of course she was Australian. She got smart and actually did move somewhere where the men would fuck you when you're fifty.

I said we were indeed at the café that day, and introductions were made. Her name was Sarah and her companion was Made (pronounced MAH-day). She told us that she'd been living in Bali for six months and was thinking about moving there permanently.

"Are you two on your honeymoon?" she asked us.

"No, this is just a vacation for us," Thomas said.

"Oh, it's just you two look so much in love. I couldn't help but notice when we were at the café." I wondered if that's a main pastime among couples—looking at other couples, trying to find out how happy they are.

"Well, thank you," Thomas said. "We are." He looked at me, his blue eyes now full of mischief.

"Won't you two have dinner with us now? It would be so nice to talk to Westerners and hear what's going on in the rest of the world. They do have CNN here, but I still feel isolated sometimes."

I really didn't want to spend our last night in Ubud with another couple, but I didn't know how to say no. Thomas at least tried.

"I think tonight is not very good for us. We're leaving for Kutu tomorrow . . ." Thomas said, relying on his usual charm.

"Please, I'm desperate for some Western companionship," Sarah said, interrupting. "Let's have an early dinner so you can have the rest of the night to yourselves. Let's go to the Lotus Café. It's beautiful there." We didn't seem to be able to refuse. "We'd love to," I said.

As we all walked down the road, Thomas and I were a few feet ahead of them. I let the silence settle between us, before I turned to him and said, "In love, huh?" And he said, "Yes. In love."

We arrived at the Lotus Café, and were seated at what seemed to be the best seats in the house, right by a pond lit up by tiny lights that showed off the ancient trees that framed it; small gargoyles lining the pond spouted water from their mouths. Towering over us from the far side of the pond was a dazzling temple, the Pura Taman Kemuda Saraswati. It was so exotic, very *Lara Croft: Tomb Raider,* but still austere. It was impossible not to be humbled by it. Thomas ordered a bottle of wine for us and we began to get acquainted. We sat down, Sarah next to me, Made next to Thomas. We were all seated perfectly to be able to look across at our beloveds.

"How long have you two been here?" Sarah asked.

"It's been a week," I said.

"How marvelous. Did you get to see the cremation ceremony two days ago? That was a spectacular sight."

Thomas and I both smiled and shook our heads.

"Did you go to the Monkey Forest? I love monkeys. I find them to be so amusing."

I shook my head, embarrassed. "No, we really didn't get to that."

"What about that trek up to Mount Batur? No?"

We both shook our heads again. Thomas leveled with her. "We didn't really leave our hotel. It's quite a romantic spot."

"Ah." She smiled knowingly. "I understand completely." She looked at Made lovingly. "Bali is an exceptional place to fall in love." Thomas took my hand from across the table and said, "It is."

"There's something about the scenery, obviously, but also just the Balinese culture, their dedication to art and beauty and worship. It is very . . . sweeping." Sarah brushed a strand of hair away from Made's eyes. "It's impossible not to be taken in by it all."

Made finally spoke. "Yes, that's Bali. It is an island dedicated to all kinds of love. Love of God, love of dance, of music, of family, and . . . romantic love."

Sarah reached her hand across the table. He held it in both his hands and kissed it sweetly. What's the crime in that?

Nothing, except it was still, for me, hard to ignore the fact that she was old enough to be his mother. Now to be fair, I feel the same way when I see a much older man with a younger woman. One time I saw Billy Joel on the street with his young wife and I thought, *He should be paying her college tuition, not having sex with her.*

But who was I to be judging Billy Joel? Or Sarah and Made. If they're all happy, so be it.

By our second bottle of wine, we had covered a myriad of subjects. Made talked about the Balinese lifestyle, of families living in a compound; the parents, children, the children's wives and families, all living in individual houses connected by a central courtyard. Made also explained a bit about Hinduism, about death and their belief that life is a cycle of life, death, and reincarnation until your soul has reached the pinnacle of enlightenment, of Samadhi.

Sarah was now reaching the pinnacle of her inebriation, and was beginning to lean on Made, putting her head every now and then on his shoulder like a teenager. A pair of Brits sitting at the next table couldn't stop looking at the two of them. Sarah was less reserved about her feelings on the situation. She talked a little too loudly.

"I know what they're thinking. They're thinking that because of my age, Made is just using me. But he doesn't ask for anything. Not a thing."

I nodded at her reassuringly.

Sarah took a sip of wine. "We met on the beach at Kutu. He came up to me and said I was the most beautiful woman he's ever seen. Of course I knew that was rubbish, but it was still very sweet."

Sarah must have picked up something from my expression, even though I was trying desperately to look supportive.

"It's not what you think. He sat down in the sand with me and we just talked and talked. For hours. It was lovely."

"That sounds so romantic," I said, encouragingly. Sarah was now getting more insistent and a little loud. She started tapping her finger on the table to make her point.

"He's never asked me for a thing. I mean it. I bought him his motorcycle because I wanted to. I gave money to his family because I love Made and I wanted to help. They're very poor. He lives with me and I pay for things for us, because I can, because it's my pleasure. But he never asked me. Never! He works at a boutique just down the road. Every day. He has an amazing work ethic." She stared drunkenly and directly at the British couple and repeated it loudly. "An amazing work ethic." The couple looked at her and then toward each other. The man waved down a waiter and asked for their check.

"It's getting late. Maybe we should get going," I said as I shifted in my chair uncomfortably.

Sarah just scowled a little and curled her arms around Made. "He loves me better than any man I've ever known. And I just get so sick of it sometimes. All the looks."

Made kissed her on the forehead. "Some people. They don't understand what we share. It's okay, my love."

"Yeah, well, all those people are assholes," she said, now loud enough for the whole restaurant to hear. "Assholes." Then she looked at me.

"Besides, Julie, show me one relationship that is truly equal—show me one couple that are both feeling exactly the same things for each other at exactly the same time. You show me that, Julie. Show me *now!*"

The whole restaurant was now looking at us. I didn't really want to answer.

"Exactly. It doesn't exist," Sarah said, banging her fist on the table. "*It doesn't exist.* So what if I give him and his family money? So what? He loves me. That's all anyone needs to know. *He loves me.*"

The bill came and Thomas paid it faster than I've ever seen anyone pay a check, and we made a quick exit.

As we walked down the road, I felt a little shaky. I walked faster. I couldn't get away from them quickly enough. To me, she truly was a desperate woman. Desperate for the world to see them as a true couple. And desperate not to allow herself to see that the man who has loved her better than any man she has ever known is doing it as a part-time job. *In my opinion.*

This past week had been a miracle; I had been so happy that I prayed to the gods, Hindu and otherwise, for it to never end. When I thought about going back to my life of concrete sidewalks and appointments and lunches and unemployment, of dates and parties, it took everything in me not to start shrieking. If Thomas had asked me to stay there with him for the rest of my life, never live near my family or friends again, just stay there and build a life with him in Bali, I would have said *yes yes yes* in a heartbeat. It's like he had opened up this little trap door in my heart, one that was covered all those years by a bookcase and rugs, and he unleashed more need in me than I ever thought I possessed. All I wanted to do at that moment was fling myself at his feet and beg him to never ever leave me.

Instead, I just kept walking. Fast.

We went back to our little villa and immediately collapsed into our lush canopied bed. We wrapped our arms around each other and started kissing, our bodies pressed tightly against each other.

Back in the States

It's never a good thing when both people in the relationship are depressed. It's extremely helpful always to have one person capable of comforting and bucking up the other at any given moment. Serena and Ruby weren't in what you might consider a classic intimate relationship, but Serena was sleeping on Ruby's sofa, and both of them were having a hard time getting out of bed. This particular morning, Serena woke up and for a moment had completely forgotten her quick stint as a swami—until she sleepily ran her fingers through her long blond hair and realized that it wasn't there anymore. Then, she started to cry.

Ruby was in the other room having a nightmare about the last pit bull that she'd hugged before he was taken away. His big brown eyes looked so . . . unsuspecting. She woke up, sobbing into her pillow. If someone had slipped into Ruby's apartment they would have been able to hear them both in a muffled fugue of sorrow.

Finally, Ruby stopped crying, realizing she was awake. As she lay collecting her thoughts, she heard Serena's quiet sobs from the living room. She was confused as to what to do. All she knew about Serena was that she had decided to shave her head and join a yogi convent after getting her stomach pumped for alcohol and chicken wings. She wasn't sure exactly how well she wanted to get to know Serena. But Serena was crying in Ruby's home.

So Ruby got up out of bed. She was wearing flannel pajamas with pictures of tiny dogs on them. She put on her fuzzy white slippers and walked out of her bedroom and down the hall. Vanilla was in the hallway, rubbing up against Ruby's leg. Serena heard Ruby walking toward her and quickly clammed up. There's nothing worse than a stranger seeing you cry. If there's one single reason to live without roommates it's that you can cry in private. Serena pretended she was asleep, hoping Ruby would go away. But Ruby stood by the pullout bed. She waited a moment, then whispered.

"Serena, are you okay?"

Serena moved around a bit. "Oh, yeah," she said, fake-groggily. "I'm fine."

"If you need anything, let me know, okay?"

"Okay. Sure." Ruby then padded down the hallway and got back into her bed. As she pulled the comforter over her head, she thought, *This is what my home has become. Sad Girl Land.* Then Ruby started daydreaming. Which is something she did a lot. In fact, during her darkest times, it's the thing that always managed to keep her going. Daydreaming of a better life. On this particular day, for some reason, she began to daydream about what her morning would be like if she had a small child in her home. She wouldn't have time to stay in her fluffy bed with her downy pillows. She would have gotten up already to fix breakfast and make up the lunch box and get her child dressed and ready for school. Instead of that idea exhausting her, it made her smile. Ruby realized she couldn't wait for the day when she didn't have the time to think about herself. It was then that she realized this really was such a day. Serena may not have been seven, but she was in need. She was depressed and crying, and if Ruby remembered correctly, Serena was meeting with her old boss in about an hour. This morning, Ruby could be of help. She threw off her comforter, jumped out of bed, and padded back down the hall. Serena was no longer crying, but she was in a fetal position, her arms cradling her head, covering her eyes, breathing softly.

"Serena. Can I get you anything? Some tea or coffee? Maybe an egg or something?"

Serena just shook her head into her arms. Ruby stood there, not knowing exactly what should happen next. She thought about what mothers do in this type of situation. They wouldn't take no for an answer. That's what they would do. They would go make something even after the person had refused all help or comfort. So Ruby turned back around and went into the kitchen. She poured some water into her teakettle, turned a burner on, and set the kettle down. She then opened up her cabinet and perused. She assumed Serena was a tea drinker, being the yogi she was. Ruby remembered that she had bought a box of green tea once, in her one attempt to start drinking it for its amazing antioxidant attributes, even though no one had ever successfully explained to her what an antioxidant was. She reached deep into the shelf and pulled out the green tea and, when the kettle whistled, made Serena a cup. Ruby opened a little container of Fage (a thick, tasty Greek yogurt) and got a spoon. She walked back to Serena, deciding to push the intimacy a bit by sitting right on the bed. She touched Serena's arm.

"Would you like a cup of green tea? It's right here."

No answer. Ruby's instincts were kicking in and she knew to just wait. After a moment, Serena slowly pushed herself up and leaned against the back of the sofa bed. Ruby thought that, with her shaved little head and her puffy eyes, Serena looked an awful lot like a baby ostrich.

"Thanks, Ruby. I appreciate it," Serena said weakly. She took the green tea and sipped it. Hallelujah. Ruby felt her heart swell with maternal pride. "Do you want to talk about it?" asked Ruby.

Serena looked down into her tea and didn't speak. "I just had no idea how nice it felt to be in love." The corner of Serena's lips started turning down and tears formed in her eyes. "It made me so stupid."

Ruby took Serena's hand and just softly said, "I'm so sorry, sweetie."

Serena continued. "And then it wasn't even real. It was all a fake. So how could I have even been in love if it was all a lie? Was I so desperate to be in love that I just made it all up?"

Ruby truly didn't know what to say. But she tried to be helpful. "Maybe this was just a rehearsal. Maybe you needed this one to open you up to be in love with someone who's worthy."

Serena glanced at the container in Ruby's hand.

"What is that?"

"It's Greek yogurt with honey. Really thick and yummy. Want to try?"

Serena nodded subtly. Ruby dipped the spoon into the yogurt and held it out for Serena to take. But instead, Serena leaned in and opened her mouth, as if holding the spoon would take more energy than she had. Ruby placed the spoon in Serena's mouth. Serena smiled. "That's good."

"Don't you have a meeting soon?" Ruby asked gently.

Serena nodded slowly. She took a deep breath. "I guess I should get up."

But before Serena swung her legs out of the bed to get up, she looked at Ruby.

"Thank you, Ruby."

Ruby smiled. She was good at this.

After Serena left, Ruby started thinking that maybe there was a way around this whole single-motherhood issue. She realized that maybe she didn't have to do it alone. There were many ways to get a father into this situation. As she walked down the street to her office, which was conveniently just blocks away, she started thinking about who could possibly knock her up. It came to her instantly. Her friends Dennis and Gary. They were her friends with the most stable relationship she knew of. They had been together three years and lived in a beautiful loft on Eighteenth Street in Chelsea. Ruby lived on the Upper West Side—but she would be happy to move to Chelsea so they could share parenting duties. She thought she remembered them talking about having children one day. She couldn't believe she didn't think of it before. They were the two most nurturing people she'd ever met. Often, one person in a couple is the really sweet one, and the other is more the "bad cop" kind. But with Dennis and Gary, they are both so caring that when you go to their house you feel like you've entered a magical bed and breakfast where everything is soft and cozy and your every need is taken care of. Ruby met Gary when he lived next door to her five years ago, and they've been close ever since. When Dennis came along, he and Ruby liked each other immediately. They got together fairly often, one big happy family. Ruby started playing it out in her mind. She would have primary custody of the baby, but they could be around as much as they wanted. And best of all, she wouldn't have just one dad for her kid, she'd have two. She would have the freedom to go out and still have a life, because Dennis and Gary would be there to take the child. Maybe they could even find apartments in the same building.

Ruby wondered exactly how this would all happen. Whose actual sperm would it be? Gary or Dennis? They're both deeply good-looking, both ridiculously fit. Dennis is a little more stocky than Gary. But Gary has terrible eyesight. But Dennis is starting to lose his hair. But Gary was her friend first; maybe it would be better if it was Dennis's child, so he wouldn't feel left out. She had read somewhere that sometimes male couples mix the sperm together and play a semen version of Russian roulette. Ruby could see it all. The child in a BabyBjörn carrier, dressed all in pink. Or blue. Ruby carrying the blue or pink baby around, as it gurgled and babbled. The blue or pink baby walking around the apartment, she and Dennis and Gary clapping and laughing. And then maybe she'd meet someone. And that someone would think she's so cool with her crazy, modern clan and he'd fit right in. Maybe he'd have kids of his own and they'd be this kooky progressive mixed family. She loved the idea so much she couldn't wait another moment. She pulled out her cell phone and made a date to see Dennis and Gary for lunch.

On the day of the lunch, Ruby had decided to dress "maternally." She wore a loose-fitting peasant blouse, loose pants, and a cute pair of flats. The way the blouse fit, she almost looked pregnant already and that was exactly the plan: Let Dennis and Gary see what it would be like if she was already carrying their child. How soft and womanly and maternal she could be. Unfortunately, she wasn't sure how soft anyone would seem amid the clamor of hipsters eating salads and burgers, yelling over the throbbing music.

They told her to meet them at Cafeteria, which, upon arrival, Ruby realized was a misstep. Cafeteria is possibly the noisiest restaurant in New York City. With the combination of the loud techno music and the din of the diners it was like trying to have lunch in the middle of a rave.

Ruby was nervous; she had never had this kind of conversation before. She had never even asked a guy out; she didn't believe in it and never had to resort to it. Now, she wasn't just going to propose marriage, but rather something that you could never take back. It would be a decision that would bond them together for the rest of their lives. More than that, she was about to have the nerve to ask these uber-caregivers if they thought she was good enough to be the mother of their child.

They arrived. Gary was wearing a suede jacket, impeccable, perfect, and Dennis was in a black cashmere turtleneck with a down vest over it. Very Lands' End adorable. They sat down, obviously pleased to see her.

"It's so great to see you, Ruby," Dennis said, grabbing Ruby's hand and giving it a squeeze. Ruby relaxed immediately. These men were going to think she was a good mother. They knew her good qualities better than anyone else. That she's patient, gentle, calm. So what if they had also been witnesses to a few bouts of her bone-crushing disappointment? No one is perfect. She suddenly remembered Gary once coming over and taking her for a drive in her pajamas. She had been despondent over one guy or another. He told her to get in his car "or else," and they drove all the way up to Bear Mountain and back. Ruby, in her pajamas and parka, was so touched that it shook her out of her depression and she was able to move on. Now she regretted that Gary had ever seen that side of her. He might use that touching moment against her. She silently cursed herself for not always being perfectly cheerful around her close friend. What if he thought she was too mentally unstable to be the mother of his or Dennis's baby?

She decided to just blurt it out. "I want you to inseminate me."

Ruby put her hands on the table to steady herself.

Gary turned to Dennis and said, "I told you so."

Ruby looked at them. "What?"

Gary simply shrugged. "I just had a hunch."

Ruby began her pitch. "You know how responsible I am. I never miss a deadline, no matter how depressed I am or upset I am. Not that I would be depressed or anything, because the reason why I was depressed before was because of guys, you know, giving them so much power over my life. But when I'm a mother, I could never be that depressed about some guy or anything because I would be having a higher calling. I would be a mother."

Dennis and Gary looked at each other. They looked back at Ruby, each with a different expression of uncomfortable pity in his eyes. Dennis leaned over and touched Ruby's arm.

"I'm sorry. We just gave our semen to Veronica and Lea."

Ruby sat there for a moment, taking in this new information. Then she thought, *Who the hell are Veronica and Lea?* She had never even heard of Veronica and Lea.

"Who are Veronica and Lea?" Ruby asked, a little too much outrage in her voice.

Gary answered. "They're our friends that we met doing volunteer work at the soup kitchen near our house. A lesbian couple. They're really nice."

"New friends? You gave new friends your semen over me?" Ruby said, softly but with a trembling in her voice.

"We didn't know you wanted it!"

"But you could have asked! Before you gave your semen over to strangers you should have thought for just a minute of which one of your good friends might want your semen first!" Ruby's voice was raised just a bit, but in the cacophony of talking and techno, no one even noticed. "You should have been more considerate!"

This time, Dennis spoke. "Honey, the last time we talked to you, your cat had just died and you hadn't gotten out of bed in three days."

"We came over and washed your hair for you, remember?" Dennis added.

Ruby cringed. She knew it. While they were being nice and nurturing, they had been making little mental notes on her fitness for motherhood. She felt betrayed. She made up her own new rule about how to be single: *Never let anyone see you at your worst. Because someday you might want that person's sperm or to date their brother, so you can't ever let them see you crazy or sad or ugly.* That's what she would tell me to put in my damn book the minute she had the chance. She immediately calmed down.

"I was depressed. But a lot has happened since then. I went and helped kill dogs at the shelter uptown to toughen up and now I'm ready to have a child."

Gary and Dennis looked at her, confused. Dennis went in first.

"You helped kill dogs at that awful shelter up in Harlem?"

"Yes. Okay. That's not the point." Then Ruby, being a businesswoman, decided to start negotiating. "The point is, I don't think there's anything wrong with your lesbian offspring having a half sibling in New York City somewhere. We'll arrange playdates. It'll be fun!"

"Ruby, I don't think—"

The waiter came over to take their orders. He didn't get the chance.

Ruby raised her voice even louder. "It's because I'm single, is that it? You'd rather give your semen to a couple even if they're lesbians, than one single straight woman. I get it now. Single discrimination. Fine." The waiter quietly excused himself from the table.

Ruby started to get up, but Gary grabbed her arm and sat her back down. "Honey, we're so sorry, we are."

Ruby leaned back in her chair. "I'm sorry. I didn't mean to overreact. I'm just disappointed."

"We know, sweetie," Dennis said, softly. "After we see how this goes, maybe we'd consider having another."

"Never mind. I understand." But Ruby wasn't really sure if she understood. She didn't know if the real reason they didn't ask her first was that it didn't cross their minds, or because they thought she would be a terrible mother. She didn't know if they really would consider her in a year or two, if things went well with the first child. She didn't know anything, except that she wanted to retain whatever dignity she might have left.

"I should have asked sooner," she said, trying to smile. Then the waiter came over and took their orders.

By the time she got back to her office, she had decided that this time she wasn't going to give in to her disappointment. Theirs was not the only semen in the sea. There were lots of possible fathers out there for her to choose from. And as she was walking into the elevator, she had another brilliant prospect: her gay friend Craig. A former theatrical lighting designer, he'd made a career change a few years before and now drove around selling rare and gourmet mushrooms to the high-end restaurants in the city. He was single and made a decent living, but his sperm couldn't possibly be as sought-after as the highly cultivated and high-income sperm of Dennis and Gary. She decided to give him a call. But this time she laid it all right out there from the beginning.

"Hi, Craig, this is Ruby. Can we get together and talk about you possibly being the father of my child? How about we meet at Monsoon, at, say, eight tonight? Give me a call."

When Craig called back, Ruby let it go to voice mail. He agreed to meet her.

At 8:15 Ruby walked into Monsoon, a low-key Vietnamese chain restaurant with great food and unpretentious décor. This time she had decided to have him sitting there waiting for her—it put her in the power position. She sauntered in, wearing an extremely expensive top from Catherine Malandrino and high heels. Not knowing what his reaction would be to this big question, Ruby decided she should at least try to look wealthy. Even though she desperately wanted something from him, she was going to make sure she had something, too. She sat down. Before she had a chance even to say hello, Craig blurted it out.

"I'm HIV positive, Ruby. I never told you."

Ruby's stomach flipped. She hadn't even entertained this as a possibility, mainly because she assumed he would have told her if he was. So she just assumed he wasn't. She realized now that that was naïve of her. She was also flummoxed as to what the appropriate reaction was. Being HIV positive today means something so different than it used to. Does she say she's sorry? Does she ask how he is? How his T cells are? What kind of cocktail he's on?

"I'm sorry to hear that. Are you . . . ?"

"I'm fine, I've been on drugs for years, no side effects. I'm going to live to be a hundred."

"I'm so glad," Ruby said, relieved. "Do you want to talk about it?"

"No, I'm okay, I just thought you should know, now, because of . . . everything."

Ruby nodded. They both got quiet. She thought about this news for a few minutes. Then she came back to thinking about how badly she wanted this child. She had known Craig since college—longer than she'd known Gary. He was an incredibly sweet person, and loyal and kind and consistent. He would be a great father.

"You know, I heard you can do a wash now," Ruby said.

"What?"

"You know, an HIV wash. On your sperm. Before you inseminate someone. They can clean your sperm of the HIV before you inject it in them and everyone is fine."

Craig fidgeted in his chair. "Really?"

"Yeah. I read about it in the *Times* science section, a year ago I think. I think you might have to go to Italy or somewhere to do it, but it can be done." Ruby didn't want to seem too pushy, but at the same time, she was determined.

"Oh." Craig paused, sipping nervously at his tea.

"I know you might be worried about how it could affect me and my health, but I could do research . . ."

Craig put down his tea. "I know about the wash."

Ruby brightened up. "Oh, you do? So, does it seem doable? Is it something you might be interested in—"

Craig interrupted. "Ruby, I don't want to hurt your feelings and I didn't think you'd suggest the wash . . ."

Ruby looked at Craig, confused. "I don't understand."

"My friend Leslie already asked if she could do the wash. She's forty-one and she—"

Ruby pushed her chair out and slammed her hands on the table. She began to speak without thinking.

"No no no no, I don't want to hear it. I thought I was being generous by being willing to do the wash. I had no idea you were *fielding offers* from women who were willing to do it."

"I was surprised, too. But Leslie liked that I went to Brown and was tall," Craig said sheepishly.

"Who is this Leslie person anyway?" Ruby's hands were flapping in the air, gesturing at no one in particular.

"She's my Pilates instructor."

Ruby pushed her chair back into the table and leaned over to Craig. "Your *Pilates instructor*?"

Craig looked at her helplessly. "Ruby, if you had asked me first I would have been happy to . . ."

Just then, the waitress came over. "Do you know what you'd like to order?"

Ruby stood, her coat still on. "Yes. I would like a little, healthy baby girl or boy, ten fingers and toes, with one responsible, kind, coparenting partner on the side. I mean really, is that so much to ask?"

The waitress gave Ruby the death stare, which signified "I'm not going to acknowledge you until you say something not crazy."

Ruby took a breath. "No, thank you. I'm not hungry." She then turned to Craig. "I'm so glad you're okay, and I'm so happy that you're going to be a father one day. But I think I'm just going to go home now if that's okay with you?" Craig nodded as Ruby quickly stood up. She leaned down and gave Craig a big kiss on the cheek, turned, and walked out the door.

Back in Bali

Our hotel in Kutu was another obscenely luxurious villa, this one with its own little backyard and private swimming pool overlooking the ocean. I know. Insane. Thomas had gone to a business meeting an hour ago. The bad news was, I missed him terribly. This was the first time we had been apart in over a week and it was horrible. I'd become completely emotionally dependent on him. I was never a possessive girlfriend, even in my teens and twenties, but if I could have sewn a pocket into my skin and tucked Thomas inside me, I would have. I didn't want him to ever leave my side.

It took all my energy to fight the urge to stay in that hotel room and refuse to leave it for the rest of my born days. But Thomas had told me Kutu was a big surfer beach, so I decided to go watch the surfers; finally I might not look so out of place in my surfing trunks. But I was also curious if I was going to see some gigolos waiting to tell some lady that she was the most beautiful woman they had ever seen. And I wondered if the beach would be full of older women waiting for their day to be Made.

The beach was dotted with surfers, all waiting for the next wave. The beach wasn't crowded yet, and as far as I could tell, there were no gigolos or women waiting to be gigoloed.

As I sat in one of the chairs provided by the hotel, a young Balinese man came up to me with a big plastic bag.

"Excuse me, miss, would you like one? Very cheap."

He pulled from his bag something that looked like a Rolex watch—

I'm going to go out on a limb and say I don't think it was real. I shook my head.

"But look, they are so nice, very cheap. Buy one."

Being a New Yorker, I know how to get my point across. I shook my head forcefully, and said loudly, "No thank you." He got the message, picked up his bag, and walked away.

The surfers had found a wave and I watched them doing their best to ride it. They made it look so easy, most of them keeping their balance until the wave deposited them gently on the shore.

My thoughts quickly drifted back to Thomas and the fact that he was going to be going home in less than a week. Back to Paris, to his wife. It started to dawn on me that in only a few days, I might never see him again.

I began to think again about what a great deal this had been for him. A nice little vacation he must be having from the monotony of marriage. And he could go home guilt free, because he had been completely honest with me about his open marriage, and his wife didn't seem to mind. He had a perfect arrangement. I was starting to get pissed off.

Just then, an older Balinese woman came up to me and asked if I wanted my hair braided. I said no, forcefully, with one very big shake of my head. She moved on.

It also began to dawn on me that I might not be the only woman Thomas had done this with. I know, sometimes I'm a little slow. I realized that this might be where he takes all his lady friends. In fact, he might've known he was going to Bali and made sure he had a girlfriend lined up for the trip. Who knows? All I knew for certain was that I had bought it all, every last romantic bit of it, like a tourist snapping up a fake Rolex.

A man came by with an armload of t-shirts. But before he could speak, I barked "No!" and he scurried away.

I then had the thought that no woman in my situation should ever allow herself to have. I started to imagine Thomas telling me that he wanted to leave his wife for me. I imagined him with tears in his eyes, begging me to be with him, he loved me too much, he couldn't bear living without me.

I shook my head, trying to dislodge this dangerous thought as quickly as possible. It was going to be terrible saying good-bye. I wondered if there was a way to just guilt him into staying with me. If there was a way I could seem as pathetic and vulnerable as possible and just cry and plead with him to stay. I've seen it work on the soaps.

A young Balinese man came up and sat down on the chair right next to me.

"Excuse me, miss, but you are the most beautiful woman I have ever seen on this beach. I had to come over and tell you that."

And at that, I said, very loudly, *"Okay, that's fucking it."* I stood up from my chair, grabbed my towel, hat, and beach bag. He jumped at my little outburst, but I have no idea what he did next, because I walked away from him quickly without ever looking back.

I can tell you that at that moment, I had never felt so completely, literally, utterly, whatever, insulted in my life. He actually mistook me for a woman who was desperate and lonely enough to believe his line of bullshit.

As I walked back to our little villa of lies, it occurred to me that maybe this Balinese boy had read my mind. Maybe he sensed that I was a woman at that moment scheming on how to make myself so pitiable that a man might be guilted into staying with me.

Maybe that kid knew *exactly* whom he was talking to.

As I stomped down the stone path, I realized that it had to stop. I desperately loved Thomas, I wanted desperately to have someone in my life, and in New York I had been desperately lonely. But as I got close to the door of the villa, I also decided that this was fantastic. This was going to be my saving grace. I was a desperate woman. Good. Now that I knew this about myself I could be on guard for it. It wasn't going to ambush me suddenly and force me to do something embarrassing. Not me. Because the truth is, there's absolutely nothing wrong with feeling desperate—*it's just that under no circumstances are you ever allowed to act it.*

I started throwing all my things into my suitcase: my clothes, my toiletries, everything. As I was running around the room grabbing up my things, Thomas walked in with a big smile on his face.

"Julie, I've missed you—" He saw my suitcase on the bed and looked immediately distressed.

"But, what are you doing?" he said, panicked.

"You're going home soon anyway, back to your wife and your life. It's better I leave now, before things get . . ."

I stopped. It was very important for me not to cry. "I just want to leave, now."

Thomas sat on the bed. He put his head down, thinking. I kept running around the room, looking to see if I had missed anything. When Thomas finally looked up, he had tears in his eyes. My first thought, because I'm from New York and fucked up, was that he was faking it.

"I spent this entire meeting thinking of you, Julie. I couldn't keep you out of my mind. I missed you so much."

I stayed firm. It was easy for him to have all these romantic notions, with his nice, big Paris safety net. I spoke to him a little coldly.

"You've been through this before, I imagine, so you understand. This was going to end in a few days anyway, so it's just ending a little sooner. That's all." I zipped up my suitcase. This time I had a plan. "I'm going to go to China. It's really interesting, I read that there are so many more men there than women, due to the policies involving—"

Thomas stood up, grabbed me and kissed me.

"Yes, Julie, I admit it, I've been through this before. But this feels so very different. Please, please, let me go with you wherever you are going next, please. China, Zimbabwe, wherever. I can't leave you, I can't. Say you'll let me stay with you, please. I beg of you." He pulled me close to him, his hand around my head, clutching at my hair, desperately.

Back in the States

I'm going to try to be brief with this because it's upsetting, but I'm not sure if I'll be able to because I need you to have all the details. The details are important.

Ever since the Sam incident, Georgia had actually been feeling pretty good about things. There's nothing like deciding not to see a perfectly good man to make a girl feel a little up on herself. She had been going on some dates with a few men she met online, none of them really for her, but not disasters, either. Dale had been taking the kids as often as Georgia asked, and she also had a long list of reliable babysitters. She might not have been paying as much attention to her kids as she should have, but she was feeling optimistic. So there had been some improvement.

She met Bryan at a parent-teacher conference at school. They were both waiting out in the hall, on those tiny chairs, and they struck up a conversation. His son was six and in the same class as Georgia's daughter. He was of average height, with a thin face and bright cheeks—he looked Scottish. He had been divorced for three years. They got on the subject of their respective marriages and breakups, bonding over the toll it takes on everyone involved. By the time Bryan was called in to speak to the teacher, he had asked Georgia if he could call her. Which he did. That night. Two days later, they went out. They had dinner and he walked her to her building and they kissed and kissed in front of her house and he said he had had a great time and asked if he could see her again. He called her the next day, to tell her what a nice time he had had and to make plans. They made a date for two nights later. This time she went to his house (his son was with his mother) and he cooked her a delicious pot roast and they ate and talked and he was very sweet and they made out on his bed, very tenderly—but not without passion. He called her the next day and asked her when he could see her again. She told him she was free Tuesday or Thursday and he said, "Well, Thursday feels too far from now, so how about Tuesday?" Well, how about that. Let me say it to you again, because Georgia repeated it to me, over and over again, long distance, in the ensuing Many Long Days of Bryan. He had said "When can I see you again?" And Georgia had said "Tuesday or Thursday" and he had said "Well, *Thursday feels too far from now, so how about Tuesday?*" Got it? Okay. This kind of insanely consistent, straightforward, I-am-incredibly-excited-to-have-met-you-but-not-so-much-that-it's-unbelievable behavior went on for the next week and a half. They spoke on the phone nearly every day, and all things pointed to one thing only: "game on." This was something real with a consistent, affectionate man who had not, in anything he said or did or mumbled or joked about, revealed himself to be anything other than a man who was ready and excited to enter into a relationship with Georgia. No red flags, no vague or direct warnings, no "I just need to let you know" conversations. Again, Georgia had the feeling you have when things are finally clicking. Suddenly, it's easy. Suddenly, you didn't know what the fuss was all about. She became a little smug, and thought to herself yet again, *I knew it wouldn't be that hard to find a great man.*

And then they slept together.

It was a Saturday night, and Georgia had to get home to her sitter. There had been enough affection and tenderness to cushion her post-coital exit, so she didn't feel like a complete slut when she had to leave. She went home, paid the sitter, and went to bed, happy and secure. She had done everything right. They had laid the groundwork of friendship and established a rhythm of dates and calls that obviously suited them both. So when she woke up Sunday, as her eyes popped open, her first thought was Bryan. She remembered the sex. She still actually *felt* the sex. And a big, easy smile came across her face.

It would be safe to say that Georgia had been fairly impatient with her two children ever since Dale left. For some women, having their children during a time like that would give them a sense of comfort—of still be-longing to something. But for Georgia, the day-to-day tedium of raising her children only served to underscore whatever misery and loneliness she was experiencing at that moment. So when Beth screamed for Georgia to hail a cab because she didn't feel like walking the half a block back to the apartment, well, maybe Georgia hadn't exhibited the same kind of patience she did when she had had a husband.

But this Sunday she woke up smiling, with nothing but patience and adoration for her two young children. She got them up, got them dressed, made them breakfast, and took them for a walk along Riverside Drive. Beth was on her bike, Gareth was on his scooter. She barely looked at her phone because there was no need to. She was dating a nice man whom she had just slept with for the first time, and she would be talking to him sometime today as she usually did.

So when Georgia saw that it was four o'clock in the afternoon, she didn't even flinch. He was probably busy with his son. "He probably doesn't want to call when he can't really talk," Georgia said to herself. She took her kids for an early dinner at their favorite Chinese restaurant and went home.

But by eight o'clock, when Beth came out of her room and asked for her third glass of water, Georgia snapped. "What did I tell you, Beth?! No more water. Go back into your room." Beth started to whine. "I SAID GO BACK INTO YOUR ROOM!"

Bryan hadn't called. Georgia turned on the television. She started having the tiny stirrings, the first whisper of a feeling, but it was there: panic. And when panic starts to creep in, even on tiptoe, a woman's mind goes on overdrive. At least Georgia's mind did. It may have seemed that she was watching television but in reality she was summoning all the creative powers she could muster to keep that rumbling of panic at bay. Sometimes after an intense sexual experience a man might need to take a step back, just as a cooldown, to compose himself emotionally. Maybe he was really busy. Maybe something happened to his son. Maybe he's not feeling well. There are so many reasons why he might not have called.

I'm not going to be one of those women who go crazy just because a guy didn't call, Georgia thought to herself. *It's not a big deal. He'll call tomorrow.* "I SAID GO BACK TO YOUR ROOM," Georgia screamed at Gareth when he appeared in the hallway. Georgia tried to put it out of her mind, but the dread wouldn't really leave her. Wisely, she went to bed. Tomorrow was another day. And tomorrow he would call.

When Georgia's alarm clock rang at six thirty the next morning, the first feeling that hit her was excitement. *Yay! Bryan is going to call me today!* She wondered how long she would have to wait. Georgia tried to put it out of her mind. She got up and looked at what she could make the kids for breakfast. She sighed. It all felt like drudgery. She took out eggs and bread and got to work. The kids woke up and first Beth didn't want eggs and then she didn't want the oatmeal that Georgia made, and then she wouldn't eat the toast because Gareth touched it for a second. Which is when Georgia told Beth that there are many children that don't get a choice of what to eat for breakfast and she better eat what's on her goddamn plate or she'll go to school hungry. Which is when Beth threw a piece of toast at Georgia and stomped angrily into her room.

After that it was an all-out brawl to get them to school. Screaming, tears, names were called. And that was just from Georgia. *Ha ha.* At school she looked around for Bryan, but he wasn't there. She walked back home, exhausted, and checked the clock. It was nine. Nine o'clock. *What is he doing right now?* Georgia wondered. *What is he doing right now that is more important than calling me?* She decided to get productive. It was time for her to look for a job. Ever since the divorce, she had been putting that off, wanting to punish Dale with her financial needs. But now it was time to move on. She knew that that is what a smart, empowered woman would do.

It was then that she had the most comforting, peaceful thought she had ever had in her entire life.

She could call him.

Oh my God! She could call him! She loved it. Now, she knew that it was always better to not call the guy, but this was different. This was killing her. This was not empowering—waiting by the phone for some guy to call. This was not in any way what she called women's lib. She was going to call him. But Georgia did know enough to get a second opinion. Unfortunately, she ended up getting a second opinion from Ruby because she couldn't get me on the phone (I was with Thomas in Bali, I'm sorry!) and Alice didn't pick up when Georgia called. If Georgia had spoken with either Alice or me, we would have said, "Don't call, don't call, don't call."

In my book there are many reasons why you shouldn't call, but the main one is that it's the only way to find out what his intentions really are. You need to know how long he can go without talking to you, unencumbered by your meddlesome phone calls, emails, or texts. If you call, you are contaminating the evidence. But we weren't available and Georgia called Ruby, and Ruby is all heart, all emotion, and you could basically get her to say anything you wanted her to.

Georgia quickly explained the situation to Ruby, then asked, "So, there's nothing wrong with calling him, right? I mean, there's no rule saying that I can't call him, is there?"

Ruby shook her head as she clicked on the NYU Medical Center website. She was searching the Net for information about artificial insemination. "I don't think there's a rule, per se, but I have a feeling there's a strong suggestion out there not to call."

"I know. But I can't get any work done. It's driving me crazy! I just need to know what's going on!"

Ruby didn't know Georgia well, but she could tell when someone was becoming mildly hysterical. Then Georgia pulled out the real trump card, the defense for calling, which only highly experienced daters can argue against.

"But maybe something happened to him," Georgia pointed out. "What if something has happened to him and I'm sitting here with my pride instead of treating him like any other friend who I was expecting to hear from and didn't? I would be worried and I would call him."

It seemed like a completely logical argument. (Why-oh-why didn't Alice and I pick up our phones?)

"You're right. If he was just a friend of yours, which he is, you would call him and find out what's up."

"Exactly!" Georgia said happily. "I have the right to treat him just as I would any friend."

She hung up on Ruby and started dialing Bryan's phone as quickly as she could get her fingers to move.

Like someone who has just taken a shot of migraine medicine, Georgia was ecstatic that her pain was going to be alleviated momentarily. As she dialed, she felt proactive. Strong. There's nothing worse than feeling powerless over your own life. Or helpless over some guy.

Now if she had spoken to me or Alice, we would have both said something like "He's not your friend. Sex changes everything. That's the sad truth of it. *Assume he's fine.* Assume his life is exactly the same as it was the last time you saw him. And if you find out later that his son was bitten by a rare South American bee and Bryan had spent the past few days sleeping in the highly-contagious-disease section of Mount Sinai Hospital, well, send him a nice email and apologize." But we were not there for Georgia. So instead, she gleefully dialed.

She left a message. She knew there was a very good possibility she'd get his voice mail, and she was ready.

"Hey, Bryan, this is Georgia. Just calling to say hi! Hope you're well." And then Georgia hung up, almost proudly. *Well. That took care of that.* She let out a triumphant sigh. The worry, the dread, the panic, whatever you want to call it, had been lifted. She knew immediately she had done the right thing and she felt like a superwoman.

For exactly forty-seven seconds.

Then an awful realization hit her and gave her a feeling of doom unlike anything she had experienced. It dawned on her that she was now just waiting for him to call *again*. All she had done was give herself the briefest pause from the agony of waiting for him to call her. And now she was back to waiting—*but it was far, far worse. Because now she had actually called him.* Now if he didn't call, he would not be simply taking his time calling her after having slept with her, he would be actually *not returning her call.* She had doubled the misery.

So now, to speed things up a bit: The rest of the day went by. Bryan didn't call. And Georgia literally had to take to her bed. The kids were picked up by a sitter who stayed and made dinner for them. Georgia was still lying in bed at nine o'clock, when the church bells rang, the doves sang, the clouds parted, and the angels played their harps.

Because he called. He called, he called, he called. Georgia doesn't know when, in all her born days, she had felt such deliverance. They chatted. And laughed. The knot in her stomach went away. Oh my God, she didn't know what she was so worried about. Women can get so crazy sometimes! They talked for about twenty-five minutes (of course Georgia was keeping track) before Georgia started to wrap up the conversation. Right when they were about to hang up, finally, Bryan started to make plans.

"So. We should get together soon."

"Yeah. That would be great," Georgia said, two days of stress and worry releasing from her body.

"I'll call you this week and we'll make plans," Bryan said.

"Oh-h-h. Okay," Georgia stammered, confused. She hung up the phone and her first thought was, *What the fuck? Why did he have to call her to make a plan when they were already on the phone now?*

Now she began the next phase of the disassembling of a dream. She became obsessed with figuring out what she had done wrong. What had she done that made him go from "No, Thursday is too far away" to "I'll call you this week and we'll make plans"?

So Georgia waited again. Tuesday, Wednesday, Thursday. She tried to put it out of her mind. She got herself a couple of job interviews. She met up with Alice and they did some shopping. She tried to yell at her kids less. The shameless devil on her shoulder was telling her that if she wanted to see Bryan so badly, she should call him. That there's nothing wrong with a woman asking a man out; it's the twenty-first century, for goodness sake. But on Friday, just as she was about to pick up the phone, a stay of execution was granted. And he called and asked her out for

Tuesday night. Tuesday night? Well, okay. He must have known that you shouldn't ask a woman out for the weekend on a Friday night; that's not polite. And she guessed she could ask Dale to take the kids.

So they went out on Tuesday night. Georgia remembered why she liked him so much. Every once in a while the nagging thought would enter her head, What would have happened if I had never called him last Monday? Would he have ever called me? But she put it out of her mind as quickly as it came in. They went back to his house. They had sex. And Georgia got another shot of the love/sex drug that would make her obsess about him for the next four days, during which all he did was text her once to say, "Hey, let's get together soon!" But this time she did not call him. She was resolute. More than needing to see him, to have sex, and to be validated, much more than all of that she needed to know how long he could go without seeing her. Now, that required strength, stamina, and emotional fortitude on a level that had never been asked of her before, not even in childbirth. And the only way she was able to muster this Herculean restraint was to call and torture Ruby and Alice. (And me, when she could get me on the phone.) The conversations went something like this:

Georgia to Ruby: "But I just don't understand. If he didn't want to go out with me, why wouldn't he just stop asking me out? But if he does like me, why doesn't he like me as much as he did in the beginning?" Ruby would have no good answer, because really, how do you answer that?

Georgia to Alice: "Maybe he's never going to call me again. I mean, he said he was going to call me but he didn't say when. Is it so hard to make a plan for the future? Even a tentative one? What does that mean when you don't want to make a next date while you're still on your current one? Is he that busy? Does it feel like too much pressure?" And Alice, a girl after my own heart, just kept saying, *Don't call him, don't call him, don't call him.*

I guess it would be fair to say that Georgia, whose sanity was really not that fully present to begin with, had now officially completely lost it.

There are some people who have catastrophic results when alcohol and their blood mix together. One could say the same thing for Georgia when it came to mixing her disposition with longing. Some people can suffer through it; some people can overcome it and move on. Georgia was felled by it. Like an aborigine with a bottle of Wild Turkey, Georgia spiraled out of control. She took to her bed again. She would get the kids to school, come back, put on her pajamas, and go back to bed. It seemed like the best way to have the time go by as quickly as possible until he called. If he called. And, in Georgia's defense, she was always able to get back up and pick the kids up from school, bring them home, and make them a snack. And then she would take to the sofa. It was as if someone had squeezed all the air out of Georgia, and now she was the carcass of a balloon, broken and lifeless, lying on the sofa, popped. Okay, maybe it wasn't just Bryan. Maybe it was the culmination of the trauma of divorce, of missing Dale more than she wanted to admit, of becoming a single mother, of having jumped in too quickly to the brutal world of dating. Or maybe it really was that she was desperate for Bryan to call. Who knows. The love drug she had ingested turned out to be toxic and she was slowly being poisoned to death.

Finally, he called. At nine o'clock. Wednesday night. Bryan told her that he was at a little coffee shop across the street from her. Were the kids with her or could she come out?

The kids were indeed with her. So that's what she should have said. But she wasn't in her right mind. She needed to see him in person and find out what happened. What did she do wrong? She needed to know so she wouldn't make the same mistake again. She didn't want to confront him; she just wanted the quiet, possibly brutal truth. So she said that the kids were with her, but her sister was there, so she could run out for a few minutes.

I know! But you have to understand; Beth never, *never* under any circumstances ever gets up in the middle of the night. She could drive you to your wits' end before she goes to bed, but once she is asleep, a bulldozer ripping through her bedroom wall wouldn't wake her. And as for Gareth, it was the same. Also, he was old enough that if for some reason he did wake up, he could read the note that she would leave him, reading "Back in FIVE minutes! Don't be scared!" She knew that what she was doing was dicey. But she was desperate to get this over with. So she wrote the note and ran out of the apartment, down the stairs, and across the street to the coffee shop. Bryan was sitting by the large window, and when he saw her walking across the street, he started waving with a big smile on his face.

Georgia sat down and tried to be casual. She knew it was all about not seeming like a hysterical woman. She must not cry. She must not have Trembly Voice. Can't have Trembly Voice when talking to a man about Things. You must have Casual Lighthearted Voice.

"Can I get you a coffee, or is it too late?" Bryan asked, politely. Georgia just shook her head, too busy trying to slow her breathing and quiet the pounding in her chest to speak. "I'm sorry to call you at the last minute. I was just grabbing a cup of coffee and thought I'd take a shot you were free."

Georgia finally spoke. "I'm so glad you called. I've been meaning to ask you something." So far, so good. No trembly voice. "I was just wondering, it's not a big deal, but it did cross my mind, that you don't seem that"—Georgia added a casual shrug and wave of her hand—"excited about me anymore. And that's okay, but I was just wondering if I had done something wrong. Because it seemed like you were excited about me, and now you're kind of . . . not." Bryan caught this gentle lob of emotional vulnerability with utter grace and chivalry.

"Oh, Georgia, I'm so sorry you feel that way. Of course you didn't do anything wrong. Of course not. I think you're fantastic. I didn't know it felt like that. I'm so sorry. I just got busy with school and . . . it's only been a few weeks, right? So I guess I thought we were just taking it slow . . . ?" Georgia looked at him. It made perfect sense. It had only been a few weeks. He was really busy with school. He thought they were just taking things slow. For a moment, she felt like a jerk. Why did she get so worked up over this? He didn't do anything wrong. He was just being *responsible. Levelheaded. Grown-up.* But then she remembered something. She remembered "Tuesday Thursday." This was that guy. When she met him he wasn't Taking It Slow Guy. He was Tuesday Thursday Guy. And once a girl knows what it feels like to be dating Tuesday Thursday Guy, no matter how much she wants to pretend she believes that he's busy or taking it slow, she can never forget that that same man thought that Wednesday, cruel, relentless Wednesday, and Thursday, that nasty, interminable Thursday, were far too long to go without seeing her.

She tried to imagine now what she had been hoping he was going to say in this moment. "I'm so sorry, Georgia, you're right, thank you for re-minding me that I'm in love with you. From now on I will see you twice a week and call you every evening to wish you a good night." Or, "Well, now that you mention it, Georgia, what happened is that because of my recent divorce, I equate sex with commitment, and from the minute I penetrated you I knew I needed to keep you at arm's length because ulti-mately I'm never going to be able to love you and deep down I knew that already." Whatever closure she was trying to find, Georgia realized it wasn't going to be discovered at the Adonis Coffee Shop. And her two children were upstairs without adult supervision.

"You're right. Of course. We're taking it slow. Absolutely. It never hurts to just check in, right?" Bryan nodded agreeably. She looked at her watch. She had been there exactly four minutes.

"You know, I should get back. I have a feeling my sister wants to get home."

"Sure, okay, that sounds fine," Bryan said. "I'll give you a call soon."

"Definitely," Georgia said. Very casually.

She walked away from the coffee shop with a nice, relaxed stride be-cause she knew Bryan would be watching her. But the minute she was inside her building she bounded up the four flights of stairs and into her apartment. No fire. No dead bodies. She walked quickly to her children's rooms. Beth was sound asleep. She breathed a huge sigh of relief and walked down the short hall and peeked into Gareth's room.

That's when time seemed to stop.

Gareth wasn't there. She raced to her room and was relieved to see him sitting on her bed, frightened but perfectly fine. It was what he said next that truly terrified Georgia.

"I called Daddy."

Georgia took a deep breath, in a gasp. "What? Why did you do that?"

"I was frightened. You weren't here. I didn't know where you were."

"But didn't you see my note? I left it on the pillow next to you! I said I was going to be right back."

He shook his head, his little-boy fear turning into large droplets of tears practically jumping off his face.

"I didn't see it!" he wailed. "I didn't see it!"

Georgia grabbed him and held him tightly. She rocked him and kissed his head and tried to do whatever she could think of to make up to him for the last four minutes. She stayed there for what was probably ten minutes, possibly less, when she heard Dale burst in. Georgia put Gareth down and tried to head him off at the pass, running into the living room so he could see that she was home and everything was okay.

"I'm here, I'm here!" Georgia whispered emphathically. "Everything is fine."

But Dale was not going to be placated so easily.

"Where the fuck were you? Are you out of your mind?"

Georgia took a few steps back. This was bad. Very bad.

"Seriously, Georgia, where the fuck were you?"

Georgia was dumbstruck; his fury and her blatant guilt left her with no words to use in her defense. "I . . . I . . . It was an emergency."

"An emergency? What kind of emergency could make you leave your kids alone? *That's* the fucking emergency."

It was then that Georgia started to cry. She didn't want to, she couldn't help it, but she did.

"I'm . . . sorry . . . it was just . . ."

"Was it some guy?" Dale walked toward her, menacingly. "Did you leave the house for some fucking guy?"

Georgia heard the way it sounded, heard her insanity in Dale's accusation. And she just cried harder.

"I'm sorry. Please. It won't happen again."

"Damn right it won't happen again. I'm taking the kids, Georgia."

Georgia immediately stopped crying, as if instinctively she knew that her full faculties were needed for this attack.

"What?"

"I'm hiring a lawyer. I want full custody. This is bullshit."

Georgia let out a scream, but it also came out as "WHAT?"

"You heard me. It's over. The dropping them off with me whenever you have a hot date. The yelling at them all the time. The teachers say they look dirty, they're acting out at school. You obviously would rather be single and go out and get laid, so now's your chance."

Georgia stammered. "You can't do that . . . you can't."

Dale started to leave, but he turned back to point right at her. "You should be happy. You'll get to go out every fucking night of the week if you want to. Don't try to fight it, Georgia, send me a thank-you card instead." And with that he walked out of the house. If he had looked to his left before he did, he would have seen Beth and Gareth standing in the doorway, having heard everything.

Georgia sat down at the kitchen table and started to let out a sob. She realized she had just endangered her children and now her own motherhood because of her desperation—the desperation that she had no idea how deeply she felt until it was too late.

8

There's Really So Few People Who Have It All So Try Not to Bother with That Whole Envy Thing

On the plane from Singapore to Beijing, it felt as if Thomas and I were on the lam. Every moment we spent together now felt almost criminal; it was an act of rebellion against the agreement he and his wife had for their marriage. They were allowed to leave each other and their marriage for up to two weeks at a time. Now, he wanted more. It was like choosing to escape from a Club Med.

When he called his wife from our hotel room in Bali to tell her that he was going to be away a while longer, I had left the room. The whole thing really wasn't pretty. No matter how I tried to rationalize it, I was participating in something that was probably causing someone else anguish. I wasn't sure of this, because, as I said, I had left the room. When I returned, I couldn't help but ask him how it went.

Thomas, looking very serious, just said, "She wasn't happy."

I didn't ask anything else.

So, now, going to Beijing, it all felt a little illicit, a tiny bit dirty, and somewhat dangerous. So of course some panic was to be expected. Right before we got on the plane I had taken a full Lexomil. But still, as we got up into the air, I began to feel a tightening in my chest. I'm not sure if Thomas was trying to distract me from a panic attack or if he was just trying to distract himself from his domestic concerns—but he decided to play the part of my research assistant on this trip. He had heard about my phone call from Candace, so I think he was also slightly concerned I wasn't getting enough work done. He began filling me in on what he had learned.

"This is a very interesting thing, I think, to find out about this woman drought. I think we must get to the bottom of this." He glanced over at me, slightly worried. "The Lexomil should start working soon."

There was a group of fifteen people, all together, chatting excitedly a few rows ahead of us. There seemed to be four couples and seven women traveling alone, all Americans. They were swapping photos and sharing stories. There were two others who appeared to be their guides. As I tried to slow down my breath and take my mind off my oncoming terror, I eavesdropped on their conversations.

I looked over at Thomas and whispered, "They're going to China to adopt children." I nodded my head toward the group. Thomas looked up at them. I stared at the women who appeared to be without partners. They seemed so excited, as if they had won the lottery and were going to pick up their winnings.

"It's amazing, isn't it? They're choosing to be single mothers. I think it's very brave," I said as my body started to relax.

Thomas looked at the women, and then back at me. "Do you want to have children, Julie?"

I tensed up again. "Well. I don't know. I think if I met the right person I would. I don't know if I could ever do it alone."

The truth is, ever since I met Thomas I had been thinking about children. It was such a cliché, but it was true. I had met someone I loved and suddenly I was imagining having his children. I was embarrassed at how quickly I became so predictable. Of course, it was not a fantasy that ever got very far, since I quickly reminded myself that my beloved was already married. But it had engendered such startling new images in me: Thomas with me at the birth, us lying together in bed with a baby, or clapping at the child's first step. The idea of a man and a woman falling in love and raising a child together did right now seem like kind of a genius idea.

Thomas nodded. "You would make a very good mother." He put his hand on my cheek. He kept it there a long time, and just gazed at me. I wanted to ask him if he wanted children. What his plans were for the future, for a family. He would make a fantastic father. But I reminded myself that none of those plans would include me. So I broke away and closed my eyes. I started feeling a little sleepy.

Thomas decided to get some investigating done before everyone started sleeping or watching movies. There was a woman who I guessed was in her thirties who was sitting across the aisle from us. She appeared to be Chinese and did not have a wedding band on. Thomas leaned over to her and smiled.

"Excuse me, do you speak English?"

The woman looked up from the book she was reading.

"Forgive me for asking such a question, but my friend here has been traveling the world talking to women about what it's like to be single in their culture. She's going to Beijing now to talk to Chinese women. I was wondering if you might have any knowledge of this subject."

The woman glanced over at me. I tried to put on the most trustworthy face I could, no matter how groggy I was. She was quite pretty, and looked sweet; possibly a little shy. I wondered if she would be offended at this brazen question.

"I do, yes. I'm single and I live in Beijing."

Thomas turned to me, as if to give me a little nudge.

"Hi, my name is Julie." I leaned over Thomas and extended my hand to her. She shook it.

"My name is Tammy. Nice to meet you. What is it that you would like to know?"

"Well, there have been reports in the news, that because of the one-child policy of the eighties, and all the girls that have been adopted, that there is now a woman drought in China, and the men are having a hard time dating."

Tammy laughed and shook her head. "Maybe in the countryside, yes, but not in the cities, not at all."

"Really?" Thomas asked.

"Really. The men have it so good in Beijing. They can date as much as they want, and when they do settle down, they often have mistresses. The rich ones at least."

Even with my Lexomil, I started to get depressed. "Seriously?"

Tammy just nodded her head, amused. "Yes, unfortunately. Your theory is not correct at all."

I leaned back on my chair. This was not what I had wanted to hear. I whispered to Thomas.

"So we're going all the way to China to find out that the men here have a hard time committing and like to cheat?"

Thomas laughed. "This is not good news—for us, or for the Chinese women."

I leaned over Thomas again to talk to Tammy. This would be my last attempt at conversation before I passed out. "So what do you do about this?"

Tammy shrugged. "I never date Chinese men. I think they're awful."

"Never?"

"I haven't had a Chinese boyfriend since I was a teenager. I only date foreigners. Australian, German, American. But never Chinese. Never."

Thomas was interested as well. "So tell me, where do you meet these men?"

"I work for an American company, so my last boyfriend I met at the office. But there's also a bar I like to go to, Brown's, where there are a lot of expats."

"Brown's?" Thomas repeated. "Like the color?"

She nodded. "Yes, it's in the Chaoyang District. It's a lot of fun."

Thomas looked at me. "So, to Brown's tonight? Yes?"

"Yes," I mumbled, and then fell asleep.

When we got out of the cab at our hotel in Beijing, it was quite a scene. We were staying at one of the nicer places in the center of the city. In front of us, some very fancy woman had gotten out of her big black car and twenty to thirty photographers snapped away as she walked into the lobby. We walked inside, right behind her, where there were another dozen important-looking people waiting to greet her officially. Then they whisked her away into an elevator, for what I assumed would be some kind of press conference. When we finally were allowed to walk up to the reception desk, I asked who the woman was.

"The vice president of Spain."

This, it seems, was the perfect introduction to Beijing. Things were happening here, from the high-rises being built everywhere you turned your head, to the influx of businesses trying to get a piece of this growing global power, to the vice president of Spain stopping by for a visit. This was the new China. And Thomas and I had a very important job to do. I had to go to a bar tonight and talk to women about dating.

It was a little sad. Our first night in Beijing and we were having beers at an English pub and eating buffalo chicken wings. There was a DJ who was playing "Get Right with Me" by Jennifer Lopez and the place was packed with foreigners of all shapes and sizes. I heard German, British English, Australian English, American English. There were some Italians in the bunch and a couple of French people. And yes, some Chinese as well. The crowd seemed to be mainly in their thirties, and everyone was having a good time dancing, talking, and flirting.

Thomas was still taking his job as assistant cultural observer seriously, and soon enough he was talking to some German men at the bar. I let him go it alone, thinking he might be able to get more information out of them than I could.

A young woman, around twenty-five, came up to me and handed me her business card. Her name was Wei and her card said she was a "tourist consultant."

"Hello, my name is Wei. Where are you from?"

"New York," I said loudly, trying to be heard over the music.

"I love New York," Wei said, laughing. "I love New York so much!" She laughed even louder. She had long black hair that went straight down her back and she was wearing a short black skirt and tall black suede boots. She couldn't have been cuter.

"Do you know that show *Sex and the City*? I love it so much!" Again, with much laughter. "Me? I am Samantha. That's who I am!"

I raised my eyebrows, understanding exactly what that meant, but not knowing exactly how to respond. "Oh, wow. That's great. So you must be having fun being single."

She laughed again. "Yes. I love being single. I love it. I am so happy not to have to be married and having babies. I love my freedom!" She laughed again and pointed to her card that I was now holding.

"If you need any help while you're in Beijing, anything, you let me know. I work for a travel agent. We help people with everything they need."

"Thank you, that's very nice of you." But not wanting her to leave just yet, I added, "So, are you here for business tonight, or just to meet a nice expat boy?"

Wei laughed again loudly. "Both! You are so smart!"

I laughed with her, trying to be polite, and asked, "So, are you not so interested in Chinese men?"

Now Wei stopped laughing. Her eyebrows furrowed and she pursed her lips.

"Chinese men are boring. All they care about is money. They don't know how to communicate. They don't know how to be romantic." Then she shook her head in disgust. "No, only Western men. They are much more fun."

Wei looked over and saw a tall blond man that she knew. She started waving and laughing. "Ben! Ben!" She turned to me. "What do you do in New York?"

"Well, I was a book publicist, but now I'm sort of . . ."

"Really? I am writing a book about my crazy life in Beijing. Just like New York!"

"Wow, that's great," I said enthusiastically.

"I must go, but I'll come back, okay?"

"Yes, of course."

Wei ran up to the guy named Ben and gave him a big laughing hug.

Just then, Thomas came back. "Julie, I have been working very hard for you. We have much to discuss." He pulled up two available bar stools and we sat.

"I spoke to two German men who said they were here to meet Chinese women."

I smiled, enjoying his enthusiasm about this subject. "Really? What else?"

"They said that they like Chinese women more because they are more devoted than Western women. With their German women, they said, it's too much about power and negotiation. But with Chinese women, they let them be men, they don't try and change them."

My eyebrows rose again. Thomas shrugged. "I'm just telling you what they told me."

"Well, this really is perfect then. Western men are here to meet Chinese women, and Chinese women are here to meet Western men."

"Yes," Thomas said, narrowing his eyes. "I'm very upset I didn't think of this idea. There is a lot of money to be made in this."

Just then, Wei came back over.

"We are all going to Suzie Wong's next. It's much fun. You must come." She then burst out laughing.

They say that to understand the Chinese people, you have to understand their language. So at Suzie Wong's, as Thomas and I sipped our Long Island iced teas in a little side room that we shared with two Chinese businessmen, Jin and Dong, we were given a lesson in Mandarin.

Jin broke it down for us. First of all, there are four different tones in the Mandarin language. So for each word, it may have four different meanings depending on how you say it, sometimes more. For instance, the word *ma,* said in a straight, flat tone, means "mother." But said in a tone that sort of dips slightly and then comes back up, it means "troublesome." When you say *ma* with a deeper dip, almost as if you are disapproving of something, it means "horse." When you say it sharply, it means "to curse." Now add to this that you have two different ways of learning the language, either with pinyin, which is when it is spelled out in Roman letters, or in the original Chinese characters. All forty thousand of them. These two men told us that in school it takes most Chinese people—who, by the way, *speak Chinese*—four to six years to actually learn the language.

So. The next time you want to make fun of some Chinese person's inability to speak English, just keep in mind that that person, even if he or she is just a short-order cook at your local Chinese restaurant, can kick your ass at one of the hardest languages in the world. And think of this: when it takes that much discipline and determination simply to speak your own language, you could easily end up with a work ethic that just might help you take over the world. *I'm just saying.*

After two rounds of Long Island iced teas, I was able to move them from Mandarin to the language of love.

"So tell me, is it true because of China's recent history, that there aren't enough women for the men?"

The two men started laughing immediately. Jin said, "No, where did you hear that?"

I thought for a moment. "Um, I think the *New York Times*? And maybe *60 Minutes*?"

Dong shook his head. "Maybe in the country, but here? This is not true at all. This is a very good time to be a single man in Beijing. A very good time."

Jin nodded in agreement. "It's not difficult to find women to date. But frankly, I prefer Western women."

I perked up a bit at that. "Really? Why?"

"The Chinese women have become very materialistic. All they care about is how much money the man makes."

I turned and looked at Dong. "Do you agree?"

Dong nodded. "I had a girlfriend who when we broke up after two years, asked me to pay her seventy thousand yuan."

"For what?" I asked, confused.

Dong shrugged. "I don't know. For her time?"

"Were you the one that ended it?" Thomas interjected. "Was she angry?"

Dong hit his hand to the table, his voice raised. "This is what was so crazy. She broke up with me!" He shook his head at the memory of it. "Western women, they're better. More independent. Less materialistic."

In terms of dating and China, it seems the grass is always greener on the other side of the world.

After the full effects of our drinks took hold, Thomas and I made our way down to the dance floor. There were some Westerners here and there, but this was a place where trendy locals came to mingle.

Wei was on the dance floor with a few of her beautiful, chic friends. She saw me and waved us over.

"These are my friends, Yu and Miao. They want to talk to you about being single here in Beijing."

"Wow, great," I said loudly over the music. "What do you want to tell me?"

Yu's English wasn't that great, but she made her point. "We are so lucky, to be able to be free. To be independent. To travel, to work. I love it so much!"

Her other friend, Miao, agreed. "I can have sex with whoever I want. It's very exciting to me!"

Just then I saw Thomas take out his cell phone, which must have been vibrating in his pocket. He looked at the number and his expression became quite serious. He made a motion to me that he was going outside to take the call.

We all started dancing to Shakira's "Hips Don't Lie." I was jealous of these women, in a way. They were experiencing the joy of newfound independence. The world had opened up for them only a few years ago, and now they had options, from what shoes to buy to what kind of man to sleep with. I wish I could see singlehood in that way again, with that kind of excitement and delight. I looked at all these made-up, miniskirted, and writhing cuties and I was envious. They were young, they were single, and they were having the time of their lives.

After a few songs, Thomas was still nowhere to be seen. I excused myself and walked outside. Thomas was leaning against the wall of the neighboring building, still on the phone, talking intimately, emotionally. My stomach tied into a little knot. Again, my French was limited, but I knew that there was some kind of negotiation going on. There was arguing and explaining and cajoling.

I knew she was calling him right now and demanding that he come back home. And I knew that she knew he would ultimately listen to her—because he was hers. I was just borrowing him and everyone knew that.

"Okay. Je comprends. Oui." He hung up.

I decided to just be brave and say it first.

"You can leave tomorrow if you need to. I don't want to keep you . . ."

Thomas wrapped his arms around me. "But I don't want to leave you; this is the problem." He kissed me on the forehead. He gently said, "She is threatening to come here and drag me back home." I must have looked quite alarmed, because he added, "I've never done this before. She understands this is different."

I said quickly, "Well, then you have to go home. That's it." I felt myself get choked up but I swallowed hard and continued. "This has been very nice, but you're married. *You're married.*" I took a quick, deep breath to control myself. It worked. I looked up at him, calmly. "We knew it had to end. So. This is it. It's okay. It's been fantastic. It will be a beautiful memory." I then looked down at the sidewalk and took another deep breath. I was proud, I didn't fall apart. Thomas nodded.

Thomas wrapped his arms around me again. "So, in three days I must go back to France." It was now official. There was a bottom line.

"This agreement my wife and I had, it has worked very well up to now. Very well."

I buried my head into his chest.

"You are a very exciting woman, Julie. So funny, so filled with life. I had no idea this would happen."

He kissed me on my forehead. "But that is life, I guess. This is what happens when you keep yourself open." He tightened his grip around me. "I am very sorry for all this drama."

We stood there for what seemed like forever. He was going to go back to her. This would be just another story in their crazy life together. She would win. Of course she would win; she should win, she is his wife, his history, his promise to the world.

"I love you very much, Julie. I hope you know that."

It was merely a consolation prize, that admission, but it was nice to hear anyway. We went back to our hotel and lay on the bed together, our arms wrapped around each other until we went to sleep. It was too sad to do much else.

Back in the States

Serena had always, deep down—and maybe not so deep down—resented them all. Let me phrase that better. It wasn't resentment; that's too strong a word. It was a little touch of envy. It's the hazard of any job where one is being paid to take care of someone who is wealthy enough to hire someone to take care of them. At first Serena chalked it up to being in such proximity to wealth. And it wasn't ostentatious, wasteful, stomach-turning wealth. Theirs was something much, much more enviable. For the three years that Serena was the cook to a famous movie star, his lovely former-model wife, and their one young son, Serena got to see firsthand that money does indeed buy happiness. Don't let anyone tell you differently, because the equation is simple: Money buys you the freedom to do more of the things you want to do, and less of the things you don't want to do. Thus, you are spending more of your time happy, less of your time unhappy. Therefore, money buys happiness.

Then let's just talk about where money can let you live in New York while you are spending more of your time being happy. You can live in a five-thousand-square-foot loft on West Street off Franklin, in Tribeca. The entire back wall of your huge loft can have windows facing the Hudson, so when you walk into the apartment you feel as if you've just boarded an ocean liner.

Money also made everyone look good. The wife, Joanna, was gorgeous and fit, Robert was gorgeous and fit, and their son, Kip, was adorable mainly due to winning the genetic lottery, but he also wore perfect cute boy outfits that made him look even more adorable than his DNA already did.

Since Serena had gone back to work for them, she would sometimes look at Joanna jetting off to some board meeting for some charity, going to the gym, taking her son to the park, or just sitting next to Robert on the couch reading the paper with him, and Serena couldn't help but just be envious. Joanna's DNA made her beautiful, which allowed her to be a model, which allowed her to meet Robert, who of course fell in love with her, and which then gave her this extraordinarily blessed life.

And when Serena was able to stop noticing all the important, profound things she could be jealous of, she could then move on to the more superficial things. And for Serena, that meant literally their things. They had the most amazing kitchen: a Viking stove, a Sub-Zero refrigerator, an overhanging pot rack, an entire cabinet just for their accompanying lids. Serena was able to go out and buy every type of olive oil infusion you could imagine: rosemary-infused olive oil, basil-infused olive oil, roasted-garlic-infused olive oil. And then there was the forty-five-dollar bottle of balsamic vinaigrette. And the appliances. The gorgeous Kitchen-Aid mixer. The ice-cream maker. The panini-maker. It was Disneyland for cooks. Her favorite part of the kitchen was the long, narrow column of shelves that housed all the CDs in the house, as well as a CD player and an iPod and speakers. Because you must have music when you cook and dine. Money = happiness, see?

Now the truly wonderful part of this story is that this very fortunate, wealthy, happy family happened to love Serena. Because for all the people who could have worked for them, learned their habits and their little eccentricities, and have been around when their son was misbehaving and they didn't feel like being charming parents, Serena was the one you'd want to be there pretending to be invisible.

And she's a damn fine cook. They say the turnover for private cooks is two years, because every chef, no matter how hard they try, has a style of cooking that after two years people naturally get tired of. So when Serena quit her job with them and went to the yoga center, she had already outlived her shelf life by a year. That's because Serena could cook anything. And one of her favorite things was to find a new recipe and try it out for fun. And one of this family's favorite things to do was to eat the new recipes that Serena made. And she had no idea how much they appreciated her. When Serena told Joanna she was leaving, Joanna was gracious and wished her good luck and hoped she would be happy. Serena had no idea that after she walked out of their apartment, Robert laughed and said, "Well. I guess I won't be having another decent meal in this house ever again."

When Serena began working for them the second time, something was different. She realized that there were a lot of things she really liked about this family that she didn't even notice until they were missing. For one thing: Robert. He was actually an enormously likable, down-to-earth guy who might lumber around the kitchen in a spare moment and start joking with Serena.

"What are we having for dinner, See?" he'd ask. "See" was his nickname for her. Serena assumed it was less an endearment and more because he was a movie star, and don't all movie stars like to call people by nicknames?

"Chicken with a mustard sauce and broccoli rabe," Serena might say, which is when he would invariably make a face and say, "That's disgusting, I won't eat that, you're fired." Like clockwork. It's not very funny the first thirty times it's done, but by the thirty-fifth, well, it makes things kind of feel like home.

It's not that Robert was no longer there; he was. But he seemed different. More subdued. Joanna seemed a little distracted, and everything Serena did for them, from organizing the pantry to giving the pots and pans a good cleaning, was met with such an enormous amount of gratitude that it confused her. She knew something was going on, but she didn't ask, because as I mentioned before, the main job of a household employee is to go as unnoticed as possible.

But one day, while Serena was preparing broiled salmon and a big green salad for lunch, Joanna and Robert walked into the loft after being out at an appointment. Robert smiled and clapped his big hand on Serena's shoulder.

"How ya doing, Eagle?" he said. That became his new nickname for Serena the first day she walked into their home with her new head of no hair. Robert put his hand on Serena's scalp and told her she looked like an eagle. As in bald. But this time, he could barely get out a smile when he said it. He just walked away down to his bedroom. Joanna looked like she was about to cry, or explode, or collapse onto the floor. She smiled a tight smile and tried to remain professional. She cleared her throat and began to talk.

"I know this is a complete change in what you're used to, and I know this is absolutely not in your area of expertise, but I was wondering if from now on, if you would be interested in starting to cook a raw food diet for us."

Serena was startled. A raw food diet is incredibly complicated and time-consuming and she had no experience with it whatsoever.

"I know it's an extreme diet, but there'll be a doctor consulting with you on a daily basis, and we have all the cookbooks you'll need, and a list of things for you to shop for." Joanna took a deep breath. Her voice was trembling a bit. "Would you be willing to try? I know you can make that awful food taste delicious for us," she added, trying to make a joke.

Serena said of course, she would go shopping that very day and start tomorrow. There was no need to say anything more. In this loft with the views of the Hudson and the KitchenAid mixer and the CDs in the kitchen, Serena began to understand that the charming, handsome, down-to-earth man of the house was very sick. And no one in this house could possibly be happy. At all.

· · ·

Ruby had run out of gay men to get her pregnant, but she still couldn't shake the whole baby thing. She knew she could adopt, but ever since she thought of having someone impregnate her, she couldn't help but want a baby of her own.

Which is how it came to be that Alice, only one week later, was coming over and sticking a needle in Ruby's ass.

Okay, maybe I need to explain. Ruby decided to look into artificial insemination with a donated sperm. She picked her donor father—Ivy League, Jewish, tall—and got the ball rolling. A blood test showed her hormone levels needed a little boost, but with the right drugs she could get pregnant on the first try. Of course, she could also end up with quintuplets, but Ruby wasn't going to worry about that. What she did worry about was that there was no way she could stick a needle in her own ass for two weeks. She tried it at the doctor's office and couldn't even stick a grapefruit. The thought of actually piercing her own flesh made her sick. No matter how much she wanted to get pregnant and hold a squealing baby of her very own, she would never be able to stick a needle in her own butt.

Her first thought was Serena, who was still living with Ruby until she found her own place. Serena had been looking in Park Slope, Brooklyn, for an apartment because she found out the hard way how high the rents in Manhattan had gotten. (Never give up your New York apartment, never give up your New York apartment, never give up your New York apartment.) It looked like she would find something soon and Ruby wasn't worried; on the few occasions that they were actually in the apartment at the same time, she enjoyed Serena's company.

Ruby walked into the living room, where Serena was sitting, reading. Ruby didn't know exactly how to broach the subject, so she just started talking.

"So. You know how I mentioned that I was thinking of maybe having a baby on my own?"

Serena put down her book and nodded. This didn't seem like it was going to be one of their casual roommate we-happen-to-be-in-the-kitchen-at-the-same-time conversations.

"Well," Ruby continued, "I've decided that I'm going to get the hormone shots first, to help my odds. And, I think it might be really hard to stick myself with a needle. You know?"

Serena nodded. She hoped this wasn't going where she thought it was going, but if it was, she thought it would be polite not to make Ruby have to spell it out for her.

"So do you want me to do it for you?"

Ruby breathed a sigh of relief. She loved Serena at that moment for not making her spell it out.

"Well. I know that that might possibly be the weirdest request known to mankind, but yes. How weird is that?"

"It's not weird, not at all," Serena lied. "I'd be happy to do it," Serena lied again.

"I know it's kind of a big thing to ask."

"Actually, I think if you asked me to carry your child, that would be a bigger deal."

"Well, that's true." Ruby took a beat. "We would start tomorrow. Is that okay?"

Serena was surprised. She had no idea they were talking about something that would happen *tomorrow*.

"Like, in the morning?"

"Yes. Before you go to work?"

"Okay. Fine."

"Great. Okay. Well, thanks."

And yes. It was the weirdest conversation Serena had ever had.

But in the morning it got even more awkward. There was Ruby in the bathroom leaning over the sink, her underwear slid down her butt, her butt cheek exposed, all white and vulnerable. She was imploring Serena to stick it in her ass, just do it, just do it! But Serena couldn't. She stared at Ruby's white flesh, and then at the needle in her hand, and she started to get dizzy. She looked at Ruby's reflection in the mirror.

"I can't do it," Serena said, slightly hysterical.

"You can't?" Ruby said, sweetly, but concerned.

"No. I thought I could. But I can't. I can't stick you with this. It's freaking me out."

Ruby was gentle. "That's okay, honey. If everyone was good at sticking people with needles we wouldn't have a nursing shortage, right?"

Serena felt awful. Here she was, a virtual stranger, living rent free in Ruby's apartment. The least Serena could do was stick a needle in her ass. But she couldn't do it. She was mortified. Ruby stood there with her ass literally hanging out, concerned. In order not to go off this very important schedule, she had to start the shots today.

"You really can't do it? Just today?"

Serena knew how important it was.

"Okay. I'll try. I will."

Serena took the needle, put her hand on Ruby's butt cheek, took a deep breath, and . . . still couldn't do it.

"Why don't I call Alice?"

Ruby perked up.

"Alice? That's a really good idea. I bet you she could do this without blinking an eye. Do you think she's going to think it's weird?"

"Maybe. But who cares. I'll call her and explain."

Ruby breathed a huge sigh of relief.

Two hours later, she breathed another as Alice injected the follicle-stimulating hormone drug known as Repronex into Ruby's ass.

Ruby didn't know how to ask, but she really needed Alice to give her the shot every day for the next two weeks. But there was Serena, who had no trouble speaking up because it wasn't her favor and it wasn't her ass and Alice wasn't actually her friend.

"So. We'll see you tomorrow, same time, same ass?" Serena said, her attempt at being casual.

Alice turned around and looked at them, surprised. "Oh. Do you . . ."

". . . and for the next twelve days after that?"

"You mean like every morning?"

Ruby nodded, mortified.

"Okay. Sure," was Alice's immediate reaction.

Ruby was actually oozing gratitude from every pore when she said, "Thank you, Alice. Thank you so much."

Alice flicked her hand, shooing away the moment, and said, "Please. It's nothing." And she walked out the door.

During the next week, Alice came over every morning and gave Ruby a shot.

It was then that Ruby was reminded that everything comes at a price.

Alice was now in full wedding planning mode. And like every bride that has come before her, it was all she could talk about. Every day, while she was shooting Ruby's ass full of hormones so Ruby could use a stranger's sperm to become a single mother, Alice would rattle off the latest developments on flower arrangements or what color linens she decided to use.

"Jim's mom is really into peonies, but *my* mom loves hydrangea, which you really can't have in a bouquet, because they're ginormous. So, I'm thinking of maybe hydrangea for the tables and then peonies for my bouquet."

"That sounds like a good compromise," Ruby said, bent over the bathroom sink. "I love both."

"I know, but the florist of course has his own whole idea on what it should be that does not include hydrangea or peonies." Alice stuck the needle into Ruby's ass. "I brought croissants today—do you want?"

So every day, Ruby would stand there in the bathroom with her pants down listening to all of Alice's wedding conundrums and stories and she was plain jealous. *Jealous.* Alice was Ruby's age, but she was going to get married and then get pregnant and then have children running around the playground. She was going to have a family with a mommy and a daddy. And Ruby wasn't. Alice was picking out a wedding dress. Ruby's breasts were starting to swell from the hormone injections. But Alice was doing her an enormous favor, so Ruby had to bend over and take it.

Alice started bringing over pastries and bagels for Serena and Ruby. They would sit and chat every morning before Ruby and Serena had to go to work. Alice, not being completely unfeeling, also asked them what was going on in their lives. Ruby noticed that Alice seemed to really enjoy her time with them, and soon her visits stretched from ten minutes to a half hour, to an hour. And even though Alice was annoying with her wedding talk, she was funny to listen to and, Ruby realized, good company.

Over the following weekend, Alice met Jim over at his sister Lisa and brother-in-law Michael's house for brunch. They all got started talking about the upcoming wedding, and Lisa and Michael started talking excitedly about their fond memories of their own honeymoon. Soon enough, Michael had carted out his Mac and started giving Alice and Jim a little slide show.

As they started digging into their scrambled eggs and bagels, Michael clicked on their first photo: the two of them at the beginning of the Inca Trail in Peru. They were beaming newlyweds, with Michael's arm around Lisa and her head bent in, almost leaning on Michael's shoulder. Lisa no longer needed to face the world straight on, with her head erect and her posture strong. She was in love and could smile and lean. They were up in the mountains, with the clouds seemingly only three feet above them.

"We were so far up, it was like we were walking on air," Lisa said, it all coming back to her.

"We were . . ." Michael said, putting his arm around Lisa and giving her a kiss on the lips. "Remember?" Lisa smiled and kissed him back. She then turned to Alice.

"I'm so glad you and Jim have found each other. Some people might think you guys are going too fast, but I just think when you know, you know, right?"

"Yes, it's totally true." Alice nodded, a knot tightening in her chest. Click.

"This is when we finally got to Machu Picchu. Isn't it amazing?" Michael said. He grabbed Lisa's hand and gave it a squeeze. Click.

"This is the temple of the sun. They say it was built for the astronomers of the village," Lisa said. She squeezed Michael's hand back. Click.

"This is what they call the Jail. They think they held prisoners there," Michael said, the photo showing the couple kissing, surrounded by tall rock walls. Click.

"This is the hotel at the base of Machu Picchu. It's not fancy but the view is unbelievable," Lisa gushed.

"We spent an extra day there and didn't even leave the room," Michael said, with his eyebrows raised. Lisa giggled and hit Michael in the arm.

"Michael, Alice and Jim don't need to hear that."

"Sorry, guys!" Michael laughed. "The trip was just so great. I hope you guys have just as much fun on your honeymoon, wherever you go."

Alice hoped so, too. Click.

"Michael, no!"

"What? Just a few."

"Please, we don't need to bore Alice," Jim said, laughing.

Michael couldn't resist, and decided to show Alice a few of their wedding photos. The one on the screen now was of them outside the church, kissing. Michael and Lisa fell silent, almost worshipful. Alice could have sworn that she heard them sigh in unison, in a reverie of unified bliss.

Then Lisa said the thing that took the knot in Alice's chest and twisted it into a stabbing pain. "It was the happiest day of my life."

Alice had come for brunch, but she ended up being treated to a pictorial study of love; the kind of love she always wished she would have, and the kind she knew she would never feel with Jim. Her wedding day would not be the happiest day of her life. She would never look at Jim the way Lisa looked at Michael. No matter how she rationalized it, no matter how she spun it, that was the truth. If she married Jim, she was never going to have that. She watched the photos click by of them dancing at the reception, of them cutting the wedding cake. She knew in her wedding photos she and Jim could look just as happy as they did. At their wedding, no one would suspect a thing. But she would know.

As Alice and Jim left the building and walked down the street, it was only now that she truly understood what it meant to settle. She wasn't just making the decision, "You know what, by golly, this is good enough." She was saying, *This is the level of happiness I'm willing to stop at. Forever.*

The next day, Alice brought over cheese Danish because she knew it was Ruby's favorite, to celebrate the last shot of the series. This time, however, after the injection, when they were sitting at the kitchen table, there were no swatches or magazine tear sheets or photos of flower arrangements to look at.

"I really hope you get pregnant, Ruby. I really do," Alice said, quietly, as she picked at her Danish.

"Thank you. I've gotten really excited at the idea," Ruby nodded shyly.

"It's really nice for you to have done this, Alice. I'm sorry I was such a wimp," Serena added.

"It's no problem. You asked, and I thought, Why not give it a shot?" Alice said, laughing. Ruby and Serena sort of laughed and groaned at the same time. "Besides, I think it's really brave what you're doing, Ruby. Really brave. You're going after something you really want. It's amazing."

Ruby was feeling such goodwill in the air that she felt sincerely inclined to say, "So, you haven't given us the daily update on your wedding plans!" Alice nodded.

After walking for many hours yesterday, Alice had come to a major decision. She couldn't ignore the fact that she was, in fact, settling. She also couldn't ignore the fact that her wedding day would not be the happiest day of her life. She knew that she was a strong, clever, stubborn woman—and could do whatever she set her mind to do. That night she went over to Jim's apartment. She talked it all out with him, and even though he was deeply disappointed, he knew it was what Alice wanted. And in the end, all he wanted was Alice's happiness.

"We've decided to elope," Alice said. She managed to then dodge everyone's reactions by taking a big wedge of Danish and shoving it in her face.

Ruby and Serena did indeed react—it was the last thing they were expecting Alice to say. "It just got to be too much." Ruby and Serena just nodded, pretending they understood what Alice meant.

"Every couple always threatens to do it. I think it's great that you are," Ruby contributed.

"I'm really psyched. We're going to go to Iceland next month and get married there. Just us," Alice said. Ruby and Serena sat there, at a slight loss for words.

Finally, Ruby just said, "Iceland?"

Alice nodded. "It's supposed to be really gorgeous there. And with all the darkness now, I think it's going to be really romantic."

Alice just kept chewing and not looking them in the eyes—now it was her ass hanging out there in the wind. She changed the subject quickly and they made plans to meet up soon for lunch. Then, she was gone.

As soon as the door closed, Ruby turned to Serena. "Does she look like someone who's madly in love and excited about getting married?"

Serena gave Ruby a look. "She's going to Iceland so she can get married *in the dark*. So no, no she doesn't."

Ruby, who had just spent the past two weeks seething with envy over Alice and all that she had, was now worried about her. Maybe Alice didn't have everything that Ruby wanted. But instead of that making Ruby feel good, it just made her sad. "Maybe it's time to call Julie."

RULE
9

Not to Put Pressure on You, But Start Thinking
About the Whole Motherhood Thing

(You Really Don't Have Forever)

The next morning, I woke up to see Thomas walking into the room. For a moment a shudder went through me—I realized exactly how much I was going to miss him. There he was: his humor, his intellect, his good nature, all in one beautiful package. It was all going to be ending soon and I would be devastated. I tried to put those thoughts quickly out of my head.

"Where have you been?" I said, sleepily.

Thomas's blue eyes were bright with excitement. "I have been doing some investigating for you. There is a park we must go to today. It will be perfect for your research!"

After a typical Chinese breakfast consisting of a rice congee—a watery rice porridge that can have meat or fish thrown in it—we took a cab to Zhongshan Park. Thomas had practiced saying the name of the park during the entire breakfast, but in the end I had to show the cabdriver the paper that our concierge gave us, spelled out in the Mandarin characters. As I said, Mandarin isn't something to be taken lightly.

Thomas wouldn't tell me what this trip was all about, so my curiosity was piqued. As we got out of the cab and walked into the park, Thomas finally explained.

"I read about this online—parents come to this park to make matches for their unmarried children. Every Thursday and Saturday afternoon."

"Really? You mean it's sort of like horse trading but with people?"

Thomas shrugged and took my hand. "Let's find out."

In the park we saw a few dozen people standing around a fountain. Some were sitting silently, some were chatting. But all of them were holding a big white sign to their chests. It was all in Chinese, but Thomas's research had paid off.

"They're holding up facts about their son or daughter. How old, how tall, what type of education."

These older Chinese parents meant business. Some would start talking to others, to see if there could be a match. Sometimes they would show one another photos of their children that they had been hiding from view. It seemed like a somber process, with people talking very seriously with one another, and looking at us Westerners with great suspicion. Many of the parents were just sitting there staring into space, with the photo or information of their son or daughter hanging from their necks.

I don't think these older Chinese people would be telling me how happy they were that their sons and daughters had so many options available to them, and how delighted they were that their thirty-six-year-old daughter was still unmarried. These parents were so dismayed over their children's love lives that they had literally taken to the streets. In a country with a notable distaste for public gatherings, these people were out there with signs on their chests, trying to get their children married off. These parents were experiencing the ramifications of their children's independence. It was hard not to find it depressing.

I tried to look on the bright side of things.

"Maybe we should think it's sweet. How concerned they are. And what harm does it do?"

"Or you could think of it another way," Thomas said. "Because of the one-child rule, they only have one child to care for them as they get older. Maybe they think it's better for their own well-being to have their children married off."

I shook my head. "That is so dark."

Thomas smiled and took my hand. "I know how you like the theories. I was just offering mine."

We had decided to take a little tour of Houhai, a beautiful little neighborhood that has some of the last remaining courtyard houses, or *hutongs*. These little gray structures, some attached by a courtyard, all connected by little alleyways, were once the typical domicile for most of the people in Beijing, but now were being torn down to make way for high-rises. But in Houhai, the little shops and food stands in the hutongs themselves had now become a main tourist attraction. This neighborhood just might be spared in Beijing's new development craze.

We stopped to have some lunch at one of the little "restaurants" in the middle of the hutong. It was a dirty, tiny place that basically served only dumplings and noodles. The jars of chili pepper paste that were on the table looked as if they hadn't been wiped down in years, and flies were buzzing all around. The two people working there spoke absolutely no English. In a world where it's getting harder and harder to find anyone who can't speak English or doesn't know where the nearest Starbucks is, this was a comfort. We were in the middle of something authentic, even if the only reason it was kept authentic was for the tourists. Something about it all made me get emotional. We sat there sharing a plate of noodles with vegetables, and a plate of boiled dumplings. After a few moments in silence, I spoke.

"I want you to know that this was good for me," I said, trying to sound philosophical, yet casual.

Thomas looked at me, not saying a word.

"It gives me hope, that there's love out there, there's possibility. You shouldn't feel badly about any of it. I understood your situation."

Thomas put down his chopsticks.

"My dear Julie, I don't feel sorry for you. I know you will be fine. This is what is so difficult for me."

He smiled and took my hand. I didn't want to cry in front of him, since I knew my French counterpart would have much more pride. I asked the woman who served us our dumplings where the bathroom was.

"WC?"

She pointed to outside on the street.

I was confused. I said it again. "WC?" She nodded and spoke to me in Chinese and again pointed outside. I stood up and looked out the door. A few yards away some women were walking out a doorway.

"Wish me luck," I said to Thomas and walked out the door.

In Beijing, as I soon found out, they enjoy "squatter" toilets. Even in some of the upscale establishments, they had not yet found the need for a good old Western toilet. This was something I was prepared for, having been to Rome and not being all that squeamish about these things. But walking into this public "WC" I actually experienced a bathroom situation that I not only had never encountered, but had never even heard existed.

First of all, as I walked toward this public facility, the stench was incredible. I had to stop breathing through my nose while I was still on the street outside. I considered just turning back, but I really did have to pee. I walked into the entryway and took a few steps in. I looked around. I was in one large room, no doors, no walls; just about eight squatting toilets altogether with Chinese women squatting on them. The only thing that separated each squatter was a little metal partition, only about two feet high, in between each one. So it sort of gave the feel of being in a squatting pen.

I walked in and saw this and I was actually shocked. This, for a New Yorker, is not an easy thing to be. I was shocked by simply seeing four or five Chinese women squatting and peeing together, and then I was shocked with the quick realization that I was expected to do the same.

A few of the women looked up at me and I had a strange moment of some new kind of pride. I didn't want to be a wimp about things right now. This is my life, I am in the hutongs, and this is how they pee.

I walked to one of the squatters, unbuttoned my pants, and squatted. I looked up and found I was face-to-face with an old Chinese woman who was in the squatter right across from me, only about a foot away. If we spoke the same language we could have had a nice little chat. Instead, she farted, and I looked down and finished peeing.

So I had gone from a kiss at the Colosseum to falling in love in Bali to a squatters' pen in Beijing. It was all quite clear to me. My grand affair was indeed coming to an end. There was nothing I was going to be able to do about it except get through it as quickly and with as much dignity as possible. I took out a crumpled tissue I had brought with me and dried myself off.

When we got back to our hotel, there was a message on our phone from our new best friend, Wei, inviting us to a party at this restaurant and bar called Lan.

"It's going to be so much fun! So exciting!" And then she let out her long, loud laugh.

Thomas and I got dressed up and walked to the bar, which happened to be across the street from our hotel. When the elevator opened up, we were immediately ushered into one of the more impressive spaces I had ever seen. We had to pass through the massive nightclub-restaurant to get to where our party was. The whole place was done up in melodramatic elegance, as if it were a king's palace, with velvet drapes and huge chandeliers in what seemed to be thousands of square feet. There were different restaurant spaces, bar areas, and lounges, all designed to create a different opulent mood.

We walked to the end of the restaurant where the party was taking place. We could hear the din of people talking and laughing. As we got closer, we saw that it was another beautiful crowd of Chinese hipsters, everyone fabulously attired and drinking. The minute we walked in we saw Wei.

"Oh my God, it's so good to see you, my friends!" She ran over to us in a tiny white and black sequined minidress and gave us a big kiss on our cheeks. She pushed us over to the bar and then ran off to say hello to someone else. As Thomas ordered us wine, I turned to see Tammy, the woman we had met on the airplane, standing with a martini in her hand. We looked at each other, surprised—trying to remember how we knew each other.

"Oh! Hi, I met you on the plane," I said.

"Yes, that's right. Hello."

"Hi."

Thomas came over to me with our glasses of wine.

"So tell me, how do you like Beijing? Are you learning a lot about single women here?" Tammy asked, pleasantly.

"I am, actually. Thank you. It's a very exciting time to be here."

"Yes, it is," Tammy said. "There have been so many changes, so fast—it's been very interesting to see it all."

"Really? What kind of changes?" I asked, curious.

"Well, it's only been in the past ten years that we had supermarkets. Before that, I wasn't able to touch my groceries."

"I'm sorry, what did you say?" Thomas asked.

"It wasn't until only a few years ago that we had grocery stores where we could actually take our groceries off a shelf and look at them before we bought them. Before that they were all behind the counter."

For some reason the idea of not being able to touch your groceries was fascinating to me.

"So now you're free to be single, to get divorced, to touch groceries—everything's different."

"Yes, we have so much freedom now. Not like our mothers did."

"So tell me—do women here ever think about becoming single mothers? Is that something that's done?" I asked casually.

Tammy took a bite of a spring roll and said quite matter-of-factly, "No."

Thomas and I looked at each other. It was such a definite answer. So black-and-white.

"Really? Never?"

"No. Never. It's not possible."

"But what do you mean?"

"It's not possible."

I took a pause, not wanting to push. And then I just repeated, "But what do you mean?"

"Each child is registered at birth. With this registration, they are given access to health care and other services. A child born out of wedlock is not given a registration. It's not recognized by the government. It does not exist."

Thomas and I stared at her for a moment.

"So, tell me, Tammy, what does a single Chinese woman do if she gets pregnant?" Thomas asked.

"She has an abortion," Tammy said, as if it were the most obvious answer in the world.

"What about adoption? Can't a single woman adopt one of these Chinese babies in the orphanages?" I was shocked by this new piece of information.

"No. It's not possible," Tammy said again, with complete seriousness.

"But why not? There's so many of them."

Tammy just shrugged. "Don't you see? If you let a single Chinese woman adopt, you would be allowing them to be single mothers. It would be almost the same as letting them have their own children. This will never happen. Or maybe it will happen, but not for many years."

It then began to dawn on me that all these women that were out and about in Beijing enjoying their freedom, refusing to settle, working hard on their careers, had one very big difference to us Western women. They didn't get to have a Plan B. We get to date the wrong men and have our little affairs and in the end, we still know that our motherhood isn't ultimately at stake. Many of us don't want to be single mothers, many of us will not choose it even if it's our only option, but it's still an option.

These ladies, who now get to choose from three different kinds of shampoos, don't have the option to be a mother even if they haven't found the right man. Their singleness came at a price much higher than I realized.

"So, if you're thirty-seven or thirty-eight and you want to be a mother, what do you do?" I asked.

Tammy shrugged again. "You marry the next man you meet."

She must have detected the sad look on my face. "It happens all the time."

Suddenly those parents in the park didn't seem so crazy to me.

The two gentlemen we met the night before at Suzie Wong's came in, Jin and Dong. I introduced them to Tammy. Even though Tammy made it clear that she didn't enjoy Chinese men, for a moment I had hoped that she and Jin would hit it off. They talked for a while, as Thomas and I made conversation with Dong. Eventually, Dong and Jin went to the bar to get some drinks. I decided to play matchmaker.

"I know you don't like Chinese men, but Jin seemed nice, no? I thought you two might hit it off."

Tammy looked over at Jin, who was the Chinese equivalent of the nice stable guy in the States who sells insurance or becomes a dentist, except a little more handsome and able to speak more languages.

"Please," she said, rolling her eyes. "If I wanted to marry *that* guy, I could have been married a long time ago."

I went to the bar and got myself another drink.

The next day, our last together, we decided to walk from our hotel to the Forbidden City, the main tourist destination of Beijing. Thomas took my hand as we walked down the street. It was rush hour, with cars whizzing by, and crowds of cyclists going to work. Many of the cyclists were wearing masks over their faces, to protect them from the intense pollution there—another result of Beijing's growing economy. Thomas stopped me and gave me a long kiss. It felt sad, like the beginning of good-bye.

At first glance, the Forbidden City isn't all that impressive. All you see from the outside is a long red wall with a picture of Mao Tse-tung that hangs over it all. It looks a little drab, I'm not going to lie. But once you get inside, it all changes. You are in the largest palace still standing in the entire world. What seems like miles and miles of walkways lead to the various temples and halls that all the great emperors used from the Ming dynasty on. The halls all have grand and majestic names that I couldn't help but find amusing: the Gate of Heavenly Purity, the Palace of Supreme Harmony, the Hall of Mental Cultivation, the Hall of Lasting Brightness. Even the modern antilittering signs to the tourists were filled with melodrama: "A Single Act of Carelessness Leads to the Eternal Loss of Beauty."

Thomas and I chose to do the audio tour, which was quite stressful at first. Both of us were wearing headphones and carrying around a little GPS device and trying to understand where we were supposed to look and what we were actually looking at, based on what the guide in our ears was saying.

"Is yours on yet?" I asked Thomas.

"Yes, mine is saying something about musical instruments—do you not have that?" he asked.

"No. I don't have anything . . ."

"Well, maybe you should try . . ."

"Shh . . . it's coming on. Wait, are we in the right place? Are we in the Hall of Supreme Harmony? Where's the statue of the lion? What's she talking about?"

That sort of thing. But eventually we got into a nice rhythm and we were able to walk around with the little guide in our ears that knew exactly where we were at all times, and what we needed to know. It was perfect. Thomas and I were together, holding hands, experiencing the grandeur of the largest palace in the world, and we didn't have to talk to each other about anything.

Near the end of the tour, as I was looking at one of the little temples, I glanced over to see Thomas taking out his cell phone. The light was flashing. He took off his headphones and started talking on his phone. Again, he looked fairly animated. I chose to turn away. I listened intently to my audio guide, who sounded a bit like Vanessa Redgrave. In fact, I think it *was* Vanessa Redgrave. As I was looking at the Palace of Heavenly Purity, Vanessa was telling me about how the emperor hid the name of his successor, whom only he could choose, under a plaque that said "Justice and Honor." At the same time he carried a duplicate copy in a pouch around his neck, so that if he died suddenly, there could be no high court shenanigans. As I was listening to this tale of palace intrigue, I glanced over at Thomas. He had shut the phone and had started pacing, nervously. I took off my headphones.

"What's the matter?" I asked.

Thomas ran his hands through his black wavy hair. He didn't answer.

"Ça c'est incroyable," he muttered in French.

"What?" I asked, now a little worried.

Thomas didn't answer. He just kept shaking his head.

"She's here. In Beijing."

"Who's here . . . ?" I asked, hoping I didn't understand what he had just said.

"Dominique, she's here."

It was then that I realized I didn't even know her name. I had purposely pushed her so out of the realm of my reality that I didn't even know what people called her.

"Your wife?" I asked, alarmed.

Thomas nodded. His face was getting a little red.

"She came to Beijing?" I asked, trying not to shriek.

Thomas nodded again, tugging at his hair.

"She didn't believe I would ever come home. So she's come here to get me."

I stood there, standing on the tiny steps that lead to the Palace of Heavenly Purity. There were now throngs of tourists, mostly Chinese, shoving past me.

"Where is she now?"

Thomas crossed his arms over his chest. Then he started biting his thumb. He put his hands down by his sides.

"She's across the street, in Tiananmen Square. She's coming here, now."

"How can she be across the street—how did she . . . ?"

Thomas looked at me, astonished. "I don't know. I think she just got here and told the taxi to take her to Tiananmen Square, and then she called me."

I looked at him, incredulous. "Well, what should I do . . . where should I . . . ?"

I looked around, like an empress trying to find her route of escape from the advancing army.

"Let's just take you out the back entrance and then I'll go talk to her."

"Okay," I said, my heart beating rapidly. "Okay."

We walked quickly through the Imperial Garden (it looked lovely from what I could tell) and were about to walk through the doorway that said "exit here." I turned to Thomas to tell him that I would go back to the hotel, and he could call me there—or, I don't know what, really—when I saw him looking over my head. His expression was fixed, but his eyes looked like someone had just pushed a fire alarm. I turned around, and saw this beautiful, tiny blond woman in a long cashmere coat and fashionable heels walking toward us fast. Her hair was in a high ponytail, and it bounced behind her as she stormed toward us. She had entered the gates of the Forbidden City and was about to confront us both in the Imperial Garden. What better place for a wife to confront her husband and his concubine?

Thomas is an outstandingly cool and elegant man, but even he, at this moment, looked as if his head was about to explode all over the cypress trees.

"What should I . . . what . . . ?" I stammered.

I wanted to flee, to run the three miles back to the front gate and through the streets of Beijing to the hotel and jump under the covers and hide. In two more seconds it would be too late for that.

Dominique charged up to Thomas, yelling at him in French. Then she looked over at me with utter disgust, and started to yell some more. I could make out some of the things that she said, about the years they'd been together, how much she loved him. I kept hearing that over and over again, "Est-ce que tu sais à quel point je t'aime?" ("Do you know how much I love you?") She kept pointing at me and yelling. Even if my French wasn't perfectly accurate, I got the gist of it: Why would you throw away everything we have for her, for this woman, for this whore, for this nobody. Why is she so special? She's nothing. We have a life together, she doesn't mean anything to you. Thomas wasn't defending me, but how could he? He was just trying to calm her down. Throughout all this, I have to admit, she looked beautiful—and dignified. I was amazed; she flew all the way around the world to rip him out of the arms of another woman, and she looked gorgeous and chic the whole time she was doing it. The Chinese tourists were staring, confused and a little surprised, but they kept on moving. With over a billion people in their country they didn't have the time or the space to really give a shit about anything.

I was taking a few steps backward, when Dominique just put her hands on Thomas's chest and pushed him back, hard. Now the tears were falling down her face. Thomas looked truly surprised, as if he'd never seen his wife this upset before. I turned around to go when I heard her scream out "Je suis enceinte" in French.

I wasn't sure, but I thought she'd just said, "I'm pregnant." And judging from the look on Thomas's face, that's exactly what she said.

I lowered my head and, without a word, escorted myself out of the Forbidden City. I was officially dethroned.

In one of the Chinese travel books I had bought at the airport, I read that there's a common saying to sum up the total regime of Mao Tse-tung: It had been "70 percent good and 30 percent bad." I liked that. I think percentages are a good way to sum up most things in a person's life. As I walked back to my hotel, I tried to trace my steps backward, to remember all I had done to land me now on the Street of Great Humiliation and Sorrow. I had been trying to say yes to life and play by someone else's rules and experience love and romance and go for it. Was that so wrong?

In Bali it seemed like a really great idea. Now, on West Chang An Avenue, maybe it was more accurate to say it was a 70 percent bad idea and a 30 percent good one. All I knew for sure was that I had made a French woman cry on the street, that I was called a whore, and that the man I was in love with was about to go off and start a family with his wife. As he should. I was mortified and ashamed. I had done it again. I had gone and dated a bad boy. Maybe a boy who was only 20 percent bad and 80 percent good, but a bad boy nonetheless. So besides experiencing the shame of the public humiliation and the guilt at my own behavior, now I got to add to it the realization that I was still making the same damn mistakes.

"Don't come home," Serena said. I had called her at six in the morning her time. "You can't just run home because of a man; that's insane."

"Well, what am I supposed to do?" I asked, sobbing on the phone. "I don't want to travel anymore. I'm sick of it . . ." My voice trailed off as I wept.

"Go to India!" Serena said. "I know of an ashram right outside of Mumbai. It's a great place to just go and heal. You'll feel better there— you'll see. India is an amazing place to give you perspective."

"I don't know . . ." I couldn't imagine taking another plane all the way to India. I just wanted to get back to New York, with my bed and my apartment and all the sights and smells that I'm used to. Then I realized I had to give my subletter two weeks' notice. So I wouldn't be able to go back to my apartment now even if I wanted to.

"Think about it. Don't make any big decision just yet. Give it a few hours."

"But he's going to have to come back here. I don't want to see him."

"He's not going to come back there for a while, trust me. Just take an hour or two to calm down and think."

I hung up the phone and sat on the bed. I didn't know what to do. I hated the idea of going back to New York because of a broken heart— that seemed so weak. I put my head down on the pillow, exhausted.

I woke up to the sound of the hotel phone ringing in my ear. I practically jumped to the ceiling at the sound of it. I sat up in bed and stared at it as it rang and rang. I wasn't quite sure how long I had slept. An hour? Three days? I didn't think it could be Thomas, he would call me on my cell, but I wasn't sure. I let it go to voice mail. When I went to check the messages it was Wei.

"Julie! I am having a big karaoke party right now in your hotel for some big Chinese businessmen. I'm in lounge on eighteenth floor! You and your boyfriend have to come!" And then, of course, she laughed.

The party never stopped for that one. It really irritated me. Besides calling Thomas my boyfriend, how could she be partying away as if she didn't have a care in the world? Didn't she know her days were numbered? That someday she's going to be pushing forty or fifty and she might not find everything as funny as she does now? That she might end up a single, childless woman alone in a country that considers itself communist but expects you to pretty much take care of yourself? I wasn't sure if she knew this, but for some reason—let's blame the jet lag and/or the fact that Thomas was absolutely gone from my life, *gone*—I decided it was my job to let Wei know the truth about being single.

I jammed on the little terry cloth slippers the hotel provided, grabbed my plastic hotel key card, and went out the door. I walked briskly to the elevator and got in. There were two nice-looking midwestern men in the elevator. They chatted to each other, but both of them at some point glanced down at my feet. I guess they'd never seen anyone walk around a hotel in their slippers before. I got out on the eighteenth floor, and so did they. I followed them into a large room just opposite the elevator, called "The Executive Suite." For this night it had been transformed into a karaoke lounge, with a disco ball in the middle and a large video screen. There were lots of young women prancing around in their designer outfits, and lots of Chinese and Western businessmen drinking and chatting with the girls.

Wei was standing on a little stage that had been set up, singing a song in Chinese while the karaoke machine displayed the words on the screen, along with a video of a Chinese man and woman walking along a babbling brook. I don't know what she was singing about but—wait a minute—could she be singing about—I don't know—love? Do you think? Just as she was finishing up her song and everyone started clapping, I stormed up on the little stage and stood right next to her. I looked out on this sea of twenty-something Chinese girl cuteness and men in suits going along for the ride. I grabbed the mike out of Wei's hands.

"I just want you ladies to know that you should think very carefully about what you're doing," I said loudly into the microphone. Everyone stopped talking to stare at the crazy lady. Wei just looked at me. She cupped her hand over her mouth, covering a smile.

"You think you have all the time in the world, you think that it's so fun to be so free and independent. You think you have all these options, but you don't really. You're not always going to be surrounded by men. You're not always going to be young. You're going to get older and know more about what you want and you won't be willing to settle and you're going to look around and there will be even *fewer* men for you to choose from. And you're not only going to be single, but you're going to be childless as well. So you should understand there are consequences to what you're doing now. *Very serious consequences!*"

No one said a word. Clearly, they all thought I was a lunatic. I handed the mike back to Wei. She kept her hand over her mouth and laughed.

"Oh, Julie, you're so funny! You are so funny!"

Back in the States

It was the day Ruby was to be inseminated and she didn't have anyone to accompany her. And, really, what could be more depressing than that? By this point Ruby was bloated. Fat. Her breasts felt as swollen as if she were already pregnant. She imagined someone pricking her with a needle and having the water just come gushing out of her, and bringing her back to her normal size again. She had also been really emotional for the past three days, which she attributed to the hormones, but, really, let's face it, it could also be because she was about to be ejaculated into by a syringe and then possibly spend the next nine months pregnant and alone. I'm just saying.

Her good friend Sonia was supposed to be her plus-one to the ejaculation, but she canceled at the last minute because her daughter was sick. Ruby didn't want to call Serena because Serena had told her what was going on at her job and she didn't want to bother her. She called Alice, but she didn't pick up. Ruby would have asked her gay male friends but she was still mad at them. The only person left was Georgia. They really didn't know each other very well, and Ruby thought Georgia was a little crazy, but maybe it would be better to go with a crazy person than no one at all? She wasn't sure.

But then, Ruby considered the alternative—getting in a cab, going to the clinic, lying on a table, getting shot full of semen, hailing a cab home. Alone. So she picked up the phone and called Georgia. Alice had told her about the daily shots so she wasn't taken completely by surprise and she said yes immediately. Georgia was desperate to have something to do besides think about the upcoming custody fight with Dale and the visit with the court-appointed social worker that was happening later that day. The kids were at school, as opposed to at home, unattended, and she was free to think about someone else's life for a change.

When Ruby got to the clinic, Georgia was already outside. Ruby relaxed. It was nice to have someone there for her, waiting for her.

"Hey Ruby," Georgia said, sweetly. "How are you feeling?"

Ruby just smiled and said, "Fat. Nervous."

"This is really exciting," Georgia said as they were about to walk through the revolving doors. "You might become a mother today."

"I know. Isn't that weird?" Ruby replied, putting her hand on the revolving door and pushing it.

Georgia followed right behind Ruby and said, "You know what? *It's all weird.*"

The waiting room was mercifully quiet. There were only two women there, both pregnant—which seemed like a good sign to Ruby. Ruby signed in and she and Georgia sat down to wait.

"I think it's fantastic that you're doing this. Being a mother is one of the most wonderful experiences in the world. Really," Georgia said.

Ruby smiled. She was happy to hear that right now.

"You'll never really be able to understand it until it happens to you, but it's like this awesome responsibility is given to you—to take care of another human being on this planet. That little person becomes everything to you." Georgia seemed to be lost in thought. "It's incredibly sweet."

Ruby looked at Georgia. For once, she seemed soft. Vulnerable. Gentle. Not crazy.

"So, you're going to do it as a single mother. What does it matter?"

Georgia added. "We all end up getting divorced and becoming single mothers anyway. You're just starting out that way."

Ruby thought that was a little bleak, but perhaps Georgia was just trying to make her feel better about being single. Ruby glanced over at the magazine rack filled with *Woman's Day* and *Redbook* and *People*. Georgia continued her pep talk. "It's a fuck of a lot better for the kid this way."

Now Ruby wondered where this was going.

"At least with you they won't be subjected to an asshole father who wants to go to court to prove that you're an unfit mother. At least there won't be that."

"What?" Ruby said, taken off guard.

"Oh. Yeah. That's what's going on right now. Can you believe it?"

Ruby never let her gaze stray from Georgia, so as not to reveal in any way the thought crossing her mind, which was "*Well, actually . . .*"

Georgia took a breath. She picked up a *Parents* magazine and started to flip through it. "But today is not about me. It's about you. And my point is that you shouldn't feel badly about this. Why deprive yourself of having children just because you don't want to be a single mother? By the time we're fifty, everyone we know is going to be a single mother." She stopped to look at a photo of the "Five-Minute Brownie."

"The problem with single mothers is we're all competing for the same men—the ones who are willing to date women with kids. I mean, how many of those guys are there in New York? How can we all possibly find one?"

Ruby had the impulse to put her hand over Georgia's mouth and not take it off until her name was called. Instead, she leaned back in her chair, closed her eyes, and sighed. Maybe it wasn't a good idea to have invited Georgia to her insemination party after all.

"Ruby Carson?" a nurse called out, and Ruby stood up immediately. Georgia sat up and squeezed Ruby's hand.

"Do you want me to go in with you?"

The image flashed through her mind of Georgia sitting there while some doctor or nurse put a syringe of semen in her woo-woo.

"No, that's okay, you can stay here, I'll be fine."

"Okay. But if Julie was here, she'd be in there with you, so I just wanted you to know that I would."

"Thank you. I appreciate it. I think it's really fast. I'll be fine."

"Okay," Georgia said, a little relieved. "Have fun!"

Ruby was undressed and sitting on the examining table. She felt like a little girl, her feet dangling down, clutching at her paper robe. She remembered her first gynecological exam. She was thirteen, and was brought by her mother right when she got her first period. She sat there, just like now, waiting, not knowing what to expect, but understanding that it was a rite of passage, one that would usher her into a whole new chapter of her life, as a woman. The only difference then was that her mother was with her; her mother who now lived in Boston; her mother who raised her as a single mother, by the way; a mother who was always extremely depressed. Her father left them when she was eight, and her mother never remarried.

She closed her eyes and tried to think fertile thoughts. But all she could see was her mother sitting at the kitchen table, smoking, staring out into space. She thought of her mother coming home late at night from work, carrying the groceries. She thought of the three of them at the kitchen table—Ruby, her brother Dean, and her mom—quietly eating together. Her mother, too tired, too depressed to talk, her brother and she trying to lighten things up, with mashed-potato fights, with milk coming out of their noses. She remembered her mother's anger; then often, her mother's tears.

"Don't you know how hard I work? Don't you understand how tired I am?" she shouted once as she got up and grabbed a sponge and walked over to the wall to attack a big gob of mashed potato. Ruby remembered that they laughed at her in that moment. She seemed like just a grotesque caricature, not a real person. It seemed funny to them at the time, their mother with all that crazy emotion. Of course at that moment, at the sight of her children's smirks and giggles, Ruby's mother broke down and cried.

"I can't take it anymore! I can't!" she said as she threw the sponge in the sink, letting out a series of sobs as she leaned against the kitchen counter, her back to her two children. "Burn the whole house down if you want to," she screamed as she raced out of the room.

Ruby remembers the feeling she had in the pit of her stomach in that moment. She didn't know what it was at the time, but as she got older, she found herself recognizing that feeling over and over again. She had it when she saw a blind person, all alone, tapping along a busy Manhattan street, or once when she saw an old woman fall down on the ice. It was pity. At ten years old, she was giggling at her mother because she didn't know how else to process the sick feeling in her gut of feeling sorry for her own mother. As she became a teenager, as she saw her mother have a string of boyfriends, all in differing shades of lame, she processed the pity in a whole new way: she hated her. Not like this is the most unique story ever told, but for Ruby's last two years of high school, she stopped speaking to her mother. Yes, they didn't get along, yes, they fought about things like curfew and outfits and boyfriends, but more importantly, Ruby just couldn't stand pitying her anymore. So the less she engaged with her in any way, the less Ruby had to feel that queasy, awful feeling in the pit of her stomach.

Now here Ruby was, feeling her naked body sticking to the sanitary paper covering the table, and waiting to be inseminated by a doctor. Why? Because when the music stopped and everyone had grabbed their men, she was left standing alone. The race was run and she had lost it. *She had lost.* That was the only way she could see it as she sat there, naked and alone, waiting.

Maybe if I had been there it would have been different. Maybe I would have joked with her and said the right thing and made her feel that what she was about to do was the beginning of a life that, though hard at times, would be rewarding beyond measure. There would be life and joy and children and laughter. But I wasn't there, and I didn't say anything genius, and Ruby started to slide down into that hole like so many times before.

In the middle of her slide, Doctor Gilardi came in. He was in his early sixties, with a distinguished head of white hair and skin that had the kind of tan that came from entitled living. Ruby chose him because he was handsome and gentle and she felt that, as the man inseminating her, he would in some way be the father of her child.

"So," he said with a smile. "Are you ready to go?"

Ruby tried to be chipper. "Yep. Knock me up, Doc!"

Doctor Gilardi smiled. "I'm just going to examine you one last time, and then the nurse will come in with the specimen."

Ruby nodded and lay back, put her feet in the stirrups, and opened her legs. The doctor wheeled a chair over and sat down, ready to take a look.

Lying there, Ruby felt that old feeling again. She wondered if it was called "pity" because it was always felt in the pit of your stomach. It didn't matter how the word was made, all she knew was that she felt it now, for herself. There in the paper robe and the fluorescent lighting and the absence of any man anywhere in the world who loved her, she was pitiful. She thought about all the men she had dated and spent too much time grieving over. There was Charlie and Brett and Lyle and Ethan. Just guys. Guys it didn't work out with, for whom Ruby had cried and cried. She knew they weren't jerking off into a cup right now so some surrogate mother could have their children. She was sure they all had girlfriends or wives or whatever the hell they wanted to have. And there she was, about to be a lonely, sexless, depressed single mother.

The nurse came in carrying a big cooler. She opened it up and the smoke of the dry ice came billowing out. Out of it she took a canister that looked like a large silver thermos. This was filled with Ruby's children.

"Here it is," the nurse said, sweetly. Doctor Gilardi stood up and took it from her. He looked at Ruby.

"Everything looks fine. Are you ready?" A million thoughts came to Ruby at this moment. About going home afterward to her empty apartment. About taking a pregnancy test and finding out she was pregnant. About not having a man there with her, who would be ecstatic about the news. About being in the delivery room with her friends, her family, but no man. But the one thought that truly made her cringe in pity was the memory of her mother crying, talking to some friend on the phone. "I can't take it," Ruby remembered her mother saying through her tears. "It's just too much for me. It's too much. I don't know how I'm going to do this, I don't!" And then her mother crumpled into a chair, sobbing.

Ruby shot up, yanking her feet out of the stirrups.

"No, I'm not ready. I'm not ready at all." And she turned to the side and hopped off the table. She held her robe together as she said, "I'm so sorry to waste your time, I'm so sorry to waste all that good sperm, and I'm really, *really* sorry that I just wasted over seven thousand dollars, but I have to go."

• • •

It was eleven thirty in the morning. Georgia opened her refrigerator door for the twelfth time in five minutes and stared inside. She had milk. And eggs. And bread and vegetables and fruit and little cheese sticks and fruit juice boxes and pudding cups. She had some cooked macaroni and cheese in some Tupperware, as well as some pieces of fried chicken wrapped up in plastic. She thought this would be a very homey touch, showing that she had cooked a nice meal the night before—what said "good mother" more than some leftover mac and cheese and fried chicken?

She did not have a good attitude about this interview. It was a mother-fucking humiliating motherfucking interview with some bullshit social worker or psychologist or whoever who was going to come into *her* home, and look into *her* refrigerator and ask *her* questions about how she was raising *her* kids. And then this woman, this bitch, this do-gooder, "I'm so noble" *busybody* was going to decide whether she would be allowed to keep *her* children. Georgia slammed the door of the refrigerator.

She thought that perhaps she should get into a better mood before the social worker came.

She paced around her apartment. "This is serious," she said, to herself. "This is as serious as it gets." She tried to breathe. In and out. In and out. She started thinking about bad mothers. The mothers she saw on the streets, screaming at their kids, slapping their kids, calling their kids names like "stupid" and even "you little asshole." She thought about all the stories she had read in the paper about women who had burned their children with cigarettes, or abandoned them for three days, or let them starve to death. She stopped pacing and looked around her lovely apartment in the West Village. *There's no way they're going to take my children away from me. I'm their mother, for God's sake.* Then she thought about crazy-ass Michael Jackson and his diabolical Neverland and his dangling his child out a window as he greeted his fans. *And he got to keep* his *children*, Georgia thought to herself as she walked to the bathroom. She opened the door to the medicine cabinet and looked around at the Band-Aids, baby aspirin, real aspirin, bandages. Was there anything she didn't have in her medicine cabinet that was going to make her seem unfit? She couldn't believe Dale had the nerve to call her an unfit mother. Okay—So, fine. She left the house once with the children unsupervised. Georgia closed the medicine cabinet and looked in the mirror. That *was* really, really bad. But doesn't every parent once in their fucking parenting life do something really, really negligent? Was she the only one in the whole world that's made a mistake? Georgia stared at her face in the mirror. Okay, so it was over a guy. That was also really bad. It was. She had spiraled and lost her bearings and she went a little nutso. Okay—so, fine. She didn't dangle anyone over a fucking balcony.

She walked out into the living room and looked around. Were there any sharp objects around, any dangerously jutting corners on the furniture that could make her seem like an unfit fucking interior decorator? Georgia, still burning with rage, walked into the kitchen and looked into the pantry. Ah, the pantry. What's better than a big pantry? This almost relaxed her, the corn muffin mix and the chocolate chips and the vanilla extract and the flour and the coconut flakes. Her mother had once told her that every home should have the ingredients to make toll house cookies at all times. She never forgot it. *Now does that seem like the thinking of a motherfucking unfit mother?* Too angry. Much too angry. She was trying to just breathe when the doorbell rang. Georgia wanted to burst out crying. But she didn't. She took a breath and walked calmly to the door. She breathed again, but as she put her hand on the doorknob she couldn't help but think, *Dale will burn in fucking hell for this.*

She opened the door with a smile. Standing there was a short man with a gray ponytail and mustache. She knew his type immediately. Liberal do-gooder social worker throwback to the sixties. He smiled benignly. Georgia smiled benignly back. She hated him. How would he know what a good mother was? He was a man, just like Dale, and he could just kiss her ass.

"Please come in," Georgia said sweetly and waved him in. He walked in and quickly looked around the apartment. Georgia's eyes moved with his. She could see what he saw: a clean, privileged, well-cared-for home.

"My name is Mark. Mark Levine."

"So good to meet you, Mark." *So good to have you come into my fucking house and judge me.* "Can I get you anything to drink? I have coffee or

tea, grape juice, orange juice, pear juice, grapefruit juice, tap water, bot-
tled water, sparkling water, Gatorade . . ."

"A glass of water would be fine, thank you," he said.

Georgia went in the kitchen and opened the door to the refrigerator
wide, revealing its maternally full contents. She saw him notice it, and
she smiled to herself as she pulled out the Brita pitcher and filled up two
glasses. "Why don't we talk in the living room, Mark?"

"That would be fine."

They walked to the living room and sat down. Georgia wondered if
she should put coasters down on the coffee table—would that make her
seem like a good mother because she had an attention to detail, or a bad
mother because she was too anal? She decided for the coasters. She sat
back and sipped her water and looked at Mark Levine.

"I know this must be a particularly difficult time for you," Mark said,
gently. "I'll try to be as sensitive as possible, even though I'm going to be
asking you some personal questions."

"Ask away," Georgia said, cheerfully. *Asshole.*

"Well, to start, it's always good for us to inquire about your relationship with your ex-husband. How you feel about him and how you talk to
your children about him."

*My relationship with him is great. That's why you're sitting in my fuck-
ing apartment deciding whether my children should be allowed to live
with me.*

"Well, considering the situation, I think we're getting along remark-
ably well. I encourage him to see the children. I was, and still am, perfectly ready to work out some kind of official custody arrangement with
him."

Mark looked at his notes. "He mentioned that you had some problems with his new girlfriend."

Georgia's stomach did a tiny little flip as she took a sip of her water.
"Well, yes, she is quite young, and he did just meet her." She looked up at
Mark Levine with wide, innocent eyes. "Wouldn't any mother have con-
cerns?"

Mark Levine nodded his head. He checked his notes again and then
gently said, "He mentioned that you called her a 'whore'? 'Gutter trash'?"

Georgia looked him dead in the eyes. *So this is how it's going to be, asshole.* "Have you ever gone through a divorce, Mr. Levine?" Georgia asked, as neutrally and as calmly as possible.

"Yes, unfortunately, I have."

"So then you understand there is a period, a small regrettable period, when emotions are heightened? When we might do or say things that we regret later?"

"Of course," Mark Levine said with an obligatory tight little smile. He continued to look down at his notes. Georgia imagined drilling a hole in his forehead.

"And these feelings, possibly of resentment toward his new girlfriend, did you make your children aware of them in any way?"

Georgia answered this one quickly. "Of course not. Even the most . . . I don't know . . . unsophisticated parent knows by now that you should never *ever* bad-mouth your spouse or his friends in front of the children."

"Of course," Mark Levine said delicately. He took a breath. "So when your husband said that Beth had called his girlfriend a 'cheap Brazilian whore,' would you say that . . ." Mark Levine paused, not really knowing how to finish that question or if he really needed to.

"That's an absolute lie," Georgia said, lying. "This just goes to show what lengths my ex-husband will go to in order to portray me as some kind of vindictive, out-of-control monster." Georgia got up from the sofa and just stood with her hands on her hips, then off her hips, then on again. "Do I look like the kind of woman who would call another woman a 'cheap whore' in front of my four-year-old daughter?"

Mark Levine looked up at her and didn't say anything.

And then it began. She started talking.

"Not that it's not painful, mind you, to find out your husband of twelve years has decided to leave your marriage and break up your home and start seeing a woman almost fifteen years younger than him. A woman whom he wants to introduce to your children, to go to the park with them, maybe go get Chinese food in Chinatown, maybe all go see a movie, like one big happy *family.*" Georgia was now pacing around the apartment, in front of Mark Levine sitting on the sofa, behind Mark Levine sitting on the sofa.

"Like it's completely appropriate to live with your wife and children one day, and then the next being like 'Hey, kids, I want you to meet my new girlfriend.' Does that seem appropriate to you? *I*, meanwhile, am just trying to go on a few dates, just trying to find a decent man of an appropriate age who *one day*, a long, long time from now, when my children are healed and well and strong, I *might* bring home to meet them. Yet, I am the one that gets criticized. Judged. Now tell me, Mr. Levine, is that fair?"

Again, Mark Levine said nary a peep.

"Truly, Mr. Levine, does my husband's behavior seem like that of a man who is sensitive and understanding of the needs of his children? Or does he seem like a man who is perhaps in a sex-induced haze because he's getting fucked three times a night by some Brazilian *whore*." Georgia stopped dead in her tracks. Mark Levine put down his pen and looked up at Georgia, expressionless.

"I . . . I mean . . . shit. Shit. Fuck." Georgia realized how she sounded. "I mean, I mean . . ." Georgia sat back down on the couch and shut up for a minute, tears welling in her eyes. She looked up at Mark Levine.

"You have to understand. This is an incredibly stressful thing. To have you come in here, and ask me questions . . . it's very upsetting. And then you put the word *whore* into my head. I mean, you used the word *whore* first, you put it in my head and then I was upset and then, pop!"—Georgia made a gesture with her hands by her head to signify, well, a pop!—"it came out of my mouth!"

Mark Levine closed his notebook.

"I completely understand. This must be a very difficult time for you." It was clear from Mark Levine's body language that he had seen enough and was about to get up and go.

"Yes, it is. I hope you understand that. We're talking about my children. About whether my children are going to get to live with me. What's more important than that? What could be more stressful than that?"

Mark Levine, again, left the question unanswered. He stood up to go. Georgia had nothing left to say. She had run out of rope to hang herself with.

"I think it's best if I come back another time. The next time I'll talk with you and your children together. Is that okay?"

Georgia stayed motionless on the sofa. "That would be fine, thank you."

Mark Levine let himself out.

After about a good ten minutes of Georgia staring out into space, frozen, unable to cry or scream, she stood up. Without thinking, she walked to the kitchen and opened the refrigerator door. She stood staring at the milk and the bread and the eggs and the fruit and the vegetables and the sparkling water and the chicken and the mac and cheese for a very long time. She closed the refrigerator, leaned against the door, and began to cry.

• • •

Serena was doing everything by the book. She had begun pureeing vegetables, making salads, and getting recipes for things like hemp pesto and zucchini "pasta." She was not cooking anything over 110 degrees. She was making sure every single vegetable was organic and then scrubbed within an inch of its raw life.

Serena, as I mentioned before, knew that part of her normal job description was to be as unobtrusive a presence as possible in their home. But now she was trying to be invisible. This family, with whatever hardships they were going through, at least deserved some privacy. This seemed to be exactly what Joanna and Robert wanted and fortunately, they seemed to be getting it. The press didn't have a clue what was going on. There were no friends, no family traipsing in and out. Their loft was a solemn yet tranquil oasis. So Serena attempted to be the invisible sprite floating on the outskirts of their suffering. She wanted to feed them, nourish them, keep them going, perhaps without them even remembering she was there. She would try to bear no witness, leave no footprints. Instead, she attempted to put all her "presence" into the food. Some of her yoga training remained, and she began preparing the food as if doing a meditation. She began visualizing her healthy life force pouring into the food; she pictured all her healing energy radiating out of her fingers and imbuing the raw food with magical curative powers. In her own small way, with her zucchi-getti and her sunflower seed patties, Serena was trying desperately, quietly, to save Robert's life.

But as far as Serena could tell, none of it was working. From her perspective, all the medical equipment that started getting wheeled in clanged and banged like a death knell and the beautiful loft now looked like a hospital ward. From what Serena could tell, as she drifted like a ghost in and out of their home, Robert was going in for chemo once a week and it seemed to be making him incredibly sick. Any other normal person going through this would be in the hospital right now, but because of who he was and how much money he had, they had managed to bring the hospital to him.

And at eight o'clock every morning, Serena would use the key they gave her and let herself in. Joanna would invariably walk out of her bedroom and greet Serena with a bright "Good morning!" Serena would smile and meet her with as cheerful a "Good morning" as she could muster, and then she would cast her eyes down and walk to the kitchen and get to work. They both had it down to a science. Serena would prepare lunch and dinner and snacks for Robert and Joanna (who was also on the raw diet to support Robert) and then a different dinner for Kip. She would stay all day in the kitchen, which was a big open one that everyone had to walk past to get anywhere, but Serena always kept her eyes down, never acknowledging that anything was even happening for her to see.

But that day, around two thirty in the afternoon, as Serena was moving her hands over some broccoli sprouts, praying over them, meditating on them, Joanna walked up to her, looking ashen, her voice shaky.

"I'm sorry, Serena, I would normally never ask you this, but Robert's having a hard time breathing. The nurse is on her way, but I don't think I should leave now to pick up Kip. I know it's not your job, but I was wondering if you could pick him up from school? Just this once?"

"Of course, I can go. Of course," Serena said, immediately taking off her apron. "It's Tenth Street, right?"

"Yes. He comes out the front door usually right at three. But if he sees you, he might . . . he might get nervous, so if you could . . ."

"I'll make sure he knows everything is okay, and you just got busy."

"Thank you. Thank you so much, Serena," Joanna said, closing her eyes in relief.

Serena took this opportunity to actually look at Joanna straight in the face, which she almost never did. She was a beautiful woman, the kind with naturally jet black hair and white, porcelain skin. She had just a few absolutely adorable freckles dotting her nose. She also looked very tired. Serena quickly got on her coat and left.

As she walked over to the school, Serena thought about having to make conversation with Kip. She really didn't understand eight-year-old boys and would have to say she didn't really even like them all that much. Every seven- to thirteen-year-old boy Serena had ever come into contact with had seemed to be a maze of uncommunicativeness and superhero obsessions and video games. Really, who could care less, except their mothers, whose job it was to blast through that crap with maternal good-ness and feminine tenderness so they could rest easy knowing they weren't raising the next generation of hazing frat boys and date rapists.

Kip was no different. He was all Xbox and Club Penguin and bore-dom. He was impenetrable and somewhat spoiled and Serena was always more than happy to be invisible around him and he was more than happy not to notice that she even existed. Especially now with her crazy short hair. The only person in the whole world who could get him to light up, giggle, act silly, and talk nonstop was his father. When he wasn't working, Robert would pick Kip up after school, and they would burst through the door, sounding like they were in the middle of an outraged debate, both refusing to back down from their impassioned positions. It might be about who they thought it would be better to be, Flash or Batman, or which they would rather eat, dirt or sand. They might take off their shoes and try to settle the argument by seeing who could slide the farthest in just his socks. Robert would tickle Kip and reduce this stoic pre-man to fits of squirmy laughter.

Now, Serena was standing in front of the school practicing the casual, cheerful, but not too cheerful expression on her face that she would have when Kip first saw her. An expression that immediately showed him, before his stomach could leap anywhere near his heart, that everything was fine, there was no emergency, and this was just a pesky little devia-tion from an otherwise normal day. The doors opened and teachers and children started streaming out of the school. Kip took one look at Serena and his eyes grew wide, his normally impenetrable face filled with fear. Serena got to him as quickly as possible to allay his fears.

"Your mom's busy but everything's fine. She just got tied up with a few things."

Serena hoped to God that she wasn't lying. She knew there were probably a million reasons why his breathing was labored and was sure the nurse was there right now taking care of it. Even though Robert was sick, even though things looked very bad, still, from her narrow perspective she couldn't imagine Robert would actually die. Movie stars don't die of cancer. Name one young, handsome movie star who died of cancer. None. They just don't.

"Let's go home and you can see for yourself," she said as she put her arm gently on his shoulder.

As they turned the corner at Watts Street, they both saw the ambulance at the same time. Serena instinctively went to put her hand on Kip's shoulder but he was already running. They were only half a block away and Serena could see Joanna coming out of the building next to a stretcher. Serena began to run, too, to catch up with Kip. Her greatest fear as she watched the stretcher come out was that there would be a sheet covering his head. *Please make it not covering his head.* As she got closer, she saw Robert on the stretcher with an oxygen mask on his face. Alive. Joanna was crying as she walked quickly behind the EMS workers. She looked up and saw Kip. She tried to return her face to that of a cheerful mother, but she couldn't. Kip was now right by her, crying, too.

"What happened?" Kip screamed, his voice childish and raw.

"Daddy was having a hard time breathing," Joanna said, the one sentence she was able to get out calmly before she started to sob again. Serena didn't want to intrude, but she went to Joanna and put her arm around her. Joanna then turned and buried her face into Serena's shoulder. She began to sob deeply.

Serena looked over at Kip. He was staring at his mother with enormous confusion and terror in his eyes. He turned away the minute he saw Serena look at him.

Joanna quickly picked her head up and looked at Kip as well. She wiped her eyes and went over to him. She crouched down to talk to him.

"I have to go in the ambulance with Daddy . . ." she began to say. Kip didn't let her finish her sentence; he just started screaming.

"No! No!" he wailed, as he stomped his feet and flailed his arms around.

It was then that Serena noticed something out of the corner of her eye. She looked up and saw it and it started moving before she had even a moment to think about it.

The "it" was not an object, it was Steven Sergati. Steven Sergati was a man who proved that sometimes you can indeed absolutely judge a book by its cover, because he looked like a weasel. Or a rat. His long, slicked-back black hair slid down his back, ending in a long little rodent tail. His pointy eyes hid behind a pair of five-dollar glasses, bought cheap because they had gotten broken so often. His four front teeth jutted out into a little point that would be perfect for gnawing on phone wire, which he had probably done at some point in his life for some nefarious reason. He was the most beaten-up, sued, spit-upon snake of a cockroach of a paparazzo in all of New York City. You weren't a VIP bouncer in New York City if you hadn't given, at some point, Steven Sergati a beat-down. Preferably in some alleyway where no one saw you do it. This man was infamous for disrupting film shoots, breaking into buildings, frightening young actresses, and stalking one particular celebrity for so long and so relentlessly that the celebrity had to get a restraining order against him. He had been seen screaming at a young television star as she walked down a lovely tree-lined New York street with her newborn, shouting that she had a fat ass and no one was going to want to fuck her anymore—just so he could get a photo of her being a new mom and scowling like Medea.

Serena recognized him from a news article Robert had shown her about him last year. Robert had his own grudge against Steve, since he had picked Robert and Joanna to stalk for a period when Kip was two. But six-four Robert, a former college football player who had just finished playing an action hero, was not someone who was going to wait for a judge. And there happen to be a few little alleyways on this one strip of Tribeca. So Robert was one of a group of celebrities, which included Sean Penn, Bruce Willis, and George Clooney who had been known to issue Steve a beat-down of their own. That was the only restraining order Mr. Sergati needed and he left them alone after that.

But there he was. He had been waiting for the right moment, when he knew his enemy was vulnerable, to stage his next attack. Joanna was about to get into an ambulance with her dying husband as their son Kip, his face red and contorted, was stomping his feet and shrieking in full view of the snapping camera. Even Serena, who was not media savvy in the least, knew that a photograph of Robert's son wailing as Robert was whisked away in an ambulance would fetch a great deal of cash.

Before she knew what she was doing, she placed Kip behind the ambulance out of view and marched across the street. Not a march, really, more like a stride that sped up as she got closer to him—the way a lioness would move just before she caught an antelope and tore its rear legs off.

Steve, who was used to this sort of thing, stood up straight, raised both his hands in the air, and said, "I'm not doing anything illegal. You can't stop me!"

The only good thing about Steve Sergati was that he was painfully skinny. So it was easy for Serena to shove him down, grab his camera, and then smash it on the ground, but not before she got the digital card out of it.

"I'm going to call the cops!" Steve shrieked, in his high-pitched rat squeak. "I'm going to sue you, you bitch! You can't do that to me! I know everyone! Everyone."

Then Serena, the former swami, leaned down and got right in his face, her nose practically touching his.

"Listen, motherfucker," Serena growled in a voice that was no longer hers, "I own a gun. And if you come anywhere near this family ever again I swear to God I will blow your fucking head off." And then Serena stood up and just looked down on him lying on the ground and added, "Please. Try me."

Across the street, Joanna and Kip were looking at her as if they'd just seen a ghost. But, in fact, it was the exact opposite. For at that moment, Serena was no longer circling on the outskirts of their lives like a mist. She had plunged right into the middle of it all. She walked back across the street to the stunned Joanna. Right now there was other business to attend to.

"I haven't had time to call anyone . . ." Joanna stammered. "Do you mind staying with Kip until . . ."

"I'll stay as long as you need me. Please don't worry."

Joanna looked at Kip. "I'll call you the minute I get there, okay, sport?"

Kip nodded. The doors of the ambulance closed, and Joanna and

Robert were whisked away. Serena turned to Kip, this distraught eight-year-old male creature, and didn't know what to say to him. He took care of that for her.

Kip watched as Steve Sergati got up and rambled shakily away. Then the boy looked up at Serena, his big eyes filled with awe.

"Wow. You kicked that guy's *ass*." This was the first time in all the three years that she knew him that Kip had actually spoken to her directly.

Serena smiled. "Yeah, I guess I did." And then Serena, the superhero, took Kip back upstairs.

· · ·

The afternoon after her canceled insemination, Ruby decided to go visit her mother in suburban Boston. Every now and again, a girl just needs her mommy.

On the train north, Ruby tried to figure out why she was going. What did she want to get from her mother? As the train rode through Connecticut, and she looked out at all the little houses with their covered-up pools, and their doghouses and their plastic jungle gyms, she decided that she needed to know if her mother really was as miserable back then as Ruby remembered her to be. Maybe it wasn't such hell raising her and her brother. Maybe her mother wasn't as unhappy as Ruby's childish memories made her out to be.

She rang her mother's doorbell. She lived on a quiet little street in Somerville. No one answered. She rang again, surprised—Ruby had called and told her she was coming. She walked down the driveway, around to the back of the house. Shelley was in the back raking leaves. She was now sixty-eight years old, with dyed light brown hair, which had streaks of gray in it and was cut in a short, curly little bob. She had Ruby's body—round, voluptuous, but with the added weight that comes from deciding to grow old gracefully rather than spending every spare moment at the gym. Unseen, Ruby watched her mother for a moment; she looked hearty. Comfortable in her own skin. She wondered how happy she was these days. Her mother looked up.

"Ruby!" she said, coming over and giving her daughter a big hug. "It's so wonderful to see you!"

Of course it is, because you're my mother and I'm your daughter and all mothers are always happy to see their children. There must be a reason for that.

"You look great, Ma," Ruby said, meaning it.

"So do you! So do you! Let's go inside!"

After Ruby showered and changed, she walked into the kitchen, where her mother had the tea ready. "I made some cinnamon toast, too! Just like the old times!" Ruby smiled, thinking that was such a nostalgic thing to do. Every time it snowed, there would always be cinnamon toast waiting for Ruby when she came inside. It was her mother's little tradition, one that was passed down from her own mother. The tea for them was an adult tradition, one that they shared down to the idiosyncratic detail. They both liked weak American tea—Lipton will do just fine, thank you very much—and when together, like today, they knew implicitly that they would share a tea bag between them. She sat down at the table.

"Tell me all about New York. What's going on?"

Some people have sophisticated mothers, ones they can talk to about their abstract thoughts and who can tell them where to go to buy the one bra they're looking for.

That was not Shelley, which never bothered Ruby a bit. Because what you got instead of someone who might have seen that documentary about Sudanese refugees was a mother who reacted to everything you did with complete wonder and glee. You got someone who wanted to hear everything about Manhattan and your business and your life because it was all still so exciting to her.

"Well, a new restaurant opened in the Village," Ruby said, "but no one can get in because it's always filled with the owner's friends. It's pissing everyone off."

"Really? That's so interesting. Are there a lot of celebrities there all the time?"

"Every night."

Ruby's mom just shook her head. "That's not right."

Ruby smiled. "It's not." She sipped her tea and picked up a piece of cinnamon toast. She took a bite.

"Mom. I've been wondering. About what it was like for you."

"What it was like how, dear?"

"Well, you know, as a single mother."

Shelley rolled her eyes. "Oh, it was hell. It was awful. I had a miserable time."

"Were you lonely?"

"Honey, I was so lonely that I thought about killing myself on a number of occasions. I'm not joking. It was horrible, it really was." Shelley sipped her tea. "So who is the owner of this restaurant? Is he famous, too?"

"Yeah, sort of. He runs a magazine." Ruby tried to get her mom back on track. "So, it really was just as awful an experience for you as I remember?"

"Oh, I'm sure it was worse than you remember. It was the worst time in my life," she said, with a little laugh.

Ruby took another sip of her weak tea and burst out crying. She put her elbows on the table and her head in her hands. "I'm sorry, Mom." Ruby looked up at her mother. "I'm sorry you were so unhappy. I'm so sorry."

Ruby's mom put a hand on Ruby's arm and leaned in close, smiling. "But don't you see? I'm fine now. I'm happy. I have friends and my garden and I go out all the time."

Ruby started to sob even harder. "It's too laaaaate! You needed to be happy back then! So I could think it was okay to be a single mom! It's too late!"

Shelley looked at Ruby, trying to take this in. She didn't feel attacked, just terribly sad. She touched Ruby's shoulder. "But honey, you're not like me, you're nothing like me! If you want to be a single mother, you won't be like me at all!"

Ruby leaped out of her chair, with tears streaming down her face, her voice choked and trembling. "But I'm just like you. I like tea and I'm depressed and I stay in bed and I cry a lot and I'm really, really lonely."

Ruby's mother got up and put her hands on Ruby's shoulders. "Well, if you're so much like me, then do what I did. Get yourself to a doctor and get yourself on a nice antidepressant. Lexapro worked for me."

Ruby looked at her mother, surprised.

"What?"

"I've been on an antidepressant for the past year. It's changed my life."

"You . . . what?" Ruby stammered, still trying to process this news.

"There's no reason for you to be walking around depressed. There's no good reason whatsoever. You should get a prescription, too."

Ruby sat down at the kitchen table again. It was shocking. Even after the countless nights spent crying, the days of not being able to get out of bed, Ruby had never even considered taking an antidepressant. It hadn't even crossed her mind. And yet here in the suburbs, her unsophisticated mother had beaten her to it.

She spent the rest of the day sitting at her mother's kitchen, crying. She told her about the fertility drugs, about not being able to go through with it, about how she remembered how miserable her mom was, and how it made her leave the doctor's office. It was Shelley's turn to start crying.

"I'm sorry. I'm so sorry, I should have tried harder to hide how unhappy I was, I'm so sorry."

Ruby continued to cry as well, saying, "It's not your fault. How could you have hidden that? You did your best, I know that. I do."

"Yes, but I wish someone had told me . . ."

"What?"

"That it was also my job, besides feeding you and getting you dressed, and making sure you did your homework, it was also my job to somehow make myself happy. For you. So you could see that. I'm so sorry."

Ruby reached over and held her mother's hand. "There's no way you could have done it all. There's no way." Then she and her mom sat there the rest of the day, talking and holding hands, making each other feel better and sipping their Lipton tea.

· · ·

Georgia's children were staring at Mark Levine. Mark Levine was smiling a wide, closed-lipped smile, as if he had just caught something in his mouth that he didn't want to let out, but wanted to make sure everyone knew he was happy.

"So," he began. "How are you two today?"

Beth and Gareth looked at him blankly. Georgia had some sort of satisfaction at this. Her kids instinctively knew he was an asshole and that they shouldn't talk to him. His lips went back to their closed smile. He tried again.

"I'm here because your mother and dad want me to find out how you two are doing now that your dad isn't living here anymore."

Silence.

"For instance, I heard that one night you were left all alone, isn't that right? And were you scared?"

Georgia looked down at her hands. She felt beads of sweat popping up on her forehead. She had never before realized how much energy it could take to *not* kill someone.

Again, silence. Blessed, hostile, sullen, child silence.

Mark Levine looked at Georgia. "Maybe it would be best if I spoke to them on my own?"

Georgia looked at him, startled. "But . . . I didn't know that you're allowed to . . ."

"We are absolutely allowed to question the children without you in the room. For your protection, I have a tape recorder so it's not just my word you'll have to take."

Georgia, of course, wanted to protest, but considering how the last meeting went, she decided to restrain herself.

"Of course you can. I'll just go into my bedroom and shut the door."

"Thank you," Mark Levine said. "This shouldn't take too long."

Georgia stood up and looked at her children. Her children who were now her judge, jury, and executioner. Her moody, fibbing, childish, adorable, bratty, unpredictable children who were now going to have every word they said written down as if they were the Dalai Lama. Georgia glanced at Gareth. *Last week he had an imaginary friend who was a giant tarantula. Yeah, talk to them about who they want to live with. Motherfucker.*

"Now you talk to Mr. Levine, okay? Tell the truth and answer all his questions. We both want you to just say how you feel, okay?"

She then walked slowly and confidently back to her bedroom. When she got to her room she closed the door and threw herself on her bed, buried her face in a pillow, and let out as loud a scream as she dared. After a moment, she sat up and stared into space.

Georgia wondered how she had gotten here; to a place where a court might rule that she was an unfit mother. She thought about her marriage. Images started flashing before her eyes of the fight she had with Dale on the street once about how he never picked up the mail. She thought about how she would snap at him in the morning, because he always dumped coffee grounds on the counter—and there's nothing she hated more than having to wipe up coffee grounds and then wrestle them off the sponge. She thought about how stupid she thought he was for never knowing how to use the microwave, or how angry he would get when the paper wasn't delivered correctly, but would never bother to call and complain about it. She wondered when she started disliking him so much, and when she became so unrestrained in making him aware of that. It must have been after the kids came. She heard that was common in marriages. Why was that? After they are done procreating, do women subconsciously decide the man has fulfilled his duty, and so they let him know in big and small ways that they have no use for him any longer? Why would she feel that way? It was not like she wanted to be a single mother. It was not that she wanted to go out and date again.

She thought about Sam and buying herself all those flowers. She thought about dancing on top of the bar and the man telling her to get off because he wanted a hotter girl to get on. She thought about chasing the guy down at Whole Foods. It was all coming in flashes, each image more humiliating than the next. And of course, she thought about the Bryan frenzy that caused her to feel the need to run out of the house, leaving her two children alone.

She realized then that she really had gone crazy. And she had no one to blame but herself. In the marriage, she felt entitled to have unbridled irritation for Dale at any time, with any provocation. Then, being left by Dale made her feel entitled to act without any restraint whatsoever. Somehow she had lost control of herself, and now she had lost control over her own motherhood. She sat wondering what her kids could possibly be saying about her. She remembered when she was called to the school after Gareth had hit another boy. She came and talked to the principal while Gareth sat on a bench in the hall outside, nervous and ashamed. *Well, the tables have certainly turned, haven't they?*

After about twenty-five minutes, which was an eternity, Georgia decided to peek her head out and see what was going on. *I am their mother, after all.*

"Just making sure everything is all right!" Georgia said, with her body in the bedroom, her head leaning out into the hallway.

Everyone was where they were before, the two kids on one sofa facing Mark Levine on the other. No one seemed particularly traumatized, no one seemed particularly angry at her.

"We're actually done, perfect timing," Mark Levine said.

There was nothing in his demeanor to suggest that anything particularly earth-shattering or indicting had been said. He gave Georgia his usual tight smile, said good-bye to the children, and left.

Georgia looked at her children. They didn't seem upset or angry. But still, she wanted very badly to ask them to act out the entire twenty-five-minute interview. But instead, Georgia did something she hadn't done in a very long time; *she showed restraint.* Georgia walked into the living room and up to Beth and Gareth and sat down next to them. She gently asked, "Are you guys okay?" They both nodded. She looked at them carefully, to see if there was anything that needed to be done. "Do either of you have any questions?" They didn't say anything. They looked okay; unharmed.

"Okay, then. Who wants a snack?"

10

Remember That Sometimes There Are More Important Things Than You and Your Lousy Love Life AND Get Your Friends More Involved in Helping You with Your Lousy Love Life

Basically, I cried all the way to India. And by this point, I didn't care who saw me. The man next to me asked if he could change his seat (which he was able to do) and two flight attendants asked me if I needed anything.

When I arrived, a friend of a friend of a friend of Serena's from the yoga center, a woman named Amrita, was going to meet me. I had no idea what would make this perfect stranger be willing to do this, but I was very grateful. I didn't have the will to be adventurous and strong. I had an image of India of lepers begging on the streets and cows running rampant. But I also read *Time Out Mumbai* between crying jags on the plane, and I couldn't imagine that a city where they had a *Time Out* review of performance art would also have cows and begging children. So, I didn't know what to expect.

As I walked into the airport, the first thing I thought was that it didn't look very different than any other airport I had been to, just less modern. It had the white walls and floors, fluorescent lighting, signs telling you where to go. But after I got my bags and walked outside, I knew I was in India. There was chaos everywhere. Men standing next to their dilapidated taxis were calling loudly to passengers coming out of the airport. Cars were jammed up against one another, honking and trying to get out of the parking lot. The air was thick and hot. There was an odd, unidentifiable odor everywhere.

If I weren't meeting Serena's extended friend, I might have had a nervous breakdown right there. But as soon as I walked out, a beautiful woman with long, thick black hair, and wearing jeans and a loose-fitting cotton tunic, came up to me. "Excuse me, are you Julie?"

"Yes I am. You must be Amrita."

"I am. Welcome to Mumbai."

We got into her little car and she took off. It was dark, so it was difficult for me to really see out the window. But I thought I could make out makeshift huts and lean-tos on the sides of the road, and people sleeping out on the street, but I wasn't sure. I was hoping I was mistaken.

Amrita cheerfully asked me about my project.

"I heard you're writing a book about single women all over the world."

I cringed. It was really the last thing I wanted to talk about. I straightened her out.

"I'm here just to find comfort. I've heard it's such a spiritual place."

Amrita nodded, silently. Well, she didn't really nod. She had this odd little habit of bobbling her head in a way that made you not really sure if she was saying "yes" or "no." She also had a habit of honking an enormous amount while she was driving, a habit most of the other drivers shared with her.

As Amrita tapped on her horn, she said, "Most of the yoga ashrams are outside of Mumbai. Were you planning on going to one of those?"

"Yes, my friend Serena suggested one."

She kept driving and honking. I squinted out the window and saw a young couple zip by on a moped. The woman was wearing a sari and it flapped in the wind as she rode sidesaddle.

Amrita spoke again. "I think this idea of how to be single is a very good one. There are many decisions we have to make when we're single. Very important ones."

She furrowed her thick, black eyebrows. She seemed to have something on her mind. I couldn't help but ask . . .

"What decisions do you have to make?"

Amrita shrugged. "I'm thirty-five. My family is pressuring me to get married. I have been dating, hoping for a love marriage. But . . ."

She looked like she was about to cry. Here's the last thing I felt like hearing about: someone else's lousy love life. But I took a deep breath and listened.

"The last man I dated had no money. I paid for everything. Dinners, movies, even trips. My family thought I was crazy. They said he was using me. One time, we went shopping, and he asked me to buy him a sweater. And I did! Then he broke up with me, just like that."

Tears started to fall down her cheeks. I felt like Angela Lansbury in *Murder, She Wrote*. Every time she went anywhere, even on vacation, the poor old gal stumbled across a murder. Everywhere I went, relationship dramas seemed to unfold.

"He said I was too independent, too focused on my career." The tears kept falling. She kept driving and honking. I nodded, trying to be sympathetic.

"Yeah, well, it seems like he didn't mind your career when it could buy him a sweater."

Amrita bobbled her head vigorously. "Exactly. I think I dated him so long because my family hated him. I thought they were being racist, because we're Brahmins, and he's Vaishya. But now I see they were right."

I looked out the window again and saw what appeared to be an entire family on a moped. A father, mother, son, and daughter all squeezed in together. I blinked. Yep, that's what I saw.

I was extremely tired. I was so grateful to Amrita for allowing me not to have to take a cab from the airport, but I really just wanted her to shut up.

"So now, I am letting my family find him. They have been looking on the matrimonial sites and have picked out some men for me. Their horoscopes look good, and so I'm going to start meeting them."

Okay, that woke me up. Matrimonial sites? Horoscopes? As we drove into the city through narrow streets, she told me about the popularity of the matrimonial sites, which are just like dating sites but for the specific purpose of arranging marriages. She told me that often it's the family that puts the son or daughter's photo up.

"Well, that's kind of great, sparing the actual people the embarrassment and hassle of doing it themselves."

Amrita's eyebrows rose. "But that's not why they do it. They do it because it's understood that parents know better who would be a good match for their children than the children themselves." I thought of my own romantic decisions. This idea was beginning to make sense to me.

She also explained the important role the horoscope played in matchmaking, all about the planets and moons and birth time—I got the impression that it wasn't the same kind of astrology that the *New York Post* employed to tell me what kind of day I was going to have.

"If the astrology is not a good match, I won't even meet the man." I was definitely not in the West Village anymore.

We parked near where I would be staying, a modest "economy" hotel in South Mumbai. As Amrita helped me roll my luggage down the street, I realized that these single Indian women have something that we American women don't really have: a backup plan. They can go out into the world, discarding their families' outdated views on marriage to look for love on their own—and if it doesn't work out, their moms and dads and aunts and uncles and cousins and sisters-in-law are more than happy to swoop in and get things cracking.

"Would you like to meet my sister tomorrow? She decided on an arranged marriage, and she's very happy."

I looked at Amrita, surprised. I was planning on spending the day crying and then maybe figuring out how to get to the ashram Serena recommended. I was over the whole "research" aspect of this trip and was looking forward to just doing shoulder stands and drinking mango lassis.

"I think it might be good research for your book." I didn't know how to tell her that I'd rather gnaw off my arm and beat myself over the head with it until I passed out than go talk to a happily married couple about how in love they are. So instead, I said, "I'd love to."

"Good. I'll pick you up at noon? Is that okay?" I agreed and checked in.

My room was small, with two double beds, a television, and a desk. It was no marble-covered Bali bungalow, but then we're not in Bali anymore, are we? Or China. We're in India. And I still didn't quite understand what that meant.

The next day, I was back in the car with Amrita. The difference between driving with her then, as opposed to the previous evening, was the difference, well, between night and day. As we spoke about her sister Ananda, it was difficult for me not to notice the poverty now fully visible outside my window. On the highways, you could see crumbled and dirty buildings that seemed more like bunkers than places to live. But going into the town where we were supposed to be meeting her sister, I saw the images that one might see taken by any photojournalist in any third world country: the naked children on the street walking next to what had to be raw sewage. Children, not in school, but playing on heaps of rubble. Older children banging on pieces of tin scraps, as some kind of menial job. And mothers walking around, barefoot, in and out of their little makeshift huts, right on the side of the road. When our car came to a stop, a little girl banged on my window. She had a dirty face and big black vacant eyes, and she kept putting her fingers to her mouth, in a gesture that seemed to be her way of saying she was begging for money for food. Amrita saw me look at her.

"Don't give these children money. It's all organized crime. They have to give the money to someone who is in charge of this neighborhood. They go to you because you're white and they think you'll feel bad for them."

I looked at the girl as she kept putting her fingers to her lips. Well, I did feel bad for her, actually. Was I really supposed to just drive by without doing anything? Yes, I was. And we did. As we drove through this village, right by the ocean, I decided I didn't want to become the cliché. I didn't want to be one of those tourists who go to India and then come back and tell people with that tone of overwrought pity in their voice, "Oh, India, the poverty there, it's just *unimaginable*." This wasn't my country, this wasn't my problem, and I don't know a damn thing about anything.

We drove up a road and into a high-rise building with a wraparound parking lot. Over to the side there was a lawn area, green and lush with trees and bushes and benches. This seemed like a fancy place to live, by Mumbai standards, even though the building, no matter how high-end, seemed to be covered in a thin layer of soot. But come to think of it, that could be said of all Mumbai.

The few things I felt I knew about India before coming here was that one must never, *ever,* drink the water. This was such a serious issue that I read you shouldn't even brush your teeth with the stuff, and as much as possible, turn your face away from it when you were showering.

But here I was, sitting in front of this woman, a woman who had allowed me into her home, who was about to talk to me about her marriage just to help me with my book, who was now holding out a glass of water for me to take.

"You must be thirsty; it's very hot today."

I took the glass and watched her watch me not drink from it. Not wanting her to think that I thought her water, and thereby her home, was dirty, I took a sip.

"Thank you. I appreciate it." I imagined the germs and the parasites now swimming down my throat and into my intestines.

"Amrita told me that you are writing a book about love and being single all over the world?" Ananda asked.

I nodded my head politely. "I am. It's been a very interesting experience."

Ananda and Amrita sat on a sofa together, with me in the armchair across from them. One of Ananda's daughters, around five years old, came and sat on her lap. She had short black hair with a little pink plastic clip pushing her bangs back.

"So, Amrita said that you decided to go with an arranged marriage, instead of a love match?"

Ananda nodded her head. She seemed excited to speak. "Yes. I had just finished my master's in psychology. I wasn't sure what I was going to do next, but I was thinking about going to get my doctorate. I had been dating on my own, like Amrita."

I looked at the two of them. I had found Amrita to be very attractive, but now seeing her with her sister, I saw that Ananda was probably the one who was considered the prettiest. She was more petite than her sister, and her delicate features made her seem a bit more regal.

"I wasn't like Amrita. When my parents would tell us every now and then that they had a boy they wanted us to meet, Amrita would always refuse." She put a hand on Amrita's shoulder. "I would at least humor them."

Amrita shrugged her shoulders, a bit regretfully, it seemed to me. She jumped in to help with the story. "So one day, my parents said they wanted her to meet someone. So this man came with his family to our home. The families talked for a bit . . ."

"And then we went on the terrace to chat. He seemed nice. After twenty minutes he asked what I thought. I said, 'Okay, why not?' So we came downstairs and told our parents that we would get married."

They both started laughing at the memory of it. Ananda continued. "My parents were shocked. You should have seen their faces. They thought this was going to be another boy I just sent away."

Amrita added, "When she called me and told me, I thought she was playing a joke on me. It took her a half hour just to convince me that she was serious . . ."

I was so confused. "But . . . I don't understand . . . was it love at first sight? Were you just tired of dating?"

Ananda shrugged. "I don't know. He seemed nice."

I looked at her, with her five-year-old snuggled beside her. I didn't know how to ask this politely, but here I was and there they were, so . . .

"And so . . . it worked out? You're happy?"

"Yes!"

Amrita decided to elaborate for her sister. "She's very happy. He's a very good man. It's one of the reasons I'm letting my parents help now. Because it worked so well for her. I always thought it was just a fluke, that she just got lucky. But now, I don't know. Maybe my parents and the horoscopes do know best. Maybe if I meet someone whom I have no expectations about whatsoever, there's more of a chance it will work out."

Ananda smiled. "Tonight, she's meeting two men, one after the other. It's different than when my parents got married. Amrita would never be forced to marry someone she didn't want to marry. We get to decide."

I thought about all the women I knew in New York and around the world, who might want to rethink the whole idea of letting people get involved in their love lives. Maybe one way to deal with looking for your mate after a certain age is to put an APB out on him. Maybe it was time to notify the authorities, set up roadblocks, and send out a search party.

"How long did you date before you married?" I asked.

"Two months," Ananda said. "We saw each other once or twice a week."

At this point, it seemed like just as valid a way of doing things as dating someone for five years and then finding out he can't commit. Or going to Bali with a married man and pretending he's not married. It's so crazy it just might work.

Amrita drove me back to the hotel. Through the slums and the huts and the sewage and the shoeless children. Again Amrita noticed my discomfort at it all. She tried to make me feel better. "They're not unhappy, these people, you know?"

I looked at her, not sure what she could possibly mean.

"This is what they know, this is their lives. They're happy. They don't have the same expectations as you or I."

I looked out my window and saw a toddler, a gorgeous tan child, about two years old, standing by the street in the dirt in front of his little "hut." He was adorable in a little pair of pink shorts and a white t-shirt. Finally, a sweet sight. And just as I was taking in this adorable sight, a waterfall of pee gushed down his legs, completely soaking his shorts and forming a puddle right around his bare feet. I watched him as he just stood there, unfazed. My stomach immediately tied up in a knot. It was clear he was not going to be cleaned up any time soon. And at that, the car moved on.

After I wished Amrita good luck with her two dates that night, I went to my room and took a shower and then went to sleep.

After my nap, I decided to get dressed up and go to a trendy restaurant suggested by *Time Out Mumbai* called Indigo, right down the block. As I walked in, I saw what must be considered the beautiful people of Mumbai. The men were in jackets and jeans and pressed shirts; the women in dresses and heels. I think I even spied a few gay Indian men, which somehow comforted me and made me feel at home. I took the stairs to the top floor, which opened up onto a roof-garden restaurant with an enclosed lounge area off to the side.

I went into the lounge and straight to the bar. I ordered a white wine

HOW TO BE SINGLE

and I sat down near three done-up Indian ladies in their thirties who were all smoking and drinking and talking very loudly in English. As the bartender served me my drink, I remembered an image from the drive back to the hotel: an Indian family who lived outside under a highway; three of the children were running around in the dirt, playing, while the mother sat there with their belongings in a little circle around her. Then my mind flashed to the little boy peeing on himself. I shook my head, trying to dislodge the image.

"I was just remembering a little boy I saw today. On the street. It was very upsetting."

The bartender nodded. "You know, these people. They're not unhappy."

That old chestnut again. "You mean they like living in the dirt and banging on tin for a living?"

"It's what they know. It's their life. Yes, they're happy."

I sipped my wine and nodded at him politely. Clearly, I just didn't get it.

To the right of me, these three women were discussing something of the utmost importance. And, being me, I decided to start more assertive eavesdropping. It seemed that one of them was having problems with someone she was dating. He didn't want to see her as much as she wanted to see him. She was telling her friends that she liked him, so it seemed crazy just to break up with him, but at the same time she hated not getting to see him. She was very agitated, waving her arms around, running her fingers through her hair. Her friends were trying to help, asking questions and giving suggestions.

I almost fell asleep right there at the bar. I mean, really. I didn't come all the way to Asia, by way of Europe, South America, and Australia, just to hear this shit. Congratulations, Mumbai ladies. I'm so happy that you have worked hard for your independence and your singleness. You've gone against tradition and your family and you are going out and getting jobs and living in your own apartments and having drinks at bars and taking men home with you. Now that you aren't being forced to marry men you don't love and have children you don't want, this is how you are rewarded: you get to sit in bars just like the rest of the women all over the world and complain about some guy not liking you enough. Welcome to the party. Isn't it fun?!

If I were being ambitious and inquisitive I would have asked them if they would ever go back to the way it was. I would have asked them if they would ever consider marrying someone their parents set them up with when they were a bit older. I should have asked them if they felt it's worth it to refuse to settle, even though it might mean they stay single for a long, long time. But I didn't because I couldn't care less about them and their stupid dating problems. I just cared about me and my stupid dating problems. I paid for my drink and left the lounge. I walked down the stairs—and with each step downward, so went my mood.

As I headed back to my hotel, I was deeply depressed. I decided that I felt cheated. *Great, that's all I was given. A couple of weeks of love. That was it for me. And now I have to go back out there and look for it again. But this time he has to be someone whom I like just as much as Thomas, but is also completely available to me. Yeah. That's going to happen soon.*

The next morning I decided to stay in bed. You can do that when you're all the way across the world and you're depressed and there's no one that's calling trying to cheer you up. I stayed in bed until one in the afternoon. I hadn't done that since I was a teenager and it felt great. Then the phone rang and it was Amrita. I asked her how her fix-ups went last night.

"Well, they really weren't my type. But they were nice. My mother and father have two more for me tonight."

"Wow, they've been busy," I said, trying to seem interested. Which I wasn't. I pulled the covers to my chin and tucked myself tight into my bed.

"Yes, they have. It will be very interesting to see who comes tonight," she said, brightly.

I rolled over to my right side, while moving the phone to my left ear. "You sound a little excited about this."

Amrita laughed. "I have to say, I am. It's really nice to have someone else worrying about my love life for a while. It's a great relief, actually."

I thought about this idea for a moment and I liked it: handing the crisis that is your singlehood over to other people and make it *their* problem. I wondered how I could stay in India, get adopted into a family, and make them take care of all this shit for me.

"Anyway, I was wondering if you wanted to come tonight to watch. For your book."

I rolled onto my back and rested my arm on my forehead. "Well, actually. I was planning on going to that ashram today at some point . . ."

"You can do that tomorrow. Tonight you'll get to see me meet these men. It will be like those reality shows you Americans enjoy so much. Very voyeuristic."

"But isn't this a private thing between families?"

"Yes, but no matter. I'll tell them you're visiting from New York, and had nowhere else to go. It'll be fine."

As it was already one in the afternoon and I hadn't gotten out of bed, I realized the odds of me finding my way to this ashram today were slim. So I agreed to go. After all, it would be great research for my *book*.

Just then the hotel phone rang again. It was Alice. I had sent her my travel info because that's what one does when they don't have a husband or a boyfriend looking out for them. Can you tell? I was a little bitter.

"Julie, hey, how are you?"

She sounded distressed, so I lied. "I'm good, how are you?"

I heard Alice take a deep breath. Then, "I don't think I can go through with this, you know? The marriage. Iceland. I don't think I can."

"Why not?" I asked, even though I knew the reason.

"Because I'm not in love with Jim. I love him, I'm so fond of him, but I'm not in love with him. I'm not."

Now, this is the part of the story where the best friend tells her *of course you shouldn't marry a man you don't love. Of course you shouldn't settle. Of course there will be someone better out there for you.* But I was in Mumbai, for God's sake. I couldn't be held responsible for what I did or said.

"Alice, listen to me. *Listen to me.* You marry him, do you understand me? *Marry him.*"

There was a long silence on the other end.

"Really?"

"Yes, really. This whole falling-in-love thing is bullshit, it's an illusion, it doesn't mean anything, and it doesn't last. Are you and Jim compatible?"

"Yes."

"Do you two respect each other? Do you like to take care of each other?"

"Yes."

"Then *marry him*. We have been brainwashed to have these high expectations. Marry him and love him and make a family and have a good life. The rest is just a lie."

"Really?"

"Yes, really. Go through with it. You'll regret it later if you don't."

And with that I hung up the phone and went back to sleep for a while.

Amrita picked me up at my hotel to bring me to her parents' house. She was dressed in a long, gold Indian tunic, over a thin pair of black cotton pants. She was wearing red lipstick and a little mascara. She looked quite beautiful.

"I could have taken a cab. You shouldn't have to worry about driving me on a night when you might be meeting your husband," I joked.

Amrita shook her head. "The cabdrivers will rip you off if you don't know where you're going."

And then we were at it again—driving through frickin' Mumbai. Getting another glimpse of its house of horrors. At one point, we stopped at a red light, and I heard a loud crack on the window of my car. I looked over and saw a young girl at my window. She had banged her head against it to get my attention. She was around seven years old and was holding a baby in her arms. Then she took one of her hands and brought it up to her mouth, over and over again. I looked over at Amrita, my mouth open, tears forming in my eyes. She was unmoved. She drove on.

After a few moments in silence, I tried to form a question, anything to try and understand things. I asked her, "Do these children go to school?"

Amrita bobbled her head. "Some do, but most don't. These people are mostly Muslims, so they don't really believe in education. They want their children to start businesses."

"You mean like selling peanuts on the street?" I asked, a little sarcastically. I really wasn't getting it.

Amrita nodded her head. "Yes, like that." We drove the rest of the way in silence.

We arrived at another large high-rise, this one so tall and pristine it looked like it had been built and painted the day before. We drove past tennis courts and an outdoor swimming pool. In the lobby, a uniformed man waited to let us in.

Amrita's parents politely greeted me at the door and invited me in. Amrita's mother, Mrs. Ramani, was dressed in a traditional blue and white sari, with a long-sleeved cotton t-shirt underneath it. Mr. Ramani wore simple trousers and a button-down shirt. There were also three other older women sitting in the living room, with another older man. They were introduced to me as Amrita's grandmother, uncle, and two aunts. I was invited to sit down on a sofa next to Amrita's grandmother. Amrita's mother brought me a glass of water. Like hell I was going to offend anyone right now, so I took a nice sip and set it down on the coaster next to me.

Amrita sat down and they all started speaking in Hindi, and from what I could tell from the gestures, one of the aunts was complimenting Amrita on how she looked. Then the father started talking for a bit, and everyone was listening very intently.

"He's telling us about the first man that I'm going to meet. He's an engineer who works for the city, something to do with the gas and the oil lines. Our horoscopes are very compatible, and he has no problem with the fact that I work."

"And her age. He does not need a young wife," her father added.

Everyone nodded their heads gratefully.

"He lived in the States for two years. He's very modern," Amrita's father told me.

I felt extremely awkward being there, in the middle of all this. I didn't know where I should be when the man and his family arrived.

"Would you like me to go outside or to another room when they come . . . ?"

Amrita's mother looked at her husband. The husband thought for a moment. In that moment's pause, I jumped in with "You know, when the family gets here, I'll just go outside and get some air. So you can have your privacy."

The mother and father looked at each other. The father bobbled in agreement. "You can go in the other room with Amrita, while we talk."

The doorbell rang and Amrita's mother went to the door. Amrita nervously waved for me to get up and we scurried into a nearby bedroom like two teenage girls.

We waited there, sitting on the bed cross-legged.

"What are they talking about?" I asked.

"The parents have to make sure they like each other. This is very important. They both must feel we come from good families."

"And what makes a family seem like a good family?"

"Well, first, these men are all from the Brahmin caste, like my family, so that already is very helpful."

"Does the caste system really matter anymore?"

"Not as much as before, but with things like marriages it does."

"Really?" I thought the whole system was long gone.

"In a way, yes. The Brahmins, my caste, were the priests and teachers, the intellectuals. Then you have the people who were the farmers. Then the people who were the laborers. It's very similar to your country, with the blue-collar and the white-collar workers, but here it comes from a long tradition, and we've given them names."

"But what about the untouchables. Is that what those people are? The ones on the street?" I asked Amrita.

"Yes."

"So they are born poor and they're going to die poor, with no hope of advancing themselves?"

Amrita bobbled her head. "The government is starting to help them, but this is what they know."

I didn't want to get into a political argument with her while she was backstage before her big date, but still, it was a hard topic for me to comprehend. Amrita could sense my disapproval.

"You tourists, you come to Mumbai and you see the poverty and you take your photographs. You go home and you think you've seen Mumbai. But that's not all Mumbai is. That's not all that India is." She sounded defensive. I thought I should change the subject.

"So, what else do the families talk about together?"

"They want to know if the father has a good job, if the other siblings are responsible and have good jobs. Mostly, they want to know if they are all well educated. That's very important."

After an hour, Mrs. Ramani knocked and walked in.

"You can meet him now," she said, with a timid smile on her face. "His family is very nice."

Amrita looked at me, gave a little shrug of "here goes nothing," and walked out the door. I sat back on her childhood bed. I was exhausted. I sat there for a few minutes staring at the wall in front of me. Just as I started to drift off, the door opened again and Mrs. Ramani came in.

"His family has left. She is going out for a walk with him. Come out and sit with us."

I quickly jumped up, trying not to look as if I had just fallen asleep in their home.

"Thank you. That would be nice."

I sat down on the sofa. Amrita's family was still all assembled. We were just awkwardly staring at one another, so I decided to jump right in with my so-called "research."

"I find it interesting how important a role astrology plays in marriages here in India."

Mr. Ramani bobbled his head emphatically. "It is everything. We saw matches online, from very good families, from our community, with good jobs. But the horoscopes were not compatible. So it could not be."

Mrs. Ramani bobbled in agreement.

"We don't have that in America. It's a very odd concept to me," I said.

Mr. Ramani got up and started to walk around the living room, explaining it all to me like a schoolteacher.

"It's very simple. A marriage must be composed of three things: you must be emotionally compatible, intellectually compatible, and physically compatible. If you don't have all three, a marriage will not work."

I was surprised by the "physically compatible" part. I had assumed that the sex life of the couple was the least of anyone's concerns.

"Relationships start out very fast, with a burst, a lot of attraction, but it does not last. This is because they were not compatible. The horoscopes can tell you if they will be truly compatible. Who can predict that? Not the couple. Not the family. But the horoscope can."

As he was talking, I became more and more intrigued. If this was true, then it meant that these people had figured out years ago something that still perplexed us stupid Americans. How do you know if your relationship will last? If you were to go solely by the incredibly low divorce rate in India (1 percent), one could assume that they might be on to something. Of course, there are many more factors at work, such as how different their expectations are when they go into a marriage, as opposed to ours. I decided to continue my probing.

"If you don't mind me asking, where does romance come into this?"

Mr. Ramani kept pacing around the room. What appeared at first to be his enthusiasm for teaching me about Indian culture now seemed to me to be nothing more than a case of nerves. It dawned on me, as I watched him yank his hands in and out of his pockets and walk around the room, that he was simply a nervous father waiting for his daughter to come home from her date.

"Romance. What is romance? Romance means nothing," he said, as his lips curled upward in distaste.

Mrs. Ramani seemed to agree. "This is a very Western idea. With Indian marriages, you don't think about romance. You think about taking care of each other. I take care of him," she said as she pointed toward Mr. Ramani, "and he takes care of me." She put her hand to her heart. I smiled agreeably. The image of Thomas taking care of me when I was having my panic attack on the plane quickly flashed in my mind. It felt like a tear through my flesh.

Mr. Ramani continued. "These men you see, who try to be romantic. They say 'Honey baby this, honey baby that.' If he can say 'honey baby' to you, that means he can say 'honey baby' to the next girl. These words don't mean anything."

I thought about Thomas. How he called me "my darling." Until his other darling came halfway across the world to take *her* darling back.

Mr. Ramani glanced at the clock. Amrita had been gone almost an hour.

Mrs. Ramani asked, "So, how old are you?"

"I'm thirty-eight."

"And you aren't married?" The two aunts perked up at this question, looking at me and waiting for my answer.

"No, no, I'm not." My glass of water was still on the coffee table and I nervously took a sip.

The grandmother seemed to understand what I had just said, but she spoke Hindi to Amrita's father. He translated the question she had for me. "Why are you still unmarried?" Ah, *that* question again. I considered which response I should use this time. After a few seconds, I just went with the obvious. "I guess I haven't met the right guy yet," I said.

Mr. Ramani translated, and the grandmother looked at me sadly. One of the aunts spoke up in English. "Isn't your family looking for someone for you?"

They all looked at me intently. I shook my head. "No, we really don't do that in the States. We don't get our families involved like that."

"But don't they want you to get married?" Mrs. Ramani asked, the unmistakable tone of worry having crept into her voice.

I am much more comfortable when I do the inquiring. I took another sip of water. "They do, very much. But I guess they think I'm happy the way I am."

Now the uncle spoke up. "This cannot be," he said. "The human being is designed for many things. Loneliness is not one of them."

I swallowed hard. I tried to nod in agreement. My stomach tightened into a little knot again.

Mrs. Ramani leaned into me, and said, as a statement of fact, "We are not meant to go through this life alone."

I tried to force out a smile, but the blood started draining out of my face. I looked at all of them staring at me. And, being the good emotional wreck that I was, tears started rolling down my face.

"May I use your bathroom?" I asked, my voice shaky. Everyone looked at one another, not sure what to do.

Mrs. Ramani stood up. "Yes, yes, of course, please come with me."

I sobbed for a few moments in the Ramanis' toilet, as quietly as I could. After about five minutes, I heard Amrita's voice and what sounded like a lot of commotion. Bored with my own drama, I blew my nose, splashed water on my face (which, may I remind you, *never works*), and went out. Just as I got to the living room, Mr. Ramani turned to me smiling, and said, "We have a match! They are going to be married!"

Amrita was beaming. His parents were smiling and hugging their son. Her now-betrothed, a tall man with very thick black hair combed away from his face, and a thick black mustache, looked like he was about to start dancing a jig. I just stood there with puffy eyes watching the whole scene unfold before me like a Merchant-Ivory film.

When the hugging and kissing started to slow down, Amrita came over to me. She took my hand and walked a few feet away from everyone else. "He was so nice. We just talked and talked. We have so much in common. He's really funny and smart! I'm so lucky! I can't believe I'm going to get married!" She hugged me, laughing. "I would never have met this man on my own. Ever!"

I couldn't help but marvel at the speed of all this. In New York, if you like the guy a lot—you go on a second date. Here, you plan the engagement ceremony. But if you consider how truly miraculous it is to meet anyone you want to go on a second date with, maybe they have the right idea. Maybe wanting to go on a second date with someone is proof that you might as well just get engaged, give it a shot, and nail that shit down.

Mr. Ramani had taken out a bottle of champagne that he was saving for just this occasion, and Amrita's mother was handing out glasses. Both families were absolutely ecstatic. The reason was obvious: these two lost souls who were floating around for years, unmoored, loose strands in the fabric of society, who were not designed for loneliness, had now found their place. They were now a couple within two families, that would start their own family. In this one decision, in this one hour, they had given themselves a place in the world, neatly carved out, ready to go.

Besides the fact that I was intruding on an extremely private moment, I also realized that if I didn't get away from all this matrimonial glee I was going to hurl myself out a window. I asked Amrita to call me a cab, and I left as soon as I could.

And then another car ride. Luckily it was again night, so most of the children who were normally playing and begging in the streets were now sleeping on blankets or cots along the side of the road with their families. It was bedtime in Mumbai. Still, there were some older children out, and as we came to a stoplight, one little girl, her right arm amputated below her elbow, used the truncated limb to bang on the window, her left hand putting fingers to her mouth.

The cabdriver looked at the girl and back at me. "Don't give them money. It's all an act. It's all organized crime."

I looked out the window. That was a really great act she had going there, impersonating a poor child from India who had only half a right arm.

"Why doesn't the government help them? Why are they being left on the streets?"

The cabdriver just bobbled his head. The perfect answer for what is I'm sure a complicated question. The little girl was still banging the car with her stump.

For just a moment, I imagined what this must look like. Me, this white American woman, all dressed up, staring at this child, and refusing to open the window, refusing to help. I looked at the child, this dirty girl with matted, long black hair. This was her place in the world. This was her caste. She lived on the streets and she probably would do so her entire life.

"Fuck that," I said quite loudly, and I opened my purse and took out my wallet. I opened the car window and I gave her five dollars. And I did that very same thing to the next four children who came begging to the car during that drive. The cabdriver shook his head in disapproval, and in my mind, I told him that he could kiss my ass. Because here's what. I hate to be a cliché, but the poverty in Mumbai is really appalling. The quality of life for these people is nightmarish. The fact that no one seems to care was even more outrageous. I was the American tourist who could only see Mumbai for its poverty. I was the American tourist who would go back to New York and say, "Mumbai, oh my God, the poverty. *It's awful.*" That would be me. Guilty as charged.

By the time I got to the hotel, my stomach was feeling a bit upset. But ever since I arrived in Mumbai, due to the spicy food, the air that smells like burning rubber, and the overall misery, my stomach had been in a general state of displeasure anyway. So I didn't think much of it. I walked into the hotel elevator and breathed a sigh of relief. I'm telling you, those car rides in Mumbai could suck the light out of the sun.

As I rode the elevator to my room, the images of those children popped into my head again. They wouldn't go away. It was like a horror movie that played in a loop, that I was unable to turn off.

I took a shower, hoping that would somehow soothe my stomach and clean off the car ride. I thought about how concerned these families were for one another, concerned with getting everyone married off, making a family, becoming part of the larger society. And here were these people, these families, just outside on the street, who would never be allowed into this society for the entirety of their lives. And these other families, the families in the houses and apartment complexes with the champagne and the education, these families didn't care one bit about those others.

As the water hit my face, I tried to tell myself that this is such a complicated issue, something that I couldn't begin to understand in just a few days. But all I could think of was the emptiness in those children's eyes. Their robotic waves as I drove on, as if they were merely shells of flesh, impersonating children.

By the time I got out of the shower, I felt nauseous. I went to the bathroom and discovered I had diarrhea. And that, folks, was the rest of my night: bathroom runs and sweating, all the while having images of small dark figures sleeping on the streets, standing in their huts, begging for food. I was sick and alone in Mumbai.

I slept till noon the next day. Then, I stayed there. I couldn't bear the thought of going outside one more time. I needed a Time Out Mumbai.

Then I thought about Amrita's mother. She was right. We aren't meant to go through life alone. It is against our human nature. Single people should be pitied. We are living with a glaring deficiency in our lives. We are being denied love. And let's face it, it's kind of true, all you need is love. I have everything but that, and my life feels very empty.

I realized how pathetic I sounded, even to myself. But I didn't care. For me, when I am feeling sorry for myself, which is often, I like to just really indulge in it, to really push myself to feel as badly as I can. Call the cops if you want to shut it down; otherwise this pity party is going to go on all night.

But here I was, in India. Where literally the streets were teeming with people in the worst cases of need. Children with no homes, no food, no clothes, no *hands*. Could I really sit there and cry because I didn't have a boyfriend?

I hoped the answer was no, but I wasn't sure. I got on some clothes and went down to the tiny concierge desk. There was a beautiful woman with thick dark eyeliner working the desk. My hair was disheveled and my eyes were puffy. I can't imagine what she must have thought of me.

"Excuse me," I asked, my voice rough from not having spoken all day. "I was wondering if you knew of any organization I could volunteer for. You know, to help."

The woman at the desk looked very confused. This was not the sort of request she was used to.

"I'm sorry, what do you mean?"

"I'm just wondering, if I could spend a few days helping, you know, the people here. On the streets."

I assume she thought I was a madwoman. She smiled politely and said, "Just one moment, I'll ask my colleague." There was a door that led to some back room, it seemed, and she disappeared behind it, for ten minutes. Finally, she came back.

"I'm sorry, but we really don't have any kind of recommendations like that for you. I'm sorry."

"Really, there's no place I could go to just volunteer for a bit?" I asked again.

The woman bobbled her head. "I'm sorry, no. It's not possible."

Just then, a young woman who worked at the front desk, around twenty, interrupted.

"Excuse me, are you interested in volunteering somewhere?"

I nodded and said, "Yes."

Her eyes lit up. "Three of my friends and I get together on Saturday nights and we go to the outdoor festivals. We buy food for the kids who are standing around and we take them on the rides. We're going to-night."

"Can I join you?"

She bobbled her head. "Of course, I will meet you here in the lobby at six. You can come in my car."

I almost smiled. "Thank you so much."

"It's no problem." And then she stuck out her hand. "I'm Hamida, by the way."

"It's nice to meet you. I'm Julie."

"It's nice to meet you, Julie."

That night, I stood in a sea of what seemed to be the entire population of India. We were at an outdoor festival for some important Muslim Baba (spiritual leader) in Mumbai. There were crowds of teenagers, there were families, there were couples, all shouting and laughing. There were about a half dozen big Ferris wheels, all lit up, which made the entire scene feel like one big dusty circus. Indian music came out of the loudspeakers, as well as a man's voice talking nonstop in Hindi. It was absolute chaos.

I was standing with Hamida and her friends Jaya and Kavita, who were sisters. They were both very modern-looking young women, with nice jeans and cute designer tops. Jaya and Kavita were born in London and their father was a businessman who had come back here for work. Never having seen that kind of poverty before coming to Mumbai, they were appalled. They had met Hamida at the fancy private school in Mumbai that they attended, and they all decided to do something to help.

So this was what they did. They would go to fairs and find children who were running around unescorted or who were out begging for money, and offer to take them on rides and buy them food. It wasn't much, but it was something.

Of course, since I was there, the white lady, it was like bees to honey. In a matter of moments, five children came up to me altogether, with their hands to their lips. I looked at Hamida and her friends, waiting for them to take charge. Hamida started speaking to them in Hindi. They suddenly got very quiet, as if they didn't understand what she was saying and were slightly afraid.

"This happens all the time," Jaya whispered to me. "They're confused. They never heard of someone asking if they want to go on the rides."

Hamida kept talking to them, pointing to the stands of food and the Ferris wheels.

The children seemed truly puzzled. Kavita started talking to them as well. I could tell it was difficult to get them to switch gears from beggars to children—like someone asking a puppet to realize it's actually a little boy. Finally, after much cajoling, the women were able to walk the children over to a stand that was selling ice cream. They bought all the children ice cream and gave them the cones one by one. The children started licking away at them happily. Soon enough, they were smiling, and we were able to get them on a Ferris wheel. We piled them on it, making sure there was an adult with each group of kids. As the Ferris wheel turned round and round, the children began smiling and laughing. They pointed out to the horizon, amazed at what they could see up there. They screamed and waved at each other from the different seats they were on.

We did a variation of that for the entire night with as many kids as we could find. We ran around with them, bought them some real food and treats, and took them on a few other rides. I didn't speak any Hindi, obviously, but I was able to do some funny dances and make some funny faces that cracked them up. It was exhausting, I must admit. I looked at these three young Indian women and felt enormous admiration for them. They had figured out how to go straight to the heart of the matter. They spent their Saturday nights not with their boyfriends, at parties, or at bars, but at these noisy, dirty fairs, breathing life back into a few children if only for a few hours.

When I got back into my room, I collapsed on the bed, covered in dirt and ice cream. As I thought about the night and the children, I was filled with a lightness. I had helped some children. I was not a selfish person, but a kind one. I wasn't a pathetic crybaby but a noble mother to the world . . . But then, like having a scab that you just have to pick at, my mind started drifting toward the image of Thomas and his wife summering in the countryside with their baby crawling on the green grass; them opening presents on Christmas; them lying in bed all together, on a lazy Sunday morning. I tried to push them away, force them out of my mind. I began to pace, to clear my thoughts, and I happened to glance back at the full-length mirror with the overhead lighting. I saw the cellulite covering my upper thighs. I looked down and swore I saw the first signs of cellulite on my knees.

I couldn't help it. I'm sorry. I started to cry. And yes, I wasn't crying because of those poor little children, I was crying because my heart was broken and I now had knee cellulite.

This was certainly not my proudest moment.

Back in the States

Alice was in her bedroom, with the suitcase out on her bed, already packed for Iceland. They weren't leaving for three days but she was ready to go. It hadn't been that stressful a task, packing, as she assumed they were going to be in the dark the whole time, so it really didn't matter what she wore. But just as in finding a husband, Alice doesn't like to wait until the last minute.

She had spent some time picking out just the right dress for the big day. She found it last week with Jim's sister, Lisa. She had settled on a "winter white" skirt and jacket set, woolen, with the sleeves of the jacket and the hem of the skirt trimmed in mink. It wasn't politically correct, but it was cute, very *Doctor Zhivago*. She made a mental note to donate money to PETA after the honeymoon.

It was nine o'clock in the morning and she didn't have a damn thing left to do. She didn't have to go give Ruby her shot. Obviously, she didn't have to meet with any wedding planners or florists or deejays anymore, because there was no wedding. Alice had spun it to Jim (and Jim had subsequently spun it to his family) that she realized getting married was an incredibly intimate event, and she wanted to share it with just Jim. And that it always was Alice's dream to get married in Iceland—which it wasn't, so just add that lie to her guilty list along with the dead minks. The only way they got away with this plan, among all the families, was by promising to have some big party when they got back from their honeymoon.

So now Alice was sitting on her bed with not one thing to do that entire day. She wasn't being a lawyer, she wasn't being a bride-to-be, she wasn't even being a friend. She reminded herself to call Ruby in a few days to check in about the news. She wondered how to make that phone call: *Hey Ruby, I was just wondering—are you pregnant?* She then realized it was one of those situations where it's better not to ask. The news would get to you when it wanted to. She went into the kitchen and poured herself a cup of coffee and thought about how similar that was to dating. She couldn't bear the fake-casual phone calls the day after a big date.

"Hey Alice, it's Mom, I'm just sitting here vacuuming, and I was just wondering how it went last night . . . ?"

"Hey, Al, it's Bob. Didn't you tell me you had a big date last night? How did it go?"

"Hey, Al, it's me, how'd it go with Hedge Fund Guy? Tell me everything."

As Alice sat and sipped her second cup of coffee she let a feeling of relief wash over her. Those days were over. No more phone calls. Now she had the time to think about Ruby and be one of those annoying people, calling, saying, *Hey Ruby, are you pregnant?*

Unfortunately, Alice's mind did have the time to think about the real current event—her marriage to Jim. She had the impulse to actually squeeze the sides of her temples together to somehow push whatever integrity or bravery she had left in her psyche out into some kind of action. But it never came. Because all she ever thought about was how she never wanted to go out on another date. She knew it was weak. She knew she was settling and she tried to care. She tried to feel guilty about that, as opposed to the minks. But instead, all she kept remembering were all those dates and all those phone calls and she knew that she wasn't going anywhere.

But she did decide to call Ruby anyway, and ask her how it all went. When she picked up the phone, Ruby answered and told her everything. How she had left at the last minute; how she saw her mother and realized she was from a long line of depressed women; how she was now *really* depressed. She also told Alice how she hadn't seen Serena in days. Alice was worried. She was worried for Ruby, and she was worried for Serena. Finally, she had something else to think about.

• • •

Mark Levine was sitting at the head of a conference table. Dale and Georgia were sitting across from each other, on opposite sides of Mark Levine. Georgia, of course, was a nervous wreck. She had no idea what the children had said to Mark Levine, and consequently, she had no idea what Mark Levine was going to say to them. If he recommended something that they didn't agree with, she would have to hire a lawyer and spend enormous amounts of money and end up in court. But she was ready to do that if need be. She wasn't going to let squirrelly Mark Levine be the final word about where her children should live if she didn't want it to be.

Georgia looked over at Dale. He looked odd, a bit disheveled. He hadn't shaved for the big day. He managed to throw on a blazer, but didn't bother to put on a tie. *Finally,* Georgia thought to herself. *It's finally hitting him. What he's done to me. What he's done to his family.*

Mark Levine had just opened their file. Georgia and Dale sat there in silence; Dale had his hands in front of him on the table, picking at a cuticle.

"So. As you know, I've had a chance to speak to both of you, individually, as well as speaking to your children. It's my recommendation that—"

But before Mark Levine could finish, Dale interrupted.

"I think the children should stay with Georgia," Dale said, with his eyes still on his cuticle.

Georgia, startled, looked at Dale and then looked quickly back at Mark Levine. Did she hear correctly? She had to make sure.

"What?" Georgia said.

Dale now looked up at both Georgia and Mark Levine. "She's a really good mother. She's just been going through a hard time. So, she made a mistake. I don't think she would do it again. Would you?"

"No. Never."

Mark Levine took off his glasses and rubbed his eyes. He looked at Dale. "Are you sure about this?"

Dale nodded, his head pointing down again toward the table. Georgia thought she noticed his eyes welling up with tears. She decided to engage him in conversation so she could see for sure.

"Really, Dale, you're positive?" Georgia asked. She didn't really care if he was sure, she just wanted to see if he was crying. Dale looked up at Georgia for a split second and mumbled, "Yes. I'm sure." He was, indeed, all teary. Dale quickly looked down again. Georgia felt a wave of all sorts of emotions well up inside. She felt sorry for him, how sad he looked, gratitude for his change of heart, regret for how everything turned out, and when it all mixed together like that in this one giant surge, it felt exactly like love.

"Well, I believe I can agree to that," Mark Levine said. "I was going to recommend—"

"Do we really need to know?" Georgia interrupted quickly. "I mean, if we're in agreement. Do we need to know what you were going to recommend?"

Mark Levine pursed his lips, and said politely, "No, I guess you don't. But I do feel it's my duty to encourage you to find a way to manage your anger. It's absolutely unacceptable to ever show your children anything but a supportive, cooperative relationship between you and your ex-husband."

"I absolutely agree, Mr. Levine. Thank you."

"Do you want to talk about visitation rights?" Mark Levine said to Dale.

"Can I have them every other weekend?" Dale said. "And dinner once a week?"

Georgia nodded, and said, "Of course, and if you want to see them more often than that, I'm sure we can figure something out."

Dale almost smiled and then looked down again.

Mark Levine got up from the table. "Well, I'm glad this ended so amicably. I'll have them draw up the papers." Mark Levine began to exit the room and cast a look backward, at Georgia and Dale still sitting there. "Will you two be all right in here?" Georgia and Dale gave various facial assurances that they would not in fact start choking each other the minute he walked out of the room.

The door closed behind him and Dale put his head in his hands, his elbows on the table. Georgia leaned over and touched his elbow. Dale was truly crying now. The only time she had seen Dale cry like that was at his mother's funeral. At that time, she found it profoundly sweet. She remembered she had stood there, rubbing his back as he cried in the parking lot of the funeral home. She felt an overwhelming love for him at that moment; an understanding that this is what a husband and wife go through together, births and deaths and tears, and she had been touched and proud that she was able to be there for him. Similarly, today, she felt a deep love for Dale. In that little conference room, she understood that history is something not to be underestimated, and even if the present was gone, a shared history must be respected and, she would go so far as to say, cherished. As she touched Dale's elbow, trying again to comfort him during a moment of intense grief, she knew that he must be having a similar experience. The weight of the dissolution of their shared history and the fracturing of their family was finally being felt. And although she felt great tenderness for Dale at this moment, she also felt vindicated. Finally, there was reflection. Finally, there was regret. Finally, there was gravitas.

"She left me," Dale suddenly blurted out, as he lifted up his face and flashed his big wet soppy tears to Georgia. She thought, hoped, prayed she hadn't heard him correctly.

"Excuse me?" Georgia asked, with a little of her old contemptuous tone sneaking into her voice.

"She left me, Georgia. Melea left me." Dale grabbed Georgia's arm and squeezed it as he turned his head away from her. "She said she didn't want to date a man who had children. It was too complicated."

Georgia took a breath and asked him, calmly, "Is that why you didn't fight for the kids? Because you had wanted to raise them with her?"

Dale, in his vulnerable state, was too weak to lie or even avoid.

"I thought she'd be a great stepmom."

There were a lot of things that Georgia felt entitled to do or say in this moment. She could have screamed at Dale that he had merely seen his children as props in his imaginary dream life with Melea. She could have screamed that he should be thinking about the dissolution of their twelve-year marriage, that by their failure they had now added their children to the statistics of children of divorce. That, because of what was going on right this very minute, there might be psychological re-percussions for their children that they might not see until years from now. And that he didn't seem to be noticing any of this, because he was too busy crying over some Brazilian whore—yes, in her mind she could call her a whore, fuck Mark Levine—whom he'd known for just a few months.

But Georgia knew that now was not the time to think about Dale or their lousy love lives. Dale was busy enough thinking about Dale. Now was the time to think about her two gorgeous children of divorce, and how she could make their lives filled with as much joy and stability and discipline and fun as possible. That's what it was time for. That was all she was entitled to—that and only that.

*   *   *

Oftentimes, morning brings better news. The sun rises, people are rested, and the brightness of the day helps things look less bleak. But there are those horrific times in a person's life when things are so bad that the morning just brings a fresh hell of pain, or a new sobbing realization of the doom that has befallen you. For Serena and Kip, that's how this

morning began. Kip was sprawled out on the couch, his head still in Serena's lap, when he woke up crying. Then he stood up suddenly and
screamed, "I want to talk to my mother! I want to talk to my mother!"

"I'll call her right now," Serena said, jumping up and grabbing the
phone. It was six in the morning. She could only imagine what Joanna
had been through that night. Kip stood there, tense, breathing heavily,
his eyes watery, as Serena dialed the phone.

"Joanna? It's Serena. Kip wants to talk to you." Serena passed the
phone to Kip. He took the phone slowly, as if it might blow up in his
face.

Kip listened, quietly. Serena had no idea what Joanna was saying to
him. Was Robert all right? "Uh-huh," Kip said. "That's really great, Mom."
And he hung up the phone.

Serena stood there and looked at Kip.

"Dad's coming back home," Kip said, relieved, and went back to the
sofa and sprawled on his stomach. He picked up the remote and started
watching a movie Robert starred in where he played a cowboy looking
for his lost son.

Robert is coming home? Is that good news or bad news? Serena had no
idea. She just started doing the only thing she knew how to do in this situation.

"I'll make you an omelette and some bacon—does that sound okay?"
she called out to Kip.

"Yep, thank you, See," Kip said, staring at the television. Serena quietly went to work.

At nine, Joanna called Serena and filled her in on the details. His
breathing had not improved and he had been put on a ventilator, which
definitely was not good news. Joanna told her that Robert's mother and
brother were flying in from Montana, and Joanna's parents were flying in
from Chicago. She hoped Serena wouldn't mind letting them in. Serena
didn't. She just wanted to be of help; anything she could do was fine by
her.

The phones began to go crazy. Joanna had started making calls at the
hospital and when people couldn't get her on her cell, they started calling
the house. Close friends, acquaintances, colleagues, agents, managers,
were all calling. Unfortunately, news had gotten out to the press as well,

and photographers started to camp out in front of the building. Flowers began arriving; food, too.

By noon, Joanna's parents had arrived. They were an unassuming elderly midwestern couple, both short and gray and cute, wheeling in their little suitcases and taking off their coats. Kip met them at the door and they must have both stood taking turns hugging him for about fifteen minutes. Eventually, they looked up and saw Serena.

"Hi, I'm Ginnie," Joanna's mother said as she stretched out her hand. "Joanna has told us so much about you, Serena."

Serena shook her hand. "I'm just glad I could help."

"Oh, you've been much more than that," Joanna's father said as he stretched out his hand. "I'm Bud."

"Now," Ginnie said. "What can we do to help?"

Serena saw that these were two sturdy people who dealt with grief and hardship with good old-fashioned hard work. So Serena had Ginnie do laundry. She asked Bud to be in charge of the buzzer. In the meantime, Serena kept cooking nonstop and answering the phone. Kip kept watching the movie over and over again, comatose, mummified.

At two o'clock, Joanna called from the ambulance and told them they'd be home in five minutes. Everything was ready. Their bedroom was spotless, thanks to Ginnie's polishing and vacuuming. There was food to last them for days. And the throngs of photographers outside were under control because Bud got fed up and called the cops, so now there was a police presence outside. Go, Bud.

No one knew exactly what to expect. They all just sat around, waiting until Joanna and Robert came home.

Theirs was an industrial-size elevator, one that opened up directly into their loft. When they finally arrived, a whole new reality entered the home. Robert was on a stretcher rolled in by two paramedics. There were two women dressed in white scrubs who followed, as well as one man in green scrubs who was apparently the doctor. Joanna came out in the middle of the crowd. She was stoic, pale, and looked much older than she had when she left the house twenty-four hours earlier. They all filed toward Robert and Joanna's bedroom. Robert was unconscious, and no longer had a breathing tube down his throat. There was only one IV in him now, rolled along by one of the nurses as they all walked away.

They've brought him home to die. Serena finally allowed herself to think it. She wasn't the only one. Kip began to wail the moment he saw his father rolled out.

"Is he going to wake up? WHEN IS HE GOING TO WAKE UP, MOMMY?"

Joanna went over to hold him but he ran away.

"NO! NO!" Kip ran into his room and shut the door.

At two thirty, Robert's mother arrived from Montana. She was a frail woman, in jeans and a turtleneck. Her little feet were in New Balance sneakers and her thin hair was in a light brown, tight little perm. She obviously had had a long, sad flight, and seemed to be reserving every ounce of energy she had left for her son. When she walked in, she kissed Joanna hello, nodded to everyone else, and went into Robert's room.

By five o'clock, friends had started to arrive. Not just friends, but intimates. The inner circle. The inner, inner, inner circle. It was about twenty people; twenty lovely people who were all, every last one of them, deeply appropriate, speaking quietly, somber but not morbid, occasionally joking and idly chatting, but never without sensitivity.

Serena did crowd control, not with the guests, but with all the food they brought with them. With each person that came, a cake or a bottle of booze or a platter of something was given. Serena unwrapped everything she could, found places to store the rest, and began operating as if she were suddenly the hostess of an impromptu party. She ordered in paper goods, set up a buffet table, and by seven o'clock had set up a full bar.

By nine, Serena had put soft jazz music on the stereo (jazz was Robert's favorite) and it didn't look as if anyone was going anywhere. Serena had not witnessed anything like this before and she was struck by the weight and depth of what she was experiencing.

Moreover, this was no normal group of people—there were recognizable actors and actresses, a newscaster, and a writer who had won an Oscar for best screenplay. Serena began to understand that what she was witnessing was primal. This was a tribe, these show biz folks; one of their own had fallen and so they gathered. Because that is what human beings have done at times of grief since the dawn of man. They gather. They hold one another, they cry, they eat.

As the hours went by, they all continued to talk and drink and then suddenly, someone would start crying, and then someone else would start crying, and everyone's eyes would become moist, and the mood would suddenly be grim and quiet. Men would weep openly, women would just stand with each other, hugging. These people were show people who weren't embarrassed by their emotion, but they weren't show-offs, either.

Every time Joanna would come out of the bedroom, everyone would quiet a bit, waiting. Joanna would look at one of the guests and say, "Would you like to go in and see Robert now?" They would nod, silently, put down their drink, and walk away toward the bedroom. Even as she was living through the nightmarish event of watching her husband die, she was still taking care of the needs of others. She was slowly letting everyone pay their last respects. Clearly, it must not be long.

Throughout all this, Kip hid in his room. There was one young actor, Billy, who had just made his first romantic comedy and was about to become a huge star, and Kip allowed him to come in and play video games together. But that was it.

Joanna walked into the kitchen, where Serena was, to put down a glass of water she had just finished. "I know he must hate this." Serena turned to look at her.

"Having all these people around, in his home, talking and laughing, when his dad is—" Joanna stopped herself. "But later, he'll remember. He'll remember all the love, all the people who were here because they loved his father."

Joanna put her face in her hands and began to cry. Serena walked around the kitchen counter and put her arm around her. At the moment of touch, Joanna quickly stood up and composed herself. "I'm fine. Really. I'm going to go back in." She turned to walk away and then she turned back, with a start.

"Oh my God, Serena. All this time, you've been here—is this okay?

Do you have to be somewhere? I . . . I haven't even had a moment to ask you if you need to go, or—"

"I'm fine. I don't have to be anywhere. Please, don't worry about me again, please."

"Thank you."

As Joanna walked away, Serena realized that she truly had nowhere else to be at that moment. There was no one in the world who needed her as much as these people did right now. There was no boyfriend, no child. She had called Ruby and told her what was going on so she wouldn't worry, but that was it. In a room where it seemed people were practically fused together in their grief and love, no one wanting to leave Robert, no one wanting to leave each other, Serena felt weightless. Untethered. And if it weren't for this group who needed right now to be fed and cared for, Serena felt like she might just float up and away into the sky.

The doctor kept coming and going from the apartment, stopping in every few hours to check on Robert. His name was Doctor Grovner, but everyone called him Henry. He was a family friend of Joanna and Robert's who happened to be an oncologist, which is why Robert was allowed to go home and get the fantastic care he was being given. At eleven thirty that night, the doctor arrived again and went directly in to Robert. At midnight, everyone in the living room heard Robert's mother crying in the bedroom, with Joanna saying, "It's going to be okay, it's all going to be okay."

Doctor Grovner came out. Everyone was already quiet. Anxious. Tearful. He said quietly, "It won't be long now." Billy, who was now back in the living room, began to sob, and Joanna's mother went over and patted his hand gently. Another woman just dashed into a bathroom, where she was heard wailing. Another beautiful woman, someone Serena recognized from starring opposite Robert in one of his movies, just started rocking back and forth. Joanna came out next. She smiled and went directly to the kitchen, where Serena was. She was carrying a wash-cloth and went to the sink to dampen it. She wrung out the excess water. Serena had been filling up an ice bucket with ice, when Joanna came over. Joanna came up to Serena and said, gently, "You don't need to, please don't feel you have to, but if you want, you're welcome to come in and say good-bye."

Serena burst out crying. She put her hand immediately to her eyes and turned away from Joanna, embarrassed. She quickly wiped the tears away and turned back to Joanna and smiled. "I'd like that."

Serena walked into the bedroom. It was dark. There were two windows that looked out onto the Hudson, the lights from New Jersey twinkling in the distance. The room was otherwise lit only by candlelight, everything designed for the maximum amount of peace. Robert's mother was sitting in a chair by his bed, holding his hand, her eyes closed. The nurse was in the back of the room, almost invisible in the shadows. Joanna sat down in the chair on the other side of Robert and stared at him. Kip was not there. Robert no longer had his breathing tube in him, and his breathing was very light. He was pale, thin, unrecognizable. The first word that popped into Serena's mind was *outrageous*. It felt outrageous that Robert, strong, virile Robert, Robert sliding around the floor in his socks and punching Serena in the arm and teasing his wife mercilessly, was now lying in this bed, looking like that. It was an outrageous indignity for him. A man who deserved nothing but to lead a long, loved, and loving life, with friends and a marriage to a woman that he adored and a child that he should see go to college and fall in love and get married. Not like this. Not thin and pale and with grieving friends gathered outside his door.

Joanna looked at her husband. Whatever the thought or memory or emotion it was that passed through her mind, it was the one that broke her. She lowered her head on the bed and began to sob, her back heaving up and down as she gasped for air in between her cries. It was pure grief that Serena was witnessing; undiluted, unself-conscious suffering from the deepest part of a person's being.

In a flash, Serena understood everything. She understood about life and tribes and weight and connections and friendship and death and love. She understood everything she ever needed to know about what it means to actually *participate* in the experience of being human. She knew in that instant, more than she had ever known anything in her entire life, that life is about risking it all and loving passionately and engaging in the world in a way she had not done in all her regimented, disciplined, pleasure-denying life. She had begun to feel it with Swami Swaroop, but after that debacle, she promised she would never put herself through that again. She assumed she just would go through the rest of her life alone, unharmed. But in that room, in that moment, in the most dark, grotesque, cruel light imaginable, Serena saw what she would be missing. She kept her eyes on the sobbing Joanna. She would never be able to explain it sufficiently to anyone, but it was then that Serena knew, more surely than she had ever known anything, that it was time for her to join the party—the ugly, magnificent, cruel, sublime, heartbreaking party.

RULE

11

Believe in Miracles

A few hours after Robert passed away, Serena called Ruby and told her. It was impossible to hide the news from the press, so his death was all over the television and radio anyway. Ruby called Alice and Alice called Georgia.

Serena had gone out just to get some fresh air. People were still filing in and out of the house, now to visit Joanna and Kip, to pay their respects. It looked like she was probably going to be there for a while, so Serena decided to go outside for a quick break. There were crowds and news vans and reporters, but Serena was able to walk through them unnoticed. She kept her eyes down and kept walking past the police barricade. When she finally looked up she saw Alice, Georgia, and Ruby, all looking at her with a collective look of care and concern, and she burst out crying. They all rushed up to her and put their arms around her. She stood there, crying and holding on to them, all the emotion of the past days just pouring out of her. They huddled around her, shielding her from any busybodies, as she wept, her shoulders heaving, the sobs erupting out of her. When she finally looked up, her face red and wet, she looked into their faces. Ruby, Alice, and Georgia were not her good friends; in fact, they were merely acquaintances. Yet here they were.

"I can't believe you all came. Thank you . . . thank you," she said, her voice still jagged with sobs.

Alice put her arm around Serena's shoulders. "We wanted to come."

Georgia said, "We're here for you. So don't you worry."

Ruby added, "Do you want to take a walk?"

Serena nodded. They headed down to the river and sat on a bench facing out over the water. New Jersey was on the other side, with its new buildings going up and the giant Colgate clock telling them the wrong time.

Serena said, "She loved him so much. He really was the love of her life. I can't imagine what she's going through. I can't."

The other women nodded. They hadn't a clue, either.

Ruby shook her head. "It's hard to imagine ever meeting the love of my life, but then to lose him? And so young?"

Georgia thought about Dale and their life together. *Had he been the love of her life?* At one point, yes, she guessed he was. But not now. So maybe he didn't count. Now she had to hope there was a man out there who was the real love of her life. "I hope she feels lucky. To have had so much love in her life."

Serena nodded. "I think she does." She blew her nose on a tissue Alice had given her. "I think so."

Alice spent the whole taxi ride home thinking about that term—*the love of your life.* She thought about Joanna and how different she must have thought things were going to be for her. And, of course, Alice thought about how she was about to take a flight to Iceland to marry someone who wasn't the love of her life.

When she got home she walked into her bedroom. She looked at her suitcase on the bed, packed and ready to go. Their airplane tickets were on her bureau. Jim was about to come over for dinner. Alice sat on her bed. What does it mean, anyway, "the love of your life"? She wished Serena had never said those words. Now she couldn't get them out of her head. She glanced at her fabulous winter white fur wedding suit. She thought about how, when you introduce your husband to people here in

America, there is the assumption that he is the love of your life. That you fell in love with him and decided to get married. It might not be true, but that's what you're led to believe. Now, if you lived in India or China or who knows where, people might not assume that. They might just assume your families arranged it or you married for convenience or whatnot. But here, in America, when you talk about your husband, the assumption is that at some point in your life you were in love with him enough to marry him. Alice wondered if she would be okay with living that kind of lie, knowing she did not marry the love of her life. She had hoped that in the weeks leading up to Iceland she would magically fall head over heels in love with Jim. But it didn't happen. She was always mildly bored with him, and then guilty for feeling that bored. So she would give him more of her attention, she would try to find him as engaging as she possibly could. But in the end, he wasn't the love of her life and he never would be. At best, he would be the man of whom she was very fond and to whom she was very, very grateful.

The love of her life, the love of her life. As Alice took a shower, she realized it came down once again to one thing: What did she believe in? In other words, what kind of life did she want to live? Did she really think the love of her life was out there? Did she think it was wise to go back out into the wilds of being single just in the hopes of finding him? What was she holding out for? As she toweled herself off, she realized that she didn't want to be the girl who refused to settle. She didn't want to be the girl who believed that life is short and it's better to be single and looking for "the love of your life" than to just give up and settle. She didn't want to be that girl. She thought that girl was stupid. Naïve. Alice liked being practical; she was a lawyer, so she preferred to be realistic. Waiting and searching for the love of your life was *exhausting*. It might even be delusional. Again, yes, she knew that some people win the love lottery and get to fall in love with someone who is also mad about them, and their life together is harmonious and filled with love. But she didn't want to be the girl who stubbornly held out for what might never come.

She sat back down on her bed, wrapped in a little towel, and she began to cry. She started sobbing; she hugged her legs as she put her head on her knees and rocked and wept.

She realized she *was* that girl.

That girl who, at thirty-eight, couldn't give up the dream that she would meet a man who made her heart soar and that they would share a life together. She cried knowing it meant that she had to worry about whether she was ever going to start a family, that she would be thrust back into a world where nothing was guaranteed and all she really had was hope. She knew it meant that she would be single again.

When Jim came over, Alice was dressed but hadn't stopped crying. He walked in, rolling his big suitcase. Alice told him right away.

"You deserve someone who knows you're the love of her life," she said, sobbing. She then began to tell him, in a torrent of words and tears and apologies, that she couldn't marry him—not in Iceland, not here, not ever.

Now his eyes filled up with tears. "But you're the love of *my* life. Doesn't that mean anything?"

Alice shook her head. "I don't think I can be the love of your life if you're not the love of mine."

Jim paced around the room. They talked and talked. He got angry. Alice apologized over and over again. And in the end, he understood. He forgave her and wished her the best. He left Alice in her living room crying, devastated. From her point of view she seemed to be much worse off than he was. She looked at him as he walked out the door, shaken, heartbroken, and she felt tremendous guilt. But she also knew that he would fall in love again. He would meet someone and get married and have children and be very happy. As for herself, Alice wasn't so sure. So she lay down on the couch and cried some more.

When I called Alice the next morning and found out what happened, I was relieved. What was I thinking, encouraging Alice to marry Jim? Who exactly did I think I was, giving her advice about anything, let alone marrying someone she didn't love? But Alice still sounded more depressed than I had ever heard her. I thought about coming home and being with her. But then I had a better idea.

"Why don't I meet you in Iceland? Use your ticket."

"What do you mean, spend my honeymoon with you?" Alice asked, not making it sound so fun.

"Well, yeah, Iceland is supposed to be amazing. I've always wanted to go." It's true, everyone I know who's been there has said it was fantastic. I didn't remember exactly *why* they said it was so great, but no matter. "I think you need to get away for a bit."

"Yeah, but maybe not to the place where I was going to spend my honeymoon."

"Please, it's Iceland in the middle of the winter, not Maui. You'll be able to forget that part of it." And then I added, "I promise. Come on, let's do it, it will be fun."

At the Mumbai airport, I walked into the ladies' bathroom. There was an elderly woman in there, wearing a worn purple sari with white flowers, and her eyes were haunted, just like so many other eyes I saw while I was there. I thought she was functioning as a bathroom attendant, but I wasn't quite sure. As I came out, she handed me a paper towel that I was quite capable of getting for myself. Then she put her fingers to her mouth. This city was relentless. She could have been my grandmother. And she was in the bathroom of the Mumbai airport begging for money. I gave her all the rupees I had. Then I did the only thing I knew how to do at the time. I took two Lexomil and hoped for the best.

I woke up, groggy, as the pilot was telling us to get ready for our descent—the Lexomil had gone the distance. We must thank God for these small blessings in life.

The funeral for Robert was held two days after he passed away. Joanna decided that she and Kip were going to go back with her parents for a week or two, just to get away from the press and the chaos and the memories. She gave Serena two paid weeks off—which Serena had absolutely no idea what to do with. So when Alice called her to check up on her, and told her that her marriage was off and that she was meeting me in Iceland, Serena quickly jumped on board.

"Could I come, too? I mean, I know . . . it's your honeymoon . . . I was just thinking . . ."

"Of course, you can come—of course," was Alice's immediate response. "I'm not sure what kind of food they have there, if it's really hospitable for vegetarians, but . . ."

"Oh, fuck that," Serena said. "Everything in moderation, right?"

Alice smiled. "That's right."

In the meantime, Ruby had never really recovered from opting out of the insemination. She was sliding again, thinking about what she had lost, what a mistake that was. She thought about the idea of taking anti-depressants, like her mother, but couldn't imagine it. A depressed single woman taking antidepressants—that sounded so *depressing*.

But she was trying very hard to fight the slide. She was on the floor of her bedroom doing sit-ups, trying to get her endorphins going. After meeting with Serena, and hearing about Joanna and Robert, she was re-minded just how short life is and how you shouldn't be wasting any of it crying over regret and things that could have been. But nevertheless, as she was doing her crunches, she was thinking about how that sperm might have made a baby and how cute he or she would have been. Serena popped her head in the room and mentioned that she had just spoken to Alice and she was going to Iceland with them. Ruby stopped crunching.

"I've always wanted to go to Iceland! Reykjavik is supposed to be amazing! Can I come, too?" Ruby said, excited. Serena looked surprised.

"Um, I would think so . . . you might want to call . . . ?"

"I'll call Alice to make sure." And with that Ruby hopped on the phone.

After their meeting with Serena, Georgia had also gone home thinking about the love of her life. She wondered if it was a cop-out to think maybe her children could be the loves of her life. She knew that they weren't a replacement for a man or an intimate relationship—but it was love. They were two people whom she loved more than anything else in the world. Two little people who, for as long as any of them were alive, would always be her children. And this coming weekend, they were going to be with Dale. And now that she wasn't spending all her time hating Dale and chasing after men, she literally had nothing to do but be lonely. So when Alice called her up and told her that Serena, Ruby, and I were joining her in Iceland for her honeymoon that would never be, well, she decided to whip out that credit card and climb on board, too.

I think you can tell a lot about a place by the ride from the airport. I'm always a little disappointed if there's no sense of foreignness about it. There's nothing like flying twenty hours just to look out your car window and see the same old telephone wires and concrete. But the drive from the airport in Reykjavik to the heart of the city was through a landscape that I had never before seen or even heard about. The only way to describe it was lunar; imagine landing on the moon, which happens to be covered in a lovely green moss, then discovering that it's inhabited by lots of really good-looking blond people.

Now as I arrived on this moon, I couldn't have been feeling more sorry for myself. I was still humiliated by what happened in China, and still traumatized by Mumbai. I wanted to be somewhere as far away from there as possible. Reykjavik seemed like it was going to be just the place.

When I got to the hotel, I was exhausted. It was a tall, corporate-looking skyscraper, owned by Icelandair—not very quaint for Iceland or a honeymoon choice. I checked into Alice's suite. She would be arriving in the morning, so I would have the room to myself for the night. The room Alice booked was spacious—with a living room and kitchenette and king-size bed. But it was more suited for a busy executive than amorous newlyweds. I imagined Alice getting married in the dark, then coming back to this minimalist room to have cold executive sex, and I got ashamed all over again. *Why had I encouraged her to go through with the marriage? Who do I think I am anyway? I have no business calling myself a friend, and certainly no business writing a book about anything.*

At 7 A.M. I was woken up by my four friends barreling into the room. It was still pitch-black out and I was a bit disoriented, particularly from seeing my normally disparate friends all arriving in one bunch, in Iceland. It took me a minute to get my bearings.

"Thank God I booked this room for last night. You should see the mobs of tourists in the lobby. It was ghastly," Alice said as she took off her parka.

"It's true, there's just dozens of poor slobs who just got off some red-eye flight, nodding off on the sofas, waiting for check-in," Georgia said as she sat on the bed.

"Which is at, like, three," Ruby added, exploring the minibar. Then she turned around and stared at me. "I'm so glad to see you! It's been so long!"

I sat up, leaning on the copious pillows, and crossed my legs. "It's so good to see you! I missed you all so much." Serena leaned over and gave me a good, long hug. It felt like she might just burst out crying right there, but she let go and got up.

"I have to pee," she said, sniffling.

Alice looked around. "So this was where I was going to spend my honeymoon, huh? I guess I didn't research that very well, did I?"

"Why don't we go downstairs and have some breakfast and then go to the Blue Lagoon?" I said, brightly, seeing that things in this room could turn morose very quickly.

"What's the Blue Lagoon?" Ruby asked.

"It's a natural thermal pool—a big tourist spot, but the locals go, too. I read about it on the plane."

Alice added, "Jim and I were going to go there the day after our wedding."

"Well, let's go," Georgia said. "We can sleep later!"

They went downstairs to the buffet while I changed. As I was putting on my jeans, my cell phone rang. It was an "unknown" number so I assumed it was from the States. When I picked up, I heard Thomas's voice.

"Hello, Julie? It's me."

Don't you dare say "it's me" when you call. As if we're still intimate. I wanted to throw up.

"Please, leave me alone," is all I managed to get out.

"I'm sorry, Julie, I am. I just needed to tell you again how sorry I am. This all was very difficult."

"I don't really want to talk to you right now. I'm sorry. It's too sad for me." I closed my phone. I leaned against the desk for a moment. If I let myself cry again, I would never get out of this hotel room. So I took a breath and went down to breakfast.

Alice, being Alice, had rented a car at the airport, and had directions to the Blue Lagoon ready. So we all piled in and drove the forty-five minutes out there. It was still dark out, so it was difficult to see where we actually were. But as we got closer, it appeared as if we were driving to a big hole in the ground puffing with smoke. We got out of the car and marched through the turnstile and into the locker rooms, where we put on our bathing suits and showered. We walked right out into the pool.

It was freezing, so we quickly got into the water, which was warm and soothing. There was soft sand under our feet. We walked around for a bit, crouching so that the warm water covered our whole bodies. We settled into a little corner where steam was gushing out of the crevices of some rocks. It created a little shower for us while we soaked. The view was stupendous. The sun was rising so the sky was filled with pinks and blues. There was a geothermal power plant next to the lagoon, and while it spoiled the view a bit, it also puffed out clouds of steam that spilled over the mountains. We definitely weren't in America anymore, and I wasn't quite sure if we were even still on planet Earth.

As I sat there taking in this otherworldly beauty, Georgia was having an entirely different experience.

"Here's the thing with hot springs—the water's so cloudy, there's no way to tell how clean it is." I didn't know how to answer her. I was too relaxed to worry.

Alice reassured her. "I read all about it. The water gets pumped out regularly, so it's always being cleaned."

Georgia looked around. "Good, because I'm sure people come here with all sorts of skin problems that they're hoping to get cured. It could be really gross in here."

Serena looked at Georgia. "Why don't you just try and enjoy the water? It feels so good."

Georgia nodded. It was Saturday, and tourists and locals alike were starting to wade in. Two women sat near us. One blond, the other with darkish red hair. They both were in their early forties and very tall and beautiful. They were speaking what seemed to be Icelandic.

"Excuse me," Georgia called to the women. "Do you know if the water here is clean?"

The women looked at Georgia. I was worried that this might appear to be a rude question, but the women didn't seem to mind. They also didn't flinch at her assumption that they understood and spoke English. Yes, we're Americans.

"Yes, it's clean," the blond women said, in a thick Nordic accent. "I come here all the time."

The other one shrugged. "I don't like it as much, swimming with all these people, but I think it's clean."

Georgia smiled at them sweetly. "Thank you so much. I appreciate it." Georgia crouched down even lower in the water and let it come up over her neck.

Alice looked around. "It's so strange to be here. Tonight would have been my wedding night . . ."

I tried to keep her level. "But you must know you did the right thing, don't you?"

Alice shook her head. "I don't know that. I don't know that at all. What if he was my last chance? What if I'm never going to have another boyfriend again, let alone another husband?"

Again, no one knew what to say. How could anyone predict the future? We were all trying to heal our battle scars here in the Blue Lagoon, and no one had a lot of optimism to share.

Georgia spoke first. "All you need to know is that you tried very hard to go through with it, and you couldn't. That's your answer. You didn't have a choice."

Alice nodded as if she understood. But then her face crumpled into tears. "But why couldn't I? What's wrong with me? What am I holding out for?" I waded over and put my arm around her.

Serena had been fairly quiet since we got here, but now spoke up. "Our time is so precious. You're holding out for someone who you really want to spend all your time with. Otherwise, there's no point to it."

Alice wasn't so sure. "Maybe there is a point to it. Just so you don't have to be so alone."

And at that, I burst out crying. I had been holding it in since my phone call with Thomas and it just came out right then and there. "We're so fucked. We are. We're screwed. We're this generation of women who are just as lonely as any other, but we're just unwilling to settle or compromise to get ourselves out of it. So we're all just waiting for the fucking needle-in-a-haystack guy who we're going to love, who's going to happen to love us, who we're going to meet just at the time when we're both available and living in the same city." Tears were now streaming down my face. "We're totally fucked."

Ruby burst out crying as well. "Oh my God, you're right. You're absolutely right."

Serena had tears streaming down her face, too. Georgia looked at all of us whimpering and tried to lighten things up. "This is not the kind of honeymoon I expected."

We tried to laugh, but we were still crying too hard. The two women who were sitting near us were looking at us, concerned and puzzled. They were talking to each other in Icelandic, while they both looked over at us. We were making a spectacle of ourselves, all the way on the top of the world, and people were noticing. Georgia looked over and for some reason felt the need to explain.

"We're just all going through a very hard time right now. That's all."

If I had to guess, I think it must have been fairly shocking to see such an outpouring of emotion, here in the relaxing geothermal hot springs, amid a sea of reserved Scandinavians and happy tourists.

"Do you need any help?" the redhead asked.

Georgia just shook her head. "No, we'll all be fine, um, someday, hopefully soon."

The blonde couldn't help but inquire further. "What is the matter? May I ask?"

Georgia looked at us all. She pointed at each of us, one by one. "Alice just called off her wedding, Julie had an affair that went very badly, Serena watched someone die, I almost got my children taken away from me, and Ruby is clinically depressed."

The two women nodded, looking sorry that they had asked, and went back to talking among themselves. They looked so rugged, these women, with their strong jawlines and their dark eyes. They turned to the rocks and started rubbing them, taking the mud from the rocks and putting it on their faces. They leaned back and let the steam and mud work its magic.

Georgia looked at them, impressed. "Wow, these ladies know their lagoons."

We stayed in the pool for another hour. We didn't necessarily come here to be healed from a skin disease or get a natural lava facial, but we definitely needed a good cry, and that we did.

When we were back in the locker area, the two women whom we were sitting near walked in and glanced around at us. We were all taking off our bathing suits. I was in my bikini top and surfer shorts. From the looks of the two women, and from my own common sense, I realized that here in Reykjavik, far away from vanity and supermodels and plastic surgeons, I looked like a clown in crazy balloon pants.

Georgia seemed to be fascinated by these two women and couldn't stop staring at them. Finally as they were putting their coats on to go back into the wintry day, Georgia spoke to them again.

"Excuse me, I was just wondering if you could tell us a good place to eat tonight in Reykjavik?"

The blond woman nodded. "There is a very nice place, Silfur, at the Hotel Borg. We are eating there tonight with some friends. It's a little expensive, but has very good *fis*." I assumed this meant "fish" but I didn't want to interrupt.

The other woman added, "There's also a place called Maru, very nice sushi, and Restaurant Lækjarbrekka is more casual, but very good food."

Georgia nodded her head gratefully at them. "Okay, thank you so much!" They walked out, saying polite good-byes to all of us.

"I don't know what it is, I just love those two ladies," Georgia said. We all put on our coats, and our gloves and hats and scarves, and braced ourselves. It was time to leave the lovely, warm amniotic sac of the Blue Lagoon, where we got to feel sorry for ourselves and everyone else we knew, and venture back out into the cold winter air.

After we took naps, we all dressed for dinner in our Nordic finest— turtlenecks and down vests and sturdy winter boots. It wasn't snowing, but it was windy and cold, around ten degrees Fahrenheit. The ladies gathered in my room; everyone was doing her best to make sure there wasn't any downtime on Alice's wedding night. We drank some white wine in the room and tried to keep things light.

"Thank God we didn't go to Finland. I heard Finnish men's penises look like logs of Roquefort cheese," Georgia said.

We all shrieked in our own different ways.

Ruby was appalled. "What?"

"My girlfriend told me that. That they looked, well, marbleized."

"Oh for God's sake, how am I going to ever get that image out of my mind tonight?" Alice asked, almost spitting up her drink.

"Well, here's to us not going to Helsinki for your honeymoon," Serena said, raising her glass of white wine and smiling.

We stood around in the hotel room laughing. Alice was having a good time and we were all getting a little tipsy.

We took two cabs to the restaurant. We chose the restaurant Silfur, basically because we knew those two women were going to be there and Georgia wanted to stalk them. We walked in, and immediately realized we were underdressed; this restaurant was bathed in art-deco elegance, and we looked as if we were going to dinner in an igloo. A trendy igloo, but an igloo nonetheless. We took our seats and immediately ordered white wine. All the waitresses in the restaurant were blond and beautiful. They suggested we order the fis, particularly the lobster. As we were looking at the menu, with all the crazy, crazy Icelandic words on it (chicken breast is, phonetically, "koo-kinkablinka"), the two ladies from the Blue Lagoon walked in with two men and two other women. I saw them see us and look at each other. I nodded toward the door and Georgia turned. The waiter was seating them at the table next to us and Georgia waved. "Hi! We decided to take your suggestion and come here!"

The blond woman smiled politely. "I'm so glad. I know you're going to like it." She then put out her hand and said, "I'm Sigrud. This is my boyfriend, Palli. And these are my two friends Dröfn and Hulda." Dröfn was a woman in her late twenties with long white-blond hair and a huge mouth with big white teeth. Hulda was in her late forties, with blond hair in a close pixie cut, a pierced nose with a tiny little stud in it, and large hoop earrings dangling down from her round, pretty face. The redhead from the lagoon introduced herself as well. "I'm Rakel, and this is my husband, Karl." Even if I hadn't had a few glasses of wine in me, I wouldn't have had the foggiest idea how to pronounce all their names.

We introduced ourselves. Georgia explained to the others, "We met at the Blue Lagoon today. We're from New York and we were all a little depressed."

Karl nodded. There was something about his demeanor that immediately broadcast a kind heart and good humor. "Yes, well, Rakel kind of mentioned it." The whole group started smiling. "Why are you so sad? You're in Reykjavík now; this is where you come to have a good time."

Ruby joined in. "Well, that's what we're trying to do now. We're out to have a good time!"

Karl looked at us all and said, "Come, you must sit with us. We'll all eat together."

We all looked at one another. They were a big group as it was, and so were we—it seemed like a very burdensome idea. Rakel and Sigrud joined in immediately, though.

"Join us. We'll have some fun," Rakel said.

Sigrud added, "We don't have any friends from New York; come."

Georgia didn't need to be asked twice, and soon enough we were all crammed into a large circular table for ten, even though we were eleven. Soon the white wine (or "veet veen," as they called it) was flowing and we were regaling them with our tales of woe. Somehow it all seemed quite hilarious when we told it to these folks: Ruby's stint at the animal shelter, my China calamity, Georgia's domestic nightmare. Hilarious. The only thing that could never be spun as comic was Robert, and Serena didn't bring it up.

Karl egged us on. "So Julie, tell me about this book you're writing."

I groaned loudly. "I'm not writing it anymore. I'm going home and giving the money back to the publisher. I hate my book. I don't know what I was thinking."

Serena spoke up. "It's a book about what it's like for women to be single in all different cultures."

One of their friends spoke up, "That sounds very interesting. Don't you want to talk to Icelandic women?"

"Actually, I don't want to talk to any women anywhere, ever again, about this subject."

Georgia tried to explain. "She's just a little burned out. I'm sure it would be really helpful for Julie to talk to Icelandic women."

Somehow, Georgia steered the conversation to her two new favorite people, Sigrud and Rakel, asking them about their men. Rakel and Karl didn't get married until after their two children were eight and ten years old. Sigrud had two children with a man named Jon, whom she only married after their two children were four and seven, but now she was with Palli. Dröfn and Hulda both had children, were single, never married, and no one seemed to give a damn about any of it.

I refused to find any of this interesting. My irritating friends, however, were eating it up.

"So you're telling me that you're married, not married, single mother, not single mother, none of it really matters to anyone here?" Ruby asked, interested.

They all sort of just shrugged and said, "No."

Georgia was also intrigued. "So, you don't worry that a man will be put off by you having a child?"

Dröfn seemed actually offended by the idea, looking at Georgia as if it was the first time she'd ever heard of such an idea. "How could that be? If he loved me, he would have to love my children."

Georgia just nodded her head, like *Well, yes, of course I knew that.*

Rakel added, "You have to understand, most women here have children. Many are single mothers. We had a president who was a single mother."

Sigrud added, "If the men here didn't want to date single mothers, they really wouldn't be dating very often."

The table of Icelandic people laughed and agreed.

I just wanted to talk about Björk and if the people in Iceland think she's weird. Anything but this.

Serena now was getting into the act. "It doesn't sound like the church or religion plays a big part in things around here."

Again, the table nodded. "Iceland is mostly Lutheran. The church is run by the state. But no one goes. It's just tradition."

"This is so interesting. It's like we landed on a crazy planet untouched by the church or religion, whose people are guided instead by their own natural, instinctual morality. It's fascinating," Alice said, excited. I had to admit it. Even I was starting to get a little intrigued by these odd people.

They were all going out afterward to see their friends play in a band at a big nightclub in town called NASA. We were invited along, thankfully. We were all growing very attached to them and didn't really feel like leaving them just yet.

We walked into a large nightclub, just like any you might find in the States, packed with tons of people dancing and drinking. The band was playing a jolly mix of Irish and Icelandic music that just made you want to jump around with drunken joy. I had no idea what these men were singing about, but they seemed to be damn happy about it. The Icelanders walked straight to a little VIP area by the stage, and we followed right along. There were tables all ready for them—their friend from the band had arranged it. It was the perfect way to spend Alice's wedding night. Karl bought us all a round of shots—something called Black Death—and we all drank up, except for Serena, who apparently was pacing herself.

I looked out over the crowd. Hulda sat next to me and said, "The problem we have here, is that the men are very lazy. They don't know how to make the first move, so the women have become very aggressive. So then, the men now never have to make the first move. It's a terrible circle."

I nodded. Just as she said that I saw a gorgeous blond woman, in her late twenties, grab the man she was dancing with and start kissing him.

Hulda continued. "This is the other problem. Everyone here sleeps with each other right away. No dating like you do in the States."

It seemed to be another fica situation.

"Do the women mind if the men don't call them afterward?" She had drawn me into the conversation, damn her.

Hulda shrugged. "Sometimes yes, sometimes no. Icelandic women are very strong. We're Vikings, remember?" Then she added, "Besides, if we want to see them again, we can always call them."

She made it sound so easy.

The band started playing "The Devil Went Down to Georgia." We decided this was our cue to get out on the dance floor and start jumping up and down. We did this for hours. We danced and we drank and we met more and more Icelandic men and women—each one seemingly more free-spirited than the last. And the men were handsome and nice, but they are not the story of Iceland. To me, the story of Iceland is the women. The strong, beautiful, Viking women.

Eventually, we went back to our little area and stood by a railing looking over the crowd. Georgia surveyed the situation. "Well, if all these women are mothers, there must be an awful lot of babysitters in Reykjavik."

Alice looked out on the sea of people. "If anyone would have told me that I would be thirty-eight and single and childless and going to Iceland after I called off my wedding, I would never have believed them." I didn't like where this conversation was headed.

"I know. I really didn't expect my life would end up like this, either,"

Georgia said. "I'm divorced. I'm a divorcée. My parents are divorced. I thought it was the last thing that was ever going to happen to me."

Ruby threw in her two cents. "When I was little I didn't think I would be thirty-seven and crying all the time."

And Serena added, "I thought I would have so much more in my life. I thought I would have so much more *life* in my life."

"What's going to become of us?" Ruby asked.

I looked at us all, one big sinking ship about to go down. I got an idea. It seemed brilliant at the time but I was also drinking something called Black Death.

"We need to go somewhere," I shouted to them. "Tonight was supposed to be Alice's wedding night. We need to do something to mark it. We need to do a ritual."

Alice's eyes lit up a bit. "What kind of ritual?"

"I'm not sure yet. It's still in formation." I walked over to Sigrud and Rakel. I now had the notion that I wanted to drive my friends to a beautiful place in the middle of nature. Rakel suggested Eyrabakki, a sleepy little town right on the water. They asked me what I was going to do and I told them I wanted to perform a healing ritual for all of us. They thought it was a funny idea and agreed to join us, and Hulda and Dröfn agreed to come as well. On my way out I grabbed a huge stack of cocktail napkins. When we got out of the club, it was four in the morning. Rakel and Dröfn drove because they were the only sober ones who knew where we were going. Suddenly I had become the Icelandic den mother of the bunch. We all piled into cars and took off.

About twenty minutes later, we had arrived in Eyrabakki. It couldn't have felt more desolate. There was a small street that ran down the center of it, with rocks and water on one side and tiny unlit cottages on the other. It looked as if you could walk from one end of the town to the other in five minutes. We parked our cars in front of what seemed like the town supermarket and started walking toward the rocks. The wind was whipping through the air now, making it feel like it was many degrees below zero.

As we walked onto the rocks, Sigrud said, "It's a shame that you needed water for your ritual. There are other places much more magical. We could have gone where the elves are."

Alice, Ruby, Serena, Georgia, and I turned and looked at her. "Excuse me?" I asked. "Did you say elves?"

Sigrud nodded. "Yes, of course. But they live more inland."

Serena jumped in. "You believe in elves?"

Rakel nodded, very seriously. "Yes, of course."

I looked at them and said, "Elves? As in . . . elves?"

Hulda nodded as well. "Yes. Elves."

Georgia looked intrigued. "Well, have you ever seen them?"

Hulda shook her head. "I haven't, but my aunt has."

Dröfn said, "There is a famous story of these men trying to build a new road very close to here. Everything kept going wrong, the weather, the machinery would break down, all sorts of things. Then they brought in a psychic, who told them that it was because of the elves. They were on sacred elf land. The men moved their construction just a few miles away, and they didn't have a problem again."

I turned to Sigrud. I tried to be polite, but I still needed to get to the bottom of the elf situation.

"Well, what do they look like?"

Sigrud shrugged and, as matter-of-factly as if she were talking about what she had for dinner, said, "Some are small, some are tall, some wear funny hats."

Ruby laughed; she couldn't help herself. "Funny hats?"

Rakel laughed, too, understanding how it sounded. "Yes, and they live in houses, but we just can't see them."

I just shook my head and laughed. "You don't believe in marriage or God or religion. But you believe in elves?"

They all smiled and laughed. Sigrud giggled. "Yes."

"Well." Serena laughed. "That proves it. Everyone needs something to believe in."

We all walked toward the water. It was cold as hell and my initial enthusiasm about this wacky scheme was beginning to wane. I realized that we all could be asleep right now in our beds, if it weren't for me and my crazy ideas. We gathered at the water's edge. Everyone looked at me, expectantly. I decided it was time to start.

"Okay. So. I decided that we need to acknowledge in some kind of way what we're all feeling."

Everyone was quiet. Then Ruby said, "What are we all feeling?"

"I think we're feeling that there are a lot of things we're not going to be anymore. We're not going to be young brides. We're not going to be young mothers. We might not even get a husband and a home and two little children that we've borne ourselves. That doesn't mean that we won't get a husband, or children. But this is to acknowledge that it's not going to happen the way we thought it might. The way we hoped it would."

Georgia looked at me. "Wow, Julie, way to harsh my mellow." My American friends laughed. I don't think the Icelandic ladies understood.

I passed out the cocktail napkins I stole from the nightclub to Serena, Ruby, Georgia, and Alice. I didn't want to impose this ritual on my Icelandic sisters.

"Okay. So. I don't have pens or pencils, so I want you to instead put your disappointment into this napkin. I want you to imagine what you thought your life was going to look like now and I want you to put that in the napkin."

I closed my eyes and thought about what I imagined it was going to look like. I had a very specific expectation of what it was going to be. I never dreamed of marriage and children and always dreamed I would live a glamorous life in New York doing fun things with my fun, exciting friends. I knew that I would watch all my friends get married and have children before me—and then, at the last minute, just at the last minute, which, in my mind, *was last year,* my guy would show up, and he would, against my protestations and despite my cynical nature, sweep me off my feet and make me a wife and mother. That's how I pictured it would go. I was going to be the last entry, but I *would* get in. I never imagined that it might not happen. I put that all into my napkin.

Alice thought about her old boyfriend, Trevor. How she had planned on spending the rest of her life with him. She had imagined having a few children with him and growing old with him. She remembered all the holidays they had shared, all the ornaments they had collected at Christmas, and how she thought they were going to keep collecting them for years to come. She remembered how he had told her that he didn't want to marry her, and she told him that she thought it was time he moved out.

Ruby thought how she had imagined her happy life of love with every single man she had ever dated or spoken to in the past ten years. She saw all their faces fly past her, she remembered all the different lives she had envisioned. She was going to be the doctor's wife to Len. She was going to be emotionally supportive to Rich with his fledgling contracting business. She was going to move to D.C. to be with that lobbyist, what's-his-name. All the disappointments kept scrolling through her mind. She imagined putting them all in the napkin. She liked this ritual. *Because that is what all these men were. Nothing more than a fantasy. A notion left in a bar napkin.* She wondered how she could have ever given any of them so much power.

Georgia thought about Beth's college graduation. She imagined her and Dale sitting there in the hot sun, holding hands, with Gareth sitting next to them, along with all the respective grandparents. When Beth got up to get her diploma, Dale and Georgia would clap and cheer the loudest, then look at each other and kiss—their pride for Beth and love of each other all mixing together as they hugged and kissed some more. Georgia started to cry a little at this image, this image that she hadn't allowed herself to think of in such a long time. Now, here, as the cold wind whipped around, and the sun was nowhere in sight, she felt the loss of that deeply. And tears fell down her face.

Serena realized that she had no image whatsoever of what was going to happen to her. In her perfect yogi way, she had managed to let die any expectations of what her life was supposed to be like. She had no preconceived notions to let go of. She was empty of images of what she thought her life was supposed to look like. She realized that maybe it was time to get some. For her, it was about *starting* to imagine the life she wanted. She put her blank future into the napkin.

I took out a lighter I had borrowed from Karl and went around the circle, setting fire to our napkins, one by one. As they burned quickly, I said, "It's done. We won't have those lives. They're gone." One by one we dropped the napkins on the ground as the fire got close to our fingers.

"Now we're free."

All the women looked at me. Ruby asked first, "Free to do what?"

"Free to move on. Without bitterness. Those lives don't exist. Now we have to go on and live the ones we have."

Everyone was quiet. I don't think anyone had ever seen me so, well, sincere before. I looked at Sigrud, Rakel, and Hulda. They looked surprisingly respectful and solemn. I looked at them and wondered what they were thinking.

"Do any of you have anything you want to say?"

Rakel spoke up. "Congratulations, you all have just discovered your inner Viking."

We American ladies looked at each other, pleased.

We all got back to the hotel, had breakfast, then packed. Our whirlwind weekend was over. It was time to go home. Yes. It was time for me to go home. I was done with this all. Had I learned anything? Yes, I think so. Was I glad to have met Thomas? I would have to wait a little more time to find that out.

As we were heading to the airport, we were all quiet, we were sleep-deprived, hungover, and cranky, trying to hydrate ourselves with bottles of water we took from our hotel room. Alice, who was driving, decided to make a big announcement.

"Well, I just want you to know that I believe in elves."

We all looked at her and smiled, sleepily. Only Ruby had the energy to respond.

"You do? Really?"

"Yes. I do. I believe in elves. I mean, look at this crazy place. Doesn't it just seem like there have to be elves here?"

The rest of us were too tired to reply.

But I thought about this for a minute. We do all need something to believe in, so why not elves? *Or love?*

"Well, if Alice can believe in invisible people who wear funny hats, then I can believe in love. I will believe, from today on, that it's possible to find a person that you can live with and love for your whole life, who loves you back, and it's not just some psychological delusion."

Alice looked at me and began to clap. "Now we're talking," she said. I smiled. Georgia looked at us all and said, "And if Alice can believe in invisible people that mess around with poor construction workers, then I will believe that I can meet a man who not only loves me, but loves my children as well."

Serena nodded her head. "And if Alice can believe in elves and Julie can believe in love and Georgia can believe in love a second time around, I'm going to believe that Joanna and Kip are going to get through this. And someday they're going to be happy again."

"And what about you?" I asked.

"I believe that I'm going to find out how to be happy, too. Yes, me, too," Serena said.

Ruby smiled and raised her bottle of water in the air. "And I'm going to believe that we're all going to be happy. We're all going to get exactly what we want and be just fine." She took a sip of her water. "And Lexapro. I'm going to believe in that, too."

So, in a country of Viking pagans, we all found something to believe in. But I was still inspired.

"Well then," I said, "I'm going to take it one step further. If you all believe that we're all going to find love and be happy, then I'm going to believe in miracles—because that's what it's going to take for all this to really come true." Everyone laughed, but I said it with complete sincerity.

"Here, here," Alice said, raising her bottle of water. "To elves and miracles. Let's believe in them both. I mean, why not?"

We all clapped and raised our bottles in the air and agreed. "Why not?"

The plane was rolling down the runway. I was sitting on the aisle and Serena had the window seat. In front of us were Ruby and Georgia and across the aisle from me was Alice. The plane was now rattling, the sound of the wind was all around us as we started to pick up speed. It was then that I realized that with all the fogginess of being hungover and sleep-deprived, and chatting with my friends, I had forgotten to take any drugs before we took off. Besides that, I had forgotten to even bring them with me in my carry-on. I gripped the arms of my seat as the plane rattled into the air.

"I can't believe I forgot my drugs. I'm such an idiot."

Serena looked at me, my face slowly turning white. She put her hand on my arm and whispered to me. "It's going to be okay, remember? We're all going to be okay." The plane was now ascending, climbing into the air quietly. I nodded. "Right. Right. We're all going to be okay." I loosened my grip a bit.

Soon, we were in the air. Serena started reading to me from *People* magazine, and every once in a while Alice would interject with some gossip she had heard about this or that celebrity. I knew what they were trying to do—they were trying to keep me entertained so I wouldn't start shrieking. It worked. For five and a half hours, no panic. Not a drop of sweat, not a gasp, nothing. I was just like any other sane passenger on this plane. I have no idea why, but maybe it was being with my friends, not feeling so alone. Or maybe it was because of the ritual we did in Iceland, where I allowed myself to let go of all my expectations about my life—maybe it included my expectation that I was going to plunge to my death. Or maybe I knew deep down that we were all going to be okay. And in the far-off chance that we weren't, that we were all going to go down in a giant ball of flames—there was nothing I or my panic was going to do to change that. I let go of everything and just flew home.

But whatever the reason, my panic was gone.

Back in the States

Two weeks later, we all got together to hear about Alice's new job back in Legal Aid. We went to Spice restaurant in Manhattan and sat in a big booth downstairs in the VIP area, thanks to, of course, Alice. She told us all about the first case she was working on, a young kid who was accused of breaking parole but had been set up by one of his friends. She was full of conviction and passion and was excited to tell us all about it. We ordered some wine for the table, but Ruby declined. She was on a new medication, and she wasn't allowed to drink alcohol with it. And she confessed: it was an antidepressant. We all broke out into applause.

"Well, thank the frickin' lord," Alice said.

"What took you so long," Georgia said. "I might be going to take a trip to Mr. Psychiatrist any day myself."

"That's so amazing, Ruby. I know that was a hard decision for you!" Serena said. She had moved out of Ruby's the week before, having finally found an apartment in Park Slope.

"How do you feel?" I asked Ruby. She smiled happily.

"I feel kind of great. I have to say. Not like insanely happy or anything, just not so depressed. It just gives me a shelf. So I never really sink so low."

"That's fantastic," I added. And then Georgia looked at me and said, "So what are you going to do about your book?"

I grimaced and said, "I don't know yet. My publisher doesn't know I'm home, but she did just email me wondering how it was going. I don't know what to tell her."

All the ladies looked at me, slightly concerned that I was throwing my new career down the toilet.

"But don't you think you learned so much? From meeting all those women all over the world?"

I thought about it, as I took a stab at a piece of duck on my plate.

"I'm not sure."

After that, we went to a bar on an enclosed roof of one of the trendy hotels in the neighborhood. There was a deejay, but it wasn't crowded yet. We all piled our bags and our coats in a corner and got on the dance floor as fast as we could.

So there we all were, back in action. This time there would be no brawling, no stomach pumping, no chicken wings, no hogs, no heifers. We were all just out, opening ourselves up yet again, for one more night of adventure and fun and possibility.

The song "Baby Got Back" came on. Now, this is as fun a song to dance to as there is. We all started dancing our hearts out and shaking our "backs" and trying to sing along to the song and failing miserably at it.

I looked around at all my beautiful friends, dancing with each other. In these past two weeks I couldn't help but notice how these women all now called each other on their own, without me having anything to do with it. At dinner they teased each other and got annoyed with each other and knew exactly what was going on in each other's lives, like old friends. As Serena, Alice, Ruby, and Georgia all were laughing and shimmying and whooping it up on the dance floor, it hit me: I had finally gotten what I always dreamed of. While I was on the far side of the world, a girl posse was being born. And now here it was, fully formed, dancing up a storm in New York City.

I wondered again how I could sum up what I had learned from the amazing women all over the world. One thought kept creeping into my head—but I kept pushing it away. On the dance floor, with the music going and me feeling just the carefree abandon of being out with a bunch of my girlfriends, I was mortified even to think it. But I did feel it. I'm horrified even to type the words out now. But it hit me, hard—I am so loath to admit it. Shit. Goddamn it.

I think we are going to have to love ourselves. Fuck.

I know. *I know.* But at least let me just say, I don't mean we have to "love ourselves" in a take-a-bubble-bath-every-night kind of way. Not "love yourself" like "take yourself out to dinner once a week." I think we have to love ourselves fiercely. Like a lioness protecting her cub. Like we are about to be attacked at any moment by a marauding gang of thugs who are out to make us feel bad about ourselves. I think we have to love ourselves as passionately as the Romans love, with joy and enthusiasm and entitlement. I think we have to love ourselves with the pride and dignity of any French woman. We have to love ourselves as if we are seventy-year-old Brazilian women dressed all in red and white parading around in the middle of a block party. Or as if we just got hit with a can of beer in our face and we have to come to our own rescue. We have to aggressively love ourselves. We practically have to stalk ourselves, that's how much energy we need to put into this. We really do have to discover our inner Viking and wear our shining armor and love ourselves as bravely as we ever thought possible. So yes, I guess we fucking do have to love ourselves. I'm *sorry.*

Just as I was thinking all this, a cute guy with hair down to his shoulders walked up on the dance floor and started dancing/talking to Serena. He was wearing weird red baggy pants.

As they danced with each other, I heard Serena ask him, "Excuse me, but are your pants hemp?"

He nodded and leaned over and said to her, "As much as I can, I try not to wear anything that hurts the planet."

Serena nodded, intrigued. "What's a guy like you doing in a club like this?"

The guy smiled at her. "Hey, I may wear hemp but I still love to dance!" And just like that, he put his arm about Serena's back and swirled her around the room. She was laughing and blushing. For a moment as she passed by me, she gave me a look as if to say, "What are the odds of *this*?"

After dancing a bit, Alice, Georgia, Ruby, and I eventually sat down at a little table. We had a 180-degree view of the New York skyline, with the Empire State Building lit up in white and blue. Serena was now at another table, talking to the hemp lad. He seemed to be fully smitten by her, and they were laughing and chatting like two old friends.

"So . . . do you think we're witnessing a small miracle right in front of our eyes?" Alice teased.

I smiled at the thought. "You never know."

I looked around the club at all the beautiful women that were dancing, flirting, talking to men, talking to their friends. They were all out, trying to or having a good time, looking their stylish, unique, sassy best. I thought again about my travels. It could have gotten me discouraged meeting all those single women all over the world, all with their own struggles, their own needs and hopes and expectations. Instead, it comforted me. Because the one thing that I can keep with me, hold it like a tiny love note in one of my pockets, is that no matter what I've learned, or how I might feel about my single status on any given day, there is one thing I am clear about now. I am definitely not alone in this.

I am definitely not alone.

And you know what else? Miracles happen every day.

Acknowledgments

There are many, many people who helped me research this book, particularly the women and men I interviewed all over the world, and all my "hosts" who got me access to those people. The list of all of them by name might be as long as the book itself. But I am deeply indebted to all those people, particularly all those women, who took time out of their busy lives to talk to me about love and dating, with great honesty and great humor. It truly was a once-in-a-lifetime experience and I am humbled, grateful, and in awe of all of them. I thank them all from the bottom of my heart.

Specifically, I would like to mention a few people in each country who were invaluable to my research.

In Iceland, I need to thank Dröfn and Rakel for organizing the amazing meeting of the women of Reykjavík; as well as Brynja, Rakel, and Palli for their friendship, always.

In Brazil, my hero Bianca Costa, along with Tekka and Caroline of Copacabana films. Thank you to Matt Hanover from Yahoo. And Cindy Chupack for her brilliant mind that I wish I could have as my own.

In Europe, my camera crew Aaron, Tony, and James for making us laugh all the way through Paris and Rome. In Paris, my two fixers, Laure Watrin and Charlotte Sector. In Rome, Veronica Aneris and Monica De Berardinis (and John Melfi for always being there to help, in any country he can). For Dana Segal, for a friendly face during a chaotic time. To Gabriele and Domenico for inspiring me always, not just in Rome. In Denmark, Thomas Sonne Johansen and Per Dissing, thank you for being there for me on the last, coldest leg of my Europe trip.

In Mumbai, India—Hamida Parker, Aparna Pujar, Jim Cunningham, Monica Gupta, thank you all for helping us navigate a very difficult-to-navigate city. You were generous hosts to us.

In Sydney, Australia—Karen Lawson, thank you for your endless enthusiasm, humor, and boundless energy. Thank you, George Moskos, for your additional help with the blokes, and your good humor about it all, and a thank-you to Bernard Salt, for giving me so much of his time for a long, hilariously depressing interview. And a special thanks to Genevieve Read, now Genevieve Morton, whom I've never met, but inspired me so.

In Beijing, I must thank two ladies, Chen Chang and Stephanie Giambruno, for all their help making Beijing one of the most memorable trips of my life. And for Chang, for her bravely honest insights. I'd like to thank Han Bing for his additional help and Nicole Wachs for being the best companion an aunt could ever ask for.

And overall, my research and this book would not have been possible if it wasn't for Margie Gilmore and her relentless, tireless persistence, and Deanna Brown for her faith in us both. Margie, thank you again for giving me the world.

In the U.S., I need to thank the people who were there when this was just a germ of an idea and were ready to help. Mark Van Wye, Andrea Ciannavei, Shakti Warwick—and Garo Yellin, for that night when he figured it all out for me.

During the writing of this book, thank you Craig Carlisle, Kathleen Dennehy, and my savior Kate Brown.

And then to those without whom I would be nothing: Andy Barzvi for being the pushiest, most delightful agent a girl could ever ask for, it's all her fault, every last bit of it; my editor Greer Hendricks—I'm still trying to figure out what great thing I did to deserve her; and to my publisher Judith M. Curr, I'm still learning how lucky I am that she's in charge.

Thank you to my sushi and story ladies for being ready and willing to go way beyond the call of duty. Thank you to Marc Korman and Julien Thuan on whom I rely for everything. Thank you to John Carhart for all his hard work and good humor, even when he hates me. A special big international thank-you to Nadia Dajani, for taking this journey with me and being a witness to it all—and I mean all of it. The world would not have been so much fun without you. A special thank-you to Michael Patrick King, because he started it all, and will get a special thank-you always. And to all my friends and family, whose encouragement irritated me so, thank you for your patience with me. I am nothing without you.